KV-382-713

HIGHLAND SUMMER

HIGHLAND SUMMER

Elizabeth Hawksley

WINDSOR
PARAGON
THORNDIKE

This Large Print edition is published by BBC Audiobooks Ltd, Bath, England and by Thorndike Press, Waterville, Maine, USA.

Published in 2004 in the U.K. by arrangement with Robert Hale Limited.

Published in 2004 in the U.S. by arrangement with John Johnson Limited.

U.K. Hardcover   ISBN 0–7540–9557–6 (Windsor Large Print)
U.K. Softcover   ISBN 0–7540–9436–7 (Paragon Large Print)
U.S. Softcover   ISBN 0–7862–6280–X (General)

Copyright © Elizabeth Hawksley 2003

The right of Elizabeth Hawksley to be identified as author of this work has been asserted by her in accordance with the Copyright, Designs and Patents Act 1988.

All rights reserved.

The text of this Large Print edition is unabridged.
Other aspects of the book may vary from the original edition.

Set in 16 pt. New Times Roman.

Printed in Great Britain on acid-free paper.

British Library Cataloguing in Publication Data available

Library of Congress Control Number : 2003115690

CROYDON PUBLIC LIBRARIES

Lib.   No. 15553468
Class F
V   CHIVERS   P £17.99
Stk. 27 JAN 2006

To Hugo with love

ACKNOWLEDGEMENTS

I owe a debt of thanks to my mother who, every time she went to visit friends in Scotland, gamely undertook to track down books and maps, and do research for me.

I should also like to thank Mr Robert Steward, the Highland Council Archivist, and Ms Fiona MacLeod, the Archive Assistant, who were both very helpful in answering enquiries and tracking down material.

CHAPTER ONE

Robina Drummond, aged seventeen, her Journal.
Achnagarry House
Glen Nevan
Inverness-shire
North Britain

Tuesday, 2 April, 1850.
I should have started this journal on 1st January, but I forgot, so I'm starting it now.

Grandfather has died and things are going to change. I knew it was going to be different the day after he died when, for the first time ever! *Grandmama and I had a bowl of soup and a bannock for luncheon. Normally, we don't eat from breakfast at nine o'clock sharp, until dinner at five o'clock, because Grandfather* ~~despises~~ *despised people who couldn't last out. 'Old women and invalids,' he would snort. Poor Grandmama used to keep some oatcakes hidden away in a tin. And, in defiance of Grandfather's wishes, she always made tea at three o'clock.*

I've always thought it was a stupid rule. But then, I'm usually hungry. Anyway, Ishbel gives me a bannock, if I ask her. 'You're a growing lass,' she says. She has no patience with Grandfather.

March 22nd, the day after Grandfather died, Grandmama rang the bell for Ishbel and said, 'We'll be having some broth and a bannock and maybe a wee bit of cheese at one o'clock from now on.'

'That's verra sensible, I'm thinking, Mistress Drummond,' said Ishbel. 'Such foolishness, to starve oneself.' She never did have any tact, and I know that she only put up with Grandfather for my grandmother's sake. So, for the last week or so, we've been eating properly.

The day Grandfather died was bitterly cold. I was sitting on the window seat in my bedroom, looking out at Loch Nevan. The loch was frozen, a sheet of iron grey with a light dusting of snow. The sky had been grey and lowering, but then the sun broke through and I could see a pale sunbeam cast a small pool of yellow on the frozen surface. Suddenly, there was a loud crack, and a split shot across the ice from end to end, like a bullet.

At that moment, there was a harsh noise from Grandfather's room, followed by a sort of sobbing sound. A few minutes later, Grandmama came in and told me that he had died.

It was really odd.

I hadn't realized before, but there's an awful lot of waiting around after somebody dies. At the moment we are waiting for my cousin Beatrix and her husband to arrive from Edinburgh, and Mr Ogilvy, the family attorney. I'm feeling rather in the way. Ishbel and Morag are busy getting ready for the funeral. Grandmama spends a lot of time up in her room, or sitting by Grandfather's body in the library. She seems to *have shrunk, and her eyes are red. I don't know what to say. I never liked Grandfather much—I thought he was a tyrant and I hated the way he talked about 'a pack of useless women'. Ha! It's women who run this house, cook the meals, do the washing and cleaning. What does did he mean 'useless women'? Useless man, more like.*

So I'm sitting in my room, looking out of the window at the deer. At this time of year, they are down from the hill. They are starving, poor things, pawing aside the snow with their hooves, searching for something to eat. In the mornings, you can see deer tracks crossing the loch. Only the fittest survive.

I don't want to sound dramatic, but I feel like those deer. Of course, I'm not starving—in fact, we shoot hinds that are not in calf, and eat them. But I do get very tired of the endless potatoes, turnips and carrots, and of life being always the same. Ishbel complains about having to go to the spring to get water. She says her chilblains hurt. I can't blame her. We have a water butt to catch rainwater, but that's no use at this time of year.

I want to travel, to see the world.

It's funny, but since Grandfather died, I've started to remember things I haven't thought about for ages. Like India and my parents. I don't remember them very well. I remember Mama getting dressed for a party in a lacy pink gown with huge puffed sleeves and carrying a round fan of embroidered silk with an ivory handle. I thought she looked beautiful.

3

I can't really remember her face. Nor her voice. Grandmama says that I have her dark-brown eyes. My hair is a similar chestnut, I know, because I have a locket with some of her hair in it. I only remember her clothes.

My father was tall, with a tickly moustache and he smelt of tobacco. I remember far more of my ayah. She was a fat, comfortable woman, with black hair shining with oil and rings in her nose. Whenever I think of her, I get this feeling of absolute safety. Everything was all right, because ayah was there.

I remember how often I was ill in India. I used to go down with fevers, and everything was either huge or very far away. When I say 'India' I think instantly of the heat and the colours. Every now and then, something comes back to me in a sudden flash. It's like a jigsaw. A memory of a monkey stealing a piece of mango from my plate; the smell of spices and dung and heat; and then it vanishes and I can never fit anything together.

I don't know why this is all coming back now. I suppose I'm wondering if I shall only remember Grandfather in bits, too. His white beard, with crumbs of toast in it, perhaps. Or his sudden rages, when his face went purple.

After my parents died, when I was seven, I have a confused recollection of being rattled about in a bullock cart, and then the ship, and the smell of fish and tar and the wetness of it all.

At first, I hated it here. The Scottish hills weren't right, they were too small and rounded,

4

compared with the Himalayas. The rain dripped all the time; the days were different lengths. In India we had the rainy season and the dry season; the days were always the same length, and you knew where you were. The leaves stayed on the trees as they should. Everything about Scotland was all wrong.

Then there was Beatrix, my big cousin, who was six years older than me. She was an orphan, too, and the first time we met she said, 'All your bones stick out. I shall call you "Skelly", short for skeleton.' She's pretty, plump in all the right places, and she says her hair is honey blonde. Personally, I think it's the colour of dried buffalo dung. She has a small rosebud mouth and her hands have dimples on the backs.

I've known Beatrix for ten years now, and I don't like her any better than I did when I was seven.

She also has a good dowry, which I don't. In a way, I'm pleased about Beatrix's dowry because it meant that when she came out at the Edinburgh Assembly when she was eighteen, Duncan Penicuik proposed to her. They were married in 1846 and it was a relief when she went. I don't care much for Duncan either.

I've been writing for ages, and I still haven't got round to what I want to say. It's three o'clock, and the light is beginning to go. I've lit the paraffin lamp. Soon I shall have to change for dinner.

Grandfather's funeral is on Thursday, the day

after Beatrix and Duncan, and Mr Ogilvy arrive. Grandmama isn't saying much, but I know she's worried. Grandfather ~~thinks~~ *thought that females can't manage alone, and Ishbel and I think that Achnagarry will go to Beatrix, because she has Duncan, besides being the elder granddaughter. So what will become of us? Of me? Ishbel says that Grandmama had a proper marriage settlement, but I don't trust Duncan.*

Thank God, Grandfather's coffin has gone from the library. It was all right for the first few days. People came to pay their respects and he looked just the same, only very white and still. But the lout few days, his face got sharper and more sunken and, even though the library fire wasn't lit, the room began to smell. It was a relief when Callum came and nailed the lid on and he and Tam, and the two Maclaren brothers, took the coffin down the glen to the kirk.

The thaw has come at last, and Morag, who helps Ishbel in the kitchen, opened the library window, gave the place a good clean and put the chairs back ready for the will reading.

The clock has just struck half-past four. I must change for dinner.

*   *   *

5 April, 1850
The day after Aeneas Drummond's funeral, and Robina sat by the parlour window and watched the soft highland rain. It was a chill

6

spring day and the mist had come down, obscuring the slopes of Carn Dhu where it plunged into the cold peaty waters of Loch Nevan. The Scots pines on the slope down to the River Nevan dripped monotonously and she could just glimpse the dark, agitated waters of the loch through the trees.

Beatrix Penicuik busied herself with the tea-cups and saucers. 'Come Robina,' she said sharply, 'the others will be with us shortly. Don't just sit there and mope.'

Robina sighed and tucked a stray strand of hair behind her ear. 'I was just thinking that it was ten years since I came here.'

Beatrix flicked a crumb off the table impatiently. 'And what a pinched, wan little thing you were. I remember Grandmama saying that we must feed you up, not that we've been very successful!'

Robina was now seventeen and, Beatrix feared, doomed to be scrawny. She thought nothing of walking twenty miles and she had most unfeminine muscles in her arms from her wretched archery. Her one good point was her sparkling dark eyes, but even there they didn't correspond to proper standards of feminine beauty. They were too dark, bold even. A softer brown would have been better. Beatrix's light-brown eyes looked at herself in the looking-glass over the mantelpiece for a complacent moment and watched as she patted her smooth honey-coloured hair.

7

Now, in a hastily dyed black dress, Robina looked scrawnier than ever. She didn't even have any money. Whatever was going to become of her? Beatrix certainly didn't want her in Edinburgh.

Robina left the window, skipped over to the tea tray and lifted up a muslin cloth weighted down with small beads. 'Goody, scones! I'm hungry.'

Beatrix frowned. 'Try for a little restraint!' Ladies should not *be* hungry. She herself always had a large slice of bread and butter before dining out so that she could beg for 'the *smallest* slice. Really I eat like a bird!' Robina ate a hearty meal and usually had a second helping.

'Fruit cake, too!' said Robina with approval. Suddenly she felt a burst of freedom and excitement. Perhaps Murdo Gillespie would pop the question—after all, she was seventeen now, not too young for marriage, surely? And Murdo had hinted . . .

Beatrix bustled over to the fire where the kettle was singing quietly on the hob, took the tea caddy down from its shelf, unlocked it, spooned the tea into the teapot and poured on the boiling water.

'Beatrix!' cried Robina, staring at her cousin, horrified. 'What are you doing?' Every day, at three o'clock, it was Grandmama who opened that lacquered tea caddy and put the tea into the teapot.

'You can see what I'm doing,' said Beatrix, sharply.

'But . . .'

There were sounds from the library, footsteps, then the parlour door opened and Mrs Drummond, followed by Duncan Penicuik and Mr Ogilvy, came in. Duncan looked at his wife and gave a terse nod. Mrs Drummond took one look at the tea tray, closed her lips firmly against over-hasty speech, sat down in her accustomed chair and folded her mittened hands in her lap.

Beatrix, with a quiet satisfaction, did the honours of the tea tray, cut the cake and handed round the scones. Duncan's nod meant that Achnagarry was now *hers*, and let nobody forget it.

*   *   *

Robina's Journal   *5 April 1850*
I can't bear it, Beatrix has no right to take over like that! It's not fair. When everybody had gone to bed, I tip-toed along to Grandmama's room and tapped on the door. She was sitting by her dressing-table, reading her Bible, as she does every night.

But before I could say anything, she said, 'I know what you're going to say, and don't. Achnagarry is now her house, and she has every right to order things as she chooses. I could have wished that she had had a little more delicacy . . .

9

But, it's a small thing, after all. And in a day or so, they will be gone.'

'Will we stay here?' I asked.

'I expect so.'

Thank God. The last thing I want is to go and live in Edinburgh with Beatrix and Duncan. Duncan only ever thinks about money. I'm sure that if you looked inside his head you would find a cash ledger. Mr Pennyquick, I call him.

A couple more days. I shall have to button my lip.

*   *   *

The trouble with Beatrix, thought Mrs Drummond, when Robina had gone, was that she had always had it too easy. Rich (she had inherited her mother's fortune) and prettily plump, she had caught the eye of Duncan Penicuik at the Edinburgh Assembly when she was eighteen. Mrs Drummond had not been in favour of the match—Duncan was too much of a parvenu for her taste; there was a vague unpleasant rumour about his private life, and she suspected that he had had an eye on Beatrix's substantial dowry; but he was plainly doing well for himself and Beatrix wanted the match.

Her husband, Aeneas, had liked him though. Duncan had risen from nothing and had worked his way up from the shop floor of a drapery business and eventually set up on his

10

own and founded the Penicuik Universal Stores which was now a thriving and expanding business. Aeneas admired Duncan's energy and ability to read the market and, two years ago, at the onset of his final illness, was persuaded to leave the estate to Beatrix as his elder granddaughter with suitable provision for his widow. Duncan was to be the trustee. Robina would eventually inherit Mrs Drummond's own dowry of a modest £5000. Unfortunately, Robina would not have control of it until she was thirty-five, unless she married when, of course, her husband would look after it for her. Mrs Drummond quietly determined to live as long as possible.

She had protested, but in vain. Once her husband had made up his mind, nothing would move him. 'Duncan will look after you both,' he'd said. She had tried, but she couldn't like Duncan. And Ishbel, who had a cousin in Edinburgh, had told her of whispers that Mr Penicuik consorted with a shop-girl and rumour had it that there was even a child . . .

*   *   *

The Penicuiks stayed two more days. Duncan spent most of his time on the estate with the estate manager. The ladies sat quietly in the parlour, Beatrix and Robina sewing and Mrs Drummond mending a hole in her shawl with exquisitely fine stitches.

11

Beatrix said casually, 'We are planning to pull this place down.'

The needle slipped. 'Oh, how careless of me!' cried Mrs Drummond. A small bead of blood welled up from her finger and soaked into the wool.

Robina looked up. Achnagarry to be pulled down! She opened her mouth to protest, but shut it again when Mrs Drummond shook her head quietly.

'Duncan has promised me a proper shooting lodge,' Beatrix went on complacently.

'A pretend castle, I suppose?' said Robina.

'It will have turrets and battlements, naturally.' Beatrix gave a little laugh. 'But, unlike Lord Invershiel's tumble-down affair, ours will have every modern convenience. I shall insist on a proper bathroom!'

'What about winter?' demanded Robina. 'You know how difficult it is to get running water in winter.'

'We'll be in Edinburgh during the winter,' said Beatrix, dismissively.

Plainly, how her grandmother and cousin were to manage in winter did not concern her, thought Robina.

'Duncan has plans for expanding the estate,' Beatrix continued.

Of course, thought Robina. He has his eye on Dunlairg.

Dunlairg Castle, which belonged to Lord Invershiel, stood in decaying splendour at the

12

south end of Loch Nevan. Before the Forty-Five rebellion, the Invershiels had owned all the land, but fines and confiscations had deprived them of much of their wealth. Lord Invershiel's father had been forced to sell part of his estate to Aeneas Drummond and Duncan obviously hoped to buy more.

'Won't it be very expensive?' asked Robina.

'Ladies never discuss money,' said Beatrix crushingly. 'It's so vulgar.'

Robina bit her lip. It was not until the evening after the Penicuiks' departure that Rohina and Mrs Drummond could discuss it. They were once more sitting quietly in the parlour, with the peat fire glowing softly in the grate.

'Oh, Robina!' burst out Mrs Drummond suddenly. 'Your grandfather should have thought of this!' It was a measure of her distress that she should utter a word of criticism against her husband. 'Beatrix talks of our being here as "caretakers" when the new place is built. How can I bear to stay?'

'Well, don't,' retorted Robina. Her dark eyes were sparkling angrily. 'Why should we stay for Beatrix and Duncan's convenience? Why not go? You've always said that the climate here affects your rheumatism.'

'Go?' echoed Mrs Drummond. 'Go where?'

*　　　*　　　*

There was a third house on the shores of Loch Nevan. Nevan House was a neat unpretentious place, surrounded on three sides by trees, with a well-scrubbed front doorstep and lace curtains at the windows to stop prying eyes, although there was nobody living near enough to be inquisitive. It was the home of Mrs Gillespie, the minister's widow, who lived with her only son Murdo, a tall, thin, intense young man of about twenty-one, who had just come down from university in Edinburgh and would shortly be following his late father into holy orders.

Murdo had evaded his mother's ever-watchful eye and was striding down towards the bridge which crossed the loch where it flowed into the River Nevan. He was going to meet Robina, and he was suffering from a sense of undeserved disappointment. He had fully expected that Robina, together with her cousin, would be named joint inheritors of the Achnagarry estate, and he had just learned that Beatrix had inherited it all, and that Robina would get only her grandmother's fortune of £5000.

The trouble was that he had made Robina an offer, well, not exactly an offer, he'd been too canny for that, but an understanding certainly. He was miserably aware that a court of law might well regard it as legally binding and he was not sure what to do. He did not want to find himself in a Breach of

14

Promise case.

Still, £5000 was not to be sneezed at and it might be wiser to jolly things along for a while, until something better turned up. It was just as well that he was going away, he thought.

Robina stood on the bridge and watched, with a flutter of the heart, as he strode towards her. His thin black hair was carefully combed with a centre parting and his large fair forehead always seemed to her to epitomize intelligence. He came up and bowed. Robina timidly took his arm and together they leaned over the grey stone bridge and looked down to where the loch emptied itself into the Nevan.

'My mother wants me to go to her brother in Edinburgh. I must make my way in the world,' said Murdo. 'You understand that, don't you, Robina?'

'Oh, yes,' said Robina, blinking hard.

'It will not be for long. Four or five years, probably.'

He didn't say, but Robina knew that he was dependent on his mother and that he must do as she wished.

'I would never wish to stand in your way,' she said proudly.

'You are only seventeen,' Murdo stated. 'We shall write to each other and in five years' time . . .' He let the rest of the sentence hang delicately in the air.

Robina put her hand briefly on his shoulder, but felt by the sudden tension that it was not

15

welcome. She dropped it.

'It is right that you should feel it,' Murdo assured her. 'Women feel these things more than men. I shall picture you here, so mind you come to the bridge and think of me.'

'Oh, I forgot to tell you,' cried Robina, 'Grandmama and I are going to live in Nairn.'

'Nairn!' echoed Murdo in displeasure. He wanted Robina to stay at Achnagarry. She was his back-up, if he didn't find anybody richer. He certainly didn't want her off meeting other men.

'We think the seaside will be better for Grandmama's health.'

Murdo shook his head. 'Moving—at her age. I think it very unwise.'

Robina found herself apologizing.

'We shall write to each other,' declared Murdo, with a stiff smile. 'It could not be thought improper, we are such old friends.'

'Oh yes!' cried Robina. Writing to a gentleman to whom one was not related practically constituted an engagement. Or at least the promise of one.

The future suddenly looked brighter.

*   *   *

Robina's Journal
Met Murdo this afternoon. He's so good-looking, and there's something about the way his hair grows. I desperately wanted him to speak. *I*

16

wouldn't mind a long engagement, truly I wouldn't. But all he said was that he had to go to Edinburgh. His mother wants it and I know he has to go. I just wish she liked me.

But he's asked me to write! Of course, I said 'Yes!' But he didn't kiss me. He never has, and we were quite alone. When I touched his shoulder, I knew he didn't like it. It was awful. I felt so embarrassed.

He wasn't happy about Grandmama and me going to Nairn. I hope it was because he was jealous! I wanted to ask him for a lock of hair, but, in the end, I didn't dare.

Oh, Murdo! XXXXXX

*　　　*　　　*

Once she had made up her mind, Mrs Drummond was not unhappy about moving to Nairn. It was a small town on the Moray Firth, not far from Inverness, and, with its mild climate, just coming into fashion as a health resort. There were some elegant town houses, newly built, overlooking the sea. She would take one of those.

Mr Penicuik, though, was not so pleased. He had counted on Mrs Drummond being at Achnagarry to oversee all the problems and irritations that were bound to arise with the building of the new lodge. He wanted her on the spot, not thirty miles away in Nairn, where she could be of no help. When Beatrix's

17

expostulations had no effect, he wrote a stiff letter, pointing out that, by the terms of her husband's will, her jointure from the Achnagarry estate was payable only if she stayed there. Otherwise, she would have to rely on the income from her dowry and, a mere £250 a year, he reminded her, would not keep her in the manner to which she had become accustomed.

Mrs Drummond, with praiseworthy restraint, did not mention this letter to Robina. Instead, she wrote to Mr Ogilvy asking for his comments, and when his reply came that there was nothing to be done, she lowered her sights, and asked him to find them some suitable lodgings in Nairn. She would have to forgo the town house she had had in mind, and settle for somewhere cheaper, but she was not going to submit to Mr Penicuik's blackmail.

Mr Ogilvy contacted his kinsman in Inverness, and, a week or so later, Mr Francis Ogilvy wrote to say that he had found them some pleasant lodgings in Wellington Road. Mrs Drummond replied thanking him, and it was arranged.

Robina spent the weeks before their departure saying goodbye to all her favourite haunts. Murdo had left. The builders had already cleared the site for the new Achnagarry Lodge. They were using Achnagarry House as a base, and already there was constant interference from Beatrix, who wrote frequently demanding that something or other be done. Robina was glad they were leaving. She said as much to Donald Fraser, who had been her grandfather's ghillie.

'The lodge will have turrets and battlements,' she told him. They were speaking in Gaelic. Donald smiled grimly. 'Like Dunlairg?'

'I suppose so—but modern.' She made a face. 'It'll mean more work around here.' Donald took a pragmatic view. Thirty years ago, many of his family had been forced to emigrate to America. Those who stayed were always aware that they might be next. Anything which helped the local economy was to be welcomed.

'Seasonal work, though,' Robina pointed out.

'Better than nothing.' At least Mr Penicuik couldn't evict them and then expect them to return during the stalking season.

'I shall miss it,' sighed Robina. 'I've lived here for ten years.'

'Aye. I remember when you came, a wee yellow thing, like a skinny rabbit.'

Robina laughed. 'Have you heard from Hamish?' Hamish was Donald's son, now serving in India with his regiment.

'We had a letter at Christmas. He's doing fine, is Hamish.'

'I miss Hamish,' said Robina. He was a few years older than herself and it was he who had shown her the way to the crannog on

19

Loch Tearmann.

Crannogs were artificial islands, which some said were built by the fairies. This one, in a loch high in the hills, had a secret underwater causeway leading to it. The first few steps were natural looking stones above the water line. Then there was the underwater causeway, built of ancient wooden planks and invisible from the surface because of the dark brown peaty water. To find it you aligned yourself from the last stepping stone to a boulder which projected from the hillside on the opposite side of the loch, and then it wound across the water.

Hamish had shown it to her during her first summer at Achnagarry and sworn her to secrecy. 'I discovered it last year during the drought,' he'd said. 'One day, the loch was really low and I saw the causeway. The next night there was a storm and the loch filled up again. But I remembered it.' He had explained how you found your way across. So many paces aligning yourself to the boulder, then you turned and aligned yourself to the waterfall coming down from Doire Meurach and did another twenty paces, then another realignment and so on. Robina had learnt it by heart.

It had been their secret, and she always felt that it was her special place. The loch was mysterious and dark. It looked deep and the locals said that it was haunted by a water horse, for sheep had been known to disappear there. Of course, Robina realized, it could not be that deep, at least not where the causeway ran, and she had never seen the water horse. She spent a lot of her childhood on that island. At least Beatrix could never get at her there.

Even now, Robina didn't mention the crannog to Donald. She left him and went indoors to beg a couple of bannocks from Morag to put into her satchel. She would go to the crannog on Loch Tearmann and say goodbye.

It was a stiff climb up the hillside, pushing through the tough heather and up on to the crest. Then there was the walk round the peat bog, showing the mark of generations of peat cutting. She skirted the bog, turned right and continued up the hill, this time through juniper bushes. There was a derelict shepherd's hut, and the remains of shielings up here, summer pastures for the cows, but deserted now since the clearances a generation ago. She stopped by one of the swift-flowing burns and cupped her hand for a drink. Looking back she could see Loch Nevan and the steep slope of Carn Dhu with Mrs Gillespie's house nestling under it; Achnagarry House with its Scots pines was to the right and, to her left in the distance, the moss-covered turrets of Dunlairg Castle.

Robina stood for a long time taking it all in: the egg-yolk yellow of the gorse by the road up the glen, the bog myrtle, the birch and alder by the burn. Soon the heather would colour the hill-side purple and, later, the mountain ash berries would glow orange and the bracken turn to gold.

She would not be there to see them.

The dark waters of Loch Tearmann lay between the slopes of Carn Fliuchbhaid and Doire Meurach, formed by ancient glaciers and fed by waters of a dozen peaty burns. In the middle was the crannog. Robina looked round, as she always did; she did not want to be seen crossing. Nobody, not even the water horse. She ran down to the loch's edge, took off her boots and stockings and stuffed them into her satchel, hitched up her skirts, climbed on to the stepping stones, aligned herself with the strangely shaped boulder on the slopes of Carn Fliuchbhaid, and wound her way across to the island. The water was bitterly cold.

It was a good place for defence, she thought. There was a tumbled mound of stones in the middle, the remains of some ancient building. Nowadays, the crannog was covered with myrtle and alder. There were three birch trees just behind the stone mound, good lookout points; Robina had often climbed them as a child.

She undid her satchel, took out a small towel, dried her cold feet, rubbed some colour back into them, and put her stockings and boots back on. There was a favourite place she liked to sit, with her back against a birch tree, and which looked out over the hidden causeway. She clasped her hands around her knees and became quite still as Ham ish had taught her. He had pointed out the shy red squirrel, made her listen for the tell-tale cheep cheep of the long-tailed tit busy in the birch trees, and the small scurryings of a wood mouse.

Her mind began to relax. Grandfather was gone. That part of her life was over. She must look forward, not back. Yes, she would miss all this, but it was still there; she had it all in her head and it wouldn't disappear.

Perhaps one day she would be able to bring Murdo here. She would show him the causeway and all the treasures of her secret place. But even as she thought it, the vision disintegrated. Somehow, Murdo and the crannog refused to stay together.

*   *   *

Edinburgh, 1852
Mr Alan Ogilvy sat in his office in Heriot Row, glanced at the clock on the mantelpiece and frowned. Duncan Penicuik had saddled him with a most unpleasant duty, that of telling Penicuik's mistress, Mary Ritchie, that their affair was now over, and that she would have to leave her cottage in Musselburgh. If it hadn't been for the fact that he, and his father before him, had served the Drummonds for several

23

generations, and that Mr Penicuik brought him a lot of business, he would have refused.

Mr Ogilvy knew many family secrets—it was part of his job—but they were usually respectable secrets, like trust funds to be administered for a dotty aunt, or the paying off of some youthful debts, not a sordid affair with a shop girl. Mr Ogilvy was a fastidious man, a celibate bachelor whose religious convictions were deeply felt, and the thought that 'a woman of that stamp', as he put it, was about to pollute his office, was profoundly distasteful.

Mr Penicuik himself had been brazen about it. 'Pay her off, Ogilvy,' he'd said. 'People are beginning to talk, and I don't want it getting to Mrs Penicuik's ears. Bad for business, too.' Besides, he was bored with the woman. She was no longer the adoring sixteen year old he'd taken up with. In future, he would indulge those sort of pleasures when he was away from home, on business in London or Paris.

'How high are you willing to go, sir?' asked Mr Ogilvy, removing his gaze from the stern features of Mr Ogilvy, senior, hanging over the mantelpiece, and fixing them on Mr Penicuik's florid face.

'As little as possible. Whatever will keep her quiet—within reason.'

So now Mr Ogilvy was awaiting Miss Ritchie. He imagined a buxom blonde, shockingly over-dressed and reeking of some

24

cheap scent.

At that moment, his clerk put his head round the door. 'Miss Ritchie to see you, Mr Ogilvy.'

'Show her in.' He sat down at his desk. The door opened.

A young woman in her twenties, with a clear, pale skin, brown eyes and dark hair, neatly smoothed under her bonnet, came into the room. Holding her hand was a small boy of about four, with a mop of dark curls. He was clutching a little wooden horse on wheels. He glanced up apprehensively at the stuffed deer's head on the wall, with Mr Ogilvy's hat perched on one of the antlers, but said nothing.

A child! thought Mr Ogilvy. Mr Penicuik had never mentioned that there was a child. Slowly, he rose to his feet. 'Please sit down, Miss Ritchie. Perhaps your little lad would like to sit by the window?' This was no drab, he thought angrily. This was a respectable young woman. What was Mr Penicuik about?

Mary settled her son on a chair by the window and told him to be a good boy, then sat down by the desk and waited quietly.

Mr Ogilvy cleared his throat. 'I have been instructed to tell you that Mr Penicuik feels that the time has come for your . . . er acquaintance to be terminated.' He looked up. The woman across the desk said nothing. She glanced anxiously at her son, but that was all. 'He . . . he has decided that it would be better

25

if you moved right away.' He could see her gloved hands clench and her face become taut.

'I see,' she whispered.

'My dear,' said Mr Ogilvy, compassion overcoming his usual professional manner, 'I feel it would be best if you told me how you came to be in this unhappy situation, then I shall know how best to help you. You may rely on my discretion.'

'Very well, sir.' The voice was soft and well-spoken. Her brown eyes looked at him for a moment, then she took a deep breath and said, 'I met Mr Penicuik when I was sixteen. In those days, he was the under manager at Macdonald's, the drapers.'

Mr Ogilvy nodded encouragingly.

'My father was the manager there, and he took Mr Penicuik under his wing. He came to supper from time to time. Father admired the way he had worked his way up from nothing. We all got on very well—that is, my father, Mr Penicuik, and myself. My mother was an invalid. I . . . I think Father hoped for a match between us. I . . . I hoped so, too.

'Then Father died suddenly, shortly after my mother's death. I was left alone. My mother's illness had been expensive and there was very little money, and I have no close relatives.' She paused and blew her nose firmly. 'I . . . I have no excuse, Mr Ogilvy. I knew it was wrong. But when Mr Penicuik suggested an "understanding", I agreed to it. I believed that we would be married one day and I was so scared of life on my own.

'He found me a little cottage in Musselburgh and looked after me. I became "Mrs" Ritchie.' She paused again, struggling with her tears.

'Take your time,' said Mr Ogilvy, gently.

'There is little more to say. I realized, finally, that we would never get married when he told me that he was marrying Miss Beatrix Drummond. Two years later, I found I was with child.' Her voice trembled and she stopped.

'Mrs Ritchie,' said Mr Ogilvy at last. 'I will say frankly that I consider Mr Penicuik's conduct has been disgraceful. To seduce an innocent girl, whose youth and situation should have been enough to protect her, is beyond belief.'

'Thank you, sir,' said Mary. 'But what am I to do? I have saved very little. And I have Jamie to look after.'

'How much does Mr Penicuik give you at the moment?' asked Mr Ogilvy, picking up his pen and dipping it in the ink.

'Eighteen shillings a week.'

'Eighteen shillings!' The man's a miser, thought Ogilvy in distaste. He was worth ten thousand a year, at least.

'You will need more than that,' he said firmly. 'I am sure that Mr Penicuik will want young Jamie to have a proper education.'

Mary said nothing. Duncan had several times expressed the view that Jamie could struggle, just as he had had to. 'Make a man of him,' he'd said.

Jamie, who had been watching the carriages out of the window, turned round and said, 'I think that my mother is very pretty.'

'Sh! Jamie,' said Mary, blushing.

'Well, she is,' declared Jamie.

'So she is, my little man,' said Mr Ogilvy. Jamie nodded, satisfied, and turned his attention back to the street outside. 'Now, Mrs Ritchie, is there anywhere in particular that you'd like to live?'

Mary shook her head.

'In that case, I suggest Inverness. It's a fine town, with plenty of good schools, and I have a kinsman there, who will be able to help you settle in—a Mr Francis Ogilvy.'

'You are very kind. Thank you.'

'Mr Penicuik wants the business expedited as quickly as possible. I shall write as soon as it is settled.' He rose to his feet.

Mary went and lifted Jamie down from his chair. Mr Ogilvy opened the door for her and watched as they went down the stairs, Jamie still clutching his horse and holding tightly on to the banister. When they had gone, he rang the bell.

His clerk found him agitatedly walking up and down.

'Disgraceful business,' said Mr Ogilvy, when

he'd told him what had happened. 'Poor young thing. She must be Alexander Ritchie's daughter. Penicuik's a scoundrel.'

The clerk shook his head. He had never cared for Mr Penicuik, either. He was not a man who treated his subordinates well. The clerk had never received so much as a nod of recognition from him.

A week later, in Musselburgh, Mary Ritchie received a letter.

Dear Mrs Ritchie,

I have now spoken to Mr Penicuik, and he has agreed to make you an allowance of £100 (one hundred pounds) per annum, payable quarterly, until James's fourteenth birthday. After that, it will be James's responsibility to look after you.

I am sorry that I could not persuade Mr Penicuik to do more. He has, however, agreed to pay for your and James's ship passage to Inverness and to advance the sum of £5 (five pounds) towards your settling in expenses.

My clerk will be in touch with you, about the travel arrangements.

Yours sincerely
A. Ogilvy

Mary read the letter through twice. Two pounds a week! Why, it was double what she had now. She must write and thank Mr Ogilvy.

Then she thought, but it was only for ten more years. Supposing something happened to Jamie? Or herself? What would happen then?

Back in his office, Mr Ogilvy was thinking that Penicuik had been as miserly as he had feared. He had urged Penicuik to settle a couple of thousand on James, with Miss Ritchie having a life interest in the income. Surely, she was owed that seeing that Penicuik had, in effect, ruined her life? James was a nice little lad; he should be set up properly, not cast adrift at fourteen, with his mother to support as well. When the lad was old enough to understand that his father was a wealthy man there might well be trouble.

*   *   *

Simla, India. 1852
Edward Mountsorrel looked down at his wife who was sitting on the veranda of their bungalow fanning herself languidly, every now and then reaching out for a sugared almond, and acknowledged finally that in marrying Betsy he had made one of the worst mistakes of his life.

They had married five years earlier when she was just seventeen and he was twenty-one. They had both been far too young, he realized. She was pretty, with the sort of delicate femininity he found so attractive and, he now

30

knew, was indolent and stupid. But perhaps he was being unfair. She had had no education beyond the usual feminine accomplishments, was unused to responsibility, and the climate of India disagreed with her. None of this was her fault.

Betsy,' he said.

She turned and smiled. It was still a sweet smile and her blue eyes were as guileless as ever.

'Don't forget that the Granges and Captain Everton and his wife are coming to dinner tomorrow. I shall be out, so you must have a word with the cook.'

'Oh darling, must I? You know I can't understand a word he says. Can't you talk to him before you go?'

Edward sighed. 'Very well. But Betsy, you must try and take the trouble to learn a little of the language. Just think how—'

But Betsy had put her hands over her ears. 'Oh, don't go on so,' she cried pettishly. 'You make my head ache.' She stared out at the setting sun. Only another few minutes, she thought.

'Where's Charlotte?' asked Edward next. Charlotte was their daughter, now rising four, and the apple of Edward's eye.

Betsy shrugged. 'With her ayah, I presume.' She watched as the sun sank in a ball of fire; she never quite got used to the speed with which it happened. 'Good. Drinkie?'

At that moment Ahmed appeared with the drinks tray. Edward poured her a drink in silence and Ahmed lit the paraffin lamps, salaamed and left.

'Why the Evertons?' asked Betsy lightly. Captain Everton was a very attractive man and pleasingly attentive to herself.

'I want to go up to Kashmir. Everton is sending some men there and he's promised that I can go with them.'

'Oh, your silly plants again!'

'My silly plants are wanted by Kew Gardens and my scientific reputation, such as it is, depends on them,' said Edward evenly.

'Shall Captain Everton be going with you?' Betsy twiddled the stem of her glass.

'No, I believe not.'

Good, thought Betsy. She had discovered that there were certain dangerously exciting games to be played with attractive, safely married men. She gave an inward sigh. Edward had once been exciting, but now he was just dull. He was a big man and well muscled, but whereas this had once thrilled her, now she found the way he padded about the bungalow and spent the evenings writing up his notes from his latest plant collecting merely tedious. He was just like a dull old bear, she thought. Even the beard he allowed to grow during his trips away seemed to add to this bear-like quality. And who wanted to live with a bear?

Edward put down his glass. 'I must go and say good-night to Charlotte.'

In her bedroom, Charlotte was sitting on the bed behind the mosquito net, playing with a wooden doll.

'Papa!' She jumped up and reached for him through the net. It was a little game they played. She hugged him through the net, then raced to find the edge of it, pulled it up and over him and suddenly there he was sitting beside her and he was her own Papa.

'You've been drinking whisky,' she said accusingly.

'Only one glass.'

'Mama has a bottle in her cupboard with all her shoes. I found it.' She looked up at him anxiously.

Edward stroked her hair. 'Yes, darling. I know.'

Charlotte relaxed. She'd had a horrid feeling that she shouldn't talk about it, but if Papa knew then that was all right. 'Can I go riding with you tomorrow?' She had a pony of her very own, though her father's bearer always walked beside her in case of an accident.

'Not tomorrow. I have things to arrange for my trip, but the day after.'

Charlotte stroked his arm, 'I don't like it when you go away.' Mama was different when he went. She dressed up and laughed a lot. Men came to visit her and there were whispers from the ayah and the other servants. Charlotte didn't know what was going on, but she felt uncomfortable.

'I don't like leaving you, my pet,' said Edward. 'When you're older I promise I'll take you with me.'

'When I'm four?' asked Charlotte hopefully, snuggling up to him. She liked the way he felt big and safe.

'That's still a bit little. Say seven or eight, and if I'm not going too far.'

'Seven,' said Charlotte with resolution.

* * *

A fortnight later, in Kashmir, Edward thought: I must accept Betsy as she is and try to make her happy. In a few months, we'll return to Scotland, at least for a while, until my next expedition. Perhaps, back home, things will be better. It is not her fault that I made a mistake—and she *has* given me my daughter. Charlotte makes up for everything.

* * *

Mrs Drummond and Robina stayed only two winters in Nairn. They spent the winter of 1852 on the South Coast in Bournemouth and the one after that in France.

'I've always wanted to travel,' Mrs Drummond confided, 'but I married young and I never got the chance.' It would also be cheaper and Mrs Drummond was anxious to put something aside for Robina in the event of her own death. She had said nothing to her granddaughter, but she couldn't help thinking that if she died before Robina was thirty-five, then Robina would probably be put in the unenviable position of being dependent on Duncan's charity.

It was Robina who had daringly suggested France. She could practise her French, and it would be warmer, which would help Mrs Drummond's rheumatism. The invaluable Mr Alan Ogilvy helped them with all the travel arrangements and gave them an introduction to a friend of his in Avignon and somehow it was all organized.

Robina learnt to cope with foreign hotels, booking seats on trains, ordering meals and carriages—and found, after the initial terrors, that she enjoyed the feeling of independence it brought. She wrote as much to Murdo; she wanted him to know that his future wife was a capable woman, one on whom he could depend.

Murdo's reply came as a shock.

I trust that you will not allow yourself to be drawn into any contact with the French. Their morals are lax and they are, of course, Roman Catholics. The letter ended: *I was shocked to read that you*

35

actually dined *with Madame Charpentier.*
However unpleasant, Robina, it was your
duty to protest against it. You tell me they
actually sang *grace before meals! I want*
you to write and promise me that you will
never *do such a thing again.*

Dear stuffy Murdo, thought Robina
dutifully, stifling a feeling of disappointment.
Perhaps she hadn't explained it very well. If
only she could see him and really talk to him,
then everything would be all right. She found
herself censoring her letters and there were
fewer and fewer things it felt safe to write
about. Everything seemed to contain some sort
of embargo.

*   *   *

Mary Ritchie put her head down on her arms
and cried with exhaustion and loneliness. She
had been in Ardconnel Terrace, Inverness, for
two years now, and it had been a shock to
realize how much protection Duncan's
presence, however infrequent, had given her in
Musselburgh. There, he had paid for the
cottage and coals and for the night soil men,
and she had managed to feed and clothe
herself and Jamie very well on the eighteen
shillings a week he gave her.
  Here, in spite of the fact that two pounds a
week was a very good income indeed, far

beyond the aspirations of most working men, she found it a struggle. She was a woman on her own, with no noticeable male support, and thus fair game for inferior goods and short changing. She hadn't realized that there would be an annual charge for the piped water, for example, nor that a prudent housewife bought her coals and peat in the summer, when prices were low, so she had suddenly to find money she didn't have.

Then there had been that awful episode with the chimney sweep. In her innocence, she'd offered him a cup of tea and a scone when he'd finished the job, but she had not expected him to seize her by her apron strings and try to pull her on to his knee.

'What are you doing!' she'd cried, suddenly aware that the door was shut and that Jamie was at school.

'Come on, lass,' said the sweep impatiently, gripping her tightly by the waist. 'How's about a wee cuddle?'

'Certainly not!' Mary gave her apron a sharp tug. It tore. Her eyes filled with tears. 'Go away,' she pleaded. 'Just go away!'

The sweep got to his feet. 'Why did you ask me in then, if you didn't want a bit o' fun?'

'I was being kind!'

'Kind is it? There's another word for it, I'm thinking.' He picked up his jacket. 'That'll be sixpence, then.'

Silently, Mary counted out six pennies. The

sweep picked up his brushes from the corner and, to her relief, left the house. Mary locked the door after him and fell back against it, her heart still thudding.

That episode had taught her that she simply couldn't afford to be friendly; her position was too vulnerable. In those early years, it was a struggle not to allow depression to overcome her. It was difficult to make friends. She was not one of the deserving poor, and thus on the list of one of the charitable ladies of the town who visited; nor was she one of the Gaelic-speaking working folk, though she lived near them. It seemed to Mary that she was avoided and mistrusted by both sides. A wife without her husband, particularly a young and pretty girl, was always suspect.

'What happened to your man?' asked an impertinent neighbour, one day. 'Fisherman, is he?' Fishy, more like, she thought.

Mary shook her head, her colour rising. 'He works abroad for the railway contractor, Mr Brassey. He's in Canada.'

'Why aren't ye there wi' your man, then?'

'He said it wasn't suitable for us.'

The woman said no more, but her silence was eloquent.

Mary hated the lying. She couldn't help blushing whenever anybody asked her about her 'husband', but what else could she do? It was Mr Alan Ogilvy, in Edinburgh, who had suggested the story: 'You will find it much more comfortable if it's thought that your husband works abroad,' he'd said. She'd had no choice; unless she wanted to be ostracized, she had to pretend. There was nobody she could confide in; she wasn't even sure how much Mr Francis Ogilvy knew.

It was Mr Francis Ogilvy who had found her the little house in Ardconnel Terrace and suggested which school would be suitable for Jamie.

'It's a church school, which teaches in English,' he told her. 'Not all of them do. If your little lad turns out to be bright, then they will help you to apply for a bursary in due course for the Inverness Academy.' Secondary education had to be paid for, but there were a few bursaries available for bright boys from poor homes.

When Mary visited the school, she found that Mr Ogilvy's name was one which opened doors.

'Mr Ogilvy recommended us, ye say?' said the dominie, who had been inclined to look askance at this young woman, coming alone with her son. 'A verra respectable man.' He nodded his head, satisfied. 'I think we can take young James.'

Mary closed her eyes in relief.

*   *   *

Peradeniya, Ceylon, 1854

39

Edward Mountsorrel, returning unexpectedly early from a plant expedition, arrived at the bungalow he had rented for his wife and daughter, ran up the steps and shouted that he was back. Immediately, the *khitmagar* came out smiling, and took his hat and jacket.

'Everything all right?' asked Edward. 'Missy Baba? The memsahib?'

A wary look crossed the *khitmagar*'s face, but he assured Edward that his wife and daughter were both well. He glanced over his shoulder towards the interior of the bungalow and added, 'If the sahib will sit out here, I will bring him a drink.'

Edward looked at him for a moment and then nodded. He sank down on one of the chairs on the veranda, put his feet up on the stool and watched the setting sun. One moment it was hanging like a red ball over the slopes of a coffee plantation on the far hillside, and the next it had sunk in a fiery glow behind the western horizon and, almost instantly, it seemed, it was dark.

At that moment, a small sound to the left of the bungalow alerted him. He stood up and went quietly to the end of the veranda. A male figure was walking quickly and quietly across the lawn and vaulted over the fence at the bottom. For a moment, the man's fair hair and pale face showed in the last glow of the sunset, and then he was gone.

Edward stood and watched for a few

moments, and the familiar pain returned and lodged itself in his breast. He'd been able to forget it up in the mountains, or, if not forget, then push it to the very back of his mind, but, of course, it was still there, waiting for him. He sighed and went back to his chair, and found that his bearer had lit the lamps and left the drinks tray. A moth fluttered round one of the paraffin lamps, hit the glass and fell to the floor, and a lizard scurried out of the crack in the wall and ate it.

A few moments later, Betsy came out, a shawl over her arms. Edward rose.

'You're back early, darling,' she said, a faintly aggrieved note in her voice. She held up her face to be kissed.

Edward bent over her. At that moment, her shawl drooped a little and he saw the unmistakable mark of a love-bite on her neck.

'Drink?' he said, straightening up.

'Thank you.' Betsy sank down on the chair beside him. She took the drink, raised her glass to him and drank. Had he heard Bobby sneaking off? Well, what did he expect when he was away for weeks? Besides, she enjoyed the secret *billets doux* and assignations far more than the affairs themselves, if the truth were known. It was the secrecy of it which appealed to her. She also enjoyed skating as close to disaster as she dared. Edward could be such an old bear, she thought, and she liked stirring him up, rousing him to jealousy. The

41

only problem was that, nowadays, he wouldn't play the game. She was only twenty-four, she didn't want to sink into a respectable matron just yet. Anyway, what else was there to do in this benighted country? She hoped he wasn't going to be silly about it.

'Charlotte all right?'

'Of course.' Always Charlotte. 'She's with her ayah.'

There was silence. Betsy drank her whisky and smiled reminiscently at the pleasant afternoon she had just had. Bobby made her feel beautiful and . . . wanted. That was it! He saw her as a desirable woman, not just as a creature of no account who could be left for weeks on end, all because of some stupid plants.

'Who was that man?' asked Edward suddenly.

'W . . . what man?'

'The one who left your room and crossed the garden just now.'

Betsy bit her lip. He was going to be difficult after all. 'You must mean the gardener,' she said. 'There was a snake in the house earlier and I asked him to check all the rooms. I didn't think you'd want to be bothered with him, so I asked him to leave quietly.'

'Why was he creeping across the garden like that?' demanded Edward. Perhaps he'd been wrong, he thought. It had been getting dark, after all.

'*I* don't know. Shall I get the *khitmagar* to call him?'

'No, don't bother.' What was the use, he thought. Humiliation swept over him; he was that most despised of men, a cuckold; the one everybody talked about behind his back, the butt of jokes in the hill stations, places he now avoided. He *couldn't* accuse Betsy of infidelity openly, even though he knew that it was going on. There was Charlotte to consider. Betsy was a negligent mother, but she was *there.* Appearances were maintained. If he cast her off, not only would her reputation be ruined, but there would be a stigma on Charlotte, too. No, he would have to continue to play the sophisticated, indulgent husband, a rôle he found increasingly intolerable.

Betsy, watching him in the glow of the paraffin lamps, smiled and said, 'He's a silly boy to be jealous of the poor gardener.' She put down her glass and rustled over to sit on his knee. 'Look what an old bear he is,' she said, gently tugging at his beard. 'He knows his little pussy-cat doesn't like it.' She made a *moue.*

Edward kissed her perfunctorily. Too perfunctorily, for Betsy at once burst into tears, and, even while he kissed and soothed her, he realized that he was being manipulated into acquiescence.

CHAPTER TWO

Robina's Journal   Edinburgh, August 1856

Staying with the Penicuiks, and they don't improve, though I like little Madeline. I hadn't seen her since she was three, a spoilt, pretty little thing, and I feared the worst. She's now nine and much improved—though Beatrix calls her 'pert'. She's not pert, she's just taken the measure of her parents! The one I don't care for is Ewan, who is now seven. He's one of those rough, loud little boys—he reminds me horribly of Duncan. I predict that, in about ten years' time, he'll be after the housemaids. Poor little Aeneas suffers dreadfully from asthma, but he's a plucky child and tries not to let it discommode him. The awful thing is that Duncan despises him, you can see it, and I'm afraid that Aeneas knows it, too.

I'm glad we shall only be staying another few days.

One of Beatrix's dinners this evening. What a bore. Shall I wear my new French silk evening gown, just to annoy her? And the gold evening hair net? Yes, why not? She has already told me that I am 'positively skinny', and 'as dark as a gypsy'. Beatrix, naturally, always protects her complexion, lest she should become 'brown and coarse'.

Later: Murdo was there!

He turned up with a simpering Miss Glendinning, a female with a pursed mouth, like a hen's backside, and pale-blue eyes. She looked at me as though I were Jezebel! God knows what Murdo has been telling her. She is the daughter of a minister of some Wee Free kirk.

Thank God I was wearing my new silk. Beatrix was smirking, too. I suppose she always guessed about my feelings for Murdo. But now I've seen him again . . . he's such a prig. *He came over, after dinner, when we were all in the drawing-room, brought me a cup of coffee and sat down beside me.*

'I am sure that, like me, you must feel that it is time that our youthful romance resolved itself into something calmer,' he announced.

Something calmer? When was it anything else? I said, 'I am sure that Miss Glendinning will be a far more suitable helpmeet than I, in every way.' You rat! I thought. Then I noticed that his hair was thinning—he can't part it in the middle any more.

Murdo shook his finger at me in a ghastly show of archness. 'You are much too perceptive! But you are young, my dear Miss Drummond. You will recover.' He gave me the sort of sympathetic smile that made me want to pour the contents of my coffee cup all over him. 'Miss Glendinning possesses every feminine virtue: modesty, humility, and a strong sense of duty.'

'And I am sure that she has a handsome portion, to boot,' I added. I enjoyed saying that.

Soon after, he left.

I was glad when the evening ended. Part of me wanted to laugh—he was so pompous! *Had he always been like that, and I just hadn't noticed? But, instead, I cried. I have wasted six years of my life on that* stick. *Whilst I was dreaming of our future, he was on the lookout for somebody more suitable—and richer. Well, she's welcome to him.*

*   *   *

The following day, Robina found a small packet from Murdo beside her breakfast plate. In it, he enclosed all her letters and requested the return of his. There was nothing else with the letters. He'd never even asked for a lock of hair, even though it curled prettily. She could see Beatrix eyeing her. Robina gave her a bright smile and said, 'An unwanted correspondent, that's all.'

As soon as she could escape from the breakfast-room, Robina went up to her bedroom, crossed over to her writing case, unlocked it and took out a packet of letters tied with a red ribbon. She read them through slowly. His last one was only a couple of months ago and he had signed himself *Ever your most devoted, M. Gillespie.*

She could sue him for breach of promise— doubtless Duncan would be pleased to help her; in fact, he'd probably approve of her

46

sharpness in recognizing that there was some financial gain to be had. But for what? In order to exact compensation from Murdo, she would have to undergo the humiliation of having some lawyer agree that she was unlikely to receive another offer. Did she really want that?

No. A thousand times no. She looked again at the date. Murdo must already have met Miss Glendinning—he must have known that he was going to break it off, or, as he put it, 'allow their youthful romance to fade naturally into the calm of friendship.'

She stripped off the red ribbon, pushed the letters back into their envelopes, made a parcel and posted it. She did not include a letter. What was there to say? At the back of the writing desk was a handkerchief of his and a small broken tortoiseshell comb. She threw them, together with the ribbon, on to the fire.

She pushed her own returned letters to the back of the writing desk. Some day she would reread of her own folly. But not today. She had suffered enough humiliation for one day.

*   *   *

Death in the tropics can come with appalling suddenness. In 1857, the Mountsorrels were in Singapore, where Edward was plant collecting for Kew Gardens. At the tea-planter's evening party, Mrs Edward Mountsorrel had fluttered like a gaudy butterfly among the guests, her hyacinth-blue glacé silk gown, with its prettily floating silver ribbons and frothy falls of lace, swirled about her as she danced. As the starchy chaperons of the company murmured behind their fans, Edward forced himself to remain unmoved. He stood, arms folded, watching his wife twirling in the arms of Mr Northam and made no comment beyond, 'I see Betsy's enjoying herself.'

His companion glanced at Betsy's face, coquettishly turned towards Mr Northam and said curiously, 'You don't mind?'

Edward gave an indulgent laugh. 'She's young and pretty. Let her dance. I know I'm not a fit partner for her—too clumsy. She always complains that I tread on her toes.'

The other man was silent. If pretty Mrs Mountsorrel wasn't having an affair with Northam, she soon would be. But it was none of his business.

'I hope she didn't eat that fish tonight,' was all he said. Fish, in particular, could be fatal in the tropics. He would never serve it himself.

Later, in the carriage going home, Betsy chatted happily about what Mr Northam had said about her gown, and how Mr Quattrell had complimented her on her dancing, and then fell silent. Edward, only half-listening, gazed out of the window at the silhouette of an old temple, black and silver in the moonlight. Another humiliating evening endured, he thought. There had been that awful moment when he had gone into the smoking-room and a hush had fallen upon the company and he had known . . . Oh God, he couldn't bear to think about it: the sudden jovial talk, or worse, the pitying, or contemptuous glances. There was a small moan from the figure beside him. When he looked round, he could see Betsy slumped down and pearled beads of sweat on her upper lip.

'Betsy! Are you all right?' He felt her forehead. It was clammy. 'Quick!' he shouted to the driver, 'My wife is ill—get us home, fast!'

When they reached the bungalow, Betsy's maid took one horrified look at her mistress, put her hand to her mouth and fled. Soon there were shrieks from the servants' quarters and when the doctor came an hour later, the house was deserted save for Edward, Betsy, Charlotte and her ayah.

The doctor looked at Betsy for a moment. 'Probably cholera,' he said. 'I can give her some laudanum. It will ease her at any rate. I'm sorry, there is nothing I can do.'

'My daughter, Doctor!' cried Edward.

'She should be all right, sir. She was not at the dinner. Just keep her away from her mother.'

Betsy died the following evening after a series of painful convulsions. She never regained consciousness. Edward tried not to feel as though a burden had been lifted from his shoulders.

*　　*　　*

'Mother,' said James Ritchie, 'what happened to my father?'

Mary Ritchie paused in the act of putting drop scones on the griddle. She'd been dreading this question for years. She straightened up and turned round to took at him. Jamie, now twelve, was growing fast. His thin bony wrists were shooting out of his shirt cuffs, and his dark tufty hair was sprouting like grass. It seemed as if she were always either letting down the tucks she'd made in his shirt sleeves, or cutting his hair.

He was sitting at the kitchen table, his homework in front of him, with a candle casting a small pool of light on his book. He looked back at her, his brown eyes serious.

Other boys had fathers, he thought. Even if their fathers were dead, they knew about them. It was embarrassing not to know. When he'd asked her before—he must have been about seven—she'd said, 'He works a long way away, Jamie. He sends us money, but he doesn't live with us.'

'Oh,' Jamie had said, ' 'Cos Duggie at school said that he must be dead.'

Jamie thought of this now. What if his father were in prison? Was that it? But, if

50

he were, surely he wouldn't be sending them money? James knew that money came, because, every quarter, Mr Francis Ogilvy gave it to his mother, and Mother had been saving some. 'For a rainy day,' she'd said.

Up to now, when people asked, Jamie had always said, 'My father works abroad,' but more and more that felt like a lie. How *could* it be true? He never even wrote to them.

Mary turned back to check the drop scones and turned them over.

'I think you're still a little young to know,' she said. But she couldn't help thinking that in less than two years' time he would be fourteen and the money would stop. He'd have to know then, and would it be fair to spring it on him? She frowned down at the drop scones, tested them, then transferred them on to a warm plate.

'The boys say things at school,' said Jamie, sensing her uncertainty. 'I need to know, Mother.'

Mary sighed, and sat down at the table. She looked at him. He was a clever boy, doing well at the Inverness Academy and mature for his age, but once you knew something, you could never *unknow* it. Was it right to burden him with it now? Bastardy was such a stain. He would feel it terribly—and maybe blame her.

'What do they say?'

'That I'm a rich man's bastard,' said Jamie, picking at his nails. 'That my father's in prison.

51

That he's dead.'

Mary winced.

'I don't *mind*, Mother. Well, I do, but not as much as not knowing.' He could cope, he thought, if he knew what he was coping *with*.

'If I tell you, Jamie,' said Mary seriously, '*if* I tell you, it must stay a secret. It *has* to, otherwise the money stops coming, and we can't afford that, do you understand?' He has a right to know, she thought.

'Yes, Mother.' Jamie shut his exercise book. 'I promise.'

Let me tell this right, she prayed. Let me say it so that he understands, but doesn't take on the burden. 'Your father's name is Duncan Penicuik . . .' she began. Jamie listened. Eventually, there was silence. Mary stared down at her hands.

'So, when I'm fourteen, the money stops, just like that?'

'Yes. Though Mr Alan Ogilvy says that he will try to persuade Mr Penicuik to continue until you are twenty-one. That's why I've been saving what I can—so that you don't have to leave school. You're clever. You could go to university and get on.'

'Is that why you teach at Mrs Findlay's?' He hadn't liked it when she'd started going out to work. Duggie had said, 'Is your mother a washerwoman?' and sniggered—until Jamie had hit him.

Mary nodded. She was an assistant at

Raining's School two afternoons a week. It only brought in four shillings, but it all helped.

So I'm a bastard, thought Jamie that night, lying in the small attic room with the sloping ceiling. His father didn't care what happened to him. How could he, when he was going to cut off the money? He wasn't even going to support Mother. He didn't care if they both ended up in the ditch.

Mother said that his father thought that he should struggle just as *he* had. He bet his other sons wouldn't have to struggle. It was strange knowing that he had two half-brothers and a half-sister. He wondered what they were like.

It wasn't fair. Why should they have everything and he have nothing? It wasn't *his* fault he was base-born. Jamie didn't want to be greedy, but he felt he was owed a chance in life.

*　　　*　　　*

The following years passed happily for Robina. She thoroughly enjoyed the freedom to travel and see new places. Marriage, she decided, was not for her; she had never met any man whom she preferred to her grandmother. When Mrs Drummond's health began to fail, they resisted all calls to return to Scotland, and settled in a little villa in the hills above Florence. Mrs Drummond made what arrangements she could to protect

Robina's future.

'Now, Robina,' she said one evening, 'I have entrusted our friend Signor Arnolfini with a hundred and fifty pounds for you when I die. I don't want you entirely dependent on Duncan's generosity.'

'Don't talk about dying!' begged Robina, her eyes filling with tears.

'Robina,' said Mrs Drummond gently, 'I am failing. Let us not pretend.'

It was there, in the Villa Scarlatti, in 1860, that Mrs Drummond died peacefully on an April evening full of the scent of syringas, acacias and banksia roses. She was buried a few days later in the Protestant cemetery. Robina dutifully wrote to Beatrix to inform her.

* * *

Robina's Journal   *Villa Scarlatti,*
       Wednesday, 25 April 1860
I'm still furious about Duncan's letter. How dare he? He has arranged for me to live with them, and he intends to take the income from Grandmama's £5000, which is now mine, or will be when I'm thirty-five, for my board and lodging. He will allow (!) me an allowance of £25 a year. In other words, I'm supposed to hand over £250 a year! I kept household for myself and Grandmama for far less than that. It's sheer robbery!

In return for this 'generosity', I'm to 'make myself useful to Mrs Penicuik'. 'Mrs Penicuik'— what's wrong with 'Beatrix'? I see what it is. I'm to be little better than an upper servant. He's enclosed a letter for me to sign endorsing this arrangement, which he assures me is for my benefit!!!

Is it legal? I'm going to ask Signor Arnolfini to have a look at it.

Friday, 27 April 1860
So much for Duncan! Signor Arnolfini assures me that I don't have to sign it. He suggests that I write to Mr Ogilvy, as one of my trustees, and say that I want nothing to do with this arrangement.

Signor Arnolfini has an angular face with one of those long thin noses like one of the de Medicis—Giuliano, I think. In fact, dress him up in Renaissance clothes and he'd look just like a de Medici. He sometimes quotes Machiavelli, with a twinkle in his eye, and I feel that I can trust him to have my best interests at heart.

He told me that Countess Kamenska is looking for a female companion to go to St Petersburg (!) with her. Should I apply?

What are my choices?

I can agree to Duncan's outrageous demand. If I do, I'd have to help with Madeline, Ewan and Aeneas. Madeline is fourteen, at the age when I'd probably have to escort her to dancing class and so on. She's a pretty girl. I liked her when I last saw her, but . . . Fourteen? A difficult *age. I don't want to find that I'm in thrall to a wilful Miss in her teens.*

I don't care for Ewan. He's the sort of boy who puts worms in your bed. Spoilt and over-indulged.

Aeneas is a nice lad. He's in bed a lot with asthma over the winter and it seems to have turned him scholarly. I'm sure I'd get on with him.

All the same, there are far more minuses than pluses. I'm nearly twenty-eight—in less than seven years, the money will be mine. It would be more sensible to allow the interest to accumulate during those seven years, and, in the meantime, support myself by being a companion to some elderly lady. I know how to look after them, I can organize travel and accommodation. It must be better than being a chaperon to Madeline and paying Duncan for the privilege!

I shall ask Signor Arnolfini to introduce me to Countess Kamenska.

Robina closed her journal, went to her writing desk, and wrote two letters. One was to Duncan, declining his offer. The other was to Mr Alan Ogilvy, making her opposition plain, and asking that the £5000 be allowed to accumulate during her minority.

Duncan and Beatrix, predictably, were furious. But by the time they had learned what Robina intended to do, it was too late, and she was in St Petersburg with the old

56

Countess Kamenska.

*   *   *

Kashmir, 1861

Edward and Charlotte stood by the open grave and watched while the body of the pack pony was lowered in. Charlotte, now twelve, a skinny girl with a tanned face and light-brown hair bleached by the sun, stood stiffly to attention, tears streaking her cheeks, and with her lips clenched. Edward nodded to the two men standing by the grave and they began to fill it in. Charlotte gave one last agonized look at the pony's body and began to sob. Edward turned to comfort her and in a moment the whole of the front of his jacket was wet with tears. When eventually she looked up with swollen eyes, she saw that his eyes too were suspiciously red.

'Papa, you've made my hair wet!' she said, smiling through her tears.

'She was a good pony,' said Edward. 'She had a brave spirit.'

'Yes,' said Charlotte, blowing her nose firmly. 'Do you remember when she kicked that pi-dog who was snapping at everybody's heels?'

Edward nodded. 'And the time she bit the *dacoit* who tried to steal my purse.'

They talked for a while until Edward judged that Charlotte was recovered enough to go back to their bungalow. The men had now finished filling in the grave and put heavy stones on top so that it would not be dug up by wild animals. He gave them a couple of annas each, and they salaamed and left.

'Tiffin with Mr Nunn and his sister, this afternoon,' said Edward.

'Bother!' said Charlotte, wiping her eyes and pushing her grief to one side. Her father sympathized with her, she knew, but he also disliked over-emotional females who were prone to tears, headaches and exaggeration. If she wanted to cry again, she would have to do so in the privacy of her room. 'I suppose I'll have to change.' She'd never met this Miss Nunn, but her father seemed anxious that she get to know a lady from Home.

'You most certainly will. Miss Nunn has just come out from England. She will expect you to be properly dressed as befits a young lady!'

'She'll be horrified to see me at all!' retorted Charlotte. She'd stopped counting the times that concerned ladies had cried out 'But shouldn't she be educated at Home?'

Charlotte had been Home several times when her father had returned after his plant expeditions, and Britain, to her, was a damp place where the sun never shone and where all the people looked miserable. It was true that she always enjoyed staying with her Scottish cousins in Inverness-shire, but she would never want to *live* there.

58

When they got back, Edward called for his bearer, and Charlotte went to her ayah, and a few hours later they rode the short distance to Mr Nunn's bungalow.

Geoffrey Nunn came down the veranda steps to greet them. 'Splendid, here you are! Charlotte, you've grown again! Come in! Come in!'

It was cool inside the bungalow and it took some minutes for their eyes to become accustomed to the shade. As they entered, a slim figure rose from her chair and came forward. Rosamund Nunn had silvery-gold hair, cornflower-blue eyes and pink lips. She was wearing a white muslin dress with blue ribbons, which were wilting a little in the heat, and matching blue kid shoes. Charlotte couldn't help staring. She looked just like a pantomime fairy she'd once seen; all she needed was a wand. Charlotte didn't often see other white women; when she did they were usually tea-planters' harassed wives, or sometimes a female missionary, not this fairy-tale vision.

Edward, too, stared. She reminded him, painfully, of Betsy as he had first known her: beautiful, feminine and heart-breakingly innocent; the sort of girl any man would be glad to lose his heart to.

Geoffrey, looking quietly satisfied, performed the introductions.

Edward remembered his manners. 'How are

you enjoying India, Miss Nunn? This is your first visit, I believe?'

Rosamund made a face. 'It's beautiful up here, but the journey . . .'

'Poor Rosie,' said her brother fondly, 'she screamed a lot and had everybody running.'

'Well, how was I to know what was dangerous and what wasn't?' Rosamund didn't seem concerned at the trouble she'd caused. 'Anyway, I can't bear creepy-crawlies.'

'I've had to employ somebody whose sole job it is to see that Rosie's room is free of insects and that there are no scorpions hiding in her shoes!'

'I know I'm a silly creature,' said Rosamund, smiling, 'but my brother is so good as to put up with me.'

Edward made some complimentary reply, but the visit was not entirely a success. He had hoped that Charlotte would be able to make a friend of Miss Nunn, to talk to a lady from back Home, somebody who might be able to give her a bit of polish. Miss Nunn was pretty, charmingly mannered and so on, but she was also, like Betsy, entirely self-centred, ignorant as only a well-brought-up white female could be, and obviously assumed that her whims would be taken seriously. Her brother was looking fondly at her now, but Edward couldn't help wondering how long that would last.

On the way home, Charlotte said suddenly,

'You don't want me to be like Miss Nunn, do you, Papa?' Rosamund had reminded her of her Mama, and Charlotte was not at all sure she liked it. She looked uncertainly towards her father. He'd looked at Miss Nunn a lot; what did he think?

'Good God, no!' said Edward. 'She's a pretty creature, but she hasn't two thoughts to rub together, and she certainly wouldn't be able to cope with organizing a plant expedition!'

'But *I* can,' said Charlotte with satisfaction.

*   *   *

A. Ogilvy and Co
Heriot Row
Edinburgh
To: F. Ogilvy, Esq   *6 April, 1862*

My dear Francis,
I have spoken to Mr Penicuik about the allowance for Mrs Ritchie and her son, now that his fourteenth birthday is approaching, and I am afraid that I have little good news for you. He will do nothing more for them. However, I have persuaded him to continue the allowance until the end of July, which will enable James to finish the school year.

I understand that Mrs Ritchie has some savings. I doubt whether she will have saved very much, but, if the boy manages to get a scholarship to university in due course, tell him to get in touch with me, and I'll see that he gets some decent lodgings.

I'm sending you a draft for £10—say it's from Penicuik.

Your affectionate cousin,
A. Ogilvy.

*   *   *

The Ritchies moved into cheaper accommodation in the lower town, in Celt Street, as soon as Duncan's allowance stopped. Ardconnel Terrace had been up on the hill, with open fields behind; a pleasant place. Here, they were down by the river and the area, though still respectable, was undeniably rougher. Their new lodgings comprised a small bedroom, where Jamie slept, and a larger sitting-room with a box bed, which was Mary's. Off it, was a tiny kitchen and pantry, and there was a privy outside which they shared with the other people in the house. Jamie's room was just big enough for a small table beside his bed, and he did his homework on it. He found an old plank of wood which, propped up on bricks, did duty for a bookshelf. Mr Francis Ogilvy gave him an old trunk, which held his clothes, and Mary used the shabby valise she had had when they came up from

Musselburgh.

It was all they owned. The furniture, such as it was, had come with the rooms, and the few saucepans and bits of crockery Mary had had to buy. They were not easy years. Mary found an extra afternoon's work supervising a girls' sewing class, but she only made six shillings a week.

'Jamie grows so!' she complained, half-humorously, half-seriously, to one of the teachers at the school where she worked. His appetite was enormous. 'I don't know where he puts all that food!'

'Aye, they have hollow legs at that age, I'm thinking,' said her colleague.

At about the same time as the allowance stopped, Jamie began to shoot up. First of all his feet grew, until they looked like boats. Then they stopped and the rest of him took over. It seemed to Mary that she was for ever trying to let down shirt sleeves and trousers or struggling to find the money for shoes. The savings began to disappear. Mary lowered her pride and, when she was offered a pair of trousers or a coat for Jamie that somebody else's son had outgrown, she accepted gratefully. Jamie did a paper round for the *Inverness Courier.* Somehow, they managed.

Jamie also met Olaf Hamnavoe. Olaf was well known in the docks and the wilder side of town where respectable people didn't go. He was a Shetlander, a big man, well over six feet

63

and strong with it. He had a weatherbeaten face, out of which shone two bright blue eyes, and his hair was red, so red that you could spot him among a crowd half a mile away.

Nobody knew much about Olaf, but rumours abounded. He'd been a whaler, said some, others that he was on the run from justice. He worked sporadically. There was usually somebody who would take him on down by the docks. His strength was impressive and he was a hard worker when he wanted to be. Then, suddenly, he would go on a 'brandy', drink himself into a stupor, spend all his money on the whores who lived in the poorest parts of Muirtown, by the docks, and then crash down somewhere and sleep it off. When he was in fighting mood, prudent men avoided him. He kept himself to himself and lived in a wooden bothy he had built out of driftwood a couple of miles out of town.

Jamie had met Olaf soon after his fourteenth birthday. He had taken to going for long walks by himself. 'I need to think,' he told Mary.

Mary nodded. He was growing up. She understood that. His school work was good and he worked hard; she must not expect to be at the centre of his life as she had been when he was a small boy. But she worried about him all the same. He got on well enough with the other boys at school, but he had no particular friends; secrecy had had its inevitable effect on him, just as it had on her. She had done what she could for him, but he had had to learn to bear the knowledge that his father had no interest in him, and that was a hard lesson.

Ever since that conversation with his mother when he was twelve, Jamie had known that he was different. He must guard his tongue, because if he didn't, then he and his mother would be stoned out of town; Jamie had taken to heart the sermons he'd heard in the kirk on Sunday; he knew what was coming to them. The only way he could cope was by walking, as far out of Inverness as possible, anywhere so long as when he got home he was too exhausted to think and could sleep. One day, Jamie was sitting on a rock by the Beauly Firth a few miles outside the town, watching a small flock of sandpipers skimming low along the edge of the sea, their wings flickering, and then landing on the sand, when a shadow fell across him. He looked up.

He recognized Olaf at once. Everybody knew him. For a moment Jamie was scared. Olaf was a big man and he'd heard stories of how he could fight, but, glancing at him, Jamie didn't think he looked violent. Olaf sat down on the coarse marram grass and watched the sandpipers.

'Do you want to see the seals?' asked Olaf eventually.

'Yes, please.'

'Come, then.' Olaf led the way with huge

strides along the beach and then up over the marram grass and round the headland. James struggled to keep up. Finally, Olaf descended again towards the beach. 'Quiet, now,' he said over his shoulder.

Jamie stopped for a moment to catch his breath and then moved cautiously, following Olaf's footsteps.

'There, see?' Olaf pointed to some half-submerged rocks just off shore. On one of the rocks, four seals were sunning themselves. One of them raised its head to watch the newcomers for a moment and then sank down again. Olaf continued to descend until, eventually, they both stood on the shore only a few yards away.

'Do they know you?' asked Jamie in a whisper. He felt awed to be so close to the seals.

'Aye, they do. Look you, yon big grey one is coming over to have a look. They are curious, see. They want to know who I've brought with me. Sit down, lad, then they'll know that you're no threat.'

Jamie sat on a small rock and watched. Olaf went down to the sea and called. It was a low sort of sing-song way of talking, Jamie thought, and in some strange language. It wasn't English and it didn't sound like Gaelic, either, but one by one the seals flopped off their rock and swam over.

Olaf squatted down. They seemed to

be having a conversation, thought Jamie, fascinated. As he watched them, the knot of tension inside him began to undo. The seals didn't care who his father was, he thought. They seemed to like Olaf, at any rate, and everybody knew that Olaf was a sort of outcast—respected for his great strength, but not really belonging anywhere.

Finally, the seals left, and Olaf stood up. 'Right, now,' he said, 'how about finding something for your supper, eh? Let's see what my lobster pots are doing.'

When Jamie arrived home that evening, he had a lobster and a dozen sprats in his bag. When he put them down triumphantly on the kitchen table, Mary looked at him with scared eyes.

'Where did you get these, Jamie?' Lobsters cost money, she knew. God forbid that . . . She didn't dare frame her thoughts.

'A friend,' said Jamie, and shut his mouth. He did not want to tell his mother about meeting Olaf.

'Jamie . . .' began Mary, concerned. 'We . . . we can't afford these. I . . .'

'They're not stolen, Mother, if that's what you're thinking.'

'But who is this friend?'

'Just a friend. He's all right. He's a kind person, that's all.'

I have to trust him, thought Mary. I can't force him to tell me. She nodded and picked up the lobster. To buy one would cost at least two shillings, quite out of her budget. The sprats could wait, she thought. They would be all right in the larder, but they must eat the lobster tonight.

*   *   *

In spite of Duncan and Beatrix's vehemently expressed disapproval, Robina continued to support herself. She thoroughly enjoyed her time in St Petersburg, and came back with a sable tippet and matching muff, which Beatrix looked at with envious eyes, when they met briefly in London.

'Aren't they a little grand for you?' she said waspishly. 'After all, you are only a "lady companion", don't forget.' Robina said nothing. Balked, Beatrix continued, 'I forgot to tell you, Mrs Murdo Gillespie died in childbirth a month or so ago. Such a sweet lady. So truly refined. Poor Murdo is beside himself with grief.'

'Murdo, beside himself with grief!' exclaimed Robina 'Surely not!' She simply couldn't picture it. He didn't have the heart. 'I suppose I'd better write and express my condolences.'

Beatrix sniffed.

Two years later, Robina was in Montpelier with a Mrs Leigh-Egerton and, a year later, in 1863, in Rome with Mrs Neil Macdonald, the mother of Lady Invershiel of Dunlairg Castle.

She returned to London at the onset of Mrs Macdonald's final illness in the summer of 1865. After Mrs Macdonald's death, Robina moved to a respectable lodging house in Montague Place, just behind the British Museum, and pondered her next step.

*   *   *

Time had been good to the Penicuiks, thought Beatrix. Duncan's business had prospered and he had enlarged the Achnagarry estate considerably, eventually buying 20,000 acres of deer forest, grouse moor and good sheep grazing from the Invershiels. Of course, it was all relative. The Invershiels still owned 30,000 acres and their title was an ancient one. What was more to the point was that she was not on the Invershiels' visiting list.

But Robina was.

Beatrix reminded herself that she had been a Drummond. She had brought £15,000 to the marriage and, later, had inherited the Achnagarry estate. Before her marriage, she, together with Robina and her grandparents, *were* on visiting terms with the Invershiels. After her marriage, that had changed. Lady Invershiel was perfectly pleasant when they met in the kirk on a Sunday, but further intimacy was quietly discouraged.

It was not one of those things Beatrix

wished to discuss with her husband. So far as was possible, she had tried to conceal the Invershiels' reluctance to be on visiting terms from him. It was ridiculous to think that, in this day and age, the fact that her husband was a self-made man should make any difference. The Penicuiks certainly had no trouble entering Edinburgh society, and Madeline had had a successful debut there.

If Beatrix were honest with herself, she had a very good suspicion as to why the Invershiels, and others, disliked her husband; it was his meanness. If they stayed the night somewhere, for example, he would never, on leaving, tip the servants properly, and Beatrix had the embarrassing job of going round again to give them extra out of her own money and make his excuses. In the early years of her marriage, she had tried to explain the convention of 'vails for servants' to him, but he would have none of it. Why should he tip them for doing their job, was his attitude. It did not improve his popularity, and Beatrix did not doubt that by now everybody who mattered knew of his parsimony. The only way she could cope with the knowledge, was by burying it and, as far as possible, avoiding the situations where his meanness became all too apparent.

'I've decided to ask Robina to spend the summer with us at Achnagarry,' she told her husband, one evening.

'Why on earth do you want Robina?' asked Duncan. He still hadn't forgiven her for refusing to live with them after Mrs Drummond's death. She could have made herself useful. That was what unmarried female relations were for, to be of service to their families, not to go gallivanting off to Russia, or wherever. His wife's cousin was no beauty, he thought sourly. Nice eyes, but that was the most you could say about her. And hadn't she been virtually jilted by Murdo Gillespie?

'Robina and Grandmama met the Invershiels in Italy several times. They were certainly on visiting terms. I used to hear about it in Grandmama's letters. And, of course, Robina has been companion to old Mrs Macdonald,' said Beatrix.

'So Robina is a sprat to catch a mackerel?' said Duncan. She looked like a sprat, too. At thirty-two, or whatever she was now, she was hardly going to be a threat to Beatrix's ambitions for their lovely Madeline.

Beatrix smiled—carefully, for she had recently lost a tooth and was self-conscious about it. 'Exactly so.'

'I don't want either of those Invershiel boys for Madeline!' stated Duncan. The Honourable John and the Honourable Henry had scarcely a feather to fly with and the Invershiel estate was heavily mortgaged, as he well knew. Duncan was aware that the

71

Invershiels didn't like him, but he wasted no sleep over it. He was a damn sight richer.

'Certainly not! No, I have my eye on one of the house guests, a Mr Edward Mountsorrel, who is Lord Glendon's heir.'

'Mountsorrel, eh? I thought he was married. Anyway, isn't he rather old for Madeline?'

'He's thirty-eight, in the prime of life.'

'Money?'

'He inherited his late wife's fortune, though he will have to settle some of that on their daughter.' Beatrix frowned. It would have been more convenient if young Miss Mountsorrel had died with her mother.

'I want to know more about him,' said Duncan firmly. These aristocrats were all very well, but all too often there were skeletons in the family cupboard. 'Does he gamble, for example? A fellow who gambles can go through a fortune in a few years. Drink? Keep expensive mistresses . . .?' Duncan allowed himself a private wink at his reflection in the looking-glass over the mantelpiece. Mary Ritchie and her son were now off his hands. Nowadays, his sexual indulgences were strictly ephemeral.

'I know nothing of such things!' Beatrix declared.

Duncan said nothing more. He liked her virtuous outrage; it showed her breeding.

'I shall write inviting Robina, then,' Beatrix finished. She had done her research into Mr

Mountsorrel pretty thoroughly. She did not think that Duncan would find anything to cavil at.

The one problem was Madeline herself, whose head was, unfortunately, turned all too often by attractive wastrels. Beatrix had no intention of allowing her well-dowered only daughter to throw herself away on an impecunious young Invershiel instead of the eligible Mr Mountsorrel.

*   *   *

George Square
Edinburgh
30 June, 1865

My dear Robina,
I am writing to invite you to come up to Achnagarry with us this summer. We shall be travelling up on Monday, 24 July, and can take you with us. I am sure that you must be longing to see the transformation for yourself.

Madeline has just had a very successful Season here in Edinburgh. We are considering asking Mr Millais to paint her, but Duncan thinks that his charges are too high. I view it as an investment—if the portrait were exhibited at the Royal Academy, for example, it would be such a cachet *for our daughter.*

Ewan is well. His school report said, 'Could do better', but what boy of fifteen wants to work! I think it's only natural for a high-spirited young man to kick over the traces a little.

I must say, Robina, Duncan and I agree that hiring yourself out, even as a 'lady companion' is most improper. It's not as if you don't have family who are willing to have you. It looks so bad. It's high time you became less selfish and thought of how your refusal might reflect on us.

Now that Mrs Macdonald has died, you can surely spend some time with your cousins? We shall be only family at Achnagarry, but we hope to see something of the Invershiels, who will be bringing up a house party. You will, of course, wish to renew your acquaintance with them. Murdo Gillespie now lives permanently at Nevan House. He has not remarried.

The train leaving King's Cross station at nine o'clock on Friday, 21 July, will be the most convenient and I shall arrange for the carriage to meet you at Waverley Station.

Your affectionate cousin,
B. Penicuik

Robina read the letter in growing exasperation. What annoyed her most was Beatrix's assumption that she, Robina, would jump to do her bidding. And why the reference

74

to Murdo not having remarried? She was reading it in the private sitting-room of her landlady, Mrs Armin. Mrs Armin was French by birth and, the moment she had learned that Miss Drummond had once lived in Avignon, not five miles from where she herself had been brought up, and spoke excellent French besides, had invited her to use her own sitting-room. It would be a pleasure to be able to speak her own language with mademoiselle, she assured her.

'Is anything wrong, *mademoiselle*?' she asked, seeing Robina's frown.

Robina explained the situation.

'But, ma *chère*, what is wrong with a little visit?' asked Mrs Armin, spreading her hands. Miss Drummond came from a good family, anybody could see that. The place in Scotland sounded delightful, with its mountains, lakes and picturesque scenery.

Robina sighed. 'I loved the house as it was. My cousin's husband has built himself a Highland lodge, complete with turrets, arrow slit windows and battlements! I really do not want to see it.'

Mrs Armin clasped her hands together. '*Un château, alors*!' she exclaimed. 'How romantic.'

Robina shook her head. Beatrix had virtually ignored Robina's own existence for the last five years. So why was she inviting her *now*? She ignored Mrs Armin's protests and declined Beatrix's invitation. *I shall shortly be*

75

taking up a situation and cannot afford to be lingering on the way. A trip to Scotland would be quite beyond my means, she wrote with a certain satisfaction. She was not going to be an unpaid chaperon, she thought, as she signed her name with a flourish.

In fact, she had no post to go to, but wasn't unduly worried. Something would come up. She'd had a tiring few months with old Mrs Macdonald. Robina had been treated kindly, but ill-health had made Mrs Macdonald irritable and the last couple of months had been exhausting.

She had been well paid and Mrs Macdonald had left her ten pounds in her will. She could afford a month or so resting in Mrs Armin's charming back garden. So she sat quietly among the roses and honeysuckle and allowed the tension to seep out of her. During the mornings, if it were fine, she would venture out to an exhibition or to look at the sights. A lone female was usually considered fair game by men on the look-out, but Robina was rarely accosted. Her brown coat and sensible bonnet did not invite male eyes, and her parasol had a steel tip.

*　　*　　*

Beatrix was furious.

'Just like Robina!' she exclaimed crossly. 'No consideration for other people. Now I

76

shall have to write again; I cannot have my plans thrown out in this way.'

Madeline looked up from where she was idly flicking over the pages of *The Lady's Magazine.* Her mother had told her that Robina's presence was important, but she could see her cousin's point of view.

'It's a long, expensive train journey,' she pointed out.

Beatrix sighed. Duncan would not be pleased to be asked for the money. Either Robina was a guest or she wasn't, he would say. If she wanted Robina to come up, and she did, then she would have to send her some money out of her own allowance.

The single fare to Edinburgh would be nearly two pounds. Then there was her return fare—for Beatrix was determined that Robina would stay only until Madeline had captured Mr Mountsorrel, and then she would go—unless, of course, she could be useful.

*   *   *

Dunlairg Castle stood on a small outcrop at the top end of Loch Nevan. It was neither a very big castle, nor a particularly important one. Built in the sixteenth century, it had five storeys, with four towers of different heights, each capped by a conical roof, which gave it an air of having been built piecemeal, as indeed it had. It was full of small closets off larger rooms, worn spiral staircases, and the kitchen on the ground floor still used the original antiquated spits. There was a well in the courtyard. The plumbing was non-existent; but a walled garden behind the castle benefited from the castle's well-rotted manure.

In the solar, there was some fine Jacobean panelling and plasterwork on the ceiling, but, as Henry Invershiel remarked with only slight exaggeration, that was probably the last time the castle had been modernized. Bonnie Prince Charlie was rumoured to have spent a night there on his fateful way to Culloden Moor. The castle also had a ghost: a lady in white who haunted the north tower.

Lady Invershiel was not at all in favour of ghosts and remarked acidly that, now the new Achnagarry Lodge was built, perhaps the white lady would betake herself there instead. God knows there were plenty of turrets for her to choose from.

On this cool summer's afternoon, Lady Invershiel, a sensible-looking woman with springy grey hair tucked untidily under her lace-edged cap, was sitting in the solar, talking to her friend, Mrs Usher. Like Beatrix, both Mrs Usher and Lady Invershiel had their eye on Edward Mountsorrel. Mrs Usher's daughter, Georgina, was twenty-seven and still unmarried. Mr Mountsorrel would do admirably, thought Lady Invershiel, who was Georgina's godmother. In any case, it was high time that he married again. She regarded an unmarried man with a good income as an affront to womanhood.

Charlotte Mountsorrel was sixteen; she would be coming out in two years' time, and she needed a mama to launch her into Society. The poor girl had spent her childhood being dragged all over the world by her father; she should now settle down properly and learn how to conduct herself in Society before her come-out.

And Georgina Usher needed a husband just as much as Charlotte needed a mama.

Georgina, who was sitting with John and Henry Invershiel at the far end of the solar, would have been horrified at these plans, had she known of them. She was a gangling woman, with a long horsy face, who hid her habitual shyness by coming out with dreadful puns. John and Henry irreverently dubbed her 'Gusher' and teased her unmercifully. Poor Georgina would react by bursting into a loud laugh, showing all her gums, then blush beetroot-red and clamp her hands over her mouth.

The truth was, Georgina didn't like men very much. She had nothing against them personally, it was just that she didn't really see what they were *for.* She could cope with the jokey relationship she had with John and Henry, but, as she put it to herself, she couldn't get interested in men in *that* sort of way.

'I despair of ever getting Georgina off my hands,' said Mrs Usher, wincing at her daughter's shriek of laughter, which could be heard right across the room. 'Whatever can be done with her?'

'She should be married,' replied Lady Invershiel with conviction. 'Running a house and having babies would soon settle her.' It would help, she thought, if Georgina wore something other than that shapeless brown gown, which looked for all the world like a sack and did nothing for her bony frame. 'That's why I've invited Mountsorrel.'

Mrs Usher looked enquiringly at her.

'He is distantly related to my husband, and is Lord Glendon's heir. He has about four thousand a year and will inherit the Glendon fortune in due course.'

'What does he do?' asked Mrs Usher.

'He is a botanist. He collects rare plants for various private collectors, and some national collections, too. He travels all over the world. He is very well thought of in his field, I believe.'

'And his character?' said Mrs Usher dubiously. She couldn't imagine her daughter trekking in the Himalayas or wherever. She was not a good rider.

Lady Invershiel considered. 'I haven't seen much of him. He stays with us every three or four years. I've always thought of him as a man's man. I don't mean that he tells coarse stories, or drinks to excess, or anything of that nature, but he seems happiest when he's out in the field.

'That's why I thought he might appeal to Georgina. I don't think she'd want a husband who was always underfoot.' She looked across at her god-daughter, who was fondling the ears of Lord Invershiel's water spaniel Clover, and thought that Georgina would probably prefer it if Mr Mountsorrel were out of the way for good long stretches of time.

Mrs Usher made a non-committal noise. Somehow, she just couldn't see Georgina married and with a baby. 'But didn't you tell me that Mrs Penicuik was after Mr Mountsorrel for that pretty daughter of hers?'

Lady Invershiel laughed. 'I believe so, but she will not get very far. Why, Madeline is only a couple of years older than Charlotte!'

'But she is quite lovely,' said Mrs Usher wistfully. She had longed for a really pretty daughter, somebody to take about and with whom to enjoy shopping. Poor Georgina had never taken the smallest interest in her clothes. 'Wasn't Mr Mountsorrel's wife a belle in her day?'

'Betsy? Yes, she was extremely pretty, but she was something of a butterfly, flitting from flower to flower . . . to put it no worse. But one mustn't speak ill of the dead. No, I think that Mr Mountsorrel learnt his lesson there. Besides . . .'

'Besides?' repeated Mrs Usher.

Lady Invershiel lowered her voice. 'Since Lord Invershiel's stroke, I've realized that something *must* be done about the estate. John needs to marry money and I've decided that Madeline Penicuik is a possibility.'

Mrs Usher was aghast. 'But, my dear Mary, have you thought? I remember you telling me a year or so ago that there were some very unpleasant rumours about Mr Penicuik's private life. Didn't he seduce and abandon some respectable girl and leave her to bring up their child quite alone, without any help from him?'

'Alas, yes. I've never liked the man,' agreed Lady Invershiel, 'and my husband refuses to have him in the house. The men on the Achnagarry estate say that he is mean—and stinginess is one thing I abhor. But Miss Penicuik will have twenty thousand at least.'

'Her breeding on her mother's side is good,' conceded Mrs Usher.

'And beggars cannot be choosers. In due course, John can offer her a title. No, I do not think that Mr Penicuik will object.'

'How shall you manage it, if you're not on visiting terms?'

'I have written to Robina Drummond,' said Lady Invershiel, with the air of a conjuror pulling a rabbit out of a hat. 'You remember her, and her situation, don't you?' Mrs Usher nodded.

'I know that she has been invited to Achnagarry Lodge for the summer. I also know that she is looking for another post, which might be of interest to you. My husband likes Robina. I shall invite her to call on us, and suggest that she brings Madeline with her.'

'Are you thinking that she might be companion to Aunt Honoria?' Mrs Usher's aunt was a difficult woman, much given to sudden rages when things did not go her way, and extraordinarily pernickety. She lived in a house on the Usher estate, and caused no end of problems. 'But will Miss Drummond agree? Aunt Honoria can be quite a handful.'

'You can but ask her,' said Lady Invershiel. As far as she was concerned, so long as Robina brought Madeline over to Dunlairg, and John charmed her, then it didn't matter what happened with the difficult Honoria. She would make it clear to Mrs Penicuik that it was Madeline only who was invited—under Robina's chaperonage.

Lord Invershiel would be persuaded to accept Madeline—he liked pretty girls—but he would certainly balk at a man of Mr Penicuik's stamp. She did not wish him to suffer a further stroke. John was a further complication; he could so easily dig his toes in and refuse to co-operate. Perhaps he had better not be told. Let Miss Penicuik's charm do its work without any interference from her—apart from a few nudges in the right direction.

It would all have to be managed very carefully.

*   *   *

Robina's Journal   Thursday, 6 July, 1865
I've just had the most intriguing letter from Lady
Invershiel. When I was with Mrs Macdonald, she
sometimes used to read out letters from Lady
Invershiel, and we would laugh over them,
because they were always so inconsequential that
it was difficult to work out what she meant. This
letter is just the same. What is going on? She
seems to have heard about Beatrix's invitation
and has assumed that I have accepted. It sounds
as if she wants me to bring Madeline over to
Dunlairg Castle, possibly to ensnare John.
Surely, Beatrix wouldn't be interested in John for
Madeline? I know he will have a title eventually,
but the Invershiels are as poor as church mice,
and I doubt whether Duncan would agree to the
match.
*   And who is Mr Mountsorrel? The name does*
ring a vague bell, but, if he is who I think he is—
a naturalist of some sort, last heard of hunting
the Tibetan kiang, *or something—what has he*
got to do with anything?
*   I do remember Georgina Usher—poor old*
'Gusher'—surely she can't be part of Lady I.'s
plans? Grandmama and I used to think that
Gusher would have done very well as one of
those intrepid women who went on pilgrimage in

the Middle Ages. I could just see her jollying people along and cracking her awful puns as she strode along some Pilgrim Way. But I cannot see her as a seductive siren—unless she's changed utterly.

More to the point, Lady I. says that Mrs Usher's Aunt Honoria needs a lady companion. Forty pounds a year!!! Hm. I shall think about it.

Next Day:

I've just had another letter—rather more civil —from Beatrix. This time enclosing five pounds. I'll think I'll go. Could be interesting.

But I'm damned if I'm going up by train en famille. I can think of nothing worse than several days of undiluted Penicuiks in close proximity. No, I think I'll go to Glasgow and catch the steamer. I've always wanted to go up the Caledonian Canal. It costs about thirty shillings for a cabin, but it'll be worth it. I can get off at Foyers and take the coach to Whitebridge. I'm sure I'll find somebody there to take my valise up to Achnagarry, and I can easily walk. I deserve a holiday.

CHAPTER THREE

Jamie swiftly learnt that there were times when you did not approach Olaf. The first time it happened, it was a terrible shock. Olaf was standing in the Citadel Shipbuilding Yard

85

in Cromwell's fort, a bottle in one hand, swaying slightly and roaring out a bawdy song at the top of his voice. Jamie stopped and stared in dismay. Olaf swung round.

'It'sh that hugger Jamesh!' His eyes were bloodshot. 'Get lost! Make yershelf scarce!' He turned suddenly and hurled the bottle straight at Jamie's head. It missed him by a hair's breadth. Jamie ran. He ran out along the headland and when he thought that nobody could see him, threw himself down on the grass and burst into tears.

A few days later, Olaf appeared again, sober and as usual. When he next saw Jamie, he walked over and said, 'Come you, I want to talk to ye.' Jamie swallowed nervously and, after a few seconds' hesitation, followed Olaf out towards the Beauly Firth.

'Listen, lad,' said Olaf, when they were sitting on the marram grass and watching some redshanks poking about in the sand, 'I'm a big man, I have big appetites. Women, drink, and when the mood comes I can't stop it, see? You been with a woman, yet, Jamie?'

Jamie turned scarlet.

'Well, there's time enough,' said Olaf tolerantly. 'So you just keep out of my way, at those times. Drink has been my ruin, lad, but a man can't help his nature.'

'Can't he?' said Jamie. How much of his father was in him, he wondered? There must be something, surely?

Olafs bright blue eyes looked piercingly at him for a moment. 'Aye, well, maybe he can and maybe he doesn't want to,' he said at last. 'I was brought up respectable, lad; I wouldn't want ye to think that it was my blessed mother's fault that I went to the bad.'

'Have you gone to the bad, Olaf?'

'I have my own code, lad, but it isn't one many people follow.'

'But you don't kill or steal,' persisted Jamie. Olaf was silent, then he said, 'I have killed once, Jamie. But he was rotten to the core. It was on a whaler and one of the crew was forever picking on me. I was only a lad then.'

'Go on,' said Jamie eagerly.

' 'Tis terrible dangerous, whaling. Ye must all work together, see. And this man had picked on me once too often. He got caught up in one of the lines and I didn't say anything until it was too late. I should have shouted for help, ye see. And I couldn't, I hated him so much.'

Jamie was silent, thinking it over.

'You think it was murder?' asked Olaf.

Jamie shook his head. 'I suppose you could say that he reaped as he sowed,' he said after a moment, 'but that's not fair either. My mother . . .' He stopped and then said in a burst, 'Oh, Olaf, my father deserted us when I was very little. He . . . he never married my mother. She was very young, younger than I am now when they met. I can't blame her, how can I? It's him I blame. How could I blame you for what happened on that whaling ship, when I don't know what I'd have done in the same situation?' All the same, a small bit of him couldn't help thinking that perhaps his mother had got it wrong. Perhaps his father wanted to know about him, was interested in how he was getting on.

Olaf patted him briefly on the shoulder. 'Life's a bugger, eh?' he said. 'We just have to do the best we can.' He stared out across the sea for a moment, and then said, 'Shall we go and see if there's anything in the rabbit snare? Poaching doesn't count as a black sin, does it?'

Jamie laughed a little shakily and got up. Rabbits and hares were plentiful; a few would not be missed. Besides, he knew that money was tight at home. A rabbit would feed them for a couple of meals.

'What have men like the Duke of Sutherland ever done to deserve rights over tens of thousands of acres?' said Olaf, as they set off. 'All they've done, seems to me, is to evict their crofters, *their own people*, mind, and put sheep in their place.'

Jamie was silent. His own father was a landowner, who had, to all intents and purposes, evicted his mother and himself.

'You thinking of your father, lad?' asked Olaf, watching Jamie's face. 'He owes you something, I'm thinking. You have your rights, too.'

*   *   *

Robina's Journal   *On board the steamer*
somewhere on Loch Linnhe
Wednesday, 26 July, 1865

It's wonderful! I hadn't realized how much I missed the Highlands until I came back. It's the way the hills sweep down to the loch, the purple heather, the birch and alder—even the soft Scotch mist and rain.

The deer, of course, are up on the tops at this time of year, but there are seals sunning themselves on rocks, and, out in the Firth of Lorn, I saw dolphins leaping alongside the boat as they swam, as if they were making stitches in the water.

The steamer is full of trippers, and an irritating woman who squeals every time she sees a fish jump. There's also a young man, wearing a brand new kilt (somebody should have told him to bury it in a peat bog for a year or so) who keeps quoting, 'O Caledonia! stern and wild, Meet nurse for a poetic child!'. Scott has a lot to answer for.

I think Mr Mountsorrel is on the boat! At least, I heard the captain say the name.

Later:

I asked the captain and he said that Mr Mountsorrel was travelling with his daughter. They are alighting at Tomassie pier. Probably going to stay with the Fergussons at Tomassie

89

Lodge.

How extraordinary! Now I've seen him, I suspect that both Beatrix and Lady Invershiel have marked him down as suitable husband material: Beatrix for Madeline and Lady I. for poor Gusher. Whether Madeline would want a husband who has a teenage daughter remains to be seen. Anyway, he's not nearly dashing enough for her.

He's one of those tall, strong, silent types. He's also very bushy about the head. His hair is too long, and almost as wild as Mr Tennyson's, though he has a lot more of it! He pads *about the deck, there is no other word for it. And he has a habit of disappearing suddenly, God knows how, because he's a big man. I can imagine him tracking some yak absolutely silently. He's probably a bit of a blockhead. Still, his daughter seems to enjoy his company, so he can't be* that *dull.*

It will be amusing to see how he copes with Madeline and Gusher.

*   *   *

I got off the steamer as we were going through the locks at Fort Augustus. It's good to be on dry land for a bit, and away from all the smuts. My cloak is filthy. I found myself standing next to Mr Mountsorrel. He obviously recognized me from the boat, for he raised his hat. I bowed.

He said, gesturing towards the steamer,

'Splendid sight! The romance of steam, eh?'

'Yes,' I said. 'I went to St Petersburg on a steamer. It was very thrilling, though I was horribly seasick.'

'So not much romance there?' he observed, smiling. His eyes are tawny, like a lion's.

'No,' I agreed. 'But, all the same, it was worth it. Being on board ship is like being in a different element. I've always liked that.'

'Me, too,' he grinned.

He has a nice smile—what I could see of it through the beard. I was just about to ask him if he was going on to Dunlairg, when the steamer's hooter went and we had to board ship. He did his silent disappearing trick. I was rather sorry.

* * *

The Glasgow steamer, which had chugged its way through the Inner Hebrides and then up the Caledonian Canal, had just left Fort Augustus, and Charlotte Mountsorrel could now see the distinctively rounded top of Mealfuavonie to her left. She was standing on deck with her father, and shortly, the steamer would stop at the private pier, which led up to Tomassie Lodge, and they would disembark.

Charlotte smiled in pure pleasure. The loch was still, except for the ripples caused by the wake of the little steamer. The hills and trees were reflected in the water and, every now and then, she could see a small bubble and the widening circle where a fish had come up to catch a midge or two. They were welcome to them, she thought, glad of the lavender oil which kept the midges at bay.

She'd seen mountains all her life, but she was especially fond of these Scottish hills, the Monadhliaths. They were mere foothills compared with the Himalayas, and the soft highland rain was as nothing beside the monsoon, but Dunlairg Castle, where they were going, was one of the few constants in her young life. Whenever she came back, and this was the fifth visit that she could remember, it remained blessedly the same.

She had lived mostly in bungalows, or even tents; in places where you had to search your shoes for scorpions in the morning, and where ants ate the wooden furniture unless you rested the legs in saucers of water, and where you slept under a mosquito net. At least in Scotland, there were none of those dangers. The midges could be a nuisance, but they weren't dangerous. She loved the muted colours of the hills, with the grey lichen-covered granite and the peaty-brown streams and the purple heather. It was a much more subtle palette of colours than she was used to, and she enjoyed that, too.

'Why aren't there any monkeys in Scotland, Papa?' she asked.

'Because it's too cold,' said Edward.

'But that can't be the reason,' objected

Charlotte. 'What about those monkeys we saw in Japan?' They had spent the winter up in the north and she remembered the monkeys with frozen whiskers and their fur sparkling with ice and snow.

'How would they get here?' asked Edward, smiling down at her. He loved her enquiring mind.

'How did they get to Japan?' countered Charlotte.

*   *   *

That evening, Edward sat with his friend Alasdair Fergusson in his snuggery in Tomassie Lodge—a room exclusively reserved for the masculine pursuits of whisky and tobacco. His gun cupboard was in one corner and his fishing rods were on racks going up the wall. There was a stuffed stag's head over the door, and several sets of mounted antlers on the walls.

The two men sat in comfortable leather armchairs, Alasdair smoking his pipe, and Edward with a glass of whisky by his side.

'Your Charlotte has grown,' remarked Alasdair. 'Pretty girl, too.'

'You think so?' said Edward, pleased. Then he sighed. 'I'll have to do something about her, though. She's sixteen, nearly grown-up. She can't keep on tramping about the world with me.'

'What have you done about her education?' asked Alasdair curiously. He had corresponded with Edward over the years and had had letters from some places with pretty unpronounceable names.

'Until Betsy died, she had a governess. But since then . . . well, nothing really. Nothing traditional, that is. But she reads a lot, and she makes fair copies of my notes and deals with my correspondence if I'm away. She pays the servants, keeps house and what not. She can lance a boil, even stitch a cut, and, of course, she's travelled widely.'

Appalling! thought Alasdair. His wife would be horrified.

Edward looked down at his whisky for a moment and then said, 'I've been thinking that I ought to get married again. Buy a house, maybe in Edinburgh. Find a sensible woman who can give Charlotte a bit of polish. See she meets the right people.'

'You mean, find her a suitable husband?'

'In due course.' Edward sighed. After Betsy died he could have taken Charlotte home. Lady Invershiel had offered to have her.

He knew that that's what he ought to have done, everybody kept telling him so. But he hadn't.

How could he have taken Charlotte back to Scotland and left her there, and not seen her for years? He just couldn't do it. Fortunately, she had inherited his physical stamina and was rarely ill. She had been a good companion, too. Remote villages had often been more welcoming when they saw a child with him. Charlotte had been his passport to a friendly reception in many places.

'The problem is,' he continued, 'it's all very well marrying some well-connected lady to see Charlotte safely buckled to some man, but then what? Charlotte is wed, and I'm stuck with the woman!'

Alasdair laughed. 'You'd have to choose her for you as well.'

Edward shook his head. His one foray into matrimony had not been a success. When Betsy had died, he had mourned not only her young life cut short, but also his ruined hopes for their happiness together; her drinking, her affairs with other men, her inability to run the household, all these had become an increasing strain. He had not realized how much, until he was relieved of it. And he had once loved her.

No, he never wanted that again.

He was not good with women, or, more accurately, ladies. He just couldn't bear the lies and subterfuges with which they got their own way. They always expected compliments and he did not have the touch which would have enabled him to do the thing lightly. Trivia had never interested him—and ladies, on the whole, were trivial creatures. Perhaps it was their nature, or possibly their education; whatever it was, he had found it better to avoid female entanglements since Betsy. He had been badly burnt and, deep down, he knew that he still carried the scar tissue. He winced, and Alasdair, watching him, wondered what memory had stirred.

Then Edward thought, that woman at Fort Augustus, now she was out of the common run. Whatever had she been doing in St Petersburg? He wished he'd asked her.

*   *   *

Jamie Ritchie, now seventeen, had turned out a fine-looking young man. He was rather above middle height, slim, with his mother's brown eyes and thick dark hair. At the Inverness Academy he was seen as a very promising student, but something of a loner. He was there on a bursary, which marked him out as coming from a poor family, and he had had, over the years, to endure a number of jibes about it. His teachers knew that, and admired the quiet dignity with which he had met the baiting he'd received. What they did not know, was the hidden knowledge about his parentage which Jamie carried round with him, the shameful secret which must never be told.

Today, after school, the headmaster had summoned Jamie to his study. Jamie walked down the corridor, which always seemed to smell of overcooked cabbage, and whose panelled walls were scored with years of roughly gouged out schoolboys' initials, and knocked on the headmaster's door.

'Ah, Ritchie! Come in, lad. Sit down.'

Jamie sat.

The headmaster steepled his fingers together and beamed across the desk. 'I am delighted to inform you that the University of Glasgow has offered you a scholarship to study mathematics under Professor Blackburn.' He handed Jamie the letter.

Jamie scanned it. 'Thank you, sir,' he said formally, his voice flat.

'Aren't you pleased, Ritchie?' asked the head. 'It's a great honour, you know.'

'Yes, sir, of course I am, but I'm not sure if I can accept it. The scholarship pays my fees, but how am I to live? And I'm worried about my mother, too.'

'The Academy has applied for a bursary from the town to support you whilst you are there. I know the chairman of the board and I do not think that there will be a problem. The town is proud of its scholars, you know. The bursary will probably be in the region of forty pounds a year, which will cover your basic necessities.'

Jamie's face lightened. 'Thank you, sir.'

'Discuss it with your mother, Ritchie. We'll talk about it tomorrow.' Mrs Ritchie would manage somehow, he thought. Women usually did.

That evening, Jamie went down to the New Quay to find Olaf, who had a temporary job there. He liked the busyness of the harbour, with the skeleton ribs of the ships being built, the smell of wood coming from the sawmills, the tar, the bales of hemp for the sail-makers, the horses waiting to tow a brig up the river to her berth. He enjoyed the bustle of it, the feeling that things were being made, that goods were coming from far away and that the newly built ships would, in their turn, set off for foreign lands.

He found Olaf in the timber-yard. 'I've got it!' he shouted excitedly. 'I've got the scholarship, Olaf.'

Olaf grinned. 'I knew ye would.' He gave Jamie a great buffet on the shoulder, which sent him sprawling.

'The Academy is applying for a bursary from the town for my living expenses,' added Jamie, picking himself up.

'That'll help,' Olaf nodded.

'Mother wants me to take it, and I want to go, but I'm worried about how she'll manage.'

'Your father ought to do something,' said Olaf. 'It's not right that he doesn't help.'

Jamie's face darkened. 'He's as rich as Dives. At least, he owns an estate near Whitebridge, and he has a house in Edinburgh.' It just wasn't *fair*, he thought.

'Near Whitebridge, eh?' said Olaf. 'That's not far. 'Tis only an hour or two away by steamer.'

Jamie looked at him, an arrested expression on his face.

*   *   *

Life had not handed Murdo Gillespie the well-endowed living he felt that he had the right to expect. He had duly taken holy orders, but, after doing a couple of years as curate in a very inferior parish, he failed to be offered anything better than a country parish near Kinlochewe. It was not at all what he'd wanted, or deserved. His parishioners were mostly illiterate, and the finer parts of his sermons were lost on them. Oh, they turned up all right, but the more he expounded on the torments of Hell, the more he noticed the not-quite-muffled laughter and conspiratorial glances from one to the other.

They all paid lip service to him. Aye, the demon drink was a terrible thing, they agreed solemnly, but that didn't stop them drinking for a single moment. What was worse, they kept jabbering amongst themselves in Gaelic. Murdo's command of Gaelic was very imperfect. He stumbled through a short Gaelic service once a month, but otherwise they were in English, and he was never sure how much they understood of it.

They were a load of savages. The elders of the kirk suggested that he start a school, but Murdo didn't see why he should spend his time and money in teaching children who appeared not at all grateful for his presence. Instead, and he confided this to nobody, he embarked on a hidden career, that of writing sentimental stories as Evangeline Mott for *The Ladies' Cabinet of Fashion, Music and Romance*, which earned him twenty pounds a story; the money reconciled him somewhat to the humiliations of his job.

Then, he met Janet Glendinning and her £9000. It seemed as if his luck had turned at last, especially when, shortly after his marriage, his mother died. From being the minister of a poor parish on £90 a year, he was suddenly, by his marriage and the death of his mother, worth £650 a year. He gave up the parish. He would become a man of letters, he decided. He took his wife back to Nevan House and they settled down.

He ensconced himself in what had once been his father's study, and wrote long-winded articles on the knottier points of doctrine in Leviticus, which brought him in a small income and a large correspondence. In spite of her superior earning abilities, Evangeline Mott disappeared. Janet was fond of poking her head round the door of his study and calling, Coffee, dear?' in a bright voice, and he did not want the shame of his sobriquet being discovered.

In due course, children arrived, four of them in quick succession. Nevan House was not large and the children were all healthy and possessed of powerful lungs. Murdo, who had been brought up as an only child, found the noise impossible. He tried hanging a thick baize curtain over his study door, but the noise, though now muffled, was still audible. A stout leather strap, which he did not hesitate to use, was more effective.

In 1862, Janet died, after giving birth to twins, and, to Murdo's secret relief, the babies died with her. He mourned her, naturally, but he couldn't help feeling that to have had all those children so precipitately did argue a certain lack of restraint in the performance of her marital duties. He had a nursery wing built at the back of the house and hired a respectable and God-fearing woman to look after the children. Several years passed.

Then, on Sunday, 23 July, 1865, he met Beatrix Penicuik at the kirk which served Achnagarry and the surrounding crofts and villages. Mr Penicuik, Murdo noticed with displeasure, rarely went to church, but Mrs Penicuik was there, with her children.

'Mr Gillespie! How are you?' exclaimed Beatrix, after the service. Normally, he warranted a mere bow, but this year she had decided that Murdo could be useful, and some extra affability was needed. 'How your boys have grown!'

'My two elder sons, William and Robert,' said Murdo, taking William firmly by the ear and grabbing Robert's wrist.

'What fine boys!' said Beatrix, and patted them on the head.

William scowled and Robert brushed his hair with his hand, he hated being patted like a dog. Beatrix affected not to notice. All through the service, she had been mulling over an idea. Murdo was a widower. He needed a wife. Robina had once been sweet on him. If they married, then Robina would be on hand to keep an eye on Achnagarry Lodge, and deal with all those little things which turned up and required attention.

After some small talk, she said, 'My cousin, Miss Drummond, will be coming up next week. I am sure you must remember her; you were once such good friends.'

Murdo bowed. She was still 'Miss Drummond', was she? He liked the idea that Robina had been wearing the willow for him all these years. 'Will she be staying long?'

'For the summer.' Beatrix was not going to confide her hopes that Robina would get Madeline the entrée to Dunlairg. 'You must come to tea and renew your acquaintance.'

Yes, thought Murdo, as he walked home, with William and Robert trailing behind him scuffling their shoes as they walked. Robina had £5000, a sum not to be sneezed at by a man with four children to bring up. An extra £250 a year would come in very handy. Robina must be—he did some swift calculations— thirty-two now, and she had always been a skinny thing. She would be unlikely to present him with yet more children, and, in any case, he would show restraint. It would not be difficult; skin and bones had never appealed to him. It would bear thinking on.

*   *   *

The Invershiels greeted Edward and Charlotte with genuine pleasure. Charlotte was shown up to her bedroom, a fascinatingly round room in the south turret and, as soon as she had hung up her coat and hat and changed out of her boots, she rushed all over the castle to assure herself that it was just as she'd remembered. As she came up on to the battlements, she saw a tall young man, with thick brown hair, a short moustache, and wearing a Norfolk jacket and knickerbockers. He was staring out at nothing in particular and Charlotte got the impression that something was bothering him. He turned as she came up the turret stairs.

'Oh, hello! I'm Charlotte Mountsorrel. Do you remember me?' It must be either John or Henry, she thought, but which?

John smiled. 'Of course I know who you are. I'm your cousin, John Invershiel. I saw you coming up the road,' He pointed down to Loch Nevan and the road they had ridden up, which wound along its length.

Charlotte peered over the battlements. The

road looked small and dusty and a long way down, and, from that height, the loch looked like a steel mirror. 'I remember you,' she said, with pleasure. 'You're the one who likes kippers.'

John laughed. 'You remember that!' He'd always had a passion for kippers and his mother ordered them especially, all the way from Aberdeen.

'What should I call you?' asked Charlotte. 'Cousin John?'

'You can call me "John" if you like.'

'Would that be all right?' Charlotte frowned. She'd lived in so many countries and she could never remember what was proper where.

'Oh, I think so. Cousins, you know.'

Charlotte looked at him, consideringly. For all his friendliness, his mouth turned down in a discontented way and he kept hunching a shoulder impatiently.

'My papa collects plants,' she said. 'What do you do?'

'Nothing much,' said John, kicking moodily at a loose piece of stone on the battlements. 'I'm the elder son. I'm not supposed to do anything.'

'Why not?' Charlotte liked to get things straight.

'Because I shall inherit this old pile of stones one day.'

'I can't see what that has to do with it,'

argued Charlotte.

'You wouldn't. You're only a girl.' And she was still Miss Curiosity, he thought, remembering suddenly how she used to badger him with questions.

'I like that!' cried Charlotte indignantly. She spun on her heel and walked off.

John turned back to the loch. How could a fellow do anything when the governor was so ill that he might pop off at any moment? And he wasn't allowed even to look at the estate business? The one time he'd asked if he might learn about the estate, his father had flown into a rage and accused him of wanting to see him in the grave. He'd apologized later, and said that he was just a tetchy old man, but, John noticed, he still hadn't offered to teach him anything.

Charlotte, he thought moodily, was still a brat. He remembered her from her last visit, always poking her nose into what didn't concern her.

*　　　*　　　*

Mrs Usher had seen fit to have a word with her daughter about Mr Mountsorrel. It was vital that Georgina did not come out with any of her dreadful puns, that she made an effort to dress properly, and, in short, did her best to attach so eligible a man.

'You are twenty-seven, Georgina,' finished

Mrs Usher despairingly. 'You *must* get married. You don't want to dwindle into a spinster, do you?' The question was plainly rhetorical.

Georgina heaved a great sigh and tugged at her whalebone corset in an effort to get comfortable. If only her mother would leave her alone, she thought.

'Well?' demanded Mrs Usher.

'If I had my money,' stated Georgina, 'I'd go and live in the country somewhere and breed dogs.'

'Breed dogs!'

'Yes! She's doggedly determined to breed dogs!' She gave one of her guffaws. Georgina often referred to herself in the third person.

Mrs Usher shut her eyes for one agonized moment.

'Sorry!'

'Please, Georgina, just try. I'll send Dalton to you.' Dalton was Mrs Usher's lady's maid.

Oh God, thought Georgina, that meant the curling tongs and she'd end up looking like a poodle, she knew it.

*   *   *

Lord Invershiel and Edward were sitting in Lord Invershiel's smoking-room, a round room at the bottom of the south turret, and crammed with various trophies of the chase— masks, antlers and stuffed fish—for his lordship had shot and fished with enthusiasm for the last thirty odd years. It was not a very comfortable room, the windows didn't fit and a sluggish fire in the grate blew out puffs of peaty smoke. Edward, however, didn't notice. He'd lived in far worse conditions.

'Good to see you, m'boy,' said Lord Invershiel, pouring some more brandy into his guest's glass with a shaky hand. 'You're looking well.' The Invershiels and the Mountsorrels were only distantly related, but Lord Invershiel had once admired Edward's mother, and he'd always felt affectionate towards her son.

'Thank you. I hope you're on the mend now?' Invershiel did not look well, thought Edward. His colour was too high. And surely he shouldn't be drinking brandy?

'So-so.' Lord Invershiel did not want to discuss his health, a topic which bored him. He had enough of that from his wife. 'How's Glendon these days?'

Edward shrugged. 'Bearing up. I don't see much of him. He's something of a recluse.'

'Shouldn't you know something about the estate?'

'I don't think he'd welcome that. I'm his heir, he acknowledges that, but he's never been the sort of man who likes his kith and kin around him. We exchange letters perhaps twice a year and that's about it.' It suited him, too, thought Edward. He'd always preferred travel anyway. One day, he'd have to settle down, but not yet.

'Think I should warn you, m'boy,' went on Lord Invershiel, 'Lady Invershiel has a wife in her eye for you, her god-daughter, Georgina Usher. Face like a horse. Laughs like one, too.'

'Good God!'

'Told her I couldn't see you going for poor Gusher—that's what the boys call her—you'll see why when you meet her. She's a good soul, mind, but marry her . . . ?'

Edward frowned. 'Charlotte's sixteen now,' he said. 'I suppose I should be thinking of settling down for her sake.' But even as he spoke, his mind shied away from the idea.

'See what you think of Georgina,' said Lord Invershiel, large-mindedly. 'She might be your cup of tea. Reasonable dowry, eight thousand or so, and she'll get her mother's money in due course. From that point of view, you could do a lot worse. Her mother and my wife would be delighted.'

Edward made a face. Over the years he'd had to endure an awful lot of hopeful mothers.

*　　　*　　　*

Mr Francis Ogilvy looked down at the letter in front of him and frowned. It was from Mary Ritchie and she begged for a few moments of his time. Since the last allowance had been paid over two years ago, he had had little contact with her. She had managed to save about sixty pounds and he had looked after it for her. From time to time, she had asked him for a few pounds and the sum had been slowly diminishing. There was now about twelve pounds in the account.

A few days earlier, she had dropped him a note telling him the news of James's scholarship, and he had written to congratulate the young man and sent him a sovereign. But how was Mrs Ritchie going to manage? He knew that she earned a few shillings a week as an assistant schoolteacher, but that wouldn't keep her.

He picked up his quill pen, dipped it in the ink, and wrote a brief note to say that he would be at Mrs Ritchie's disposal that afternoon at three o'clock, and sent his boy round with it to her lodgings in Celt Street.

At three o'clock, Mary arrived. Mr Ogilvy's maid ushered her into his study. Mr Ogilvy rose to his feet, shook hands, and offered her a chair.

'Now, how may I help you, ma'am?'

'As you know, we have been living off my savings and my six hours a week as assistant teacher.'

Mr Ogilvy nodded.

'The savings are running low, and I do not think I can support myself in the way I have been doing for the three years while Jamie is at university. I have decided to look for a position where I can live in. I have heard that

Dr Ross may be looking for a housekeeper and I wondered if you would give me a reference?'

Mr Ogilvy studied his pen tray for a moment. He knew Dr Ross, and a lecherous old goat he was, too. 'Have you met him?' he asked.

'No. I was thinking of writing to him in the first instance.'

'Of course, I'll give you a reference, but I think it would be better if I wrote to Dr Ross on your behalf.' He would stress that she was a respectable woman. Ross had a reputation for running through pretty housekeepers, but one who came to him recommended by a respectable lawyer, should be safe, or at least safer, from any unwanted attentions.

'Thank you, sir,' said Mary, gratefully.

Mr Ogilvy kept his misgivings to himself.

*   *   *

Robina's Journal   Thursday, 7 July, 1865
It was strange walking up Glen Nevan, the first time for fifteen years. It was just the same and yet it wasn't. I'd completely forgotten the bit where the Allt na Caorann with the rowans forms a deep pool just by the second bridge. The moment I saw it, I remembered. Now, how could I have forgotten that?

Pheemie Maclean's cottage has disappeared. All that is left is a stone outline and clumps of nettles. There's a darkened patch where the chimney used to be and a small birch tree is growing where the hens used to roost. What happened? Beatrix never mentioned anything in her letters, but then she hardly ever wrote about Achnagarry.

Dear Pheemie. She always reminded me of a mouse. She was little and she scurried round, her face wrapped in a shawl. She had those bright blue eyes that you see sometimes in very old people—but only those whose minds are still awake.

Later, I met Donald Fraser. He looks older and more bent and his hair's gone quite white. He can't be that old, though. Fifty-five? Sixty?

He waved and came down the hill with his collie—it looked just like Bran, though, of course, it couldn't have been. It was wonderful to see Donald again, though I soon realized that my Gaelic was very rusty. I kept stumbling over endings and tenses, and Donald stood there, grinning!

But, oh God, Hamish was killed a couple of years ago, and I never knew! How could Beatrix not have mentioned it? I felt really bad that I hadn't written. It was at a place called Ambela. I didn't know what to say, so I just stood patting Donald's arm helplessly. It's so awful. Hamish was their only son.

The other thing was that Hamish's colonel had written to Donald and Mhairi and they couldn't read it. Murdo promised to read it to them and, so far, two years later!! has never

111

found the time to do so. Despicable! Where's his Christian charity?

I hadn't realized how much I missed Achnagarry until I came back. It's belonging, knowing everybody, and being able to do things, small things, which make a difference. In many ways, I've loved the last ten years. I wouldn't have missed the travel and seeing new places and learning about different ways of going on, for anything. But having somewhere you can call home is important, too.

All the same, I know I can never live here again. Where would I fit in? It's not my home any more. But it's made me think. When I get hold of my money, I'm going to settle somewhere and make myself a proper life. Italy was lovely, but, however kind the people, I was always aware that I was the Signorina Inglesa. *I could never belong from the inside, as it were.*

What with meeting Donald and musing on Pheemie Maclean, I didn't get to Achnagarry until nearly six o'clock, later than I thought. Beatrix, predictably, was not pleased.

*　　　*　　　*

'Just like Robina!' said Beatrix crossly as she was changing for dinner.

'What is?' asked Duncan, who was wrestling with his cuff-links in his dressing-room. The door was half open and he could see his wife sitting at her dressing-table, and her maid

112

brushing her hair over the false pad into a smooth chignon.

'That she turns up hours after she's expected, looking like a hoyden. She *walked* up from Whitebridge, if you please! Why on earth couldn't she have hired a horse and come up at the same time as Tam brought her luggage? That way, at least she'd have had a proper escort. Suppose somebody from Dunlairg had seen her? What would they have thought! You know how important it is that she creates a good impression.

'For heaven's sake, Flora,' she broke off crossly, 'how many times do I have to tell you not to pull?'

'Sorry, Madam.' Flora made a face at Beatrix's back and carried on twisting the large sausage curls round her finger to make them lie just so and then pinned them expertly to the chignon to stop them floating loose. She picked up the hand mirror and held it so that Beatrix could see the effect from the back.

'It will have to do,' said Beatrix grudgingly.

Duncan came in from the dressing-room and picked up his evening dress coat. As he passed Flora, he pinched her bottom lightly. Flora said nothing, but her lips tightened. She moved away and went to fetch Beatrix's evening slippers.

'You would invite Robina,' said Duncan. He bent over the back of Beatrix's chair to look in her glass and smoothed his side whiskers.

'Yes, and I've had a good idea,' said Beatrix. 'She shall marry Murdo Gillespie, and that way she can be useful. She was sweet on him once, you know; and he needs a wife now he's a widower. Robina can look after his children and keep an eye on Achnagarry when we're not here.' She stretched out her feet for Flora to put on the evening slippers.

'But didn't he jilt her?'

Beatrix shrugged. 'There was no formal engagement. In any case, Robina's in no position to object; she's been on the shelf for years.'

Poor Miss Robina, thought Flora, tidying away Beatrix's discarded day clothes. She'd only met her once before, but she'd been a very pleasant lady and had spoken to Flora as though she were a real person with feelings. Not like some, she thought, with a dark glance at Beatrix's unresponsive back. She couldn't stand the way they spoke in front of her as though she wasn't there—even though it meant that she learnt things she wouldn't otherwise know. She hoped that Miss Robina knew of Mrs Penicuik's match-making.

*   *   *

In spite of her late arrival, Robina was down in the drawing-room before either Beatrix or Duncan. She was perfectly able to dress herself and do her own hair. Morag had ironed her evening gown, a dark red silk with a cream underskirt, and Robina had swiftly done her hair in a plaited chignon and pinned a fine cameo brooch to her bodice. She was well aware that her dress did not say 'poor relation' and wondered what Beatrix would think of it. Robina had learnt, when she first became a 'lady companion', that a well-cut silk dress and some good jewellery made all the difference to her employers' treatment of her.

It helped, of course, that she still had most of the £150 Grandmama had left her. She could leave any position at any time, and she made sure that her employers knew it. Some of them, like the Countess Kamenska, were not above bullying their dependants, and Robina had made sure that they never felt that they could get away with it with her. She would use the same tactics at Achnagarry.

Madeline was in the drawing-room, staring out of the window at a rain shower, which was sweeping down over the loch like a thin grey curtain. She jumped up as Robina came in.

'Cousin Robina!' They kissed.

Robina smiled, 'You're so pretty! I always thought you would be. And, for heaven's sake, call me Robina, you're grown up now.'

Madeline laughed and shook her honey-coloured curls. 'Thank you.' She looked at her cousin. Her father had said she was a 'skinny weasel' or some such thing, but he was wrong, she thought. Robina was slim, but her figure was pleasing and she held herself well. What was more, the gown she was wearing was decidedly fashionable.

'Paris?' asked Madeline, looking at the dress.

'Not quite. It was made for me by a French dressmaker who lived in Florence. So almost.'

She's not a dowd, thought Madeline. And her eyes were a wonderfully expressive deep brown. She smiled mischievously, 'Has Mama seen you?'

'Of course, when I arrived.'

'No, I mean now.'

'Not yet.'

'She won't like it,' said Madeline, indicating the dress. This dowdy cousin was not *supposed* to be attractive. Madeline hoped that she loved her parents as she ought, but she saw their faults clearly enough. Mama was planning to use Robina and she wouldn't be at all pleased that she was pretty. The summer could be interesting.

Robina saw that Madeline was looking slightly mischievous. It was plain that she did not accord her mother the same value that that lady accorded herself, but Robina didn't feel that she knew her well enough to comment, so she said, 'I haven't seen your brothers yet.'

'Ewan's a beast,' said Madeline promptly. 'Watch out for him. If there's anything you don't like, spiders for instance, for heaven's sake, don't let him know. Not unless you want one in your bed.'

'I'm all right with spiders,' said Robina, 'though I don't like wolves. When I was in Russia, we were once chased by them. It was winter and we were driving back late one evening and, suddenly, a pack of them came out from the woods. I was really frightened, though, thank God, the guard had a gun and frightened them off. But there aren't any wolves in Scotland now.'

'Knowing Ewan, he'd find a dead one somewhere,' said Madeline.

'Oh, I don't mind it dead!'

'Aeneas is a bookworm. He's all right. But Papa calls him a muff, so he tends to keep out of the way.'

'That's very sad,' said Robina, thinking privately that it sounded awful.

'You won't see them until tomorrow. They're too young to dine with the grown-ups.'

Just then, the door opened, and Beatrix and Duncan entered. Beatrix gave one look at Robina's dress, and an angry flush rose to her cheeks. Here was an unexpected danger! Robina had no business to look so . . . so . . . She was to be the spinster cousin, not look as though she was setting herself up as a rival to Madeline!

Duncan surged forward to kiss her. God, she'd improved beyond all recognition, he thought.

'Mr Penicuik,' said Robina, and held out her hand.

'Let us not be formal,' said Duncan, brushing her hand aside. Robina stepped back. 'Why not?' she said firmly. She'd met his type before and she'd learnt to make her position clear immediately.

Duncan frowned. He was not used to being thwarted, but there was nothing he could do. His wife was glaring at him, and his daughter was looking on with interest. Reluctantly, he shook Robina's hand.

Robina gave him a cool smile and decided to let him off the hook. 'I'm very impressed by Achnagarry Lodge,' she told him. 'A spectacular example of Scottish baronial.'

Duncan relaxed slightly. Appearances were misleading. She was just a gauche female who didn't recognize male appreciation when she saw it. When the gong went, he ignored Robina's claims to the honour, and instead offered his arm to his wife. Madeline shot Robina a droll look and they followed Beatrix and Duncan out of the room.

*   *   *

The moment Mary met Dr Ross, she knew that there might be trouble. He was a short, tubby man, with a tobacco-stained moustache, and a look in his eye which seemed to undress her.

'Mrs Ritchie! Come away in,' he said, holding out his hand.

His hand was hot, and Mary dropped it as soon as she could. He ushered her into his consulting-room and sat down, pulling his chair up so that their knees were almost touching.

'Well, well! Splendid!' he said, his small eyes darting all over her.

Mary began to feel uncomfortable. When he rose to find Mr Ogilvy's letter, she edged her chair back as far as she could.

'Right, here we are!' Dr Ross sat down again, saw her chair had been moved and felt a momentary flash of irritation. 'Mr Ogilvy quite sings your praises,' he observed.

Mary smiled primly. 'He has been very kind to me and my son for many years.'

Dr Ross tugged at his moustache. 'Yes, yes!' he said impatiently. She was going to be missish, he knew it. All the same, she was a tidy-looking wench and, once she was here, to hand so to speak, doubtless she'd be more amenable.

'I am an experienced housekeeper,' said Mary firmly. 'I can keep accounts, write a clear hand and am used to dealing with tradesmen.'

Dr Ross raised his eyebrows. 'Why, my dear, you can scarcely be more than twenty-five!'

'I have a son of seventeen,' stated Mary coldly, and saw, with satisfaction, his face drop. 'I understand that you have a cook and two maids?'

'Yes. And a groom-cum-outdoor man, and,

of course, my two apprentices.'

Mary's spirits rose. It would be more work, but she felt safer. 'I am asking for thirty-five pounds a year,' she said. She'd discussed this with Mr Ogilvy.

Dr Ross shook his head. 'But you want me to feed and house your son when he's down from university. That costs money.'

'I shall pay you five shillings a week for his keep while he's here.'

'Five? Pah! Ten would be nearer the mark.'

'Very well, a shilling a day,' said Mary. It would be over half her weekly wage, and she could go no higher.

'Seven it is,' growled Dr Ross, 'but I'm doing you a favour.' And favours needed returns. Thirty-nine was older than he liked, but she had spirit and she'd kept her figure. She would do.

'It's a fair offer,' said Mary indignantly. 'I can always lodge him elsewhere.'

'Oh, very well.' He reached out and patted her knee, giving it a squeeze before he let go.

Mary stood up. 'I'm a respectable woman, Dr Ross,' she said.

They all say that, he thought. Doubtless she missed having a man in her bed. She'd come round.

*   *   *

It didn't take Robina more than a couple of

days to realize that her position as 'guest' in the house was misleading. Beatrix was not good at amusing herself and demanded constant attention. She liked an audience for whatever she had to say and, after a couple of afternoons sitting on the veranda listening to Beatrix pontificating on the laziness of servants and how Aeneas was growing positively round-shouldered, Robina was desperate to stretch her legs. In her years as companion to various elderly ladies, it was an understood thing that she might have a couple of hours off, usually in the afternoon, whilst her employer had a nap. It was during these times that Robina set out to explore.

Now, she wanted to go down to the Frasers' cottage and read the colonel's letter about Hamish to Donald and Mhairi. She also wanted to go up to the crannog.

The weather, for once, was hot. Beatrix sat and fanned herself languidly and complained of the sun. She had put on a lot of weight since her marriage, and she felt the heat. When Robina suggested that they walk down to the loch, Beatrix exclaimed, 'In *this* weather?'

After a moment, Robina said, 'Beatrix, I can't sit here all afternoon. I need some exercise.'

'Very well then,' said Beatrix, 'but it's very inconvenient. Oh, there's Ewan.'

Ewan was approaching them with a catapult in his hand. He saw his mother beckoning and slouched towards them, a pasty-faced, thickly built young man, looking, Robina thought, astonishingly like his father.

'Ewan, you may take Cousin Robina for a walk.'

Ewan stuck his catapult in his belt and scowled.

Robina jumped up. 'I'll just get my hat. Be five minutes.'

Five minutes later, they were walking down to the loch. 'What do you get with the catapult?' asked Robina.

Ewan shrugged. 'Rabbits.'

'You won't get any at this time of day,' observed Robina.

Ewan glared at her and kicked at the pine cones which littered the path. Robina picked up a stone, weighed it carefully and said, 'See that rock there? The one with the patch of yellow lichen?'

Ewan nodded. Robina threw the stone, which hit the rock with a sharp crack. Ewan, reluctantly impressed, though suspecting a fluke, pulled out his catapult, chose a stone, and fired. It missed.

'Try again.'

Several more shots went wide, though not embarrassingly so.

'You need to practise,' said Robina, picking up another stone and hitting the rock. She had not practised her archery for many years, and she was pardonably pleased that her aim was still good. She wondered what had happened to her bow and arrows? Thrown out, probably, when the old house was demolished.

'My father calls you a skinny weasel,' said Ewan, after a few moments' silence.

'Really?' Robina was unconcerned. She could call Duncan a lot of things as well, if she'd a mind to.

'Don't you care?'

'Why should I?'

Another silence, then Ewan burst out, 'You're not like a female at all!'

Robina laughed.

Ewan shot her a baffled look. He liked having power over people. He liked the way Aeneas was frightened of him, and that his mother, whilst she deplored his 'low' ways, as she called them, nevertheless boasted about his exploits to her friends. Being a man meant that you were top dog—and he enjoyed that. But Robina seemed to be impervious to his status.

'I bet you can't gut a fish,' he said.

'Bet what?' asked Robina, at once. 'Ten shillings?'

Ewan gave a reluctant nod. His father kept him short of pocket money and ten shillings would just about clean him out. On the other hand, she was probably bluffing. Girls always squealed at the thought of touching a fish.

'Done,' said Robina. 'I'll meet you tomorrow morning early, seven o'clock say. We'll fish the morning rise.' She waiting until Ewan nodded again, and said, 'Good, that's settled. I'm going over to Donald Fraser's, so I'll leave you here.' She turned and walked up the hill, treading carefully by the side of the tussocks of heather. She didn't want to sprain an ankle.

Once up the hillside, she turned back to look at Achnagarry. The old house had once stood to the right of the new lodge. It had gone, like Pheemie Maclean's cottage. The level patch was now used as a washing ground and she could see a line of sheets blowing in the wind. Her gaze moved. She could just see the Frasers' cottage; its blackened thatched roof made of heather weighed down with stones to protect it during the winter storms, seemed to grow out of the hillside. As she looked, Mhairi Fraser came out carrying a stool and sat down outside the door with a bucket of something beside her. What was she doing? Shelling beans?

She'd go and see, and offer to read the letter from Hamish's colonel. It would be good to speak Gaelic again. She hadn't liked losing the words and forgetting the grammar when she'd spoken to Donald. At that moment, Mhairi looked up, shaded her eyes and caught sight of her. Robina waved.

*   *   *

Breakfast at Dunlairg Castle was a very

traditional affair. There was always cold meat and a veal and ham pie. If anybody had caught a trout or char then it would be rolled in oatmeal and grilled and put on the hot plate, together with bacon, eggs and sausages. There were muffins and toast, marmalade and butter and, for those who wanted it, porridge. Everybody was expected to help himself. Lady Invershiel was in charge of the tea and coffee.

Edward and Charlotte had risen early and gone for a walk. Edward had come back with a delicate frog orchid and some Scottish asphodel. He'd been hoping to find some Highland cudweed, but perhaps they hadn't gone high enough. He was in a good mood. He even felt ready for Miss Usher.

Charlotte had decided that life at Dunlairg Castle was going to prove interesting. Part of her regarded her new cousins in much the same way as she regarded meeting a new tribe somewhere up in the Himalayas, except that, confusingly, this time she was one of them. She had not been with people of her own kind very often. She had vague memories of life when her mother was alive. Then, there had been visits and parties, but she'd been too young to be taken about. Her mother had come in, smelling delicious and wearing something pretty, and kissed her good-night. Sometimes, she'd smelled of drink, and her eyes were over-bright and her cheeks red. Even now, thinking about it made Charlotte feel uncomfortable.

Occasionally, her parents had had a party at home, and then she'd heard noise and laughter and, in the morning, there would be wilting flowers on the table, and the servants would gossip about who had been there. But it was all hazy, like a dream.

Here, there were lots of people she knew, and she was allowed to stay up!

'Ah, here you are!' said Lady Invershiel as Edward and Charlotte came in. 'Were you out fishing? John and Henry went out and brought back some char.'

'Papa found some asphodel,' said Charlotte.

'And a frog orchid,' added Edward, going over to the side table and cutting himself a slice of veal and ham pie.

'Oh, where?' asked Lord Invershiel, mildly interested.

'Up by Crom Allit,' said Edward, 'though I had some trouble getting it. It was in an awkward spot, but I clung to Charlotte's feet, and she reached it.'

'An awkward orchid,' muttered Georgina, trying for a pun. Her mother shot her a frown. Georgina subsided.

'What would everybody like to do today?' asked Lady Invershiel. 'Anderson will row anybody on the loch who wants to fish.'

'Too bright,' said John. 'I might go up to Loch na Nan and try there. There's more shade.'

'You won't get much,' put in Henry. 'A

126

troutlet, perhaps.'

'An outlet for a troutlet,' said Georgina, nudging Henry, who was sitting next to her. She gave a loud guffaw and then her hand flew up to cover her mouth.

'I like that!' said Charlotte, and giggled.

Edward shot Georgina an amused glance. An over-grown schoolgirl, he thought, but she obviously entertained Charlotte.

'Would you like to come with me, Charlotte?' asked John.

She shook her head. 'I'm going with Papa. He wants to find some grass of Parnassus.'

'There's some in the woods down by the River Nevan,' said Lady Invershiel, thinking quickly. 'It's on Achnagarry land, but I'm sure they won't mind. I'll drop a note to Mrs Penicuik.' Doubtless, they'd be invited to luncheon and John must be there. 'John, why don't you go with them? You know where they can find it. Loch na Nan can wait another day.'

'Very well,' said John politely. Something was going on, he wasn't sure what, but his mother was not normally given to asking favours of the Penicuiks.

'Grass of Parnassus!' exclaimed Mrs Usher. 'Georgina, you'd like to go, I'm sure.'

Blasted grass, thought Georgina, but she nodded.

CHAPTER FOUR

Robina's Journal   Saturday, 29 July, 1865
The most amusing day. Beatrix got a note this
morning from Lady I., asking permission for Mr
Mountsorrel, his daughter, John I. and Gusher to
go and see the grass of Parnassus. Of course, she
was ecstatic! And it rather confirms what I think
is going on. Lady I. wants poor Gusher to
ensnare Mr Mountsorrel and John is to captivate
Madeline, though, of course, Beatrix's plans are
rather different—which is going to make life
interesting! Naturally, she wrote to invite the
whole party to luncheon here. Then, the fuss!
Beatrix rushed off to harry poor Ishbel and
Morag. Duncan and Ewan were chivvied out of
the way—fortunately, Duncan is having some
grouse butts erected—at this time of year! God
knows why, for he doesn't shoot, but perhaps
he's going to let it out—and obviously the men
need to be cursed at. At any rate, it got them out
of the way.

So, at one o'clock, Madeline and I, on our
best behaviour, with Beatrix hovering round, were
awaiting our guests.

Gusher—who hadn't changed an iota—
looked as though she'd been dragged through a
hedge backwards. She'd obviously had rather a
trying morning and she fell on my neck as soon
as she saw me.

'Robin!' she squeaked. Then she clapped her hand over her mouth. 'Sorry—Miss Drummond. Forgot.'

'Robin will do,' I said. 'How are you, Georgia?'

'She's been eaten alive by midges.'

I took her up to my room to change her shoes. She snorted 'boring green stuff' about the grass of Parnassus, took off her Zouave jacket (rather smart—perhaps Mrs U. bought it?) and flung it on the bed, then turned as if to go back downstairs. I asked her if she wanted to change her shoes. They were muddy and had bits of grass and heather caught in the laces. She said, 'Oh, lor! Must she?' I had to be kind, but firm!

Poor Gusher, she hasn't changed. She heaved a great sigh, undid a linen shoe bag and put on a pair of plain black kid shoes. I couldn't help feeling that whatever plans Lady I. had for Gusher, they weren't shared by Gusher herself. All the same, I've always rather liked her. She's awkward; she doesn't know what to do with her hands and feet; I suppose she hasn't really grown up, but she remains herself. I don't think she could lie or prevaricate to save her life.

When we got back downstairs, Madeline was standing in a corner, talking to John Invershiel—and Beatrix obviously didn't like it. She came up to me and hissed, 'Go and talk to Mr Invershiel and get Madeline over here!'

I was about to move over when a voice behind me said, 'Didn't we meet on the steamer?' It was

Mr Mountsorrel. I introduced myself. 'Mountsorrel,' he said, holding out a large paw. I shook it and as he smiled at me with those tawny lion's eyes, I felt suddenly as if something had shifted. It was odd, I've never felt like that before. I just felt different and I'm not sure why. It can't be Mr Mountsorrel, who looks even more like a bear close to.

'You must meet my daughter,' said the bear, reaching out a paw and pulling Miss Mountsorrel over.

I liked Charlotte. She's lively and pretty in a healthy sort of way, and her manners have an easy friendliness. She asked me how I'd got here after the steamer.

I told her about taking the coach from Forres to Whitebridge, getting Tam to bring my luggage up on a pony, and walking. Both pairs of eyebrows shot up and two pairs of lion eyes looked at me. I then told them about meeting Donald Fraser. Somehow, we got on to my speaking Gaelic and the bear asked if Gaelic was my first language, so I told him, no, that was Urdu.

The conversation suddenly became interesting. Charlotte was born in India too, so we began to compare notes about what we remembered, but then Beatrix came over with Madeline in tow. Madeline was looking very pretty. Mr Mountsorrel thought so, I'm sure, though it was difficult to tell what he thinks when he's covered with so much hair. I wonder if his chest is hairy, too? In St Petersburg, men used to bathe naked in the River Neva and some of them had hair all down their backs as well. Perhaps Mr Mountsorrel . . . Robina, whatever are you thinking of?

Anyway.

I left them and went over to talk to John and poor Gusher. John was standing, a faint frown on his face, looking across to where Charlotte, Madeline and Mr Mountsorrel were talking. Was he affronted by Beatrix removing Madeline, I wondered? As the next Lord Invershiel, he had every right to expect the daughter of the house to be propelled in his direction. But, alas, for John, he has virtually nothing, and Mr Mountsorrel has £4000 a year, and is the heir of Lord Glendon, beside.

I'd seen John fairly recently, at Mrs Macdonald's funeral. 'Lord, Robina!' said John. 'How are you? Georgina said you were here.' He lowered his voice. 'What do you think of the new lodge, eh?'

I'm afraid I told him all about my extraordinarily elaborate bed, not one inch of which has been left uncarved. John enjoyed it, as I suspected he might—but I shouldn't have done it! What is interesting, though, is that I don't think he suspects that his mother wants him to make up to Madeline. Lady I. must be being unusually tactful, for once! I suppose the old adage about taking a horse to water applies here —John can be stubborn.

131

But there was no time for more. The gong went and we were ushered into the dining-room. John took one look at the dining chairs with their stag's head finials and winked at me. It was strange meeting John and Gusher again. We were good friends once, in the way that one is if you are children together and have known each other most of your lives, though John and Gusher are younger than I am. I must remember to call her 'Georgina'; I nearly called her 'Gusher' without thinking. Too unkind. I can't say that I was a bosom friend of hers, but I rather liked her and, seeing her now, I feel sorry for her. She seems out of place, somehow.

In one sense, of course, I'm out of place, too. I'm not saying that my grandparents hadn't wanted to take me in. My grandmother loved me, I know, but I was living at Achnagarry because my parents had died. A granddaughter isn't the same as being a daughter. I don't think I fitted in with Grandfather's way of life, but I kept out of his way. Instead, I got to know the people on the estate. I found places where I felt at home, like the Frasers' cottage and the crannog on Loch Tearmann. Poor Gusher—sorry, Georgina— looks as though she's never found a place where she could be herself. I wonder what she wants out of life?

I rather hoped that the Mountsorrels would come over after luncheon and talk to me about India, but they didn't. However, John did tell Beatrix that his mother hoped that I'd bring

132

Madeline over to tea on Monday. But, of course, that's for Madeline's benefit, not mine.

Oh well, why should I care? I'm only here for a month or so.

I feel a bit down. Probably because I'm not used to eating so much in the middle of the day.

*   *   *

The kirk in the small village of Fidach was about five miles away and served many outlying crofts and villages. Once, Fidach had been a large village, but evictions and emigration had reduced it to a mere dozen cottages. The kirk was as plain inside as outside, austerely whitewashed, with a painted wooden board on each side of the transept, one with the ten commandments in stern black writing, and the other with the Lord's Prayer. There were benches at the back for the poor folk and a couple of pews at the front for the gentry. Murdo, accompanied by his two elder sons, sat at the front and slid his eyes sideways at the Achnagarry pew.

At first he didn't recognize Robina. When he did, he saw, to his horror, that she was wearing a hat! Surely, a properly modest female should wear a bonnet? His wife had always worn a bonnet. She had felt, as he did, that to wear a hat was encroaching on the prerogatives of the male. God had ordained that one sex should not appropriate a garment meant for the other. Murdo himself was wearing the kilt, but this did not strike him as contradictory. It was for men to make the rules and for women to obey. Had not St Paul written to Timothy the exhortation 'That women adorn themselves in modest apparel, with shamefacedness and sobriety; not with braided hair, or gold, or pearls, or costly array; but with good works.'? And certainly not with a hat!

All the same, he thought as his eyes slid round again, she was looking much better than he had expected: he could truly say that he would not be ashamed to introduce her as his wife. In fact, she was quite attractive.

When, after church, Beatrix asked him to take tea with them on Friday afternoon, he expressed himself honoured. 'You remember my cousin, of course,' she said. 'Robina, it's Mr Gillespie.'

Robina shook hands, murmured a few polite words and then said, 'Excuse me, Beatrix, I promised Aeneas I'd show him where the wren's nest used to be.' She inclined her head at Murdo and left.

A proper modesty, thought Murdo approvingly, forgetting his earlier strictures. And perhaps a touch of maidenly confusion? It pleased him to think so. He foresaw no problems.

*　　　*　　　*

Mary Ritchie stood in her tiny kitchen and tried not to feel that fourteen years of her life were about to disappear. Mr Francis Ogilvy had written to Mr Alan Ogilvy in Edinburgh, who, in turn, had written to a widowed friend of his in Glasgow, who, for the very moderate sum of twelve shillings a week, undertook to house Jamie, feed him and wash his clothes. She liked having a young person about the house, she wrote, and, if Mr Ogilvy vouched for Mr Ritchie's respectability, she would be delighted to have him. He could have the top back room, which overlooked the garden and would be quiet for his studies. She would expect him on Saturday, 23 September.

It was a relief to know that Jamie had somewhere to live. Mary wished that she could go too, just to see him settled in, but it was out of the question. Money was getting tight.

Jamie had been saving up his wages from the *Inverness Courier* and had decided to take a walking holiday. He would send his trunk on ahead with the steamer, to be collected when he arrived in Glasgow, and he would walk down the Great Glen as far as Corran and then go through Glen Coe and the Moor of Rannoch, and eventually along by Loch Lomond and so down to Glasgow. There was, in fact, a road of sorts all the way, and Mary was aware that her fears of rock falls, thieves, and treacherous peat bogs said more about her maternal anxieties than reality. Jamie was a sensible lad, she knew. He would not do anything stupid, and she must not tie him to her apron strings. She kept her worries to herself.

She had reluctantly accepted the position as housekeeper to Dr Ross, which would begin on Monday, 14 August. She hadn't liked the way he'd eyed her, but what could she do? She must just enjoy having Jamie with her for a few more days and try not to think about what lay ahead. She would have to cope as best she could.

It wasn't just that she didn't altogether trust Dr Ross—if alternative employment had been offered, she'd have taken it—but her nights had been troubled by vivid images from the past, mainly her comfortable childhood home in Edinburgh. Her old rocking horse. What had happened to it? The Turkey carpet in the drawing-room, the old walnut writing-desk, the mahogany tea-caddy, where had all these things gone? However little money her father had left, there was still all the furniture, some silver and a couple of good paintings. She now knew that these things would have brought her a few hundred pounds. How had she come to be left almost destitute? It seemed now, looking back, as if Duncan had hustled her into his bed before she'd had time to think. She had a couple of distant cousins. She should have written. Surely they would have taken her in? It must have been better than what had happened.

Except, of course, she'd had Jamie.

All she'd managed to save from her Edinburgh home, was a pair of china dogs. Jamie had broken one of them when he was a little boy, but she still had the other one, and, as she began packing, she wrapped it safely in her winter clothes to protect it.

Mary went to the hob and put the kettle on. Money or no money, she needed a cup of tea. Jamie would be back soon and she must see what she could do for supper. It would probably be cheap fish again.

She was worried about him. He'd become very silent, as if there were something on his mind. When she'd asked, he'd shaken his head and said that he was just trying to remember all the things he'd need in Glasgow, but Mary wasn't entirely convinced.

Perhaps it was something to do with Olaf Hamnavoe? Jamie had never so much as mentioned him, but Mary had learned of their friendship through several officious neighbours, who were only too anxious to tell her. At first, she'd been considerably alarmed. This Olaf was obviously the roughest sort of man; a sometime whaler, they said, a Shetlander, and one famous for his drinking and fighting. However, after some months, when she'd agonized over whether she should tackle Jamie about Mr Hamnavoe, fairness obliged her to acknowledge that he did not seem to be leading her son into bad ways. Jamie's reports at school continued to be glowing; he had not started to come home drunk; all that had happened was that he went out more and had gained in self-confidence.

Whatever Mr Hamnavoe's reputation, she decided, he was plainly being kind to her son. And, she had to admit, the gifts of fish and game Jamie brought back from time to time were very welcome.

All the same, she still worried. Jamie's mind was not easy, she could tell. Was it a girl? God forbid that he'd got himself entangled . . . but she didn't think it was that. He was a good lad. He knew what such things led to. But he often had a sort of brooding look, and Mary found it frightening. She had this awful feeling that he might be thinking about Duncan. She'd tried to tell him about his father as objectively as she could, to guide him away from any feelings of resentment, but how far had she succeeded?

Did he blame her? She'd done wrong, she knew, but she'd been only sixteen. What else was she to have done? She wiped away a tear roughly with her apron, made herself a cup of tea, sat down at the kitchen table and clasped the cup in her hands. It was a warm day, but her hands still felt cold.

She had the sudden apprehension that things were about to go wrong.

Jamie sat on a rock by the shore, not far from Olaf's wooden shack. He was watching the seals, who were swimming offshore, probably after salmon, he thought. He'd tried using a sing-song voice to them as Olaf had, but the results were not encouraging.

It was Saturday. Jamie had helped his mother with the shopping that morning and, after a quick snack of oatcake and cheese, and an apple, he had taken his home-made fishing rod, and an old hessian bag and come down to the Beauly Firth. Later on, he would see if he could get a fish or two for supper, but, just now, he was content to watch the seals and enjoy the sunshine.

He hadn't seen Olaf for a few days. On his way, he'd asked Alec Burns, who worked down by the sawmill when he wasn't being the sexton at the English church, if he'd seen him, but Alec had shaken his head.

'He said he was going over to the Black Isle.'

Jamie nodded. He was never quite sure whether Olaf's trips to the Black Isle were real or metaphorical, but he'd accepted long ago that sometimes he felt the need to disappear for a while. At any rate, Alec didn't think he was on a randy.

When Jamie had arrived earlier that afternoon, he'd walked round the bothy, listening, but could hear nothing. The door wasn't locked, but he didn't want to go in, in case he disturbed Olaf. Besides, the place stank. The wooden walls were caulked with heather and mud, and the floor was of beaten earth. The only bit of stonework was the chimney, and there was a hook to swing over the fire and an old stewing pot to hang on it. The one tiny window was high up and didn't open.

Olaf had built himself a bed frame with webbing made of deer sinew. On top of that was a sacking mattress stuffed with heather, and a cover of what smelt like badly cured deer skin. The first time Jamie had entered the hut, he'd nearly retched, but he'd got used to it. The place wasn't dirty, exactly. Olaf swept it out every morning with a besom which stood in a corner, and his few possessions were kept on a small shelf. All the same, the hut stank. But it was the place Olaf called home, Jamie understood that.

So, he sat a respectful twenty yards away and stared out to sea. Some time later, he heard a noise behind him, and Olaf came over the dunes. Jamie waited. If Olaf went straight into the bothy, he would know that he wanted to be alone.

But Olaf came over. 'I heard ye singing to the seals,' he said, grinning.

Jamie flushed. 'I was trying to call the seals, but they took no notice. What is it you sing,

140

Olaf? It's not English or Gaelic, is it?'

'Na, 'tis Norn, the old Shetland language. They understand that.'

'I didn't know the Shetlands had their own language.'

'Aye. Though 'tis almost gone now. My old nan, she spoke it, and it was she who taught me the song.'

'Would you teach me?' asked Jamie eagerly.

'What would you be wanting with Norn? They don't speak it in Glasgow.' The tone was light, but Jamie knew that if he didn't come up with a proper answer, Olaf wouldn't teach him. It had been like that from the beginning; he would explain things, but only if he thought that Jamie's reason for wanting to know was good.

'I need different languages, well, ways of speaking really, for different bits of my life,' said Jamie at last. 'I mean, in the kirk we have all thees and thous, it's a suitable way to talk to God, I suppose. In Glasgow, it will be different again. And I need the right language to talk to the seals.'

Olaf thought for a moment and then nodded. 'I'll teach ye,' he said. 'But first, let's get some supper. I see ye've brought your rod.'

It was an hour or so later, while they were fishing, that Jamie said, 'Olaf, I've been thinking about going to see my father.'

Olaf turned to look at him.

'You know I have a temporary job, just for a

month or so, with the *Inverness Courier*? Well, I was looking through some back copies, and I came across a reference to Mr Duncan Penicuik's new lodge at Achnagarry. There is a map in the editor's office, and I had a look at it. Achnagarry Lodge is six miles or so from Foyers as the crow flies. I could take the steamer to Foyers, and then walk.'

'And what would ye be saying to him?'

'I . . . I'm not sure. I thought I might show him the letter about my scholarship and the Inverness one offering me the bursary. Surely, he'll be pleased to know that I've worked hard and am doing well?'

'He hasn't cared much, so far.'

'But he doesn't know me!' cried Jamie. 'Don't you think, when he sees me, he might . . . ?'

'Might what?'

Jamie picked up a stone and hurled it at the waves. Then he said, 'Mother took me to meet Dr Ross. He's awful, Olaf. He has this hot look in his eye. I don't want her to work there, but she hasn't been offered anything else. Don't you think that, if I pleaded with him, my father might renew the allowance, or even half of it, so that Mother didn't have to go?'

Olaf didn't answer for a long time. There was a stillness about him, as if his thoughts were far away, and Jamie didn't dare disturb him. Eventually, Olaf said, 'He didn't treat ye both right, that's certain, but, Jamie, he doesn't reckon as you would have him do, I'm thinking. You may wake something in him he might not want to look at.'

'So you think I shouldn't,' said Jamie, disappointed.

'Ye'll do what ye must do. It's your choice, lad. I just don't feel easy in my mind, that's all.'

'But it was you who said that it wasn't right that he didn't help!' cried Jamie, indignantly.

'Aye, I did. And maybe I shouldn't have said it. 'Tis true enough, but many a thing is unfair that 'tis better not to try and change.'

'I still don't see why I shouldn't at least *try!*' protested Jamie.

*   *   *

Robina's Journal   *Monday, 1 August*
I haven't written for a day or so and I must, otherwise everything will overwhelm me. I couldn't sleep last night. People talk about how exhausting it is meeting new people and seeing new places, but it is as nothing to the shock of re-meeting old people in places you once knew very well. Everything has to be reassessed. Pheemie dead, Hamish killed, and the old house gone. I'm really upset about Hamish—he was a good man.

I went to the Frasers' cottage and read the colonel's letter to them. I suppose it was what one expected and I hope it gave them both comfort. 'Sergeant Fraser was a well-liked man

143

and his cool-headedness always to be trusted in a crisis. The regiment will miss him sorely.' I hadn't realized Hamish was a sergeant. It means a small pension for the Frasers, I'm glad to say. At least they won't be entirely dependent on Duncan's uncertain generosity. Poor Mhairi, she's taken it very hard. All the light has gone out of her.

Then there's Murdo. He has an irritating way of talking as if what he says must be right—and those poor boys of his are obviously scared of him. Oh dear! What could I have been thinking of at seventeen? Thank God nothing came of it.

Ewan, as Madeline said, is a beast. Podgy and truculent—a Duncan in the making. I won ten shillings off him for gutting a fish. Honestly! I lived here for ten years of my life, of course I can gut a fish! However, I gather that Duncan keeps him short of pocket money, so I returned the ten shillings—not that he was grateful, though I suppose I shouldn't have expected it.

Anyway, by Sunday evening, I was restless with inaction and boredom. So, once the house had settled for the night, I got dressed and went out. I left by the side door, which wasn't locked, went down to the loch and took the boat out.

Once I'd got to the middle of the loch, I rested the oars and just sat. It was a wonderfully clear night. The Milky Way was almost directly overhead and I could see Cassiopeia clearly. How many different places I've seen these same stars—India, Russia, Italy. In St Petersburg at this time of year you get the 'white nights', when the sky is never really dark. Here, it's the 'summer dim'.

Oh, to be alone! Wonderful. I sat in the boat and gazed.

Then I heard a splash, then another. I sat up. Coming towards me was a boat, and in it was Mr Mountsorrel. He seemed astounded to find me and asked what on earth I was doing. I gestured towards the sky. 'Admiring the stars.'

'But it's midnight!'

I said that I liked being out at night and asked what he was doing out. He seemed embarrassed but eventually admitted that he was escaping from the Invershiels. Of course, he didn't put it like that, but that was what he meant. I can imagine that he might find things trying. Mrs Usher would be trying to show off Georgina's talents on the pianoforte—which used to be abysmal—G's talents, I mean, though the pianoforte wasn't particularly good either. John and Henry would be arguing in a corner; Lord I. would be snoring gently, and Lady I. would be chatting to anybody who would listen.

I then acknowledged that I, too, was escaping. I told him that I liked being alone and that this seemed to be the only time available. I think he understood. At least he didn't go on about it being unladylike!

The evening had been awful. Beatrix had lectured me on not being forthcoming to Murdo when I met him after church, though why I should be, God knows; Ewan dangled a frog in front of me—I took it from him and put it back in the grass, where it hopped off behind a tombstone; at dinner, Duncan laid down the law about the immorality of Mrs Gaskell and Miss Brontë's novels—what on earth does he know about it? Nothing, I dare say. When I asked him which books he had in mind, he didn't know. Frankly, by the time we went to bed at ten o'clock, I was in a state of emotional exhaustion, coupled with a sort of impotent rage.

Why have I let myself in for all this? I should have known.

Anyway, Mr Mountsorrel rowed his boat alongside mine and we began to talk. I'd got the impression that he was a yak man, but he's a botanist. He collects for Kew Gardens as well as for various private collectors.

I told him about our garden in Italy and the oleanders. He's good at listening. There's a quality of stillness about him which I like. I suspect he's more intelligent than he looks. He still resembles a bear, but a clever one. Intriguing. I wonder if he knows that Lady Invershiel has him marked out for Gusher? We must have talked for about an hour, for Cassiopeia moved, and Cygnus and Pegasus came overhead.

Eventually, he glanced up at the sky and said that it must be about one o'clock. I was impressed. I hadn't realized he could tell the time by the stars as well. Then he said, 'We're meeting later today, I believe. Aren't you bringing pretty

Miss Madeline over?'

Of course. Pretty Miss Madeline. Suddenly, I felt tired.

He picked up an oar, pushed his boat gently away from mine and left.

When I was a child, I was given a pink stone, I think it was a spinel, which was faceted like a prism. I liked to turn it round and watch the light catch it and send small rainbows over the walls. I had a secret feeling that the spinel was a bit magic. I wonder what happened to it? Odd, that I should remember it now. Last night felt like a spinel moment, something special. A feeling, however fleeting, that somebody else understood me.

Oh, well.

*　　　*　　　*

Lady Invershiel was a woman of many admirable qualities; she presided over the slow decline in the family's fortunes with grace and dignity; she did what she could for the tenants on the estate, and, when she could do no more, she assisted them to emigrate; and she had certain strong convictions as to the matrimonial prospects of her sons and her god-daughter, Georgina Usher. However, her mind was not an elastic one. She would have found the notion that the objects of her benevolent attention had other wishes as to their several futures, very difficult to comprehend. What other wishes could they possibly have? John must marry money and what could he find to object to in the personal charms of Madeline Penicuik? If she and her husband could overlook Madeline's appalling father, surely John could as well? All the same, something told her that it might be wiser to leave John in ignorance of her plans; he could be obstinate. No, she would leave the lovely Madeline to work her own magic.

Then, Georgina needed a husband and Mr Mountsorrel was eminently suitable. Lady Invershiel had heard of Georgina's fantastic desire to breed dogs—well, Mr Mountsorrel would most likely be away on his trips for long stretches of time, he probably wouldn't object to a dog or two. Lady Invershiel had had to put up with her husband's water spaniel. Besides, it was good for children to have a dog about the place. It encouraged responsibility. If Georgina had a baby, then a nice friendly labrador would be just the thing.

Henry had recently qualified for the bar in Edinburgh. He had to make his way in the world. He would marry much later, in his forties. He wouldn't be able to afford it before that. And, just to be certain that he understood the position, she would make sure he knew her wishes with regard to John and Miss Penicuik.

Charlotte would come out under the aegis of her stepmother—and here Lady Invershiel was forced to admit a doubt—but Georgina would be helped by Mrs Usher, naturally. When she had written her invitation inviting Robina and Madeline to tea at the castle, it had not occurred to her that Beatrix might have very different aspirations for her daughter. If she had, she would have considered it a great impertinence. If the Invershiels had indicated their approval of a match between John and Madeline, who were the Penicuiks to disagree? As it was, she assumed that acceptance of the invitation indicated acceptance of her matrimonial plans. Mrs Penicuik, thought her ladyship, must be thanking her lucky stars—she would not else have got a title for her daughter.

*   *   *

Monday afternoon came. Beatrix insisted that Robina and Madeline go by carriage, so they had to endure being jolted over three miles of very indifferent road in order to make the right impression.

'Do you know,' said Madeline, closing her parasol, 'I've never visited the castle before.' Heavens, she thought, it's so hot! and the carriage bumps so.

'Be prepared for a shock,' said Robina. 'It has almost no modern conveniences. The last time I went, the food was still cooked on the original spits and there was a huge chimney in

149

the kitchen, large enough to roast an ox!'

'Good gracious! It sounds like Wolf's Crag in *The Bride of Lammermoor.*'

Robina laughed. 'It's not quite as ruinous! But it does have a ghost.'

There was a pause, Madeline's stomach was beginning to feel the rocking of the carriage. 'What did you think of Mr Mountsorrel?' she asked, to take her mind off her growing queasiness. 'Mama's very keen for me to attach him.'

'He seems very pleasant,' said Robina in a colourless voice. 'He's a botanist, I gather. He spends most of the year plant-hunting in remote comers of the globe.'

'How horrid!' Madeline had thoroughly enjoyed her Season in Edinburgh. Town life just suited her, she thought. She liked meeting her friends without having to go for miles in an uncomfortable carriage over an appalling road. 'Robina, could we stop? I do feel most awfully sick,' Her face had gone almost green.

Robina took one look at her cousin and banged on the roof. The carriage stopped. Robina jumped out and let down the steps for Madeline who almost fell out and went to retch helplessly into the ditch.

Robina looked up at the coachman. 'We'll walk.'

' 'Tis Mrs Penicuik's orders, miss,' said the coachman sternly. 'Ye canna be walking.'

'Miss Madeline can't be sick when she

arrives,' retorted Robina. 'If you're worried, you may follow us, but I think it would be more sensible for you to turn back.' She turned to Madeline. 'Are you up to walking, or would you rather go straight home?'

'I'll be all right in a minute or so.' Madeline cupped her hands under a tiny rill which came down from the hill and drank. 'That's better. Yes, let's walk. Anything is better than that awful carriage.' And she certainly didn't want to face her mother with all the embarrassment of a failed journey.

'What about your shoes?'

Madeline held up her skirts to expose a very pretty pair of blue kid boots. 'The road's quite dry.'

The coachman, grumbling, managed to turn the carriage where the verge was wider. 'I'll wait for ye here,' he said. He, too, didn't want to face Mrs Penicuik's wrath.

Robina nodded and they set off.

'Robina,' said Madeline, anxious to resume her former conversation, 'I'm not sure I want to marry Mr Mountsorrel. But what can I do? You've no idea what Papa is like when we don't do what he wants.'

'Perhaps he won't propose?' suggested Robina, conscious of a lightening of the heart.

'But Mama has set her heart on it,' persisted Madeline. 'Oh, Robina, if he doesn't propose, it will be because of Papa! I know it! I mean, there was a man I met at the Edinburgh

Assembly. I really liked him and I quite thought . . . but nothing came of it. And then, I overheard his aunt talking and she said that he didn't want to be connected with Mr Penicuik because of his reputation. It was awful! I'm sure there are things going on I don't know about and it makes me so very uncomfortable, and who can I ask? And he's so mean. Mama had to pay for my Season entirely out of her own money—Papa says that daughters are a mother's responsibility. She had to hire extra servants for my coming-out dance, and Papa made her pay even for them. I can't let her down.'

'Do you have any money of your own?' asked Robina.

Madeline shook her head. 'Papa has said that my dowry will be three times the annual income of my husband's. The traditional amount, you know. It is to deter fortune hunters.'

So much for Lady Invershiel's hopes, thought Robina. The Invershiels' income could not be more than a couple of thousand a year, and John would be lucky to have £300. Madeline would presumably have her mother's money eventually, but that wouldn't be for years.

Money! she thought, not for the first time, how it rules everything, especially for women. At least she would be in control of her own money in a few years' time and could live the way she chose. Madeline's position was even worse than her own.

Madeline's colour had returned and they quickened their pace. 'At least I shall see the castle,' she said in a more cheerful voice. 'Oh Robina, isn't Miss Usher a funny one!'

At the castle, they were met by the butler, who summoned a maid to show them to a room where they could take off their cloaks and see to their hair, before showing them up to the solar.

'Ah, here you are!' exclaimed Lady Invershiel, surging forward. 'Now, Miss Penicuik, you've met my elder son and Miss Usher, and you must allow me to introduce you to my younger son, Henry. Mrs Usher, this is Miss Penicuik and I'm sure you remember Miss Drummond.'

The ladies shook hands and, shortly, Madeline found herself sitting down with John and Henry Invershiel. She had not taken much notice of John when they had met before. He had been quiet and little inclined to conversation, and today he seemed moody. Henry, however, was alert and smiled readily. He was thinner than his brother, more wiry and with neatly cut dark hair. He looked at Madeline with admiration. He was well aware of his mother's hopes, but why John? Why should not *he* be the one to catch pretty Miss Penicuik? Instead, she had made it clear that he was not to poach on his brother's preserves.

At the same time, he was not to breathe a word to John, who could be obstinate and dig his heels in, when he should allow his Mama to know what was best for him.

Henry and John had always bickered, but their quarrels did not spring from any real animosity, rather from a profound difference in character. Henry had every intention of amusing himself that afternoon with pretty Miss Penicuik, but, at the same time, he would keep an eye out for John. If he saw that his brother was interested, he would leave him a clear field.

He turned to Madeline. 'I was watching you from the battlements,' he said. 'What was wrong with the carriage? Wheel loose?' The road was in a shocking state of repair, he knew.

'No, I felt sick,' said Madeline. She liked him. He had a twinkle in his eye.

Just then, Clover, the water spaniel, came over and put a paw on her skirt. Madeline leaned forward and patted her. Henry watched.

'Mama used to say "vanity rules the queasiest stomach".' He spoke with a smile, which robbed the remark of all offence.

'Not this one,' retorted Madeline.

Henry laughed. Dammit, he liked the girl. He'd half expected her to push poor old Clover away with a 'go away, you horrid dog', and make a fuss about paw marks on her skirt, but, instead, she was fondling Clover's ears, quite unconcerned about either paw marks or dog hairs. Madeline rose in his estimation. John, he saw, was looking across to where Charlotte was talking to Mrs Usher. He wasn't taking any notice of the charming girl next to him. More fool him, thought Henry.

He reached out to the cake stand. 'A muffin, Miss Penicuik? Cook's muffins are very good.'

'I'd love one,' said Madeline. Out of the corner of her eye, she could see Mr Mountsorrel talking to Miss Usher. She hoped he'd stay there.

In the other corner, Lady Invershiel was looking at John and Madeline with a gladdened heart. John had his back to her, so she did not see that, in fact, he was addressing himself to the plum cake rather than his visitor. She would leave them to it, she thought. She turned to Robina.

'I see that Miss Penicuik and my son are furthering their acquaintance,' she observed.

'So they are,' said Robina, though she couldn't help noticing that it was Henry who seemed the more interested. Fortunately, Lady Invershiel was somewhat short-sighted and hadn't realized. The cross-currents of who was interested in whom seemed to be getting more complicated by the minute.

Lady Invershiel, satisfied that everything was going according to her decree, now switched her attention to Robina. 'Come with me,' she ordered. 'Mrs Usher wishes to talk to you about her aunt. Between us, Miss Honoria is a difficult lady; it would be no sinecure.' She led the way to where Mrs Usher was sitting. Charlotte at once got up and offered Robina her chair. Robina sat down.

'I understand that you looked after Mrs Macdonald, Miss Drummond,' began Mrs Usher.

'No, not entirely,' said Robina. 'Mrs Macdonald had a lady's maid, of course, and, towards the end, a trained nurse. I was employed as a companion. That is, I took her to art galleries, the theatre, to visit friends and so on. In her last year, when she could not get out much, I read to her, wheeled her out in her bath chair, and did my best to amuse her.'

'That's what I said, you looked after her,' repeated Mrs Usher.

'I do not nurse, nor am I on call twenty-four hours a day,' said Robina firmly. 'I expect a couple of hours off at some point during the day, and at nine o'clock in the evening, I hand the lady over to her lady's maid or nurse for the night.'

'You are very fussy,' said Mrs Usher raising her brows. Free time during the day, indeed! Whatever next?

'Yes.' Robina smiled at Mrs Usher's look of consternation. 'The position can be a very pleasant one with a considerate employer, but it is also exhausting. I find it best to make my

156

position clear at the outset.'

Mrs Usher was not used to such independence of mind in one who was, when all was said and done, only a superior servant. 'Of course, you are a Drummond,' she said at last.

'More to the point, in three years' time I come into my money and shall have no need to take any sort of position,' Robina replied. 'In fact, I could, at a pinch, support myself now on the hundred or so that my grandmother gave me shortly before she died. I can afford to be choosy.'

This changed the matter at once. Mrs Usher saw that no bargaining was possible.

'My aunt is a difficult woman,' she began. 'She never married—there was a disappointment in her youth—and she likes her own way.' And that was the problem. Whenever she was thwarted, she would threaten to change her will and give all her money to charity. Aunt Honoria was sitting on £30,000 and it could go *anywhere*. Somehow, they *had* to keep her sweet. 'She has hysterics,' finished Mrs Usher, as if it explained everything.

'How very unpleasant,' said Robina. No, she thought. I really do not want the difficult Honoria.

Edward, meanwhile, was talking to Georgina, a conversation that did not run easily. Poor Georgina, aware of her mother's eye on her, was struggling to sit with her knees

157

together, not to spill her tea, and to eat her cake in lady-like mouthfuls and not to laugh or make puns.

'It's strange that we have only met now, Miss Usher,' said Edward. 'I have been coming here all my life, though admittedly only every few years. You probably know the place better than I do.'

'Yes,' said Georgina. She turned to watch Clover who was trotting purposefully towards the door. She nudged it open with her nose, and disappeared.

Edward tried again. 'Do you visit every summer?'

'Usually, yes.' What was she supposed to say, thought Georgina desperately. Nothing occurred to her.

'I think about Dunlairg sometimes when I'm somewhere hot and steamy,' said Edward. 'I remember the soft light and the cool breeze. But I always forget the midges!'

Georgina had no comment on the midges. If only somebody would come and rescue her! She looked round surreptitiously. 'Robina!' she cried thankfully, and put down her tea-cup.

Robina had left Mrs Usher and was coming round with a plate of muffins. Edward rose to his feet. For a moment Georgina looked as though she'd like to get down on all fours and crawl away, like Clover, but then, not knowing what else to do, she stood up as well.

'Have a muffin,' said Robina, offering one to Georgina. 'Nuffin like a muffin,' said Georgina, and gave one of her guffaws, before slapping her hand over her mouth and muttering, 'Mustn't. She promised.'

Edward looked rather amused.

'Mr Mountsorrel?' Robina offered him a muffin.

He took one.

'These are particularly good,' went on Robina. 'I believe the Invershiels' cook has a secret recipe, which she won't tell *anybody*.'

Georgina looked at Robina in awe. How did she do it so effortlessly?

Edward tasted one reflectively. 'Honey, do you think?'

'Yes, that's a possibility. She also does ones which are herby. They're good, too.'

Georgina, seeing that Mr Mountsorrel's attention was elsewhere, stuffed the rest of the muffin in her mouth and slipped away with a sigh of relief. She deliberately didn't look in her mother's direction, left the room before anybody could stop her, and raced down the stairs. She found Clover in the hall, sank down on the floor beside her and put her arms around her. She smelt so reassuringly of dog. Clover snuffled and pushed her nose into Georgina's bodice. Georgina hugged her. At least you weren't expected to make small talk with a dog.

'I trust you got back last night with no ill

159

effects, Miss Drummond?' said Edward.

'Oh yes! I'm used to being out at nights. I like it, especially at this time of year. The sky is a midnight blue, because it's never quite dark, and the stars are wonderful.'

'I was in South Africa, a year or so ago, looking for flowers at the Cape. There are very different stars there.'

'That must be strange, seeing other constellations. Does it feel like a different universe, with different plants and animals, too?'

Edward smiled, 'No, not quite. But it does make you realize how varied the universe is.'

'Yes,' said Robina reflectively. 'I like that. It was one of the things I enjoyed about living in Italy—that people did things differently. It was such a wonderful antidote to all one was taught as a child, to realize that other, perfectly respectable, people didn't give twopence about ideas which one was brought up to think of as God-given laws.'

'Like what?' asked Edward, amused.

Robina considered. 'Drink. My grandfather held that all alcohol was pernicious, except a tot or two of whisky for himself in the evening. Wine, in particular, being foreign, came in for especial condemnation.

'But in Italy, it was considered only civilized to enjoy a glass or two of wine with one's meal—an attitude I found far more congenial!'

Edward laughed.

But there was no time for anything more. Lady Invershiel, who had been watching them for some moments, now came up.

'Edward, Mrs Usher is anxious to talk to you about the grass of Parnassus. She wonders whether she could grow it at Usher House. Would you have a word with her?'

'Of course.' He bowed to Robina and left.

Lady Invershiel turned back to Robina. 'Really, Georgina is more trouble than she's worth! What on earth made her run away like that?'

'I've no idea,' said Robina. 'I only came over to offer her a muffin. I said something about cook's secret recipe, and the next thing I knew, she had vanished.'

Lady Invershiel was a fair woman; she could hardly blame Robina, who, after all, had propelled Madeline successfully towards John, and getting Georgina married off was only a secondary consideration, so she simply said, 'It's all most annoying.'

Robina looked across the room. Henry, John and Madeline had been joined by Charlotte, who was sitting on a small stool near John and talking animatedly. As she watched, Mr Mountsorrel walked over to join them and pulled up a chair next to Madeline.

'You're looking very well, Robina,' said Lady Invershiel, not altogether approvingly. 'That dress you're wearing might almost have been made by a modiste.'

'It was.'

'But surely . . .' said Lady Invershiel, and stopped. Forthright though she could be, even she realized that she couldn't tell Robina that such a dress was unsuitable to her current status. After all, she herself had invited her. It was just that she hadn't expected . . . She must make sure that she let Edward know, tactfully of course, that Robina had to earn her own living and that her expectations were very modest.

*   *   *

Robina's Journal   Monday evening
Things are getting complicated. Madeline has decided that she likes Henry. 'He's such fun,' she said. I can see why she might like him. He lives in Edinburgh—he's a barrister, and he should do well: he works hard and his connections are good. Madeline is a city girl, she likes town life. I really can't see her being content with being stuck at Dunlairg for months.

I tried to warn her against becoming too fond of Henry—and then I had to tell her what Lady I.'s hopes were. Madeline retorted that John wasn't remotely interested in her. All the same, she quite saw that she would have to be careful, if she wanted to continue to be invited to the castle—Lady I. is a very determined woman!

She said, 'You mean, I've got to pretend to like John while I'm there, and pretend to my parents that I like that old bear, Mr Mountsorrel?'

'He's not an old bear!' I said, unwisely.

Ah!' she cried, 'so you like him yourself! But he's marked out for Miss Usher, surely you saw that?' Madeline can be unnervingly acute.

Oh God, this is awful! Fifteen years of coping with foreign railway timetables, demanding old ladies, and making myself clear in French, Italian and Russian, has not prepared me for this at all. Madeline, however, has taken to intrigue like a duck to water. She said that we must cover for each other!

'Madeline!' I shrieked, 'I am not after Mr Mountsorrel! I barely know the man!'

'Bearly being the operative word,' said Madeline and gave a naughty imitation of one of Gusher's guffaws. I had to laugh. I can't help liking Madeline, it's like having a funny little sister. I find I can giggle with her. Strange, because I've never been a giggling sort of person. I was quite solemn as a child; I suppose it was being brought up with older people.

All the same, this 'love stuff,' as Aeneas calls it, is not an area I'm at all good at. I know it sounds pathetic, but I don't really know what's going on in men's heads. Yes, of course, I like Mr Mountsorrel. He's interesting and intelligent—I was wrong about him being stupid. I think he enjoyed talking to me, but who else was there for him to talk to? Madeline is only a couple of years older than Charlotte, but she knows how to talk to men, so of course he would enjoy talking to her. And plenty of men look for wives twenty years younger than themselves. Nor can I blame Mr Mountsorrel for giving up on Gusher. Poor thing, she gave me such a pathetic look of gratitude when I arrived with the muffins, it would have been very unkind of me to have moved away.

I foresee problems ahead.

Later:

Oh Lord, Beatrix has just told me that Murdo is coming to tea on Friday and hopes that I will be there. Now what?

CHAPTER FIVE

An uneasy truce existed at Achnagarry Lodge between the Edinburgh servants, who were brought up from the Penicuiks' town house, and Ishbel, Morag and the outdoor servants, who remained at Achnagarry all year round. The Edinburgh servants, English speakers all, looked down on 'the Highland bog lot', as the cook called them. The Highlanders, in turn, resented the way the 'Edinburgh lot' were better paid and took over the place.

In Mrs Drummond's time, the old Achnagarry House ran perfectly well with Ishbel and Morag in the kitchen and a couple of housemaids. There was a gardener, who doubled up as valet or groom whenever Mr

164

Drummond wanted him to and, so far as the house went, that was it. The new Achnagarry Lodge had the full complement of twelve servants, and Ishbel and Morag were reduced to the status of kitchen and scullery maid—and treated accordingly.

When Robina went to say hello to Ishbel, she found her peeling potatoes in the scullery. She was standing by the sink, and the set of her shoulders was eloquent of her fury. The scullery had two doors, one which led into the kitchen and the other on to a passageway, which in turn led to the boot room, the lamp-room and the pantry. Robina had come in from the passageway. As she did so, she heard the cook shout from the kitchen.

'Hurry up with those potatoes, ye lazy clod-hopper. I havena got all day.'

Ishbel bent over the sink, peeled the last potato, flung it into the saucepan of water and marched through with it.

There were more insults from the kitchen, then Ishbel came back with a trug full of carrots and threw them into the sink. She saw Robina, and raised her eyes to the ceiling. Back in the kitchen, the cook could be heard berating Morag. Robina tiptoed over and gently closed the door.

' 'Sakes, Ishbel,' she said, in Gaelic, 'is this what you have to put up with?'

Ishbel pushed her hair out of her eyes with one red wrist and said bitterly, 'Aye, all the

165

time. According to her, we're fit only for mud cabins and pig swill.'

'That's awful!'

'And we're paid less, too! Madam in there is paid twenty-five pounds a year. I get five and poor Morag only four. Even their housemaids get double what we're paid.'

'But why? The house doesn't look after itself when they're not here.'

'Indeed it doesn't! And we work in the garden under Callum Macgregor—ye mind Callum, Miss Robina?'

'Of course. Ginger hair.'

'Not so much of that now! Mrs Penicuik wants vegetables growing for when they're up. And we're bottling and making jam and such-like as well. Aye, we're kept busy.'

'Do you still dry mushrooms?'

Ishbel nodded.

Robina leaned forward and whispered, 'Does Callum still have his whisky still?'

Ishbel laughed. 'I canna be telling you that! Callum would be after skinning me.'

Robina smiled and then said, 'I'm really sorry things are so difficult, Ishbel. Tell me, do you have any trouble with Mr Penicuik, you know . . .' She pinched her finger and thumb together suggestively.

'He doesna go for me,' said Ishbel austerely. 'But poor Flora—Miss Kilbride, I should say, Mrs Penicuik's lady's maid—she has to watch out. She's noan so bad. At least she has a civil word now and then.' She glanced over to the kitchen door and added, 'I'll tell ye something, Miss Robina, though I know I shouldn't . . .'

'Go on.'

'Ye know that Achnagarry was left to Miss Beatrix?'

Robina nodded.

'Well, Mr Penicuik dismissed the old factor and got a new man in. Wallace his name is. The estate has to pay for itself, he says. But, I'm thinking Miss Beatrix dinna ken that she doesna get the income she should from it. Mr Wallace is charging for repairs and such like that are nae done.'

But surely Mr Penicuik checks the accounts?' said Robina.

She couldn't imagine that Duncan would not do so.

'Oh aye, he checks them,' said Ishbel drily.

'You mean that Mr Penicuik is defrauding his own wife!'

'Shh!' said Ishbel, nodding towards the door. 'Away wi' ye, Miss Robina. I hae these carrots to do.'

Robina left, thoughtfully. Was it true? Probably. Ishbel had always had ways of knowing what was going on. It was she who had told her grandmother that Duncan had fathered a child on a girl in Edinburgh. Mrs Drummond had checked discreetly one year, when they had visited the Penicuiks. During her annual visit to Mr Ogilvy to check on her shares, she'd taken the opportunity to ask him if the rumours were true. Much later, she'd told Robina. 'Duncan has made the girl an allowance until her son finishes his schooling,' she'd said. 'She was a girl from a respectable family, and only sixteen. Poor young thing.'

'I hope the allowance is a generous one,' Robina had said, sceptically.

She thought of this now. Both Ishbel and Morag were getting on. Had her grandfather left them anything in his will? Still, if she knew the Highlanders, she could be sure that the occasional deer found its way into the pot, or was sold discreetly somewhere. There would be a ready market in Fort Augustus, or perhaps one of the coaching inns, where questions would not be asked. Donald or Callum would know.

Her grandmother had said once, 'Servants always know things. Remember that, Robina.' So did children, thought Robina. As a child she'd been privy to lots of secrets that the grown-ups would have been horrified to know she knew. Fortunately, speaking Gaelic had meant that she was still 'one of us', to Ishbel at any rate.

*   *   *

Robina's Journal   Friday, 4 August 1865
I had the most fearful row with Beatrix.
*   Murdo came to tea this afternoon and I*

realized almost at once that Beatrix was planning a match between us. God knows why she thinks that I would want a man who had as good as jilted me once! The awful thing is that I'm pretty sure that it's on Murdo's mind, too.

It was the most ghastly tea-time. Madeline, presumably on Beatrix's orders, wasn't there, so we were à trois. Beatrix kept making sly little references to my being on the shelf and hinting that I was still sweet on Murdo. 'Robin has such a faithful nature,' was how she put it. Honestly, I felt like an old dog! I wouldn't have been surprised if she'd patted me. I could have killed her.

Murdo was being so complacent that I wanted to hurl my tea at him. He actually said, 'The virgin fruit shall not be left to wither on the bough,' or some such thing, and gave me an arch look as if to say that he was now graciously willing to pluck it.

Quite apart from being an obnoxious thing to say, it was also horribly indelicate. I think even Murdo realized that, for he hastily added, 'As the poet said.'

I said that I was perfectly happy where I was, thank you, and Murdo said, 'Such charming modesty.'!! Ugh!!!

The moment he'd gone, I had a furious row with Beatrix. I told her that whatever I'd once felt for Murdo, I now thought that he was the most dreadful man. Nothing would induce me to marry him, so would she please stop trying to *match-make.*

Beatrix said that she was only concerned for my welfare. Ha!

I told her that my welfare was none of her business.

She said that I had turned into one of those horribly bold creatures who were so opinionated that they would never be anything but dried-up old spinsters.

There were a lot of things that I'd have liked to have said. 1) That I'd rather be a dried-up old spinster than married to Duncan. 2) That she'd turned into a dumpling and 3) that her precious daughter was not remotely interested in Mr Mountsorrel, but much preferred Henry Invershiel.

Instead, I left the room.

Later, when I came down for dinner, she greeted me as though nothing had happened. All the same, I have the feeling that she hasn't given up. I shall have to watch out. I think I'd better write to Signor Arnolfini. He told me that I was to write if I ever needed help and that he usually knew of an elderly lady who was looking for a lady companion. I don't want to find myself stuck here, being pressured to marry Murdo and with no alternative but Mrs Usher's appalling aunt.

My God, the thought *of marrying Murdo! Of having a squalling baby who looked just like him. No! No!! No!!*

If it were the bear now . . . !

Aeneas Penicuik, now aged twelve, had suffered badly from asthma ever since he was a baby, a condition exacerbated by the smoke from thousands of chimneys during the Edinburgh winter. From October through to the end of April he spent much of the time wheezing, a hot-water bottle wrapped in an old bit of blanket clutched to his chest, or bent over a basin of steaming water, his head covered with a towel.

There were a number of things which triggered an attack: too much running about, dust, cats, and his father shouting at him. Reluctantly, because he did not want to have fathered a sissy, Duncan decided that boarding-school would be too much for him, and he was educated at a local school in Edinburgh, though he missed much of the autumn and spring terms.

Once he had outgrown the care of his nurse, Aeneas was very much on his own. He didn't mind. He was a quiet child and liked to sit in front of the fire with a book. He enjoyed being at Achnagarry; the purity of the air cleared up any wheezes at once.

When the old Achnagarry House had been pulled down, the furniture had been stored in the stables and then put into the new house. Beatrix had insisted on having new furniture for the public rooms, but the old pieces were used in the children's bedrooms and in the room known as the den, a smallish room which did duty as a day nursery.

From Aeneas's point of view, the special thing about the den was that it contained the books from Achnagarry House. Not the tomes on philosophy and religion, which had been in Mr Drummond's library, and which Beatrix had sold, but the Fieldings, Defoes and Richardsons and other eighteenth-century authors. Mrs Drummond had enjoyed the robustness of the eighteenth century and Aeneas, in his turn, relished the travels of Humphry Clinker and the rollicking adventures of Tom Jones. There were books of Scottish interest, too: Burns' poems, Macpherson's 'Ossian' and Sir Walter Scott's novels. They were all books they did not have in Edinburgh, Beatrix affecting to find them 'vulgar', but, each summer, Aeneas could hardly wait to meet his old friends once again.

Robina had seen very little of him. Duncan and Beatrix did not encourage children downstairs. They were children, what could they possibly have to say that was of interest? Madeline, of course, was now out and had joined the adults; Ewan, at sixteen, and the elder son besides, hovered between the two worlds—he was allowed down for luncheon, if there were no guests—but Aeneas still ate all his meals in the day nursery, served by Morag.

172

Beatrix did as a fond mother should, she went up to see her sons before going down to breakfast, and checked that they were well, and properly dressed. Usually, they had tea with her in the drawing-room, but, apart from that, they were expected to amuse themselves.

Duncan had instructed Donald Fraser to teach them both to fish. Aeneas enjoyed it, but Ewan found it very slow. Donald had then tried to teach him to row, but Ewan, impatient of being taught, seized the oars and succeeded only in dropping one overboard. Nowadays, Ewan preferred to slouch about with his catapult. He had also discovered girls, and the maids were learning fast that Master Ewan was proving to be as much of a nuisance as his father. Achnagarry bored him. There was nothing for a fellow to do. He'd tried to make Robina jump by handing her a frog after church, but she'd taken it quite calmly and put it in a safe place. She was no fun, he decided; he preferred being able to tease and provoke a reaction.

That morning, the weather had reverted to the usual Highland rain. Beatrix had retired with Madeline and Flora to Madeline's bedroom, to do some alterations to Madeline's tea gown. Robina was at a loose end.

She had not yet been to the nursery wing; it had not been part of the house Beatrix had thought to show her when she had first arrived. When she eventually found her way up there, she was delighted to find the furniture from Achnagarry House.

She opened the door slowly. Aeneas was sitting at a table, reading.

'Oh!' cried Robina. 'How wonderful!'

Aeneas looked up. 'What is?'

'All the old furniture.' Robina patted the back of a wooden armchair affectionately. 'This was Grandmama's. There should be a red cushion somewhere. Oh, and there's the old wag at the wa'.' She pointed to the clock.

She walked around, smiling with pleasure. It was lovely to see it all again. 'I wonder what happened to Grandmama's lacquer tea-caddy?'

'I like the books,' said Aeneas.

'Of course, the books. Am I disturbing you?'

'No.' Aeneas closed his book, marking the place carefully with a feather. 'I don't often see people.'

Robina looked at him. Poor boy! His parents didn't seem to have much time for him. He must be lonely. 'Do you know Mhairi Fraser, Donald's wife?'

Aeneas shook his head. 'I know who she is, but not really to talk to. I don't speak Gaelic, apart from a few words.'

'Mhairi speaks English. She used to work for my grandparents before she married Donald.' She glanced out of the window. 'The rain is easing off. Would you like to come with me and meet her?'

Aeneas jumped up. 'I'd like that.'

They went down the back stairs. Robina grabbed her hat and mantle, and they went out. The tips of the deer grass were beginning to turn orange and raindrops sparkled on the bracken behind the lodge. Another month or so, and that would turn, too. As they went, Robina told Aeneas about Hamish.

'Mhairi, may we come in?' asked Robina, when they reached the cottage.

Mhairi came to the door. Her grey hair was covered with a white, close-fitting bonnet, and she wore a large linen apron over her black skirt and grey blouse. She smiled when she saw Robina.

'This is Aeneas,' said Robina. 'I've brought him to meet you.' Aeneas took off his cap. 'Good morning, Mrs Fraser,' he said, politely.

Mhairi's blue eyes looked at him steadily for a few seconds. Then she nodded. 'Welcome,' she said formally, in English. 'Come away in, both of you.'

Mhairi's cottage was the usual 'but and ben', comprising two rooms. The but was the main living-room with a stone floor, a fireplace against the back wall and a pot hanging from an iron chain fixed to a cross-piece in the chimney. On cither side of the room was a box bed. When Robina was a child, one of them had belonged to a simple brother of Mhairi's, called Wullie. For a long time, Robina had thought that his name was Woolly, and she was in her teens before she had realized that his name was really William. The other bed had been Hamish's. There was one small window, with a wooden shutter, and the door was so low that even Aeneas had to stoop slightly when he entered. Donald, Mhairi and their two daughters slept in two box beds in the ben, the second room in the house.

Aeneas looked around with interest. The furniture, four chairs, a spinning wheel, a table, a wooden dresser and various cooking utensils, had all been made by Donald, and the place was scrupulously clean and tidy.

'I like this place!' he said. 'Everything here is all *needful!*' Aeneas's first thought was that they had an awful lot of clutter at Achnagarry, most of which they didn't need.

Mhairi laughed. 'Aye, that it is. Sit ye down, young man, and ye shall have some whisked milk and a bannock.'

Robina smiled. Aeneas reminded her of herself when she'd first arrived from India, not really fitting in, and a bit lost, somehow. It was Mhairi who had first given her a feeling of cautious belonging. She saw that Mhairi and Aeneas would get on.

*　　　*　　　*

Once the thought of her father's will had entered her head, Mary Ritchie could not forget it. It was true that her father had not

176

expected to die so soon after her mother's death, but she knew that he had made a will, for she remembered him saying that Duncan was to be the executor. Her father was a practical man. He had no other family. Who was there to inherit but herself, however small an amount it was?

It had been Duncan who had come round to the house on that dreadful day, who had taken charge, organized the funeral, seen to the house and furniture. The house they had lived in had been rented, as was usual, but why hadn't the rest of the lease been sold? What had happened to everything? Surely, her distant cousins had been told of her father's death? They must have written something, even if only condolences. Why had she never heard from them? Her mother's long illness had been expensive, but her father hadn't been bankrupt, had he? At the time, she'd been so overcome with grief and so terrified of the future, that she'd simply done as she was told.

Then there had been that night when Duncan had stayed . . . After that, there had been no going back.

Why on earth had she not remembered all this before, she wondered? It was as if all memory of that awful time had completely disappeared—up to now. At the beginning, she'd been too young, too ignorant. Later, when Jamie was born, she'd been too dependent on Duncan to risk asking him.

The moment she thought this, she realized something else. She had *feared* to ask him because, deep down, she suspected that he had somehow cheated her out of what was rightfully hers. He had posed as a family friend. Her father had trusted him. But, in the end, he had betrayed that friendship and ruined her.

She couldn't let this rest, not now she'd remembered. She'd have to do something.

She could write to the Edinburgh Mr Ogilvy and ask his advice. He knew her story. If her father had made a will, there would be a copy of it somewhere. It might not be possible, after all this time, to retrieve anything, but, all the same, she had the right to know.

Did she dare?

*　　*　　*

When up at Achnagarry, Duncan spent much of his time in the study, carrying on a correspondence with his business manager in Edinburgh. He came up for the summer, because it was the thing to do; it showed his success that he had a place in the Highlands, though, personally, he considered the annual trek to be a waste of time. He had no particular interest in shooting or stalking. Fishing was what he enjoyed best. It gave him time to think. Good business ideas often came to him while he was waiting for a fish to bite,

178

and he always carried a small leather-bound notebook and pencil around with him so that he could jot thoughts down as they occurred.

In fact, while Beatrix and the children stayed up for a couple of months over the summer, Duncan usually broke up his stay with several trips back to Edinburgh, where he stayed in great comfort at the Royal Hotel, and went out of an evening for some sexual indulgence: *his* little marital holiday, as he put it to himself.

This year, however, he had a different plan, one that had come to him whilst he was playing a trout on Loch Nevan, and he expounded it after dinner to Beatrix, Robina and Madeline.

'I am thinking of opening a Penicuik's Emporium in Inverness,' he announced.

'Inverness?' echoed Beatrix, who was pouring out the coffee. Her first thought was that it had been tricky enough to get Madeline acquainted with the Invershiels as it was; to induce Mr Mountsorrel to pop the question, with a Penicuik's Emporium so close, in Inverness, would be doubly difficult. It made it so *obvious* that their money came from trade. Why couldn't he call it the Thistle Emporium, or something suitably anonymous?

'It's been on my mind for a while,' went on Duncan. 'You'll mind the trouble we had getting everything brought here when we built the place?' Stone, glass, wood, fittings, plaster, it had all had to be brought in expensively and laboriously by boat, pack pony and cart.

Beatrix shuddered. It had not been helped by Grandmama and Robina not being around to cope with all the small day-to-day headaches. So selfish of them! It still rankled.

'I suppose that building lodges must be going on all over the Highlands,' said Robina thoughtfully.

'Just so,' said Duncan, with rare approval. 'That means business opportunities. All those domestic commodities every house needs: linoleum, furniture, household utensils.'

Madeline was thinking along much the same lines as her mother. Nobody minded nowadays if you made your money in trade, so long as you were discreet about it. Madeline had had to put up with jibes about 'Pennyquick's' Emporium all her life.

'Why don't you call it the Balmoral Emporium?' she said.

Beatrix smiled approvingly at her. With a bit of luck, in a few days' time Duncan would think of it as his own idea. She must warn Madeline to say nothing further.

'Hm,' said Duncan. Not a bad idea, he thought: instantly recognizable, showed class, loyal to Her Majesty—always profitable. He'd think about it.

'Might there not be a problem when the rush to build ends?' asked Robina.

Duncan shook his head. 'Once the lodges

are built, they'll need all sorts of supplies. Paraffin, for example.'

'But they're only occupied for a few months a year.'

'Inverness is a busy port all year round. The railway will make an enormous difference. There'll be a demand for all sorts of goods. I shall go to Inverness for a day or so, make some enquiries. See the place for myself. I may need Ogilvy to come up, so you'd better see that a room is prepared.'

'Of course,' said Beatrix.

Two days later, Duncan rode down to Foyers and caught the steamer to Inverness.

*   *   *

The moment she had waved Duncan off, Beatrix summoned Robina, Madeline, Ewan and Aeneas and told them that she was arranging a party of pleasure to visit the Falls of Foyers.

'But we've already seen them,' objected Ewan. 'Twice.'

'Well, you can see them again,' snapped Beatrix.

'Why are we going again?' asked Aeneas. Something was going on, but he wasn't sure what.

Madeline and Robina exchanged glances, but neither said anything. It was perfectly obvious why.

181

Aeneas saw them and said, 'Oh, love stuff. I see.'

'Don't be vulgar,' said Beatrix, and dismissed him to the den. Ten minutes later, she was sat at her writing desk and penning her letter.

> *Achnagarry Lodge*
> *Monday, 7 August*
>
> *Dear Lady Invershiel*
>
> *I am planning a little excursion to the Falls of Foyers on Wednesday, and I was wondering if any of your young people would care to join us? It will be quite informal. We aim to leave the lodge at ten o'clock.*
>
> *Miss Drummond, my daughter Madeline, and my son Ewan have elected to walk, but my younger son and myself will be riding. We hope to reach the Falls by half past eleven, and I have arranged for a picnic luncheon to be served at one o'clock.*
>
> *I do hope that you will be able to join us.*
> *Yours etc.,*
>
> *B. Penicuik*

Beatrix had taken some thought over the letter. It must seem spontaneous. It must be the sort of letter that Lady Invershiel could hand round. Naturally, Beatrix would prefer only the Mountsorrels to accept, but could hardly say so. She toyed with the idea of

182

offering some rare plant as an inducement, but decided that that would be too obvious. No, she would just have to put up with the family *en masse*. All she could do was hint, tactfully, that her husband would not be there, and extend a blanket invitation.

She sealed the letter, rang the bell, and gave it to Frank, the footman, with instructions that it was to go to Dunlairg Castle immediately.

Forty minutes later, Lady Invershiel broke the seal and read it. She re-read it carefully, twice, and decided that it meant that Mrs Penicuik was in favour of the match between her daughter and John. It was, in effect, a tacit approval. She read it out at luncheon.

'John,' she said, 'you'd like to go, I'm sure.'

John shrugged, but nodded. What else was there for a fellow to do?

'What about you, Edward? Georgina? Henry, I expect you're too busy working.'

'I should like to go,' said Henry, ignoring his mother's scowl. 'I can work just as well in the evening.' A day with pretty Miss Madeline was just what he needed.

After luncheon, Lady Invershiel wrote and accepted. Her two sons, Mr Mountsorrel and his daughter, and Miss Usher would all be delighted to come.

The following day it rained, but in spite of Beatrix's fears, by evening it had cleared up and the day of the excursion dawned with a pale-blue sky and only a few fluffy clouds.

At Dunlairg, Charlotte and Edward prepared themselves carefully. They both wore stout walking boots and Edward put his knapsack over his shoulders.

'What's this for?' asked Henry, flicking the knapsack with his finger. 'The Falls of Foyers isn't the Khyber Pass, you know.'

'A walker is *always* prepared, isn't he, Papa?' said Charlotte.

Thank God for a nice long walk, she thought, as they set out. She'd been feeling rather cooped up. Lady Invershiel was an energetic woman, but, all the same, she did not approve of ladies going for ten-mile walks up in the hills, scrambling about over rocks and wading through burns. She'd told Charlotte that, now she was nearly grown-up, it would have to stop. Charlotte had managed to sneak out a couple of times with her father, but he'd seemed a bit preoccupied.

Charlotte lengthened her stride. 'This is better!'

'I didn't know you liked walking,' said John, coming up beside her. 'I can't see the pleasure myself. Nothing but heather and sheep.'

'Don't be so feeble,' snapped Charlotte.

'Well, thanks!' retorted John, stung.

'Why don't you *do* something with your life, instead of always moaning about it? At least you're a man! You have choices.'

'Hardly.'

'Hardly a man? Or hardly have choices?'

'By God, Charlotte! That's too much!'

'Look! You've had a good education, you're young-ish . . .'

John laughed unwillingly. He was twenty-seven.

'. . . you're a man. You complain that your father won't let you help with the estate. Go off and do something else. He wouldn't cut you off with a shilling if you took up a different career, would he?'

'Probably not.'

'Well, then.'

'I've always wanted to work on a newspaper,' said John, after a moment. 'You know, be a roving reporter, like W.H. Russell.'

'Exposing army incompetence in the Crimea,' said Charlotte at once. She was a well-read girl. 'Good idea.'

'And what are *you* going to do when you're grown-up, Miss Interference?'

'I haven't decided,' said Charlotte. 'I shall certainly work for Women's Suffrage. *I* mean to make my mark in the world.' She grinned at John's look of horror and stalked off to join Henry.

Georgina had been thinking. Last night, when her mother had dropped a cotton reel, and Mr Mountsorrel had gone down on his hands and knees to retrieve it, the thought crossed her mind that he looked rather like a large, friendly dog. It must be something to do with all that beard. She didn't really want to marry at all, but to have a husband who was the next best thing to a dog wouldn't be so bad. The only problem was that you couldn't just pat him, take him for walks and send him to his kennel at the end of the day, there would be all that being married bit, too.

If only she knew whether Mr Mountsorrel really wanted to marry her. Mostly she thought that he didn't, but her mother and Lady Invershiel insisted that he only need a bit of encouragement. It was all very worrying.

When the Dunlairg party reached Achnagarry Lodge, they found Robina, Madeline and Ewan waiting for them. Beatrix bustled out of the house to greet them. She spotted Charlotte and at once introduced Ewan to her. It would do no harm for Ewan to impress a young girl who had her mother's large fortune settled on her.

Charlotte took one look at Ewan and detested him on sight. Georgina, who had spent the walk from Dunlairg trying to avoid Edward, surged forward. 'Robina!' she cried in relief. 'She's desperate for a drink, and . . . you know . . .'

'Come upstairs,' said Robina at once.

Madeline was watching Ewan. She moved closer to Henry. 'Ewan's got something dead in his pocket,' she whispered. She hated it when he waved dead animals at her.

Ewan sidled up to Charlotte, put his hand in his pocket and took out a dead shrew.

'Oh,' cried Charlotte, taking it carefully from him. 'A shrew. Look, Papa.'

Edward came over. 'A pygmy shrew, *sorex minutus*,' he observed. 'Give it back, Charlotte.'

Charlotte did so. Ewan scowled. Why didn't she *jump*? He made as if to put it back in his pocket, then changed his mind and threw it into a ditch. This wasn't going to be much fun.

Robina and Georgina returned and the party set off. Henry, who had watched the interchange over the shrew, came up to Ewan. 'Do you often do that?' he asked. 'Show dead shrews to ladies?'

Ewan shrugged.

'What have you done with it?'

'Thrown it away.'

'I hope you have,' said Henry sceptically. 'If I find you teasing your sister, or any of the ladies with it, I'll knock you into the nearest burn. Understood?'

Ewan's face darkened with rage and embarrassment. He'd like to get his own back, but Henry was a strong young man, and, somehow, Ewan didn't doubt that he would do as he said. 'It was only a joke,' he muttered.

'A very ungentlemanly one,' retorted Henry.

'Thank you,' said Madeline, when Ewan had moved off. 'I can't bear it when he does things like that.'

'Well, he shan't do it today,' said Henry. He held out his hand to help her over a small burn. Madeline smiled at him and took it.

187

Edward and Robina, who were both good walkers, soon outstripped the others. Like Charlotte, Robina had been feeling cooped up. She hadn't even had a chance to visit the crannog yet. At least today she'd be able to stretch her legs properly.

'Do you know the way?' asked Edward.

'Oh yes. I roamed all over when I was a child. We go up to the cairn there,' she pointed, 'then down the hill to the river E, and when we reach Stratherrick we take the little road to Foyers.'

'River *E*?'

'Yes. I know it's odd.'

Edward looked across at her. He liked the way she walked, swinging her arms easily and making little of the hill they were now climbing. Her cheeks were prettily flushed with the exercise and her dark-brown eyes were sparkling. He couldn't remember a single occasion when Betsy had voluntarily walked further than the end of the garden. Thanks to Lady Invershiel's careful interference, Edward now knew rather more about Robina, and the moment he heard how ineligible she was, how she had to work for her living, he, perversely, became more interested. At least she wasn't a useless butterfly.

'I understand that you will be taking on the task of looking after Mrs Usher's formidable aunt,' he said.

'I most certainly will not!' retorted Robina.

'I would have to be desperate to do so. She sounds the most impossible woman.'

'I am relieved to hear that you are not desperate for a situation,' said Edward. Lady Invershiel had spoken of Robina as being 'practically penniless'.

'I come into my grandmother's money when I am thirty-five,' explained Robina. 'After that, I shall have quite enough to live on. Meanwhile, I've written to my grandmother's friend, Signor Arnolfini, in Florence. He may know of somebody. I long for some sun!'

'Have you travelled much? I remember you saying, when we met on the steamer, that you'd been to Russia.'

'Mostly Italy and France. Not as much as you have. Charlotte was telling me about Japan. That must have been fascinating. I was once shown a kimono. What interested me was the way that it seemed to take no account of the shape of the body, the pattern I mean, and yet, it looked wonderful.'

'Yes, the Japanese have a superb aesthetic sense. I don't normally encumber myself with much baggage; but I came back from Japan with several crates of the most beautiful lacquered boxes and bowls. Heaven knows what I'm going to do with them!'

'Don't you have a home?' asked Robina curiously.

'There was a house in the Borders, which belonged to my wife, but I sold it after she

189

died. Glendon Hall, my uncle's home, is a base when I need one. We're so rarely in this country that it hardly seems worthwhile having a house.'

'There's a tendency nowadays to have far too much clutter,' said Robina, thinking of Achnagarry Lodge, which seemed to have stuffed heads on every wall, and knick-knacks on every surface. 'My grandmother and I lived in various places, but there were only a few keepsakes we took from place to place. One doesn't really need things, just congenial people.'

'You're very wise for one so young,' said Edward.

'I'm thirty-two!'

'And I'm thirty-eight,' said Edward promptly. 'A good age, don't you think?'

'For what?' asked Robina cautiously, feeling her colour rise. Again, she had the unnerving feeling that something had shifted slightly.

Edward smiled. 'Changing direction, perhaps?' Almost immediately, alarm bells began ringing inside his head. Why on earth had he said that? Surely he wasn't thinking of paying serious attentions to Miss Drummond?

It was just as well that neither Lady Invershiel, Mrs Penicuik nor Mrs Usher could see the party, for they would have been seriously displeased. Edward was talking to Robina, Madeline and Henry were together, Charlotte and Georgina were animatedly discussing how to set up a kennels, or rather, Georgina was talking about the kennels and Charlotte was telling her about Japanese Ainu dogs. John and Ewan were plodding along at the rear, neither saying much but both rather fed up. Ewan was not used to being ignored, and Henry's threat rankled. John was wondering how Charlotte, his chit of a cousin, could have made him feel so dissatisfied with his life. Eventually, the group reached the path which led down to the Falls of Foyers.

Robina and Madeline looked at each other. 'Time to swap partners,' whispered Madeline, with a naughty smile.

'I'd better make sure that Ewan isn't annoying anybody,' said Robina.

When they got there, they found that Beatrix, Aeneas, and the servants with the picnic hampers, had already arrived. Rugs had been spread out on the ground in the shade of the Scots pines, which sloped steeply down to the river far below.

'I like it here,' said Aeneas, running up to Robina and giving her a pine cone. 'It smells so piney.'

'Yes. It *feels* as if it's doing you good.'

In the distance, they could hear the falls. Everyone sat down, and Morag and Frank, who had come down with the hampers, handed round some drink: beer for the gentlemen and lemonade for the ladies. Robina thought wistfully of a cool glass of wine and remembered sitting under an oleander with her grandmother in the hills above Florence. Lemonade was just not the same. A couple of pied wagtails ran along the ground and bobbed their tails. A coal tit chirped in the branches of a small birch tree by the side of the road.

'Her feet are killing her,' said Georgina, bending to undo her boot-laces.

Robina rose. 'Come on,' she said. 'I know where there's a spring. You can dabble your feet in, it'll do them good.'

Georgina got up and hobbled after her.

'Can I come?' asked Charlotte.

'Of course. Madeline? What about you?'

'Ladies only,' said Beatrix, looking sternly at Henry, who had half-risen.

He grinned and subsided. Much though he would like to see Madeline's feet, he was well aware that he must keep on the right side of her mother.

'Bliss!' sighed Charlotte. They had all taken off their boots and stockings and were wiggling their toes in the cool bubbles.

It was surprising what five minutes of running water could do and everybody's energy returned. The ladies went back to the picnic rugs and the men had their turn.

'Did you make yourself agreeable to Mr Mountsorrel?' Beatrix demanded of her daughter in an undertone.

'Yes, Mama,' said Madeline obediently.

'And?'

'It's not easy to talk when you are clambering up hills,' said Madeline, though she had managed it perfectly well with Henry, and taken his hand a number of times—not all of them strictly necessary. What was wrong with her getting to know Henry better? He was hard-working and intelligent, he was sure to go far, and his birth was quite as good as Mr Mountsorrel's. So what if he were a younger son? At least he didn't look like a shaggy bear!

'I look to see you being rather more forthcoming this afternoon,' said Beatrix sternly.

* * *

Meanwhile, in Inverness, Duncan had just finished his perambulations of the town. He had gone out earlier that morning, walked up and down the principal streets and made notes. The town was a prosperous one and set to expand. It had a large tallow and tanning industry. There was a number of brewers and distillers. Now the railway was open, goods could come in far more easily.

An emporium in Eastgate, say, would be in a good position to do well. There was the Royal Navy nearby at Invergordon, the army barracks at Fort George, each with officers who would surely appreciate the good things in life at the right price. A high-class emporium, catering to the great estates, the officers and the retired civil servants, and the growing numbers of professional people, would have an excellent chance of being really profitable. He had noticed there were already gunsmiths and shops for fishing tackle. He'd even seen a taxidermist, where a stag's head with glass eyes stared gloomily out of the shop window.

He closed his notebook, and turned back to the Caledonian Hotel. He was just going up the steps when a voice behind him said, uncertainly, 'Duncan?'

He turned round and narrowed his eyes. A woman in black was standing front of him. Then he recognized her.

'Duncan,' she said again. 'It's Mary Ritchie.'

Duncan came back down the steps. 'Never heard of you,' he said, harshly. What the hell was she doing here?

'Don't you want to know how Jamie is!' cried Mary. 'Our son?' Duncan thrust his face close to hers and gripped one shoulder so tightly that she cried out. 'Now, you listen to me. I don't know you, nor your wretched son, and, unless you want me to call the police, you'd better take yourself off. Is that clear?'

'I . . . I must have mistaken you for somebody else,' stammered Mary. 'I'm sorry, sir.'

Duncan released her and watched her go. Then he turned and went up the steps to the Caledonian Hotel.

Back in his room, he sat down heavily on the bed, massaging his suddenly tight shoulder.

There was a pain running right across the top of his chest. What the devil was Mary doing here? He didn't want a woman around who knew about his disreputable past and who might try to set people against him. Perhaps he should have acknowledged her. A few guineas might have bought her silence. On the other hand, it might just have made her greedy for more.

No, his way was best. Deny everything. If it were his word against hers, he would make damn sure that it was *he* who was believed. Money still spoke, thank God. He would be bringing a lot of business to the town, creating jobs. No town council would want to jeopardize that. He poured himself a glass of whisky and, slowly, the pain eased.

Mary stumbled away, her heart pounding with a mixture of fear and shame. Then she stopped. It *had* been Duncan. She was sure of it. When he spoke, she recognized his voice, and yes, he had had that tiny scar just underneath his right ear. It *was* him. She turned and walked slowly back to the hotel, thinking fast. She took a deep breath and went up the steps.

The moment she got inside, a commissionaire, resplendent in dark-green uniform with shiny brass buttons, came towards her. He wasn't sure who she was. Not a guest, he was sure, but nor did she look like a servant who should be using the tradesman's entrance.

'Yes, madam?'

'I believe you have a Mr Penicuik staying,' said Mary, in her pretty voice. 'I used to be acquainted with Mrs Penicuik. I wonder if she is accompanying him?'

'I will enquire, madam,' said the commissionaire. He indicated a chair and went to talk to the receptionist.

Mary sat down, twisting her hands nervously in her lap.

The commissionaire returned. 'Mr Penicuik is alone, madam. Would you like to leave a message?'

'No, thank you,' said Mary rising. She gave him sixpence—reluctantly, for it represented half-a-dozen herrings—and left.

She walked home slowly. It *had* been Duncan, and he had lied to her. But what hurt more was his denial of Jamie. How *could* he? She would have been happy with a few kind words, maybe congratulations on Jamie's success. Of course, it would have been wonderful if he'd restored the allowance, but she would have been content without.

Suddenly, anger overtook her. She *would* write to Mr Ogilvy, see what she could find out about her father's will. *Do* something. She might be poor and of no consequence in the world, but there was such a thing as justice. And she wanted it, for herself and for Jamie.

Her son did not deserve to be discarded by his father like an unwanted puppy. But she would say nothing to him about this meeting, it would be too cruel.

*   *   *

Once the party was recovered from their walk, Beatrix suggested that they might like to see the falls before luncheon. They all at once rose obediently to their feet. Charlotte stifled a giggle. Mrs Penicuik reminded her of the time they were in Sarawak, where they had met the chief wife of an important man in a village high in the forest. She'd been very large and had had patterns all over her body and porcupine quills in her hair. For some reason, this imposing woman reminded Charlotte of Beatrix; perhaps it was her tone of voice which brooked no argument. Charlotte had seen one of the warriors, a man with formidable scars and a necklace of boars' tusks, scuttle off to do her bidding.

They set off. Madeline, conscious of her mother's eye upon her, dutifully attached herself to Edward. The others followed behind. The path went down in a series of zigzags, and they had to go in single file. Somebody had put up a rough handrail in the worst places. Ewan manoeuvred himself next to Henry and, at the next turn, tried to jostle him. Henry recovered his balance and motioned to Ewan to go on ahead. Curse it, thought Ewan. But there was always the way back. The roar of the waterfall got louder. Then, suddenly, they could glimpse it through the trees.

'If we go down a little further, there's a place where we can see it quite well,' said Robina, raising her voice against the noise of the water. She pointed. Edward, who was leading the way, nodded.

About halfway down the gorge was a large projecting rock, with a small platform of land behind it. They made their way across. In front of them the peaty-brown water plunged down in a series of cascades. Small rainbows arched over in the spray and sparkled in the sunlight. After the rain the previous day, the falls were at their best.

'I've never seen it like this before,' said Aeneas, deeply impressed.

'If it weren't for the falls, we'd have salmon up the River Nevan,' said John gloomily.

Charlotte considered it. She'd seen waterfalls in the Himalayas beside which this was a mere trickle. 'It's pretty, though,' she said politely. Her gaze wandered. 'Look, Papa! Roseroot!'

'Ah yes.' Edward came over. 'Plenty of saxifrage here, too.'

Georgina had turned and was looking back up the path with its twists and turns, the rocks, the slopes covered with pine needles and interesting holes underneath the roots, the various burns that plunged down to join the

River Foyers. 'A dog would love this!' she said. 'Lots of places to explore.'

Robina breathed in. There was a wonderful smell of pine, and a musky odour—deer droppings somewhere, perhaps? An orange tip butterfly danced by. She'd missed this. This was part of her childhood, part of what had made her. She was glad she'd come back to Scotland, in spite of the problems.

Finally, everybody had seen what they wanted to see and they turned to go back. Ewan said very little. He'd stood slightly apart from the others, fingering his catapult, which was stuck through his belt. He picked up a couple of pine cones and flung them into the cascade. Every now and then, he cast a fulminating look at Henry.

As they strung out along the path, Ewan slipped in behind Henry, who was following Charlotte. Edward brought up the rear. Stealthily, Ewan took out his catapult and picked up a couple of sharp stones. Then he saw his chance. There was a very narrow place where the path turned abruptly. He took aim and the stone hit Henry sharply on the ankle. Henry lost his footing and fell awkwardly, grabbing the root of a pine tree. In doing so, he knocked Charlotte, who slipped, rolled over and, with a scream, disappeared from sight.

Edward ran. 'Charlotte! Charlotte!'

Then came a faint voice. 'Here!'

Edward crawled to the edge and peered

over. About ten feet below, Charlotte was clinging to a small birch tree. One foot had found a precarious purchase on a rock, the other was swinging free.

'Hold on!' shouted Edward. He removed his rucksack and took out a length of rope, knotted it expertly round a sturdy pine, tested it, and made a slip knot the other end, and, after a couple of false tries, managed to throw it down to Charlotte. 'You know what to do?'

Robina, who was much higher, could see Charlotte clearly. The birch tree was hanging out over the gorge. The rope slithered down and dangled. Charlotte tightened her grip on the birch tree with one hand, shifted position, and reached for the rope. As she did so her foot slipped. There was the sound of falling stones. Robina, in anguish, closed her eyes.

There was a gasp from the onlookers. For one awful moment it seemed as if she must fall. When Robina opened her eyes again, the birch tree was leaning at a greater angle. Then Charlotte lunged and caught the rope. The birch tree seemed to crack. Charlotte pushed her hand through the loop, gripped the rope and nodded to her father. She let go of the birch tree and hung free, swaying over the fifty-foot drop, before grasping the rope with her other hand.

'Good girl,' called Edward, and began carefully to pull her up. John had come up to join Edward and took hold of the rope behind him, adding his weight.

'Not so fast,' shouted Edward over his shoulder. 'The rope might fray.'

With agonizing slowness, Charlotte was pulled to safety. Finally, Edward grasped her hand and pulled her back on to the path. He held her for a moment.

'I've lost my hat,' said Charlotte shakily.

'We might have lost *you*,' said Edward.

The moment Henry saw that Charlotte was safe, he turned to Ewan, grabbed him by the collar with one hand, wrenched open his jacket with the other, pulled out the catapult and hurled it over the edge. Then he marched Ewan up the hill, his face grim. Silently, the others stood aside. Nobody spoke.

Shortly before they reached the top, Henry turned towards the spring, still holding Ewan in front of him and threw him in, pushing him under with his boot. Spluttering and coughing, Ewan climbed out.

Henry had already left.

When Ewan got back to the picnic area, Beatrix was the only person who took any notice. 'Ewan, darling! How on earth did you get into such a state?'

'I . . . I fell into the spring,' he said, sulkily.

Nobody else said anything. Aeneas had turned away and was staring at a red squirrel which was washing its paws on a branch. Edward was sitting with his arm around Charlotte; they were talking in low voices.

Morag and Frank exchanged a small satisfied smile; Master Ewan was not liked below stairs. Everybody else was watching him silently.

Then Beatrix noticed the silence. Her glance went rapidly from Ewan to Charlotte. She swallowed.

'Take off your wet jacket and knicker-bockers,' she ordered. 'Frank, take Master Ewan away and help him out of those wet clothes. There should be a spare rug somewhere.'

Humiliated and dripping, Ewan squelched slowly across to where Frank, barely able to conceal a grin, was waiting.

'What exactly happened?' John whispered to Henry.

Henry told him.

'Serve him right,' said John, tersely. 'She could have been killed.'

It was a subdued party which sat down to lunch. All the glories of the Achnagarry hampers, with the pigeon pies, a joint of cold beef, jars of home-made pickles, mustard, hard-boiled eggs, salad, a jar of salad-dressing, and bread, followed by cake and biscuits, cheese and fruit, could not make this a joyous occasion. The awfulness of so near a tragedy had had its effect on all of them.

It became obvious, even to Beatrix, that the outing had come to an end. It was decided that Aeneas would walk home and Ewan would ride the pony.

'Shall you be all right, Aeneas?' asked Robina.

'I shall get wheezy climbing the hill,' said Aeneas cheerfully. 'I'll probably need to stop a few times.' Anything would be better than going back with his mother and Ewan, he thought. It would be worth a few wheezes.

Robina turned to Charlotte. 'How are you feeling now?' She couldn't help thinking that Charlotte should have been offered the chance to ride. 'There's an inn not far away. We could probably hire you a horse.'

'I'm all right,' said Charlotte smiling. 'Honestly, I am. Papa and I have had worse experiences, haven't we, Papa?'

'I don't see what could be worse than clinging to a tree over a sheer drop!'

Charlotte laughed. 'We once had to convince a tribe of headhunters in Sarawak that we were friendly.'

'Good God!'

'I knew what to do. I really was quite all right. Papa taught me the drill.'

Robina looked at Edward and then said, 'Splendid.' She was not going to make a fuss if they didn't want it. 'Morag and Frank are packing up. I think, if you're ready, we should make a move.'

*   *   *

Later that afternoon, Duncan went out again.

This time he would take a look at Muirtown, the docks area. He beckoned to the commissionaire. 'Get me a cab!'

'Yes, sir.'

A few moments later, the commissionaire escorted Duncan down the steps and held open the cab door. 'By the way, sir,' he said, 'a lady was here earlier asking for Mrs Penicuik.'

Duncan turned sharply, 'Oh?'

'A widow lady, sir. She left no message.'

Duncan shrugged, reached in his pocket and flicked the man a shilling. He climbed into the cab, the commissionaire closed the door, and the cab pulled away. Duncan leaned back against the squabs, his face grim. She knew then. For the first time a feeling of unease crept over him.

*　　　*　　　*

Robina's Journal　　　　Wednesday, 9 August
I wish Mr Mountsorrel would get rid of all that hair. I'd really like to know what he looks like underneath.
Edward. Nice name.

CHAPTER SIX

'I'm going out, Mother,' said Jamie, picking up his jacket from the back of the chair and putting it on. He was going to meet Olaf after work and go rabbiting. Alec Burns had promised to lend Olaf his ferret, and they would peg a large net over the rabbit warren and then Olaf would send in the ferret. With luck, they should get a couple of dozen rabbits at least. Olaf had taught Jamie how to gut and skin a rabbit—not a job he particularly liked, but it meant that his mother didn't have to do it.

'Are you going to see this friend of yours?' asked Mary.

Jamie stopped. 'Yes.'

'It's Olaf Hamnavoe, isn't it?'

Jamie folded his arms. 'And if it is?' he said, a touch defiantly. His teachers at school had said, more than once, that Olaf was no fit companion for a respectable young man. Jamie disagreed.

'I was wondering if you'd like to invite him to take a meal with us, before you go off to university? For supper, say.'

'You're asking Olaf *here*?'

'He's been very good to you, Jamie. If we've met, then I can tell him how you're doing when you write from Glasgow. I don't suppose he can read or write.'

'Yes, he can.'

'You don't have to,' said Mary, sensing his ambivalence. 'Just an idea.'

'I'll think about it,' said Jamie, and left.

Jamie's predominant feeling, as he walked down towards the Thornbush timber-yard where Olaf was working, was reluctance. Ever since he'd met Olaf, he'd kept that part of his life separate. He didn't know why, since his mother was not the sort of woman to cling on to a fellow. It was just that he had preferred it that way. He wasn't sure if he wanted them to meet, even if only for supper. Supposing they didn't get on? How awkward it would be. No, it would be best if they did not meet. He would forget the invitation.

On the other hand, he would like Olaf to know that he hadn't forgotten him when he was in Glasgow. He hadn't really thought of writing to him. Where would he send it? Would the postman deliver a letter out to the bothy? Would Olaf want a letter?

When he got down to the timber-yard, Olaf's shift had not yet finished, so Jamie sat down on a bollard and waited. There was something else he wanted to talk to Olaf about. He'd thought endlessly about going to see his father and had worked out how he might do it. The lodgings were being given up on Monday and his mother would be moving to Dr Ross's. The plan had originally been for

Jamie to lodge there, too, until the time came for him to go to Glasgow, but he had managed to save a bit of money from his work on the *Inverness Courier*, and his mother had refused to take it, so he had persuaded her to let him take a walking holiday and walk to Glasgow. He would take his box down to where the steamer to Glasgow docked and send it as advanced luggage, to await his arrival. He had reckoned that it would take him a couple of weeks to walk, and he planned to take any casual jobs he could find on the way. The forty pounds' bursary would pay for the rent and food, but it would not go much further. He would need some extra for books and things.

This, at least, was the plan as he had told it to his mother, but Jamie had another project in mind, one he did not tell her. He would indeed send his box in advance, but he, himself, would take the steamer as far as Foyers and walk up to Achnagarry Lodge. Or maybe he would find a cottage where he could get bed and breakfast for the night, many women would be glad of an extra shilling, and then he'd go up to the house on Tuesday morning. Yes, that would be better. The only problem was, he couldn't help thinking that Olaf would try to argue him out of it. He must talk to him again, make him understand.

What did he have to lose? If his father refused, at least he'd know. He pictured himself writing with the good news; the allowance restored and his mother able to come to Glasgow with him. They'd find some nice lodgings somewhere and she'd keep house for him. He could bring his friends home without worrying about them eating all the housekeeping money.

Mother could tell Dr Ross that she wasn't staying. Jamie hadn't wanted to think about it too much, but he hadn't liked the look in the man's eye, nor the way he watched his mother walk, as if he wanted to grab her. When he'd shown them up to the room that would be hers, Jamie was relieved to see that there was a bolt on the door.

He was doing this for his mother, he thought. For himself, he could probably manage on the scholarship and the bursary. It was his mother who was owed something by Penicuik. If it didn't work out, he need never tell her. He would simply walk back to Loch Ness and continue down the Great Glen as originally planned.

There was a voice behind him. 'Come on, lad! Ye're dreaming!' Olaf, holding a wriggling bag with the ferret in it, was standing behind him.

Jamie got up and grinned. 'Sorry!'

As soon as they got out of town, Jamie found himself, to his surprise, telling Olaf of his mother's invitation. He hadn't meant to, but somehow, it just slipped out. 'We're leaving on Monday,' he finished. 'But any day before that.'

Olaf turned to look at him, his blue eyes very piercing. 'Did she now?' he said. 'I take that very kindly. Would tomorrow do, think ye?'

'Tomorrow would do fine,' Jamie assured him. 'We eat at about half-past six.'

Olaf nodded.

Jamie had been rabbit-hunting before, and it was a skilful operation. The long net had to be pegged down very carefully, for a rabbit could squeeze through the smallest hole, but, at the same time, the net itself had to be loose, to have enough give in it to entangle the rabbits. They went first to the bothy to collect the net and pegs, and then walked to the mound Olaf had chosen.

'They know we're here,' said Olaf, as he handed Jamie some iron pegs. 'The warren is hollow, ye see, what with all the holes, and the sound carries. It could be a weasel, or a person, but they know. They'll be sitting tight.'

They worked as fast as they could and eventually it was done. Olaf inspected the work carefully before he nodded and went to get the ferret. He slipped it under the net, and they waited. There was silence for a moment. Jamie put his ear to the ground. He could hear a sort of pattering. Suddenly, rabbits shot out in all directions. The next fifteen minutes were frantically busy. By the time they'd finished there was a pile of twenty-seven rabbits. Not bad, thought Jamie, about thirty shillings' worth, he reckoned. Olaf, he knew, would give some to Alec, and perhaps a couple to the old watchman at Thornbush Brewery, whose wife was ill. The rest he would sell.

Olaf put the rabbits into a sack, and returned the ferret to the bag. Then he threw the last rabbit at Jamie. 'You take this,' he said. 'And my compliments to your good mother.'

Jamie took it and later, on the way home as he neared the first houses, thrust it under his jacket. It occurred to him that whereas, earlier that evening, he had decided to tell Olaf about his decision to see his father, but not to deliver his mother's invitation, in fact, he had done precisely the opposite. Why had he done that? Even as he thought it, he knew. He was going to see his father, no matter what Olaf thought about it. This way, he would save himself any arguments.

*   *   *

The day after the Foyers excursion, Beatrix was not well. In fact, it was more of a strategic retreat than actual illness. Nobody would say exactly what had happened, but even her maternal partiality could not ignore the fact that Ewan's behaviour had somehow caused a near tragedy, and that somebody had deliberately pushed him into the spring.

Robina and Madeline, when questioned, were very uncooperative. Aeneas said that he didn't know. Ewan just scowled and walked away. Beatrix was torn between worry about Ewan and concern lest her plan for Madeline's future be jeopardized. Suppose no more invitations came from Dunlairg?

Beatrix's absence meant that Robina was free, and she decided to go up to the crannog. She discarded her corset and removed all but one of her petticoats. Rummaging around up in the den, she found her old canvas bag in the cupboard and did what she used to do, went to the kitchen to beg bannocks, cheese and a couple of apples from Ishbel, took an old towel from the linen cupboard—a biggish one, she hated having to dry her feet on something the size of a pocket handkerchief—and set off up the hill towards Loch Tearmann.

She followed the route she'd taken fifteen years before, skirted the peat bog, up past the shielings and then stopped, as she had done then, to look back. It hadn't changed much. The moss-covered turrets of Dunlairg Castle looked the same, as did Nevan House, though a bit at the side had been fenced in, possibly for the children, for Robina could just see three small figures running about. The old shepherd's hut had disappeared and there were just a few stones and a lot of nettles to show where it had once been. She avoided looking at Achnagarry Lodge.

And herself? How had she changed? She was still Robina Drummond, she still had no proper home, but inside she felt very different. *Then,* she had been a green seventeen year old, in love with Murdo. Now, she was a well-travelled woman, who had learned to cope with a lot of practical things. In so far as it was possible, given her financial circumstances, she had control over her own life.

She sighed, and turned down towards Loch Tearmann. It looked blessedly the same. She took off her boots, tied the laces together and slung them round her neck, tucked her stockings into her bag, and set off cautiously across the underwater causeway. The water was icy, but she didn't dare go faster in case the causeway had rotted in places in the intervening years. By the time she reached the crannog, her feet were numb with cold.

Fortunately, it was a warm day; Robina dried her feet and then went to explore the crannog. To her relief, it hadn't changed. She returned to her favourite place, a grassy patch underneath a birch tree, sat down and let herself relax as Hamish had shown her so long ago. One thing she had missed, she realized, was the time to be alone. When her grandmother was alive, she'd been able to wander down the garden and just be in the shade somewhere. For the last few years, that was impossible. She closed her eyes.

Some twenty minutes later, she awoke with

a start. There was a sort of panting and the noise of breaking twigs. For one awful moment, Robina thought of the water horse. Then she pulled herself together. What was it? It was unlikely to be a deer; they were still up on the tops at this time of year.

It came closer. Robina rose to her feet, ready to run. Then she saw it. A large naked man stumbled towards her, and he was almost blue with cold. She stared, aghast. Who on earth was it? What was he doing here? She glanced towards the causeway. She could just about reach it before he got to her.

Then he spoke. 'Miss Drummond!'

Robina gasped with shock. 'Mr Mountsorrel!' He had shaved off his beard and cut his hair. She stared at him for one incredulous moment, and then turned scarlet.

He came into the clearing and sank down on the grass, his head bowed. Robina's colour receded. She found herself studying the long, well-muscled line of his back and thought, involuntarily, that he looked like a Greek statue come to life, some crouching athlete or gladiator, perhaps. He must have swum across. What on earth made him do such a thing? She forgot to be embarrassed; instead, she went over to her bag, pulled out the towel and threw it at him.

'For heaven's sake, dry yourself and get warm! You must be mad to have swum here!' What on earth does one do in a situation like this? Should she have fainted?

Edward was towelling himself vigorously, his back turned to her. Robina allowed herself to look again, and at once realized that he was a very attractive man, for her body was telling her so in no uncertain terms. Eventually, Edward knotted the towel around his waist and turned round.

'Thank you,' he said. 'I would give you the towel back, but I think the decencies must be observed, don't you?'

'Oh, undoubtedly!' said Robina, and couldn't help smiling. The situation was too absurd. Beatrix had a book about Manners and Rules of Good Society, or some such title. Somehow, she didn't think that how to greet a naked man on a crannog would be listed in the index. 'Are you hungry? Would you like a bannock and some cheese?'

'Thank you. That would be very nice,' said Edward politely. He sat down.

Robina handed him the bannock and broke off a chunk of cheese. She leaned against the birch tree and waited for him to open the conversation. Edward continued to eat his bannock. He's really very good-looking, thought Robina, surprised: a strong face, a Roman nose, firm mouth, good chin. And only a little hair on his chest. Why on earth had he allowed himself to look like the Wild Man of Borneo?

'I am escaping again,' he said at last.

'What from?'

'Lady Invershiel and Mrs Usher's well-meaning attempts to pair me off with Miss Usher.'

So he knows, thought Robina. 'Poor Georgina! She only wants to be allowed to breed dogs. It doesn't seem much to ask.' Then she added, 'How is Charlotte? I hope she has recovered from her ordeal?'

'She is well, thank you. She has gone up with John and Henry to look at the waterfalls at Allt Com Ben. They have promised to look after her.'

'That's very brave of her—to go and look at more waterfalls, I mean.'

'We've done a lot of travelling, and, after any sort of incident, the best thing to do is to talk about it and see what can be learned. We did that on the way back yesterday. But it's also important that Charlotte doesn't lose her nerve—hence the trip to the waterfalls.'

'Yes, I think you're right,' said Robina thoughtfully.

'So I took the opportunity to come here,' finished Edward.

'But why on earth did you swim across?'

'Didn't you?'

'No.' Robina stopped and looked at him. She'd have to tell him. She couldn't allow him to swim back. Edward was looking at her enquiringly. 'This is a crannog,' she said at last. 'It's man made, nobody knows by whom.

The Picts, probably. There's an underwater causeway.'

'I've read about crannogs,' said Edward. 'I just never expected to be on one.'

'They aren't too uncommon, there's another on Loch Tarrf, for example. They were defensive, built for safety in times of war.'

She wouldn't mind him knowing about the causeway, she realized. He fitted in somehow. He looked *right* on the crannog. She reached in her bag and offered him an apple and, as she did so, for one wild moment, she felt like Eve. Edward, took it with a smile, looked at her for a moment, and then bit into it deliberately.

Time passed. Robina found herself telling him about Hamish and how he'd found the causeway. Edward told her of hair's-breadth escapes from wild boar and tiger, and unnerving moments with suspicious tribes.

'Why did you decided on the shave and haircut?' ventured Robina.

'As I told you, changing direction,' said Edward, smiling at her in a way that suddenly made her heart flutter.

Robina said nothing, but her colour rose.

'It's eight years since Betsy, my wife, died. I haven't felt, up to now, that I wanted to alter my widowed position.'

'Of . . . of course,' stammered Robina. 'Charlotte is sixteen now, isn't she? You will need a wife to bring her out.' Perhaps it was

216

Madeline, after all, she thought.

'It's nothing to do with Charlotte,' said Edward, with some asperity. 'I dare say Lady Invershiel would bring her out, if I asked her. In any case, Charlotte is not at all keen on all that business. This is for *me*.'

'Oh,' said Robina, feeling the colour flood her cheeks. Why was he telling her this? His lion's eyes were looking at her in a way that made her heart lurch. 'I'm not very good at . . .' she began awkwardly. It seemed as if . . . But she might easily be mistaken, just as she had mistaken Murdo. There had been hints there too, more than hints, but, in the end, they had meant nothing, and she had been hurt and humiliated.

Edward was touched by her obvious confusion. 'Let's leave it for now,' he said. 'I'm hardly suitably dressed for this sort of conversation.' And perhaps I'm going too fast. His instinct was to plunge in, to get to know her, to commit himself, but he pulled back, partly out of concern for her, but also, half-unwillingly, to protect himself.

If it were Madeline he was after, thought Robina, then she'd rather know. 'Perhaps you have realized that Mrs Penicuik is anxious that you marry Madeline.'

Edward raised his eyebrows. 'Is she, indeed! If I'm not mistaken, Miss Penicuik is rather more interested in Henry.'

Robina nodded, conscious of an

overwhelming relief. It wasn't Madeline! 'It's very awkward,' she confided. 'Madeline's dowry is dependent on the wealth of her husband.'

'So Lady Invershiel's hopes for John are equally doomed?'

'I fear so.' He knows everything! she thought. She'd thought of him as an amiable bear, interested only in his plants, but he was a far more astute man than she'd realized.

'We're in for an interesting summer, then,' observed Edward, and smiled at her.

Robina smiled back, her feeling of constraint vanished. She looked up at the sun. 'I should be getting back,' she said, conscious of a feeling of regret. 'I'll take you across the causeway. Where did you leave your clothes?'

Edward pointed. 'By those rocks.'

'You must just have missed the causeway. I'm surprised you didn't bump into it.' She began to make her way down to the water's edge. 'It's only a few inches below the surface. When the sun's at the right angle, you can sometimes see it, if you know where to look. Mostly, though, the peaty water hides it.' She reached the water's edge and stopped. 'Just do as I do,' she said. 'The causeway is about eighteen inches across, so you should be all right, but it's not straight. Don't talk, because I've got to concentrate.'

Robina jumped lightly on to a half-submerged rock, raised her skirts a few inches and then stepped on to the causeway. The water, Edward noticed, covered her ankles, and very pretty ones they were, too. Then she began to walk. Edward followed. They wound their way across, Robina walking lightly and swiftly. Then she stopped. 'It ends here,' she said over her shoulder. 'My toes can feel the edge, so be careful when it's your turn.' She jumped on to the rocks, one, two, three, and was on the shore.

Edward followed. 'Fascinating!' he said. 'I'd have thought it would have rotted away long ago.'

'It's made of oak,' said Robina. 'It got preserved in the peat, I think. Though I don't know how often it was repaired, nor when it fell out of use, of course.'

Edward went off to find his clothes, and Robina dried her feet in the sun and put on her stockings and boots. When she turned round, Edward was dressed.

'Respectable again,' he said, and handed her the towel. Robina put it in her bag. 'I'm going that way,' she said, and pointed.

'So our ways part here?'

'Yes.' If Beatrix ever got to hear of this, she thought, there would be hell to pay. She would be packed off at once.

Edward nodded. 'I shall be very circumspect,' he promised, demonstrating an uncanny ability to read her mind. He reached out, took hold of her hand, held it in both of his, and then, turning it over, he pressed a kiss into her palm, curling her fingers round it before he released her hand.

Robina's heart began to beat so fast that she thought she would faint. She opened her mouth to say something but nothing came out. Edward smiled, turned, and in a few moments she saw him vanish over the top of the crest. Robina sank down on the nearest rock and stared, quite unseeing, at the crannog for fully quarter of an hour. When she eventually got up and walked back to Achnagarry, it felt as if she were floating.

*   *   *

Mary was not quite sure what to expect when Olaf came to supper, but she decided that if a man was well fed then that would give the evening the best chance of success. She made a rabbit stew, thick with carrots and onions, dropped suet dumplings on top, and she would serve it with plenty of potatoes. Afterwards, there would be a summer pudding. She had made it that morning with blackberries, raspberries and black and red currants. She put it to cool in the larder, the top pressed down with a saucer with a two-pound weight on it.

That afternoon, she bought a couple of bottles of beer and, on her way home, slipped into the churchyard and picked a small posy of toadflax, scabious and yarrow, with a few harebells as a centrepiece. However rough a man Hamnavoe was, he had been good to Jamie, and she would do her best to make him feel welcome.

At half-past six, there was a knock on the door and Jamie went down to open it. Olaf, his hair and beard neatly combed, and wearing his good jacket, stood on the doorstep.

'We're upstairs,' said Jamie. He led the way. 'Mother, this is Olaf Hamnavoe—my mother.'

'I'm pleased to meet you, Mr Hamnavoe,' said Mary, shaking hands. 'Sit yourself down. Jamie, give our guest something to drink.'

'I have something for ye,' said Olaf, reaching into his pocket. 'This is for ye, Jamie,' and he handed him an ivory paper-knife, 'and this for ye, Mrs Ritchie,' and he took out a small ivory box with a picture of a seal engraved on the lid.

'Why, thank you!' exclaimed Mary, opening the box. 'Did you make it?'

'Aye, when I was whaling. Whalers make such things to pass the time, ye see. Scrimshaw, they call it. 'Tis made of walrus ivory. Jamie's, too.'

'It's beautifully made,' said Mary, touched. 'I shall keep my hairpins in it.' She couldn't remember the last time she'd been given a present, apart from the small things Jamie gave her for her birthday. Duncan had never been one for presents, she remembered.

Jamie examined his paper-knife. It was long, thin and sharp. You could kill somebody with that, he thought. 'Mind you write to me, Mother,' he said, holding it up.

'You'll be buying books, and the pages will need cutting,' said Mary.

It broke the ice. They sat down to the rabbit stew and the talk flowed. Olaf told them stories of whaling ships and how he'd once seen narwhals fighting, using their long twisted horns as if they were swords. Mary mentioned that her grandmother had been a Shetlander.

'I never knew that!' exclaimed Jamie.

'I'd almost forgotten it,' said Mary apologetically. 'She died when I was about nine or ten. But I remember her telling me that the girls would take their spinning wheels, and a peat for the fire, and meet at a certain cottage for an evening of spinning and telling stories of selkies and such-like.'

'Where did she come from?' asked Olaf.

'Unst, I believe. Her name was Kirsty Tulloch. When I knew her, she was tiny and bent, with white hair and very blue eyes.'

'Like Olaf's,' said Jamie. 'The eyes, I mean.'

'Perhaps it's the Viking ancestry,' said Mary, smiling. 'Some more rabbit stew, Mr Hamnavoe?'

The evening was a quiet success. Olaf was appreciative of Mary's cooking and he asked her permission to smoke his pipe, just as he ought. Jamie lost some of the air of tension he had had over the last few weeks, and Mary felt that, for one evening at least, she was herself; not Jamie's mother, nor a poor widow, but just Mary Ritchie, who had things to say that people wanted to hear.

When Olaf rose to go, Mary said, 'Jamie, light Mr Hamnavoe down to the front door. The stairs are very uneven.'

Olaf thanked her gravely for the evening, they shook hands, and he left. Mary, listening to them talking for a few minutes at the door, thought to herself that Jamie had chosen well. He hadn't had a father since he was four. She'd done her best, but it was a gap in his life. But Olaf Hamnavoe had done some fathering of her son; he had taught him the sort of things that fathers taught sons: how to gut fish, or catch rabbits, for example. He was gruff, but he obviously liked Jamie and, from their conversation, she could see that Jamie held Olaf in respect as well as affection.

For all Olaf's reputation for lawlessness— relayed to her by several officious neighbours —he had not corrupted her son. And perhaps, who knows, he had gained something for himself. She hoped so. He was a good man, she was sure.

For the first time since her father died, she felt that she had linked up again with the young Mary Ritchie, the girl she had once been before Duncan Penicuik had come into her life. It was something to do with the evening, she thought; the feeling that there were relationships which were decent and straightforward. Not everybody behaved badly. There would be no more dithering, she told herself. The moment she and Jamie had done the washing up, and Jamie had gone to his room, she would write to Mr Ogilvy.

Later that evening, she sat down at the kitchen table and began to write.

c/o Dr Ross,
Old Edinburgh Road,
Inverness 12 August, 1865

Dear Mr Ogilvy

I hope that you will forgive me for writing, but you are the one person who knows my story, and I need some advice. When my father died in 1841, shortly after my mother, Mr Duncan Penicuik, who was my father's executor, dealt with everything for me. He organized the funeral, for example, and I suppose he must also have dealt with the lease of the house, and sold the contents. At the time, I was too young, ignorant and distressed to do anything and, of course, I was a minor. But now I wonder what happened to the money, for some of the contents were not without value. My mother's illness was expensive, but I don't believe that my father was in debt. And I know that my mother had £400 of her own which was to be mine, and which I never received.

Is there any way that I can find out about this? Of course, I realize that it may be far too late to do anything about it, and I could not afford a legal battle.

I have taken the position of housekeeper to Dr Ross, to see me through Jamie's years at university, but money is going to be very tight, especially for Jamie. If there is anything to which I may rightfully lay claim, then I should like to know of it.

I should add that I saw Mr Penicuik quite by chance outside the Caledonian Hotel, here in Inverness. I spoke to him briefly, but he denied knowing me, or my 'brat', and threatened me with the police. Later, I checked at the hotel, and it was indeed him. I have mentioned this in order to explain how it is that I am writing to you and not to Mr Penicuik.

I must thank you again for your kind offices with regard to Jamie's lodgings in Glasgow.

Yours etc.

M. Ritchie.

* * *

It might have been supposed, after the mishaps at the Falls of Foyers, that the intercourse between Achnagarry and Dunlairg would cease abruptly. In fact, the opposite seemed to be the case. There was rarely a day when the Achnagarry and Dunlairg young people did not meet. They no longer relied on Lady Invershiel or Mrs Penicuik's invitations, but instead arranged their own meetings. Of course, propriety had to be observed, and Aeneas found himself in demand as a chaperon. He sat fishing whilst Henry and Madeline talked or walked within sight nearby, and, as Henry always gave him a shilling, Aeneas was perfectly happy.

The first time, on the way home, Madeline said, 'You won't tell Mama, will you, Aeneas?'

'Of course not!' said Aeneas scornfully, fingering the shilling in his pocket. There were several books he wanted to buy when he got home to Edinburgh. If this spooning continued, Aeneas reckoned that he might just about have enough money.

Henry had not expected to fall in love. He'd started out on a mild flirtation, with no real desire to do more than to pull the wool over his mother's eyes, and annoy his elder brother. He knew he could not afford to marry yet; it would be years before he could support a wife. He was still dependent on the allowances from his father and godfather, but, somehow, increasingly, this ceased to matter.

The more he got to know Madeline, the more he felt that she was just right. She was pretty, intelligent and damnably desirable. He was sure that she would be an asset to any man in his career. It was true that her dowry would be useful, too, but, Henry decided, she was a dowry in herself.

But, that afternoon, Madeline had fallen silent.

'What is it?' asked Henry. He hadn't 'spoken'. He knew he should, and he wanted to, but speaking would make it real. He would then have to *do* something: talk to his parents; pay a call of ceremony on Mr Penicuik. He was not a coward, but he knew that his mother had other hopes, and God knows what Mr Penicuik would do. Forbid Madeline to see him again, probably.

Madeline took a deep breath. 'You do realize that I have no money of my own, don't you, Mr Invershiel?' she said. Her voice trembled as she spoke. She knew that he was fond of her, very fond, and it didn't seem fair for him to remain in ignorance.

'How is this?' Henry turned to look at her troubled face.

'Papa will settle three times my husband's annual income on me, whatever that may be,' she said, turning her head away. She started to tug at a piece of heather and crumble the flowers. 'Of course, when Mama dies, I shall inherit her fifteen thousand pounds, but that won't be for years.'

'So, if you married Mr Mountsorrel, your dowry would be twelve thousand, and if you

227

married me, it would be twelve hundred?'

'Yes,' whispered Madeline.

Henry reached out and took hold of Madeline's hand. 'I think we must talk about this.'

Madeline looked at him, tears in her eyes.

'I love you,' said Henry earnestly. 'I believe that we could be very happy together. I think you'd like the people in my world and my way of life. It's a town life, though I travel a bit, too, and I think that would suit you. I work hard and, although it will take time, eventually I should have a good income. But it won't happen for some years—five at the very least.'

Madeline nodded.

'I don't know what to suggest. Of course, I'd like to beg you to marry me at once, but that would be condemning you to many years of poverty.'

'It would also hold you back,' said Madeline, courageously. 'I've been thinking, too. I don't see that I can do anything until I'm of age, in about two and a half years' time.'

Henry leaned forward. 'Would you wait for me for that long?'

'I would try. But my parents will put pressure on me, and it is Mama who has to pay for me. Papa believes that a daughter is a mother's responsibility.'

Henry was prudently silent.

'It's *awful*!' Madeline burst out. 'I can't help it, I know he's my father, but he's so mean! I feel ashamed sometimes.'

'I think we should wait on events,' said Henry. 'I live most of the year in Edinburgh. We should be able to meet from time to time. The only thing is . . .' He looked at Madeline pleadingly. 'Do you love me?'

'Oh yes!'

Henry glanced round. Aeneas was absorbed in his fishing. He leaned forward, took her face gently in his hands and kissed her. Madeline's arms slowly crept up round his neck.

*   *   *

Robina's Journal   Saturday, 12 August, 1865
I think I must look different. I feel *different. I feel as if Mhairi has taken her whisk and churned me up. I look at myself in the glass and my eyes seem brighter, my face softer. Now I understand what is meant by Cupid's arrows. It really does feel as if I've been shot through the heart and it's left a sort of painful but sweet ache.*

But this is all very well, there's another voice inside me, a rational one, saying, 'Careful, Robina, don't pin too much on this.' Mostly I think that what he said was encouraging, but then I think of my disadvantages, and my heart sinks.

Whatever would Lord Glendon think, for a start? Surely he must be expecting Edward to make a good marriage? My dowry is barely respectable—it's certainly less than half of what he has a right to expect, and that's without taking the barony into account. My family is good, but I'm thirty-two. I've been on the shelf for years. Worse, I've been earning my own living. It is true that being a lady companion is just about acceptable, but I doubt very much whether Lord Glendon would approve.

If Lady Invershiel got an inkling of this, I'd be banned from the castle. Unfair, I know, because it's none of her business, but she's decided on Gusher, and she's not a woman to like her plans being altered. If Beatrix realized, I'd be packed off on the next steamer. There's nobody here, nobody really since Grandmama died, who is on my side. I hate this feeling of subterfuge, but what else can I do?

After Murdo, I put any wish of being married out of my head. I suppose, if I'd been tempted, I might have changed my mind, but I never met a man whom I preferred to my grandmother. Even now, I can still hardly believe the speed with which my life has been turned completely upside-down. I still don't really understand why I should feel so strongly about Edward.

I daren't believe he's serious. I fear it may just be wishful thinking on my part.

*   *   *

It was Mary and Jamie's last morning together. Mary's small bag was packed and Jamie's box was ready to go to the steamer. That morning,

230

Jamie had thought carefully about how he should present himself to his father and decided that he must be clean, freshly shaved and tidy. His best suit would be wrong; it was second-hand from a school friend who had outgrown it, but it looked almost new. It could go ahead in the box. No, he had to look clean but shabby. A jacket with neatly patched elbows would be better. He *needed* that allowance and he must look as if he did. On the other hand, he mustn't look so shabby that the servants denied him entrance.

James did not possess a calling card, but he had written, in his excellently clear hand: *Mr James Ritchie respectfully desires a word with Mr Penicuik.* He had hesitated a lot over the wording. To aspire to 'Mr' might be thought presumptuous, but, on the other hand, he was going up to university, surely he might allow himself to be 'Mr'? Then, he was damned if he were going to write 'humbly desires', like a tradesman. 'Respectfully' he could just about swallow.

Still, that was all for tomorrow. Today, for travelling, he would wear his oldest clothes. Steamers were filthy and he would be covered in smuts by the time he got to Foyers. He sat down on the end of his bed and stared at himself in the speckled mirror resting on a small shelf which did duty for a dressing-table. What would his father look like? However hard he tried, Jamie couldn't remember him.

He had a vague memory of a large man standing in their hall in Musselburgh, but that was all. He didn't know why he remembered it, perhaps because the sun coming through the coloured glass in the door turned the man's hair blue and yellow and he'd thought it curious. When he'd tried to ask his mother about him, she'd said only, 'About your height. Stockily built, blue eyes, brown hair—I can't remember.' She would say no more.

He sighed, rose, and went through to the kitchen. Mary was standing by the kitchen table. They sat down and ate their breakfast in silence. Mary had a lump in her throat which made swallowing difficult. She had never been apart from Jamie, even for one night. How was she going to bear it? But he had to go, she knew that. He had his own life to lead and she must not hold him back.

Jamie was feeling half excited, half apprehensive. Part of him wanted desperately to tell his mother what he had planned, but he bit his tongue. He was seventeen, wasn't he? A man? He should be able to make his own decisions without telling his mother.

Eventually Mary pulled back her chair. She went over to the dresser and handed Jamie some sandwiches in a battered tin box. This would keep him going. She looked at him, her eyes full of unshed tears.

'I'll write to you, I promise,' said Jamie, feeling his own eyes prickle. 'But I don't know

232

where I'll be able to post it on the way. I don't want you to be worried.'

'I promise not to worry,' said Mary, wiping her eyes with the corner of her apron, and trying to smile. Then her face crumpled.

'Mother!' She hardly ever cried and Jamie wasn't sure what to do. He patted her awkwardly on the shoulder and then, as that didn't seem to work, gave her a hug. There were some grey hairs along her parting, he noticed. Perhaps he shouldn't leave her. It wasn't fair on her.

Mary pulled herself away and mopped her eyes. 'I know you'll be all right,' she said. 'You're not to worry about me. It's just a wee cry. Now, off you go. *Enjoy* yourself, Jamie. I mean it.'

Jamie grinned, a little lop-sidedly. 'You're a mother in a million,' he assured her. He leaned forward and gave her a kiss. Then he picked up his box, put it on his shoulder, and went down the stairs.

Mary watched him go and then ran back to the window. Jamie turned as he reached the end of the path and waved, just as he always did. Then he was gone.

Right, she thought. No more crying. Get yourself together and get over to Dr Ross's.

Jamie made his way down to the ferry. He booked in his box and bought a ticket to Foyers, paid the fare and the carriage for the box and put his ticket and the receipt for the box carefully in his inside pocket, along with his wallet, the letters to show his father, and Olaf's paper-knife. Then he climbed the gangplank.

In spite of his anxieties, Jamie couldn't help relishing the adventure. He barely remembered living in Musselburgh and had only the faintest recollection of the voyage up to Inverness. It had been cold and wet and there was a strong smell of fish. But he'd been only four. Since then, he'd hardly left Inverness. Once he'd gone on a school trip to Fort George, where an officer had been a friend of the headmaster, and who wanted to show the boys what a fine thing it was to join the Seaforth Highlanders. Jamie's first thought was that the fort looked exactly like a toy fort he'd once seen, and second, that he didn't want to join the army and march up and down with a lot of other men, and be shouted at.

The only other time he left the town was to go up to see the Pictish boar stone at Drumdevan with their history master, who was interested in antiquities. They'd all got caught in a sharp shower and he'd come home with his clothes soaked and caught a dreadful cold in consequence.

But those adventures were when he was a child. Since then, he'd been out a lot with Olaf. They never went far out of Inverness, but somehow, because of those times, he felt he could cope with whatever lay ahead. He patted the paper-knife in silent thanks. Olaf had made all the difference. He understood that now.

It was a dull cloudy day, though not actually raining, and Jamie decided to stay on deck and watch Inverness slip away into the distance. The boat chugged slowly down the Caledonian Canal and then slid out into Loch Ness. The hills rose steeply on either side, purple and grey with stands of dark green Scots pine. Jamie gazed. It felt like his life, he thought. This morning, he'd been safe in the world he knew and now, all of a sudden, the view had opened out and he was sailing into a new world. He'd seen those hills most of his life, but he'd never been so close. They looked bigger, more majestic.

Foyers, when it came, was a disappointment, with only a pier and a small row of houses. He was just about to disembark, when a thick-set, bull-necked man, wearing an expensive Chesterfield overcoat and a top hat, pushed him roughly out of the way and trod heavily down the gangplank. Jamie was knocked off balance and fell heavily to the deck. Angrily, he picked himself up, dusted down his jacket and glared at the retreating figure. 'Bad cess to you,' he muttered. He gave one last look at the steamer, turned and followed the retreating bull-necked man down the gangplank. This was it.

In his office in Heriot Row, Edinburgh, Mr Alan Ogilvy sat at his desk and stared down at the two letters in front of him. Their simultaneous arrival seemed to him to be ominously coincidental. One was the letter from Mary Ritchie, and the other was from Duncan Penicuik, demanding that he come up to Achnagarry immediately. Mr Ogilvy was not normally a man given to fancies, but it was an uncanny feeling, knowing something about Penicuik's visit to Inverness which Penicuik himself had not told him.

Mary's letter, though, had shocked him. If he'd known about this business earlier, he thought, when he'd first met her, he might have been able to screw a proper settlement out of Penicuik. He'd never met Mary's father, but he knew of him. However expensive his wife's illness, it would not have affected the £400 which had been Mrs Ritchie's dowry. That, without question, should have gone to Mary Ritchie. He had been remiss there; he should have thought of it at the time of the original settlement with Penicuik.

Over the years, Mr Ogilvy had become accustomed to Mr Penicuik's habit of screwing every penny out of his business concerns, including his employees, but that didn't mean he liked it. There was no generosity in the man.

236

Very well, he would go up to Achnagarry, visit Inverness and look into this possible emporium as Penicuik wanted him to, but, while he was there, he would also have a word with his cousin Francis. Two heads would be better than one on this. But first, he must find out the contents of Ritchie's will. That shouldn't be too difficult; it should be in the parish records. In fact, Mr Ogilvy thought, smiling grimly, it would be a pleasure to deal with the matter.

*   *   *

It was just after midnight, and Edward sat up on the battlements and allowed his thoughts to drift back to the episode on the crannog. What was happening to him? Where was his hard-won rationality, the composure, the calm, all those things he had learnt during the difficult years of his marriage? They had all disappeared. He could not stop thinking about Robina. He was like a man obsessed.

Hadn't he always believed that falling in love was like the measles, you did it once, and were then immune to its pernicious effects? Hadn't he sworn that no woman would ever again turn his life upside-down? And yet, Robina had managed to do just that with one glance of those dark-brown eyes.

And, he suspected, she had done it quite unconsciously. That was more disconcerting than all the rest. He could cope with, indeed had coped with, a number of women whose interest in him had been transparent, and whose intentions were obvious. As the pursued, he had been able to evade them easily. But now, almost against his will, he found himself the pursuer. It was *he* who had made the moves that afternoon, he who had wanted more.

When he'd kissed the palm of her hand, it had been all he could do to stop himself from pulling her into his arms. He had been going too fast for her, he could see that, but what alarmed him was the speed with which his heart had taken control. He wanted Robina— but he wasn't at all sure that he wanted to want her.

Supposing she turned out to be like Betsy? He didn't think he could bear all that again; the subterfuge, lies and deceit. Even as he thought about it, he winced in remembered pain. Dare he risk it a second time?

And yet, in every other area of his life he continually took risks—it was part of being alive. Was this the one area that he had closed down for ever? He knew that he found in Robina somebody whose courage and honesty he admired, and who was agonizingly desirable. What he did not know was what he was going to do about it.

*   *   *

Robina's Journal   Tuesday, 15 August
God, it was so embarrassing seeing Edward again! I could feel the colour, flooding over my cheeks. I wanted to sink! Edward, when I dared to glance at him, just looked amused. Perhaps I shouldn't call him 'Edward', though I only do it here. I wouldn't dare call him by his Christian name to his face. Lady I. would certainly not like it, and, of course, it would be most unladylike. But how can I help but think of him as 'Edward' now?

Anyway, somehow we (the Achngarries and the Dunlairgs) have taken to meeting by the little bay halfway along Loch Nevan, and he was there with Charlotte and John. Charlotte seems to be taking John in hand. She lectures him on Women's Rights! She is the most redoubtable girl.

Edward asked me if I'd like to come out for a row on the loch, and I said 'yes'. We weren't out of sight of John and Charlotte, so the proprieties were observed! The moment we began to talk, I stopped feeling embarrassed. He told me about his wife, Betsy, and how she drank. Reading between the lines, it sounds as though she had lovers as well. She must have been mad! It's awful to say this, but it reassured me rather. Lady I. had told me how pretty she had been, and I'd been feeling that he must find me very homely beside her. I'm sorry for them both that it wasn't a happy marriage, but it certainly makes things

239

easier for me.

I wouldn't dream of having what Grandmama used to call 'criminal conversation' with a man who was not my husband. I wouldn't know how to set about it anyway. I suppose some women do and some don't. If Madeline weren't such a nice person, I could see her doing it, for example. She has that sort of self-confidence. I don't.

I told him about Murdo and our semi-engagement. It seemed only fair.

'Gillespie! The man's a scoundrel!' he said, and he looked so fierce, I wanted to hug him. It was wonderful to know that he was on my side.

'He was after a woman with more money,' I said. 'His mother wasn't an easy woman. I expect he wanted to get right away from her.' As I spoke, I realized how much things had changed. I never used to be so objective about Murdo. It must be being in love!

Edward wouldn't have it. He said that it was very underhand behaviour and quite inexcusable, especially with a young girl of seventeen. 'Hardly older than Charlotte,' he said. Of course, he's right. I hadn't thought of it like that.

Anyway, I felt a lot better! I said that I was very grateful that it had come to nothing; it would have been a disaster.

He then asked me if I could contemplate marriage with someone else.

I said that I might be persuaded. God knows how I found the courage, for it's not the sort of thing I normally say. It just came out.

Edward shipped the oars, reached out and took hold of my hand. We sat there, holding hands and smiling at each other. It was wonderful!

* * *

In his study in Nevan House, Murdo looked out at Loch Nevan. He could just see four figures on the far shore, two men and two women. Then one of the men got into a boat with one of the women, and there was something about that distant figure which made him think that it was Robina. He crossed to the window; they were well out on the loch now. He picked up his father's telescope, focused it, and scanned the water.

By God! It *was* Robina! And she was with that Mountsorrel fellow. He snapped the telescope shut and began to pace up and down. This needed some thought! He'd marked out Robina as the future Mrs Gillespie and he did not want her hobnobbing with a man who spent half his life in the jungle. It would, of course, be nothing more serious than a trip on the loch; Robina knew that he, Murdo, had serious intentions. She was well aware of his worth! All the same, he didn't like it.

Perhaps he should have a quiet word with Mrs Penicuik. Nip it in the bud.

CHAPTER SEVEN

Duncan arrived back from Inverness feeling that he'd done what he had set out to do: he'd made himself known to a number of useful people, looked over various premises, and was satisfied that the railway and harbour facilities were suitable. Inverness was ripe for a Penicuik's Emporium. Or should it be the Balmoral Emporium? It would do no harm to appropriate the solid worth of the royal name. It would give tone to the place.

He would not allow the encounter with Mary Ritchie to discommode him. It was a nuisance to find her there, but it scarcely mattered. Any trouble, and a word or two with his new acquaintances on the Inverness Council would soon put her in her place. He would be bringing a lot of money and work to the town, and he hadn't yet met a council who wouldn't bend over backwards to smooth his path.

Yes, the Balmoral Emporium could be a very profitable venture.

Back home, he kissed his wife and daughter, buffeted Ewan on the shoulder and nodded to Robina and Aeneas. He listened with only half an ear to an edited account of the excursion to the Falls of Foyers, and retreated to his study.

Immediately, the weight of his presence was

felt in the household. The maids did their best to keep out of his way, and Aeneas stayed in the den whenever could. Madeline wondered whether it would be possible to meet Henry in the easy way she had been doing. Conversation over meals was sticky.

In spite of the fact that everything was going according to plan, Duncan did not sleep well. There was a letter from Ogilvy waiting for him, saying that he would be up shortly. Everything seemed in train for a successful expansion. But there were these bouts of giddiness, and a tightness in his right shoulder. They both passed off after a while, but they were unpleasant while they lasted. Then, his mind kept returning to Mary Ritchie and that damned brat of hers, the boy who looked so like Neil.

He hadn't thought of his brother for years—the baby of the family, his mother's blue-eyed boy. How he'd hated him. He thought back to when Jamie was born—another boy, and one who had absorbed all his mother's attention, just like Neil. Even when they were making love, Mary had had one ear open for that wretched baby of hers; and every time he'd fondled her, her breasts spouted out milk—for the boy, not for him. He'd never liked the brat—Ewan was worth ten of him. Thank God he'd insisted that Beatrix have a wet nurse.

He massaged his shoulder uneasily. Perhaps he should have acknowledged Mary; found out what she wanted. He turned in the bed, trying to find a comfortable position, and was aware that his chest was painfully tight. Beatrix was snoring gently by his side. He turned again, but the pillow was hot. In the end, he got up, but, as he did so, a sudden dizzy spell made him grab hold of the bedpost. Slowly, it passed. He stood up carefully and made his way to his dressing-room, holding on to the furniture to steady himself, used his chamber pot, returned, had a drink from the water carafe on his bedside table, and climbed back into bed.

He turned his mind to the commodities he could sell at the emporium. The list grew longer and longer, and eventually he fell into an uneasy sleep.

*　　　*　　　*

Mary's first day at Dr Ross's was a portent of things to come. It seemed to her that Dr Ross was just waiting for his opportunity to pounce. It was not a question of 'if', but 'when'. As soon as she arrived, he invited her into his surgery, drew up a chair close to his and, the moment she sat down, placed his hand on her knee.

She must make her own arrangements with the tradesmen for deliveries, he told her. He would go through the household accounts with her every Friday evening after the evening surgery and he would expect her to stay within budget. The hand squeezed meaningfully. He could see her unease. Well, that didn't displease him; he liked a show of reluctance.

For a moment Mary panicked. What was she to do? If he threw her out she had nowhere to go and no money beyond a shilling or two in her purse, and her savings wouldn't last long. She felt like a rabbit in front of a stoat, paralysed. Eventually, her mouth dry, she said, 'Mr Ogilvy has expressed an interest in my welfare.'

Damn Ogilvy for his interference, thought Dr Ross savagely. Why couldn't he mind his own business? His hand lifted.

Mary closed her eyes in relief. She stumbled to her feet. 'I am sure that you have much to do, Dr Ross,' she managed, and fled.

Dr Ross had an income of about £800 a year and was considered a wealthy and respected citizen. He was never short of apprentices, each of whose fathers happily paid the not inconsiderable premium demanded. The housekeeping budget was reasonable, but not over-generous, and Mary was well aware from her own experience when she had first arrived in Inverness, that she must plan ahead. Coals must be ordered in the summer, when they were cheap, for example; chimneys must be swept in preparation for the winter.

As soon as she left the surgery, she went down to the housekeeper's room and sat down with the account books. It did not take her long to discover that there had been a considerable amount of peculation going on, and either Dr Ross's checking of the books had been slipshod in the extreme, or he had demanded sexual favours as recompense. That would have to stop. She was not prepared to barter her body for the money that the previous housekeeper had been creaming off. She must not go over budget.

The only question was, was the cook involved as well? Mrs Johnstone was a sour-faced woman with sparse grey hair, pulled back tightly in a bun. It was unlikely that she was being called on to warm Dr Ross's bed. On the other hand, she could easily have been abetting the housekeeper's depredations in return for a cut.

She spent the next couple of hours making careful lists: of the goods that came into the house and the shops they came from, and another of alternative shops that might offer a higher commission. She was going to have to do some hard bargaining. Eventually, she went through to the kitchen. Mrs Johnstone was busy cutting up kidneys. Beside her, the fourteen-year-old Ellen, a scraggy girl with thin greasy plaits, was chopping onions. Neither spoke.

'Mrs Johnstone,' said Mary, 'a word with you, if you please.'

Mrs Johnstone's lips tightened, she glared at Mary and then, deliberately, turned back to her kidneys. Ellen giggled nervously. Mary looked coldly at her.

'Sorry,' muttered Ellen.

'Finish those onions in the scullery, Ellen,' said Mary. Ellen left.

'Mrs Johnstone, come into the housekeeper's room, please. I don't think that you'll want Ellen and Minnie to hear what I have to say.'

Mrs Johnstone washed her hands, dried them, took off her apron, all with deliberate slowness, and then followed Mary into the housekeeper's room. Mary shut the door. Mrs Johnstone prepared to be obstructive. Slowly but surely, Mary demolished all the evasions and excuses and extracted from her the names of the tradesmen they dealt with, the percentage they offered, Mrs Johnstone's own cut, where she sold the dripping and for how much, and so on.

'I'm saving for my retirement,' said Mrs Johnstone belligerently.

'And I shall be saving to help my son through university,' said Mary. 'But I am a respectable woman, and I do not want any trouble with Dr Ross . . . I'm sure you understand me.'

Mrs Johnstone sniffed. 'Dripping's cook's perks,' she said. 'And candle ends.'

'Quite. Perks is one thing, greed is another.'

'Maybe things have gone a bit far,' conceded Mrs Johnstone, relieved that this new housekeeper was being sensible. Poor folks had to squeeze a bit extra here and there, otherwise where would they be?

Mary closed the account books. 'I shall go and see these tradesmen and make proper arrangements, and I shall not forget you.' Ellen and Minnie ought to be able to count on a little something for the New Year as well, she thought. A housekeeper was expected to take a bit of commission, that was only fair. Dr Ross's custom was good. His wages were reasonable, but, if he were going to make her life a misery, he should pay for it.

'The important thing is that I keep within budget and that Dr Ross and his apprentices are kept well fed and warm.'

'Aye, a man who likes his food doesn't complain,' said Mrs Johnstone in a friendlier tone. Maybe they could work together, after all. It all depended on the arrangements Mrs Ritchie made with the tradesmen. They'd better be good. Mrs Johnstone fancied she knew how to trip up this little madam if they weren't.

'One more thing,' said Mary. 'When I came to the interview, my bedroom door had a bolt. When I arrived this morning, I saw that it had been removed.'

Mrs Johnstone smirked. 'Dr Ross's orders. In case of fire, he says.' Personally, she thought that Mrs Ritchie was making too much fuss. She was a widow—she knew what was what. Let Dr Ross have his bit of fun and things would be a lot easier. 'If there's nothing else,

Mrs Ritchie, I'll get back to my kitchen,' she said. Mary nodded, and Mrs Johnstone left.

The moment she'd gone Mary put her head in her hands. What should she do? She couldn't sleep in an unsecured room. She just couldn't.

*   *   *

Jamie spent the night at the cottage of a Mrs Macallister, just outside Fidach. Mrs Macallister approved of Jamie: he was a well-mannered young man, with enough Gaelic to make himself understood; speaking English always made her self-conscious. He helped her with feeding the hens and making sure that they were all safely back in the hen house for the night. He sawed some wood and mended a wobbly chair leg. In return, she fed him well, offered him the box bed that had been her son's, and heated some water in the morning so that he could shave.

Jamie ate his porridge with an enthusiasm which gladdened Mrs Macallister's heart, accepted a bannock and some cheese for his lunch, paid her the shilling he owed, and set off. This was it! He'd done all he could. He had his note requesting to see Mr Penicuik, the letters from Inverness Council about his bursary, and from Glasgow University about the scholarship, and Olaf's paper-knife for luck.

It had rained in the night, but it looked as though it would be a fine day. Perhaps he would see his brothers and sister! Would he recognize his father after all this time? He would give up every hope of the allowance just to hear his father say, 'Well done, my boy,' about the scholarship and be proud of him. He knew he had his mother's love, and Olaf's affection, but there was this missing bit, and the nearer he got to Achnagarry, the more he realized just how much he wanted his father's approval.

He arrived at Achnagarry at about eleven o'clock. His first glimpse of the lodge was through the Scots pines on the far side of the River Nevan, and, all at once, his heart began to thump. He hadn't realized that it would be so huge. He stared at the uncompromising granite, the turrets, the battlements, the Gothic windows, and, suddenly, his mouth felt unpleasantly dry.

There was still time to turn back. But what had he to fear? His father need only say that he was not at home. For a moment, Jamie wished that he would. It would be a disappointment, of course, but he would walk round the loch, eat his lunch, and at least see what the place looked like.

He made his way down to the bridge that crossed the river and turned left up the pine cone-covered road that led to Achnagarry Lodge. As he did so, he saw two people

250

coming towards him: a girl, a year or so older than himself, a really pretty one too, with honey-coloured hair and blue eyes, and a younger boy of about twelve.

'Excuse me, is this Achnagarry Lodge?' asked Jamie.

The girl smiled. 'Yes.'

'Is . . . is Mr Pénicuik in, do you know?'

'Yes, Papa's in this morning, isn't he?' She turned to the boy, who nodded.

'Thank you.' It must be them! His half-brother and sister. He wanted to call them back, to say, 'I'm your brother!' It seemed incredible that he could have a brother and sister he'd never met. And they looked so nice!

Feeling that it was a good omen, he walked on with renewed confidence.

Normally, it was Frank's job to see to visitors, but Cook had asked him to move a vegetable hamper for her, so that morning it was Morag. Frank was used to receiving visitors. He would have asked Jamie to wait in the hall, knocked on the study door, delivered the letter, and waited for the response. Morag was terrified of Mr Penicuik and avoided him whenever she could.

'Good morning,' said Morag in careful English. 'What is it ye'll be wanting?' She wasn't sure that this young man should be at the front door at all. Shouldn't he go round the back?

Jamie handed her the note and said, 'I'd like

251

a word with Mr Penicuik, if it is convenient.'

Morag took the note doubtfully. 'I'll be after asking him,' she said. There was something vaguely familiar about the young man, but she couldn't place it. She hated having to interrupt Mr Penicuik when he was in his study. You never knew what mood he'd be in. She stuffed the note into her pocket, smoothed her hair and apron, walked reluctantly to the study, tapped at the door and went in.

'Somebody's after seeing you, sir,' she said. He looked in a bad mood.

Duncan looked up irritably. 'Who is it?'

'He didna say, sir.'

'What does he want?'

'I dinna ken, sir.'

'Didn't you ask, you stupid woman? Oh, very well, send him in.'

Morag left thankfully and went back to the hall. She jerked her head towards the study door and then fled back to the kitchen. Frank should deal with things, she thought. Then she remembered the note.

Jamie swallowed, brushed his hand nervously through his hair and knocked at the door.

'Yes!'

Jamie entered and stared. For a moment, the man behind the desk looked like a print he'd once seen of the minotaur, with its thick neck and massive shoulders. It was the man who'd pushed him so roughly out of the way on the ferry. He tried to reconcile the man in front of him with his half-remembered image of his father in the hall at Musselburgh, turned blue and yellow through the stained glass of the door, but they wouldn't fit. This man was a stranger. It couldn't be his father.

Duncan looked up, half-rose and then sat down again. Jamie could see his knuckles whiten as he clutched the edge of the desk. 'Why have you come back?' Duncan's voice was harsh. 'You're dead! Damn you, I saw you die in that flood.'

Jamie's throat went dry. He scanned the desk, but there was no sign of his letter. What had gone wrong? 'I . . . I'm Ritchie,' he said, swallowing. 'I'm James Ritchie . . . I—'

The man rose slowly and seemed to swell, like the minotaur Jamie had thought him. The face went purple. Suddenly, a huge fist banged down on the desk. 'How *dare* you!' he shouted. 'You miserable, misbegotten cur! How *dare* you come here? I told your mother I wanted nothing to do with you, d'you hear?'

'Told my mother . . .?' stammered Jamie, his face white.

'On Wednesday, damn her!'

'On Wednesday!' Jamie, feeling as if he'd stepped into some nightmare, clutched at a chair back for support.

Rage made the man opposite him shake. Flecks of foam appeared on his lips. 'Clear off!' he shouted. 'Make yourself scarce! I always hated you, did you know that? I was the firstborn, but then *you* came along and it was you who was the favourite, the mother's boy. I could never do anything right, it was always you. I tell you, I was glad when you died!'

Jamie took a step backwards. What was he talking about? He had the confused feeling that if only this man *understood*, everything would be all right. He hadn't meant to intrude. He'd written a letter . . . 'I . . . I'm James Ritchie,' he repeated, helplessly.

'Ritchie?' repeated Duncan, shaking his head slowly. 'No, he's only a child.'

'I'm seventeen,' said Jamie. 'I didn't know you'd seen my mother—'

'Liar! She *did* tell you, and you want to screw some money out of me, don't you? You think that you can blackmail me. But I'm a hard man to get the better of, and so you will find.'

The man's a monster, thought Jamie. 'No! I just wanted—'

Duncan gave a roar of frustrated rage, which reverberated round the room, lurched round the desk and picked up a heavy brass cigar case.

'But . . . but I'm your *son!*' cried Jamie, taking a step backwards. The man coming towards him was so terrifying that Jamie reached for Olaf's paper-knife.

'You're *nothing!*' roared Duncan. 'A bastard! A nameless whelp who shouldn't have been born!'

He hurled the case straight at Jamie. It caught him a glancing blow on the side of the head and he fell, blood pouring down his face. He grasped the knife and, as Duncan began to kick him, he stabbed upwards, blindly. He felt the knife slide in as Duncan grabbed hold of his throat and began to squeeze. His vision began to blur. Suddenly, there was a gasping sound and the hands loosed their grip. Jamie, his eyes blinded by blood, raised his head. Duncan had fallen to his knees and was clutching his shoulder. At that moment, the door opened and two women stood in the doorway. One of them began to shriek, a high-pitched keening sound.

Duncan fell to the floor, groaning. 'Neil!' It was scarcely more than a gasp. The woman ran over to kneel beside him. Then she looked up. 'You've killed him!' she cried. She stared, horrified, at the bloodied paper-knife and cried, 'Murderer!'

Jamie tried to get up, but he was blinded by blood and swaying with dizziness. He could scarcely swallow for the bruises on his throat. He couldn't speak.

The other woman came over and helped Jamie to rise. 'Come with me,' she said quietly. She took his arm and led him out of the room. As they left, they heard shriek upon shriek behind them and the wild jangling of the bell pull.

*   *   *

That morning, in Dunlairg Castle, Lord and Lady Invershiel were preparing to go for a drive. Lord Invershiel was feeling better than he had for some time and, as it had turned out fine, it seemed a good opportunity to take the air. It was nearly eleven by the time they set out, and Lord Invershiel had been carefully tucked up in the gig and provided with a rug and a flask of brandy in case he should suddenly have a turn. Edward came out to help him and held open the door of the gig for Lady Invershiel, who was driving.

Lord and Lady Invershiel were both impervious to the jolting over the uneven road surface, and the gig bowled along the lochside very pleasantly. They passed Aeneas with his fishing rod, and waved. Madeline and Henry, who were hidden by a large lichen-covered rock, heard the gig and sat in silence for a few minutes.

'Damned shame we had to let Glenogie go,' said Lord Invershiel, nodding towards the moor on his right, which he had sold to Penicuik. Lady Invershiel shrugged. Henry had had to be supported through his law studies and pupillage. What else could they have done?

'Now John has this damn fool idea that he wants to be a journalist!' said Lord Invershiel, shaking his head. Scum, in his opinion, feeding

256

like a louse on other people's misery and digging up dirt where they had no business to be.

'He must do something,' pointed out his wife. 'You don't want him to help you with the estate.' She didn't approve any more than her husband did, but she saw her son's point. He should be doing *something*.

'I'm not at death's door yet, thank the Lord.'

'John can hardly be expected to go on kicking his heels here.'

'A son of mine working for a *newspaper*!'

They had reached the end of the loch and turned left over the bridge and began to go up the hill. They both stopped talking. Lady Invershiel, because there was a series of bends and she had to concentrate on her driving, and Lord Invershiel because he was staring at Achnagarry Lodge and wondering how Penicuik had managed to create anything so ugly. Instead of the elegant Georgian house, with its charming pillared portico, there was now something which looked like some damned Gothic castle of Albert's—Lord Invershiel had never been an admirer of the late Prince Consort.

As the gig with its puffing horse finally reached level ground by the ruins of Pheemie's cottage, Lady Invershiel's eye was caught by a figure in front of them. A young man, his head bandaged, was walking slowly, dragging his feet, and every now and then he staggered. Then, as they drew closer, he lurched towards the side of the road and crumpled up.

In a minute, the gig was level. Lady Invershiel handed the reins to her husband and climbed down. The young man was trying to rise. He was good-looking, Lady Invershiel noticed, but his face was white and drawn and blood was seeping through the bandage. But it was his eyes that held her. They looked as though he had been through a nightmare. They had seen too much.

'What happened?' asked Lady Invershiel, never one to beat about the bush.

'Mr Penicuik! He tried to kill me!' His voice shook with the horror of that moment. In spite of himself, his eyes filled with tears. 'He's my father, and he tried to kill me!'

'Your *father*!' echoed Lady Invershiel.

'Bless my soul!' Lord Invershiel leaned forward. 'What is your name, my boy?'

'James Ritchie, sir.' Jamie had managed to stand and was clutching at the gig wheel for support. 'I . . . I've got to get on . . . They'll come after me . . .'

Lord Invershiel exchanged a look with his wife. 'Get in,' he said. 'You can't go anywhere like that. Shouldn't wonder if you're not concussed. Come on, boy, you're thin enough to squeeze in.'

Lady Invershiel helped him in and then climbed up and began to turn the gig. Jamie

258

leaned back and closed his eyes. He had ruined everything.

'Now tell me why you were visiting Penicuik,' said Lord Invershiel. He unscrewed the brandy flask and held it to Jamie's lips.

Jamie took a careful sip, for his throat hurt. 'Thank you, sir.' He began to feel a little better, at least, not so dizzy. He embarked on his story and brought out the two letters he'd not been able to show his father. Lord Invershiel read them out loud so that his wife could hear, folded them up and handed them back. 'Bad business,' he said, shaking his head. It was a foolish thing for young Ritchie to have done, but, in his view, no gentleman left his bastards unprovided for. He patted Jamie's knee comfortingly.

Lady Invershiel's hands held the reins and guided the pony, but her mind was very differently engaged.

It was no more than two miles back to Dunlairg, but before they had done more than half a mile, Jamie had fainted, and he was still unconscious when they reached the castle. As they drew up, they saw Edward. He came over.

'We found this young man by the road,' said Lady Invershiel. 'He fell whilst climbing.'

Edward looked at Jamie, assessing his condition rapidly. 'He needs attention,' he said. 'I'll deal with him.' He'd dealt with many climbing accidents in his time, and this one looked nasty. It crossed his mind briefly that somebody had already helped him, for there was a bandage neatly wrapped round the young man's head, through which blood had seeped, but he pushed the thought to one side.

'He was rather light-headed in the gig,' said Lady Invershiel. 'Spoke a lot of nonsense.'

Lord Invershiel looked sharply at her, but said nothing.

'It's not unusual,' said Edward. 'Leave him with me.' He eased Jamie out of the gig and picked him up.

'Take him to the West Turret,' said Lady Invershiel. 'I'll give orders for a bed to be made up.'

When Edward and his burden had gone, Lord Invershiel turned to his wife. 'What are you about, Mary? Aren't you going to tell Edward what the boy said? He was speaking the truth, you know.' Lord Invershiel had heard rumours about Penicuik years ago, and he had not been surprised by Jamie's story.

'Of course it's true!' snapped Lady Invershiel. 'Leave everything to me! I have an idea at the back of my mind, and it will not do for rumours about this young man to get out.'

Lord Invershiel nodded. He agreed with her there.

What Lady Invershiel did not say was that, in her view, Edward could be uncomfortably straitlaced sometimes, especially where marital irregularities were concerned. She had plans which involved James Ritchie, and she did not

260

want them spoilt by Edward's tiresome conscience. She would tell him nothing, and neither would she mention anything beyond the bare fact that they had taken in an injured climber to anybody else in the house.

She was playing for high stakes and she did not intend to ruin her chances.

*   *   *

Robina's Journal   Thursday 15 August
The most dreadful day, and God knows what is going to happen now. I'm desperately worried about young James. When I'd patched him up, I left him in the little room by the back door and went round to the stables and saddled the old deer pony—fortunately, Tam wasn't there—but all took longer than I meant. When I went back for James, he'd disappeared. I looked everywhere. I thought he might have fallen down the bank to the River Nevan—it's pretty steep, but there was no sign of him. I took the pony back to the stables and then I went up the glen, but there to nothing. He can't *have gone far—he was in no state to do so.*

Could Donald have seen him and taken him in?

Poor Madeline! She doesn't know anything, and I don't want to destroy her happiness, but if word gets out all will be over between her and Henry. No man, and particularly one who is a rising young barrister, is going to want a wife whose father tried to kill his bastard son. And it didn't help that when I got back to Achnagarry, Beatrix was upstairs hysterically shrieking that somebody called Neil had tried to murder Duncan. Fortunately, only Morag was with her, and I don't think she understood a word—she was looking terrified out of her wits, poor thing. Somebody must have carried Duncan upstairs— and he's no lightweight. He looked awful.

Morag crept up to me, and handed me the note that James had given her and which she had forgotten to give to Duncan. I read it out to her in Gaelic. I know it wasn't kind, because she threw her apron over her head and began to wail, but I had *to impress on her not to talk about James's visit. If she'd given Duncan the letter, he would have refused to see James, and this whole dreadful episode might have been avoided. Anyway, she promised to say nothing. I rang the bell for Flora, waited until she'd come, took Morag downstairs and told her to see what she could do about getting rid of the blood on the study carpet. Suggested salt.*

Later:

Duncan still alive, though very muzzy and seems to have forgotten the whole episode. His right side is affected, though it may pass. Serves him right. I wish he'd died. A man who can attack his own son in such a way! He's a monster.

At luncheon, Aeneas and Ewan very curious. Beatrix not there. I said that their father had had

262

an apoplectic fit. Neither seemed very concerned. Later, I went to the kitchen and gave the same version. Reading between the lines, none of them wanted to get involved. I dare say they had all felt Duncan's rages before. Someone, Frank I think, said what about the shouting and the visitor? I said that he had had nothing to do with it, he had already left and Mr Penicuik was shouting at myself and Mrs Penicuik. They believed me— which doesn't say much for Duncan's family life! All the same, rumours will go round and who knows what will come out?

'At least the maids will get some peace now,' Ishbel said later.

I suppose my own position is much the same as Madeline's. It's true I'm only a cousin, but I'm staying here and it's my family. Edward has to think about the effect of any scandal on Charlotte. I know that. I'm trying not to think about it.

Later:

I feel like a murderess. I looked for James all over. I don't know what to do. I could put the word out via Donald, but supposing Beatrix offers a reward? I'm sure that Donald wouldn't betray him, but there are others . . .

Oh God, it's all awful!

*　　　*　　　*

Later that evening, as Robina was going to bed, there was a perfunctory knock at her

263

door, and Beatrix came in. She threw Robina a furious glance and began to pace angrily up and down.

'Where were you?' she snapped.

'What do you mean?'

'Earlier. I shouted for you and you weren't here. This can't wait, Robina. That man has got to be found; he's a murderer and he could be dangerous. I want you to get dressed and go over to the Frasers, tell Donald that every able-bodied man must be out at first light to scour the hillside. Now!'

'Why me?' asked Robina, prevaricating.

'You speak the language. I've never been very good at it, and you saw him, Neil somebody. You can describe him: big, thick-set, wild-looking . . .'

'You're mad!' said Robina, with conviction. 'For God's sake, Beatrix. Don't you know who he was? Let this get out and there will be the most enormous scandal and you can say good-bye to any hopes of Madeline's marriage—to anybody!'

'That will do!' shouted Beatrix, her voice rising. 'I invited you here to be of some use, and so far you've done nothing. And, what's more, Mr Gillespie reported that he saw you in a boat with Mr Mountsorrel! You knew I meant him for Madeline and you've deliberately gone behind my back—'

'How dare you!' cried Robina, pulling off her night cap which suddenly seemed too restricting. 'How dare you listen to that horrible little sneak. He's a rat! For God's sake, Mr Mountsorrel invited me to come out in the boat! What if he did? He'd asked Madeline and she'd said no. What was I supposed to do? In any case, why bring this up now?'

'You should do as I say!' shouted Beatrix, almost beside herself with rage. 'Get up, you lazy creature, and go and deal with Donald.'

Robina reined in her temper with an effort. 'Beatrix! The young man whom Duncan attacked was his son! Now do you see why nothing must get out?'

'Nonsense! He said so, I suppose! The law will soon put a stop to that!'

'It's true. I've known of his existence for years. Grandmama told me. Mr Ogilvy arranged for an allowance for him and his mother, a year or so after Grandpapa died.'

Beatrix turned white and sat down abruptly. 'What!'

Robina told her the story. 'Nothing must get out,' she ended. 'If Duncan dies it will be because of the apoplexy—he was barely touched by the paper-knife, I saw the cut: it couldn't have killed him. Think! Do you really want a court case with Duncan's affair with this Mary Ritchie open to the public gaze? Duncan attacked James. The wound was extremely nasty and it could kill him. What will *that* look like in court? "Businessman kills natural son!" What is that going to do for Madeline's chances of marriage? Or for any of you?'

'Oh God!' whispered Beatrix. 'I . . . I should have thought . . . when Duncan said something about Neil . . .'

'Neil?'

'His younger brother who died. Duncan hardly ever speaks of him, they . . . they didn't get on.' Beatrix rubbed her face with her hand. All of a sudden, she looked older. 'If this got out, it would be a disaster.'

*   *   *

Robina's Journal   Wednesday, 16 August
Another awful day. Mr Ogilvy arrived. Beatrix swept him off to talk to him and I wasn't able to see him—Mr O. I mean, I want to tell him about what Ishbel said about Wallace. I don't know whether he can do anything about it, but he should know. Beatrix was back to her old self this morning. I think she regretted her outburst last night, at least, she didn't allude to it and she wouldn't meet my eye. Duncan is recovering, worse luck.

Morag found James's paper-knife under the chair. I took it. We could certainly do without that sort of evidence!

What is even worse is that I had to tell Madeline the truth. She insisted on knowing. She half knew anyway. She'd heard something from a friend in Edinburgh about the existence of a bastard son and she put two and two together. She said that she half-recognized James. 'He's got Papa's nose, and he looks a bit like Aeneas, or what Aeneas will look like when he's grown up,' she said.

Poor girl. 'I was so happy yesterday,' she said pathetically.

Decided that I had to tell Donald and Mhairi. I swore them to secrecy, and I trust them. I know it won't go any further. Donald said that he hadn't heard anything about James being picked up—and he would know. He also said that he'd have heard if there was a body—and that's true, too. There's nothing a man like Donald doesn't hear about sooner or later.

Mhairi got quite fierce. She called Duncan 'a black-hearted devil'!

I felt a lot better.

I've just had a letter from Signor Arnolfini. A Mrs Lambourn will be looking for a lady companion after her daughter's wedding in September. I think I met her once. Rather a bossy woman. I should be used to those! Still, beggars can't be choosers, and at least it will be Italy, and warm.

I don't know what to do. It's not what I want any more, but I daren't hope that Edward will . . . Not now. In any case, even if he did, how could I accept knowing that this awful scandal could erupt at any moment?

The following morning, Robina rose as soon as day broke, got dressed, took her grandfather's old field telescope from Duncan's study (not without an inward shudder, but the room was free of blood and the furniture put back) and left the house before anybody saw her. Once the day began, she'd be drawn back into the awfulness of it all, but, for an hour or so, she could be free. Already the days had a touch of autumn. The early morning air had a nip in it and the birch trees down by the loch were beginning to turn a pale gold. She turned up the hill and climbed swiftly, and soon reached the deserted shielings and the derelict shepherd's hut. Just over the hill was Loch Tearmann and the crannog, but she wasn't going there today. She had chosen the shepherd's hut because it was a good vantage point.

She sat down on one of the broken-down walls, took out the telescope and began, systematically, to scan the hillside opposite. Loch Nevan was agitated by small waves, for the wind had got up and grey clouds were scudding over the sky. It would rain before the day was out. She knew that Donald was far more likely to spot James than she was, but, all the same, she couldn't help looking for him as well. Above her a kestrel hovered. Soon it would be autumn, and the meadow pipit, wheatear and golden plover would leave for the winter and the moor would be left to the grouse and hoodies.

Smoke was curling out of one of the chimneys of Nevan House. How dare Murdo crawl to Beatrix with his tales? Did he have nothing better to do than to peer at her through his father's telescope, for how else could he have seen who was in the boat at that distance? Murdo was one person she would be glad never to see again. Thank God that youthful engagement had come to nothing.

Where could James have gone? The telescope moved carefully over the landscape, alert to any patch of white, but all she saw were sheep.

She lowered the telescope and, as she did so, her gaze caught a movement on the road along the loch. A distant figure was walking, moving swiftly, with self-confident steps. That couldn't be James, surely? Her heartbeat began to quicken. As she watched, the man looked up, saw her, and immediately began to climb the hill. Robina started to smile. The kestrel moved off. Whatever small creature it had been after was safe for another day. The sun came out from behind a cloud. She closed the telescope.

Edward's head appeared and then the rest of him. 'Good morning, Miss Drummond!'

'Mr Mountsorrel! You're up early.'

'So are you.'

'I don't often get much time to myself,' Robina explained. 'I'm taking it while I can.'

Edward sat down beside her. 'I'm glad to find you alone,' he said. 'I've been wanting to talk to you.'

'Oh?'

Edward gazed out over the loch for a moment, then he turned to her. There was something in the expression of those tawny eyes that brought colour to her checks. He reached out for her hand. 'I love you,' he said, simply. 'In fact, ever since our er . . . unconventional . . . meeting on the crannog, I've been thinking of little else.'

Robina stared down at her hands. Edward loved her! Joy rushed through her like a spring tide, swirling into all her hidden places. She looked up shyly.

'Say you love me, too,' he begged.

'Yes, I do,' whispered Robina. It sounded so strange, hearing him plead like that. She'd never expected this to happen to her. She'd built her life around the assumption that love was what happened to other people.

Edward put his arm around her.

'We'd better move,' said Robina, suddenly remembering Murdo's telescope.

Edward laughed, 'Too visible, eh? But I doubt whether there's more than a few sheep to see us.' But he stood up and followed Robina down the hill towards Loch Tearmann.

As soon as they were out of sight of Nevan

Lodge, Edward pulled her towards a flat stone and they sat down. 'Now,' he said. He put his arm around her again, tilted her face up with his other hand and kissed her. Ah! he thought, and all his doubts and hesitations melted away. This was it. This was the woman he wanted.

Time passed. A bee droned by. A lizard scuttled out and sunned itself on a nearby stone, but Edward and Robina were oblivious. Eventually, Edward raised his head and took her face in his hands, smoothing her cheeks with his thumbs. 'That was wonderful.'

'Yes,' said Robina, slightly breathless. She'd been kissed before, once by a drunken Russian count, and once by Mrs Leigh-Egerton's nephew, one summer evening after the opera, but neither incident was the toe-curling experience she'd just been through.

Edward began to kiss her again. Robina put her hands on his shoulders to steady herself and, pretty soon, they crept round his neck. Edward moved to hold her more closely.

Eventually, he said, 'Will you marry me?'

Reality struck Robina like a shower of cold water. Duncan. The horror of the attack. James. Where was he? She had come out to find him. 'I . . . I *wish* I could,' she said. 'Oh, *how* I wish it! But it's impossible.'

'Is there some impediment?' asked Edward, smiling. Perhaps Lady Invershiel had been as forthright to her as she had to him. 'A hidden husband, perhaps?'

Robina gave a shaky laugh. 'Of course not!'

'Then what?' He held her hand in both of his.

Robina hesitated. 'I am worried about a young man who was here a day or so ago,' she began, aware that it sounded very lame. 'He . . . he was hurt. Unfortunately, he left before I was able to look after him properly.'

Edward frowned. His hands dropped. 'What was his name?'

Robina's eyes flew to his face. 'Ritchie.' Had he seen him?

'Lord and Lady Invershiel found him yesterday when they were out for a drive. Apparently he'd fallen whilst trying to climb Carn Dhu, young fool. They brought him back to the castle. I've looked at his wound. There's always a danger of internal bleeding, but I think he'll be all right. He's terribly shaken and upset, of course, but he's young and strong and he'll almost certainly recover.'

'Oh! Thank God!' cried Robina, and burst into tears. Reluctantly, Edward put his arm around her and gave her his handkerchief. He had a sudden vision of Betsy crying, tears which always seemed to end in hysterics.

'I never cry!' said Robina angrily, hiccuping with the effort to stop.

Edward smiled, his heart lightening. No, she was made of sterner stuff! Anyway, what was wrong with a few tears? He thought of how Charlotte had cried when their favourite pack pony had had to be put down. Dammit, he had shed a tear or two himself. He bent down to kiss Robina's hot, damp cheek. 'Tears are good for you—in moderation, of course!'

'You don't cry, surely?' sniffed Robina, drying her eyes.

'Of course I cry! When our favourite pack pony died, Charlotte and I both cried!'

Robina smiled, he was a surprising man, she thought. That's why she loved him. Her head was resting on Edward's shoulder, and she felt as if she'd come home. But it was a stolen pleasure. How much did Edward know? Did he know who James really was? If not, should she tell him? She remembered Madeline's stricken face. She couldn't tell him. She couldn't risk it getting out. There was far too much at stake.

But she would have to tell him something.

As she was hesitating, Edward said, 'I don't understand what Ritchie has got to do with your marrying me?'

'Mr Ritchie didn't fall whilst rock climbing,' she said carefully, 'he was attacked by Mr Penicuik.'

Edward laughed. 'Nonsense. Lord and Lady Invershiel found him at the bottom of the scree near the ruins of that old cottage.'

'He was attacked by Mr Penicuik,' repeated Robina desperately. 'I bandaged him up as well as I could. Mr Penicuik had an apoplectic fit, which was just as well, because otherwise

273

he might have killed Ritchie.'

It was a preposterous tale, thought Edward. He remembered one of Betsy's stories, something about the carriage being overturned by a bullock, which had meant that she didn't get back home until nearly midnight. He'd learnt not to cross-question her too closely.

'Don't you understand?' cried Robina. 'If Mr Penicuik dies, and word gets out that he attacked Mr Ritchie, there'll be the most appalling scandal. Even worse, if Mr Ritchie dies and Mr Penicuik is accused? Who is going to want to know the Penicuiks then? And I am probably guilty of trying to pervert the course of justice by getting Mr Ritchie away. I can't let you and Charlotte become involved. I just *can't.*'

'Come now,' said Edward, coolly, 'you are over-reacting. I really cannot see that it affects us if Ritchie was attacked, as you suggest, by your cousin's husband.' It all sounded most unlikely.

'You don't believe me?' Robina stared at him, shocked.

'Ritchie will recover and be off within a week or so. Penicuik will either recover or not, and, frankly, I don't care,' said Edward, evading the question.

'But if word gets out!' cried Robina, frantically. He doesn't know the worst thing, she thought, that James is Penicuik's son, and I can't tell him. Supposing it got back to the

Invershiels. There's Madeline to think of. Then she thought, he doesn't believe me.

Robina, if you don't care about me enough to have me for your husband and let me deal with all this, then just say so.' He had a sudden memory of Betsy trying to cover up that last indiscretion, the night before she died. 'Are you hiding something from me?' he demanded suddenly.

Robina looked away guiltily. 'Can't you trust me?'

'I'm not sure I can,' said Edward, releasing her. There was something she was not telling him. His mind took another jump. 'What is Ritchie to you?'

'N . . . nothing! I'd never met him before!'

'But you know about him?'

'Yes! No! I *can't* tell you!' cried Robina. 'If it were just me, I would. Of course, I would. But there are others involved. I just can't.'

'So there *is* something?'

Robina stood up, 'I can't marry you,' she said, her voice shaking. 'I wish I could. I wish I could be open, but it's not my secret. If you can't trust me, then that's a poor basis for a marriage, isn't it?'

'Trust works both ways,' said Edward, drily. He stood up. 'This is getting us nowhere.' He was not going to get involved ever again in the sort of emotional mess Betsy left him in. 'I think we'd better forget this whole conversation.'

'Yes,' said Robina, dully. She felt suddenly cold. 'I shan't forget it, but I shall behave as if I have.' She stood up. 'I must be getting back. I don't want to be missed.'

'You go on,' said Edward in an unemotional voice. 'I shall stay here for a while.' He stood up and looked down at her white face. 'I'm sorry about all this. It's not the way I wanted it to end.'

Robina said nothing. If she'd tried to speak, she would have broken down again. She turned and stumbled down the hill, her eyes blinded by tears.

*　　　*　　　*

Jamie lay in bed in the little turret room at Dunlairg Castle and looked, without much interest, at the small Gothic arched windows. His head ached abominably and, whenever he turned his head, he felt dizzy. There was a painful void at the back of his mind, something that he did not want to remember, which lay there, like an incubus. How did he come to be here? Nothing seemed to make much sense.

There were footsteps, then the door opened and a man with eyes the colour of honey came in.

'Good,' said the man. 'You're awake. How are you feeling?'

'Weak as a kitten.' Jamie winced as he tried to sit up.

The man helped him up and put another pillow behind him. 'Your head needs to be raised,' he said. 'Now, let's see how things are getting on.' He unwound the bandage carefully and felt the bruise. 'It's not soft. That's good news. You'll have the devil of a headache for a while, and you'll have to stay put for a week or so.'

'A week!' echoed Jamie. 'I've got to . . .' What was it? He had somewhere to go, he was sure.

The man saw his agitation. 'It's all right. You're on your way to the university at Glasgow, but term doesn't start yet. You have plenty of time.'

Jamie relaxed. It didn't mean much, but it felt right. 'Who are you? Do I know you?'

'I'm Mountsorrel. This is Dunlairg Castle and we're both guests here. I'm looking after you because I'm used to dealing with accidents. Now, if I help you, could you manage to eat some broth?'

'I'll try.' He lay back, a worried frown on his face. There was something lurking in the corner of his mind, something he'd got horribly wrong. He winced and closed his eyes momentarily against the memory. But the man was holding out a spoonful of broth, and Jamie did not want to talk, so he allowed himself to be fed, and then he slept again. When Edward next came up, Jamie managed to smile, though his head still hurt. Things were a bit clearer.

'How do you know I'm on my way to Glasgow?'

'You had some letters in your jacket pocket.'

What letters? Something else hovered and then slid away again. He would think about it later. He pulled himself up. It was late afternoon and the room was darkening. Edward had brought up a paraffin lamp.

'What happened?' asked Jamie.

Edward hesitated, and then said, 'You had a severe blow on the head and considerable bruising around the neck. We'll talk about it when you're stronger.' He unscrewed a jar of ointment and began to anoint the bruises. Jamie winced. 'Sorry, but it will help.'

'There was a lady who bandaged me up,' said Jamie suddenly. He patted his head gingerly. 'Is she here?'

'That was Lady Invershiel, I expect,' said Edward, frowning. He didn't want to think about that bandage—it raised too many uncomfortable questions. 'Now, I'm going to leave you. One of the maids will be up soon with tea and muffins.' He left.

A few minutes later, Jamie heard a furious whispered argument on the stairs, and then the door opened and a young girl came in with the tray. She put it down on the bedside table and looked at him, her head on one side like a small bird.

'I'm Charlotte,' she said. 'I'm not supposed to be here, but I wanted to see you.'

'I'm Jamie.' There'd been another girl he'd seen, he was sure, but a different one. 'Have I seen you before?'

Charlotte shook her head. 'You've seen my papa. He's been looking after you. I broke my arm once, and he set it. He's very good at treating sick people.' She suddenly remembered her duties, poured his tea and then gave him a muffin neatly cut up into small pieces.

'This is good,' said Jamie appreciatively.

'I know. Cook has a secret recipe which she won't tell anybody.'

'Why did you want to see me?' asked Jamie next. His head ached, and the memories were still too painful to look at, but this girl, sitting on his bed like an interested robin, made a pleasant change from lying there trying not to think.

'I like to know what's going on, and they *always* think I'm too young,' said Charlotte promptly. 'And you needn't think that I'm a chatterbox, because I'm not.'

'If you find out what's going on, I wish you'd tell me,' said Jamie humorously. 'I'm not even sure where I am.'

Charlotte opened her mouth and then closed it again. Her father had impressed on her that the young man must not be allowed to get agitated.

'I suppose you're not going to tell me either!' said Jamie, feeling rather better. He didn't often talk to girls and this was a friendly one, and pretty, too. 'I know this is a castle.'

'Yes, it's very old and the stairs go round and round like a corkscrew. You're very high up here. I have a turret room, too, and you can see for miles.'

'Do you live here? No, I remember, you're a guest.'

'Yes. Lord Invershiel is a relation, though quite a distant one. He owns the castle. Then there's his wife, and their sons, John and Henry. I expect you'll see them when you're better.'

'A real lord!' Jamie didn't think he'd ever met a lord.

'He's only a baron, that's the lowest sort of lord,' explained Charlotte, 'and they're terribly poor. They were on the wrong side in the Forty-Five.'

'He has a castle, though.' Suddenly, Jamie remembered the old two-roomed apartment and the tiny room he'd slept in. Where was it? But then it vanished and he couldn't pull it back. He turned his head away.

'I'm sorry,' whispered Charlotte, seeing how pale he was. 'I . . . I didn't mean to upset you.'

'I need to be alone,' said Jamie, and closed his eyes to shut her out. He had an awful feeling that he might start to cry.

Charlotte gathered the tea things together, picked up the tray and tiptoed away.

CHAPTER EIGHT

Mary's first week at Dr Ross's wore on. Dr Ross had not come up to her bedroom, but she couldn't help thinking that he was merely biding his time. He certainly hadn't stopped his attentions. Every time he passed her, a pudgy hand would reach out to squeeze her buttocks or paw a breast. She put a chair under her door knob when she went to bed. It would do no more than warn her of any entry into her room, but it made her feel marginally safer. All the same, she found it difficult to sleep, and, as the days passed, her eyes looked smudged with tiredness.

She wished Jamie would write. Things would be easier to bear once she'd heard from him. But she must not expect an early letter; he had warned her that posting it might be difficult.

By Thursday, she was beginning to feel light-headed from lack of sleep, and when Dr Ross's hand reached to fondle her in the corridor outside his consulting-room, her patience snapped. 'Please keep your hands to yourself,' she said tartly. She was tired of sticking to a lady-like silence.

'Can't you take a bit of teasing?' asked Dr Ross, fingering his moustache. 'I shall want to see the accounts tomorrow at nine o'clock sharp.'

'Certainly, Doctor,' said Mary, colouring with anger.

'You're blushing, Mrs Ritchie!' he said with a smirk, and went into his consulting-room.

'Detestable man!' muttered Mary, as she went though to the kitchen.

Ellen, who was standing at the kitchen table and grating sugar from the sugar cone, heard her and looked up. 'Ye need a row of pins up here, Mistress,' she said, patting her thin chest.

Mary saw a few pins in her bodice. 'Does he pester you, too?' she asked, shocked. Ellen was only fourteen.

Ellen shrugged. It had been far worse in the workhouse. 'He called me to his bedroom once, but I didna go.' She shared a room with Minnie and they had refused to be separated. Later, when Mary looked, she saw that Minnie, too, had a row of pins.

Mrs Johnstone, who was busy making pastry, sniffed. Dr Ross had never tried to paw *her*, and she was inclined to think that they were making a pother about nothing. She had thawed somewhat towards Mary. The new arrangements with the tradesmen were satisfactory, better in some cases than they were before. When the bills were settled at the end of the month, there would be a good commission coming her way. 'Have ye heard from your son, Mrs Ritchie?' she asked.

Mary shook her head, and tried to ignore a pang of anxiety. 'I'm not really expecting anything just yet,' she said, trying to smile. 'I'm not worrying. After all, he's on holiday, I expect he's got better things to do than write to his mother!'

That afternoon, she went down to the haberdashers. She would buy some suitable pins, and see if she could find a good long hat pin as well. It was a relief to get out of the house. Later that afternoon, she would have to do the accounts—and they must be correct down to the last penny. She was not looking forward to presenting them for Dr Ross's scrutiny the following morning.

She was just coming out of the haberdashers, when a figure she recognized came rolling up the road.

'Mr Hamnavoe!' she said, smiling.

He stopped. They shook hands.

'I've been buying pins and a hat pin,' said Mary.

'Having problems with Ross, are ye?' said Olaf at once. He saw her colour mount and added, 'He has a reputation, and ye are a bonny lass—no offence meant.'

'It's difficult,' confided Mary. 'I . . . I can't sleep. There was a bolt on my door when I came for the interview, but it's been removed—in case of fire.'

Olaf shook his head. 'I'm sorry.' The man was a menace. Why didn't he visit the whores by the docks, like a sensible man, and stop pestering poor Mrs Ritchie? 'Have ye heard from Jamie?' he asked.

'Not yet. I'm trying not to expect anything too soon. I dare say the post isn't what it should be in the country.' She gave a bright reassuring smile.

Olaf nodded. 'I'm not worried, ye understand. He'll manage fine, will Jamie, but ye'll tell me when ye hear?'

'Of course. But how shall I find you?' He couldn't come to Dr Ross's. A man of Mr Hamnavoe's reputation knocking at the door and asking for her would destroy her own, shaky, respectability.

'A friend of mine, Alec Burns, is sexton at the English church. Ye go there, I believe?'

Mary nodded. She didn't ask how he knew; she was well aware that she had been an object of interest ever since she'd arrived in the town. A widow arriving with her son was always potentially suspicious. 'I'll leave word with him,' she promised.

The following morning, Mary brought the housekeeping accounts through to Dr Ross's study and watched nervously, her nails digging into her palms, while he went through them. He did it twice, making notes on a piece of paper, and she could see his frown deepen. What was wrong with them?

Eventually he spoke. 'These seem to be in order.' The accounts were accurate, down to the last penny. There was nothing which needed to be 'paid for'. He pushed the book across the desk. 'Take it.'

'You haven't signed it, Doctor.' Mary pushed it back.

'Oh, very well.' He pulled the book towards him and scrawled his signature.

'And the date,' added Mary.

*   *   *

Robina's Journal   *Friday 18 August*
I hadn't realized just how painful it would be, loving Edward. I feel as if I'm carrying a huge bruise over my heart. I can't bear to think of what I've lost—the chance of love, having a proper home of my own—something I've never had—of making a life with him. That awful quarrel—no, misunderstanding! He didn't believe me! Worse, he didn't trust me either. I've gone over and over it all, and I don't see what else I could have done? I had to say no. I love him. I just couldn't bring shame and God knows what spiteful gossip down on him and Charlotte.

I don't think he even listened. I supposed he's never experienced that sort of gossip, he doesn't understand what it would have been like—but I know. Grandmama and I had a very small dose of it in Nairn, when word went round about Grandfather's will. It was nothing compared with what this would be, yet it was unpleasant enough to make us want to leave Nairn. It's the lowered voices which stop whenever you walk past; the spiteful remarks; the picking over of every tiny detail about your life. Edward just doesn't know—but Charlotte would feel it. If this awful business came out and we married, and I brought out Charlotte, there would be houses where we would not be welcome; we would never know whether somebody was genuinely 'not at home', or whether they were not receiving us—and watching our carriage depart through the lace curtains.

The simple fact that I am connected by marriage to Duncan would be enough to put a question mark over Charlotte's head as a suitable bride. Edward might be affected too. At the moment, he does not find it too difficult to find a patron or some institution to fund an expedition. If he married me, he might find that, suddenly, he was not 'sound'. A man with a wife from a questionable family is a man at a disadvantage.

And I didn't even tell him the worst thing— that James is Duncan's son.

Edward accused me of not trusting him to sort things out. As if it were that simple! God, that it were so! It hurts, desperately, that we have quarrelled, but it hurts even more that I am so misunderstood.

How horribly swiftly things happen. A young man comes, innocently, to see his long-lost father—and the consequences are catastrophic. James could never have meant it—but his coming has hurt the lives of an awful lot of people. Madeline is especially vulnerable. Why is it the women who always pay the price?

No, I'm being unfair, it was not James's fault. The blame must be Duncan's. I suppose it is an example of Nemesis—but so often it is the innocent who suffer.

It's just that I'm not coping very well. I feel as if I have a well of anguish inside.

I must try and pull myself together. At least talk to Mr Ogilvy. Do something positive.

Later:

I managed to talk to Mr Ogilvy. Told him about Wallace and the Achnagarry Estate. He said he'd look into it. He may have to arrange to have power of attorney in Duncan's affairs. Good thing if so. I like him. He strikes me as being a man of integrity. At least he *understands the implications of what has happened.*

Duncan is getting better. His speech is slurred and he can't use his right arm, but he'll live. He sleeps a lot. Ishbel said he should have apoplexy more often!

*   *   *

Sunday 20 August

Church. Edward there. He bowed slightly but that was all. I forced myself not to look towards the Dunlairg pew. I kept feeling like bursting into tears and knew I just mustn't. My God, I couldn't bear for word to get round that Miss Drummond had been jilted by Mr Mountsorrel— because that's what they would think. Lady Invershiel would think that I had forgotten my position in the world, and it served me right. Beatrix would be furious, for a different reason.

God knows what the sermon was about. All I could do was sit there and endure.

What I don't understand is how Edward could have been so sympathetic before, and suddenly it's been turned off like a tap. How could he be like that—when he'd just told me he loved me?

Murdo came up to me after the service and said that he ought to warn me that I had been seen, on the hill behind Achnagarry, sitting on a stone wall next to a man—quite unchaperoned! The snake! He's underhand, intolerant, mean-minded and a sneak! I told him to mind his own business. I was furious!

He looked very taken aback and said that he was concerned for my reputation. I was too untutored in the ways of the world, apparently, to understand how such actions could be misconstrued. A female always needed a male's guidance in such matters! UGH!

I said that I thought that the honour of a man who spied on his neighbours was open to serious question. Such a man bore a distressing resemblance to a voyeur. I added that he had no right to talk about me to Beatrix behind my back, as I gathered he had.

He said that he had only my welfare in mind. That I must know that he was hoping that I could be his helpmeet on Life's Path, or some such thing. I said that I was quite sure that I was

288

not worthy of the honour, but I have an awful feting that Murdo doesn't understand irony, because he left looking quite encouraged! Stupid of me. I should have been blunter.

*　　　*　　　*

Mr Ogilvy had to kick his heels at Achnagarry for two days before Duncan was well enough to see him. Even then, Beatrix impressed on him that her husband must not be upset.

'He's forgotten about Ritchie's visit,' she said—and she did not want him reminded.

'I shall be careful,' promised Mr Ogilvy.

Duncan's main preoccupation was with his Inverness venture. He did not want to lose the momentum, and he agreed that Mr Ogilvy, together with his wife, would have temporary power of attorney to deal with things. 'Stuff in study,' he managed to say.

Mr Ogilvy nodded. He would draw up the document for power of attorney and have it witnessed as soon as possible. He spent only twenty minutes with Penicuik and then went down to the drawing-room, where he found Beatrix.

'I think that, while we have the power to deal with Mr Penicuik's affairs, it would be as well to do something about the Ritchies,' he said.

'I could not agree to it!' exclaimed Beatrix. The young man had, fortunately, disappeared,

289

she hoped for good. She was certainly not going to authorize any payment to James's mother.

'There is a matter which I did not want to bring to Mr Penicuik's attention just now, but which needs dealing with urgently,' continued Mr Ogilvy. 'I'm afraid it is serious, Mrs Penicuik. It concerns the will of Mr Alexander Ritchie, Mary Ritchie's father, for which Mr Penicuik was the sole executor.'

Beatrix turned pale.

'Here is a copy of the will, which is in the parish records in Edinburgh.' He handed it to her. 'You will see that Mary Ritchie should have inherited four hundred pounds, which came to her from her mother. She also stood to inherit the rest of the estate after the funeral expenses and other debts had been paid. She received nothing.

'Mr Ritchie's wife died, after a long illness, shortly before her husband, and doubtless Mr Penicuik would argue that the expense of that ate up all the money. At this distance of time, we can neither prove nor disprove it. But the four hundred pounds is another matter. That was a separate sum and was not part of the estate. Mary Ritchie should have had it.'

'Give the woman four hundred pounds and let us be rid of her,' said Beatrix, her mouth screwed up with distaste.

'I fear it is not that simple. Mary Ritchie should have had that money well over twenty years ago. There is the interest to think of. According to my calculations, she is now owed something over eleven hundred pounds.'

Beatrix sank back in her chair. 'Pay that trollop eleven hundred pounds!' she exclaimed. 'I forbid it!'

'I have had a letter from Mary Ritchie,' went on Mr Ogilvy. 'She is not threatening blackmail, but she does want what is hers by right. And I must tell you that any court would consider that eleven hundred was the very least that she could claim. There would also be damages to consider, and there might also be awkward questions about the rest of the estate. I understand that there were some good pictures and furniture.'

Beatrix's mind recoiled at the word 'court'. If any of this got out, one thing could so easily lead to another. 'What do you suggest?' she said at last.

'I think this matter should be settled out of court. On this occasion it is better to err on the side of generosity. If I wrote to Mary Ritchie and offered her, say, two thousand pounds as a full settlement of all claims, I think she would agree.' He saw that Beatrix was frowning and added, 'She has every reason to be angry. She has effectively been defrauded of money which was rightfully hers and has struggled to bring up her son and get him a good education. She needs some recognition of that fact.'

'Very well, I agree,' said Beatrix through

closed lips.

Mr Ogilvy bowed. 'I shall draw up the agreement. The important thing is to deal with this as soon as possible.' He did not say, but they both knew that a recovered Penicuik might prove obstinate. He might even try and take it to court. Mr Ogilvy knew very well that Mary could not afford such a thing, but if she found a friend—his cousin Francis, say—to handle it for her, then the result could rebound on Penicuik.

Beatrix was thinking along similar lines. Duncan could be obstinate where saving money was concerned. No, it would be better if this sordid business were settled as soon as possible. She would support Mr Ogilvy in this and she would deal with Duncan later. He had much to answer for—and she did not intend to let him forget it.

Mr Ogilvy returned to the study with a smile. He had resented having to be the instrument for Penicuik's parsimonious dealings with Mary Ritchie for a long time. Now, he had managed to get Mary £2000, the very sum which he had urged Penicuik to settle on her all those years ago. He sat back in Penicuik's chair behind Penicuik's desk and enjoyed the irony.

*   *   *

Edward was not sleeping well. For the first

292

time for years, he dreamt about Betsy. She was sitting on a swing and laughing at a young man, who looked like James Ritchie, who was pushing her. It was Betsy as he had known her, and yet it wasn't. There were no pouts or coquettish glances, no sidelong looks. She was the beautiful, open-hearted girl he had first known.

As Edward walked towards them, the Ritchie character said, 'I didn't mean any harm.'

Betsy smiled and said, 'Edward won't believe a word you say, he never does.'

'That's because you always lie to me,' Edward said, 'and each lie is more unbelievable than the one before.'

Betsy's face had changed to Robina's. She'd looked at him with those large brown eyes, exactly as she'd looked when he'd kissed her up by the shielings, and said, 'But it's the truth.'

'Yes,' echoed the Ritchie character. 'It's the truth.'

The dream faded, and when he woke up, Edward found that his face was wet with tears and that his heart was aching with loss.

He tried to argue himself back into a state of rationality. How could it possibly be true that Penicuik had attacked Ritchie? Why on earth would he do such a thing? It must be false. He groaned and turned over, trying to stifle his doubts. The Invershiels had said nothing of such a scenario, and surely they would have mentioned it, if it had happened?

A man of his age could not be guided by the ache in his heart. Hearts, as he had good reason to know, were often treacherous.

*   *   *

Madeline had come to the conclusion that it was her melancholy duty to break off her engagement with Henry. All the same, at eighteen, she found it quite impossible to believe that that really would be the end. Her mother's fury over her betrothal to such a 'detrimental', as she would see him, was one thing, she could understand that, but somehow she couldn't quite believe that James Ritchie's arrival and the subsequent collapse of her father could really destroy the reputation of the entire family, innocent or not. She understood it intellectually, but her heart couldn't agree. All the same, she realized that Henry must be given the opportunity to disentangle himself. After church, conscious of her mother's eye upon her, she talked to Edward and Charlotte, exchanged a few words with the Ushers, and then hovered.

'I'm sorry to hear about your father,' said Henry, coming over. 'How is he?'

'Recovering slowly, I think, thank you.'

'Good.' She was looking pale and strained, he thought. All the colour had gone from her pretty cheeks. He gave her hand a quick squeeze, 'See you tomorrow by the loch, as usual? Will you arrange it with Aeneas?'

Madeline nodded, and shortly after that, the Dunlairg party left.

The following morning after breakfast, Madeline and Aeneas walked down to Loch Nevan. They walked in silence. Aeneas, who had a pretty clear idea what was going on, did not want to intrude, and Madeline was wrapped up in her own unhappy thoughts. When they arrived, Henry was not there, which further depressed her mood. Perhaps it had started already, she thought. Perhaps he had heard something and had decided not to come.

Aeneas immediately opened his fly box, selected a pattern, and made a cast. He found fishing soothing, even if you didn't catch anything. You could allow your mind to wander and nobody ever said, 'Why don't you go and *do* something?' which they did if he were reading, or just sitting thinking. Aeneas already knew that he needed to be alone sometimes, and being alone, just thinking, was not something that was understood in his family.

Madeline walked up and down, trying to calm her thoughts, which were becoming increasingly uneasy. Where was Henry? It seemed so unfair that her entire future could be ruined by something which was nothing to do with her. Would that really happen? Would Henry be relieved to be out of it? She wrenched her mind away and tried instead to envisage a future where she would expiate her father's sins by a life of good works, accompanied, no doubt, by dreary bonnets and one of those shapeless pelisse-mantles she'd always hated, and which were at least ten years out of date.

If that was what was in store for her, she thought rebelliously, then she would join Charlotte in her campaign for women's suffrage or some other progressive crusade. What she would not do was behave as though she personally had done anything to be ashamed of.

She looked up and saw Henry walking towards her. He came up, raised his hat and kissed her cheek.

'How is your father?' he asked. He'd been surprised by Madeline's pallor in church. He hadn't realized that she was so fond of Penicuik. 'He'll recover, I'm sure.' He would, too. The man was built like an ox.

'It's not Papa,' said Madeline, taking his arm and beginning to walk along the loch side. 'It's far worse. I'd better tell you what's happened.' She did so.

Henry listened carefully, asked a couple of questions, and then said, 'You poor darling! What a time you've been having.' So that's who their mysterious young visitor was, he thought. He'd suspected that there was something going on, but neither of his parents had said anything. Indeed, his mother had been insistent that Ritchie had fallen whilst climbing. He'd thought there was something odd about her vehemence. He should have smelled a rat.

'Henry . . .' began Madeline. How kind he was being! How could she ever break it off? But she must.

'I suppose you are now going to be noble and end our engagement?'

Madeline looked at him, tears standing at the end of her lashes. 'It's not funny!'

'No, it isn't. But I have something to tell *you*: Ritchie is now at Dunlairg.'

'What!'

'My parents found him lying by the side of the road, brought him home, and Edward patched him up. I haven't met him. Edward guards him like a dragon. I gather that he's suffering from loss of memory—temporarily one hopes, but that he is slowly recovering.'

'Do . . . do your parents know who he is?' asked Madeline.

'I'm not sure. I suspect they do.' They'd had unexpected visitors before, but never somebody whose predicament was not discussed openly in the family circle. 'So, my darling, I think we should wait on events, don't you?'

'I can't marry you if there's a remotest

chance of harming your reputation,' said Madeline firmly. 'I'm not being noble, as you put it, it just wouldn't be right. I mean that, Henry.'

'Yes, I know. I admire your sense of honour—truly. But I'm a pragmatic sort of fellow, I think we may be able to find a way round this without either of us being made unhappy. After all, darling, surely your father's affair with Ritchie's mother was over before you were born?'

Madeline coloured and shook her head. 'I believe James is a year or so younger than I am.'

Henry made a face. Penicuik was despicable.

'I met him briefly,' Madeline went on. 'I was coming here with Aeneas and he asked us if Papa was in. It was odd. I half-recognized him. He looked like a grown-up version of Aeneas.'

'I'll tell you a family secret, shall I?' said Henry. 'The Invershiels are related to the Mountsorrels through a natural half-brother of my paternal great-grandmother. Of course, things were different then. He was brought up as part of the family. It doesn't appear to have harmed either the Mountsorrels or the Invershiels.'

'You're nobility, though,' Madeline pointed out. 'We're not—and, whichever way you look at it, Papa behaved very badly.'

All the same, when Madeline and Aeneas

298

returned to Achnagarry, both were feeling hopeful. Aeneas had caught two trout and was one shilling richer, and Madeline was still engaged.

*   *   *

Robina's Journal   *Monday, 21 August*
Things still not easy. It's being misunderstood which hurts the most, that, and being offered what I wanted most in the world—and now it's withdrawn—and through my own doing. There's a sort of bitterness which will not go away. I daren't go up to Loch Tearmann any more, in case Edward's there, and I get so desperate to be alone! It's as if I'm wearing a mask all the time, and behind it I'm weeping.

It was a relief when I overheard Beatrix shouting at Duncan! Duncan has been moved to the guest room next to mine, and I couldn't help hearing. In fact, her voice was so loud that I heard every word.

Ishbel must have been right about Wallace— she usually is about that sort of thing—for Beatrix accused Duncan of fiddling the books and cheating her out of £400 a year! Then Duncan began to make a noise like a bull, bellowing. At one point I thought he was going to have another fit. Actually, I wouldn't have cared if he had. Detestable man. All the same, it was rather awful and I kept wondering whether I shouldn't rush in and calm them down.

Of course, I didn't—I'm sure Beatrix would have turned on me if I had. But I wouldn't have missed hearing Duncan getting a tongue-lashing for anything! Awful of me, but there it is. Beatrix always told me that I wasn't a nice person.

*   *   *

Next day. Tuesday   22 August
Desperate to be alone. I decided to climb the hill next to Carn Dhu, behind Murdo's house. It's difficult terrain because in places there's a lot of scree and not much to hold on to. But I did it. At one point I saw a peregrine. It sailed out from the top of Carn Dhu and gave its harsh cry—eerie, like a lost soul. I'm afraid it was too much, it seemed suddenly to echo everything I was feeling and I burst into tears. Then I sat and looked out over Loch Nevan and across to where Edward kissed me. That was painful, too.

As I looked, I saw two figures climbing up the hill towards the shielings. It was Edward and Charlotte. As I watched Charlotte turned and looked in my direction. She must have seen me, for she waved frantically. I didn't know what to do. She turned and tugged at Edward's sleeve and was obviously pointing me out. He didn't look. Charlotte waved once more and I waved back.

He doesn't want anything more to do with me. I don't know how I'm going to bear it.

I moved away and found a small hollow

where I couldn't see them and I sat there for a long time. I thought of how it feels increasingly as if I'm only ever going to live at the edge of other people's lives. When I was a child—here, I mean, I don't remember much about India— I was at the centre of my own life. Perhaps all children are. Even though my life was organized to a large extent by my grandparents, somehow I made it mine. *Partly, I think, by getting to know the Highlanders, like the Frasers, and learning the language. It's difficult to explain, but Achnagarry had a personal significance for me— like the crannog. I belonged to it and it to me.*

When Grandmama and I left, it was 'we'. We made a life together, and that still felt as if I was in control of my part of it. Yes, that's it, a feeling of being in control of your own life, After she died, things began to change. I was then living another person's life: Countess Kamenska's, Mrs Macdonald's and so on. But somehow I managed to hold on to my own life by insisting on my spare time and doing things—like having Russian lessons with Kyril Ivanovitch in St Petersburg. And keeping my journal, of course.

But here it's much more difficult and, increasingly, I've had the feeling of being pushed out on to the edge. My wishes have no importance, my views are unheard. It's as if I'm becoming invisible. Even with the Frasers, I feel this a bit. I'm always welcome there, I know that, but I'm not really part of their lives anymore. In due course, I shall leave—and they will stay. Of course, there are exceptions. I don't feel this with Madeline or Aeneas, for example. For Beatrix, I'm here as a chaperon, a convenient spinster cousin. For Lady I. I'm a spare female who is sometimes useful.

When I write my journal, it's like writing the thoughts of somebody who is in danger of disappearing. I've lost my autonomy. I'm supposed to ask permission even to go for a walk—well, I don't, but undoubtedly Beatrix thinks that I should!

For a few moments with Edward, I suddenly felt that I had my life back again. I was loved and wanted. I could be part of creating something new, for us, together. And then it vanished.

Later.

I MUST do whatever I can to take charge of my life. I've been putting off writing to Signor Arnolfini about Mrs Lambourn—I must think seriously about that. I also want to talk to Mr Ogilvy—see how my capital stands. The moment I'm thirty-five I must decide where I want to live, what I want to do with my life—and DO it. The trouble is that everything seems 'weary, stale and unprofitable' at the moment.

Feeling very down.

*　　　*　　　*

Jamie's bruises turned from black to yellow. The head wound began to heal. Edward

302

allowed Jamie to get up and sit, shakily, in a wicker chair for a while, but he wouldn't allow him to go downstairs. Ritchie still wasn't clear what had happened, and Edward did not want him to face any questions. He particularly did not want it when the versions he had had from Robina and from Lady Invershiel were so different.

Penicuik was an unspeakable man, but would he really have wounded and then nearly throttled an unknown young man? Or was he unknown? Robina plainly knew him. And somebody, undoubtedly, had bandaged his head wound. No, thought Edward, he was not going to endure all those emotional complications women seemed to thrive on. The secret assignations; the hidden billets-doux; the drinking. No! Never again. He had played the complaisant husband before, but then he had the excuse that he was avoiding any scandal for Charlotte's sake.

Robina had spoken of scandal, too . . .

He'd be glad when Ritchie was well enough to leave.

Jamie was happy enough up in the turret room. He found that he cried easily, for no apparent reason. Slowly, bits of his life floated back, but it was all like a jigsaw puzzle with pieces missing. He remembered his home, but it was the old home in Ardconnel Terrace he remembered, not the awful lodgings in Celt Street. He remembered the Academy, the rows of desks, the wooden panelling scratched with the names of former pupils, and the smell of cabbage which permeated the corridors.

He remembered his mother taking him to be measured for his first grown-up jacket. There was something that concerned his mother lurking at the back of his mind, some urgent duty, but he couldn't think what it was. He hunched himself miserably in his chair. Some time later Charlotte found him, staring out of the arched turret window with an agonized expression on his face, his hands clenched.

'What's the matter?' she asked, sitting down on the window ledge. 'Does your head hurt?'

Jamie shook his head. 'It's not that. It's inside.' He saw Charlotte's look of alarm and added quickly, 'I can't think straight. I know there's something important I've got to remember, but I don't know what it is.' What was he doing here? What had happened to him? 'I can't *think*!' he cried, turning his head away lest she should see the shameful tears.

'I'd have a good cry, if I were you,' said Charlotte practically. 'I was stalked by a tiger once, but fortunately a lame sambur came by and it took that instead. When I realized how close a shave I'd had, I was terribly shocked. Crying helped me to get over it.'

A sudden picture of a bull-like man thrusting him out of the way on a boat, and him falling to the deck, shot into his mind. No!

304

His whole mind recoiled. The door slammed shut again.

'Tell me about you,' he said. Anything was better than thinking about himself.

'I was born in India,' began Charlotte, pulling up her legs on to the window ledge and hugging her knees. 'My father is a botanist and collects plants for various people and places like Kew Gardens. I go with him. We go all over. I've been to India, Singapore and Japan, and lots of other places.'

'Have you always travelled with him?' Jamie was intrigued.

'Not when I was little. But after Mama died when I was nine, I did.'

'Nine's still very young,' observed Jamie.

Charlotte shrugged. She was used to people thinking that she was too young to do things, and now she took very little notice.

'What about school?' continued Jamie.

'I learnt to read and write and do sums when I was little, and then I practised them, of course.'

James blinked. 'But what about French and the use of the globes and all those other things that girls are taught?'

'I speak Pushtu and Urdu,' said Charlotte indignantly, 'and some Japanese. I look after the accounts. I do *useful* things. Papa taught me how to find my way around and not get lost. I use a compass and the stars, and I can memorize where we've been. What use would globes be?'

'I suppose not much,' admitted Jamie.

'I can shoot and skin an animal. I've never had to cook, but, if I had to, I'd learn.'

Suddenly, Jamie remembered Olaf. 'I can snare a rabbit and gut it afterwards,' he said, smiling. It had not been taught at school, but it was more useful than Latin, surely?

'There you are, then,' said Charlotte.

Olaf, he thought, when she'd gone. He could picture that big, red-headed figure so clearly, and the old bothy. He didn't know how he knew him, but it was a good memory. When he climbed back into bed, he fell asleep remembering Olaf talking to the seals.

*   *   *

That evening, after dinner, Mary was in her parlour, darning one of Dr Ross's socks, when there was a knock at the door and Ellen came in.

'Excuse me, Mistress, there's a wee parcel come for ye.' She handed Mary a small packet, wrapped in brown paper.

'Thank you, Ellen.'

When Ellen had gone, Mary opened it. Inside was a wooden wedge and a brief note in an old-fashioned secretary hand. *This should deal with the problem. O.H.* Mary picked up the wedge, went over to the parlour door, slid it into the small gap between the bottom of the

306

door and the carpet, turned the handle and pulled. The door stuck.

Smiling, she pulled out the wedge.

When Mary went to bed that night, she felt secure for the first time since she'd arrived at Dr Ross's. It had been a long day. She had reorganized the linen cupboard and ordered coal for the winter. Then she had taught Minnie and Ellen how to polish the furniture properly. She had made them stand, one on each side of her at the scullery table, and shown them how to make furniture polish and apply it. She then took them into the dining-room and watched carefully while they rubbed the mixture of linseed oil, turpentine, vinegar and spirits of wine into the chairs with a linen rag and polished them with a clean duster.

'Yes, that's looks much better,' she said.

'The doctor willna notice, I'm thinking,' muttered Ellen, mutinously.

'But *you* do,' retorted Mary.

'It's beautiful, just!' exclaimed Minnie, standing back to admire her handiwork.

That night, Mary went to bed tired. She checked that the front and back doors were locked and the windows secured, took her candle and went upstairs. There was a paraffin lamp alight on the hall table, in case Dr Ross was called out on a night visit, but if that happened, it was the job of one of the apprentices to see to the person who had rung the night bell, and to get the gig ready.

Mary closed her bedroom door, put the candle on her dressing-table, touched her china dog gently, then took Olaf's wedge out of her pocket and pushed it under the door. She tried to open it. It stuck. Satisfied, she climbed into bed and, for the first time since she'd arrived, fell asleep almost immediately.

Dr Ross, in the room underneath hers, felt that he had waited long enough. His health demanded that he have a woman; he needed that release and he certainly wasn't going to frequent the whores down by the docks and pick up some disease. He was beginning to feel irritated with the way pretty Mrs Ritchie was playing hard to get.

He waited until the grandfather clock in the hall struck midnight, then he rose, put on his slippers and dressing-gown, took a candle and went quietly upstairs. Nothing creaked—he'd seen to that. At the top of the stairs, he stopped and listened. He could hear Mrs Johnstone snoring, and a creak as Minnie or Ellen turned over, but from Mary's room, there was silence.

Slowly, he turned the handle and pushed.

The door remained obstinately stuck. He tried harder. Nothing. Finally, in a fury, he put his shoulder to the door and pushed as hard as he could.

Mary, woken from the first deep sleep she'd had, couldn't at first work out what was happening. Her heart was pounding so much that, when she reached for the tinder box to light the candle, she dropped it and had to scrabble about on the floor in the dark. When, eventually, she lit her candle, she could see the door jerking. She got up. The wedge was still holding. If he manages to get in, she thought furiously, I shall scream the house down.

Mrs Johnstone gave a great snort and turned over. Minnie and Ellen clutched each other. Downstairs, one of the apprentices poked his head out of his bedroom door. 'Did you call, sir?' There was a final kick at Mary's door and the sound of retreating footsteps. There was a muffled conversation at the foot of the stairs and then the doctor's bedroom door shut with a bang.

Mary, her heart still pounding, crept back to bed.

Still nothing from Jamie, she thought. The country post was liable to delay—she must remember that. But it was a long time before she got back to sleep.

*　　　*　　　*

Robina's Journal　　　　Wednesday 23 August
I was actually asked over to Dunlairg for tea, the first time I've been there since the Falls of Foyers trip. It seems a lifetime ago. I wasn't sure who knew what about James, nor what they thought I knew, so I didn't mention anything.

Many years ago, when Grandmama and I

were passing through Paris on our way to Italy, we went to the Palais-Royal one evening. I can't remember what we saw, but it was a farce, I think by Labiche. Anyway, the plot needed a lot of doors for people to hide behind, and there was a maid who was constantly having to remember where her mistress was and with whom. I felt this afternoon as if I'd been allotted some minor role in a gloomy farce—if that's not a contradiction in terms.

Lady Invershiel and I both knew that James Ritchie was in the castle. She *didn't* know that I knew. I *don't* know how much she knows about him. It was both absurd and extremely worrying. I found myself trying to search her face for clues.

However, it didn't take me long to realize that I'd been invited so that Mrs Usher—who's leaving tomorrow—might put pressure on me to look after her wretched aunt. I was shown into the small tapestry room off the solar and left with her.

She informed me that I was penniless and that she'd heard that I had refused a splendid offer from Mr Gillespie (what offer?) 'a man of the very highest integrity'! Ha! She was therefore renewing her offer of a position as lady companion etc. etc.

I said no. Raised hands and exclamations. I stood firm. She offered me another five pounds per annum. I thanked her and declined. She burst into tears.

Oh dear! It was all rather pathetic. I mopped

her up and suggested—and I'm surprised that this hadn't occurred to her—that surely the best solution would be to allow Georgina control of her money and let her go and breed dogs with Aunt Honoria.

'Breed Irish Water Spaniels!' echoed Mrs Usher, in a voice which suggested that death would be preferable. Apparently, they are very muddy creatures. Still, what does that matter if Gusher and Aunt Honoria like them? 'But how will Georgina ever find a husband?' she wailed.

I suggested that Georgina might meet a gentleman who also breeds dogs, perhaps at some county show. Instantly, I had a picture of a bluff, hail-fellow-well-met man, with grizzled hair, and wearing a Norfolk jacket and knickerbockers. He would be kind and devoted to Gusher—and not too demanding in those areas which Gusher calls 'that sort of thing'. Perhaps he was in the Crimea and wounded in some unmentionable place, which would put him out of action as far as 'that sort of thing' went.

Mrs Usher sat, twisting her wet handkerchief in her hands. Poor thing, she must have been a pretty woman once, and I do see that having a daughter like Gusher can't be easy. All the same, it's Gusher's life, and if she wants to spend it with a lot of wet dogs, I really don't see why she shouldn't.

She sat for a moment, and then said, 'There is Aunt Honoria's godson. A country squire.' She *didn't sound overly enthusiastic.*

'Married?' I asked.

'Widowed. No children. About forty.' We looked at each other.

'Does he like dogs?' I ventured.

She nodded and slowly began to smile.

'He wasn't wounded in the Crimea by any chance, was he?' I asked.

She shook her head. Oh well, one can't have everything. Georgina will just have to put up with it. Mrs Usher left. When Gusher came in, a little later, she was ecstatic. She pounded up to me and hugged me so hard that one of my stays cracked. 'She can breed dogs!' she exclaimed. 'Oh, Robina, I promise that you shall have one of my first puppies!'

What on earth would I do with it? Still, she meant it kindly. Then she said, 'Anyway, Mr Mountsorrel doesn't want to marry Georgina. Charlotte told her. Such a relief. He says he's never going to get married again.'

My heart turned to ice. Is it true? Or was Charlotte just saying that to make Gusher feel better? We sat in the tapestry room, and Gusher chattered on about her dogs and I heard not a word of it.

This being in love bit is awful! I refused Edward's offer. We have quarrelled. I have no right to him. I know all this, and yet I feel tortured by it all. I don't understand how it could have gone wrong so fast.

The gong went and we moved through to the

solar for tea. Mrs Usher came back with Lady I., who gave me a very odd look. Edward and Charlotte were by the window. Edward rose and bowed when I came in, but he didn't come over. That hurt, too. The only person I spoke to was Henry, who was looking rather strained, as well he might.

He came over and sat down beside me. He told me, in a low voice, that 'our upstairs guest', as he put it, was on the mend. I asked him what his parents were going to do. He didn't know, though he thought that they were plotting something. I said that it couldn't be easy for him and Madeline.

He replied that it couldn't be easy for me, either, and threw a significant look in Edward's direction. I said nothing. What could I say? In fact, I had to swallow hard to stop myself from bursting into tears. All in all, it was not an easy visit. I was glad when I could leave without incivility.

Got home to more drama. Beatrix was wearing her martyred look. She wasn't going to tell anybody what the matter was but she was going to make absolutely sure that we all felt thoroughly uncomfortable.

A miserable day.

*   *   *

However pleased Mary was to have repelled Dr Ross, she was increasingly anxious at hearing nothing from Jamie. It was nearly two weeks since he'd left. That Sunday, she had had no message to give Alec Burns for Mr Hamnavoe, save that she still hadn't heard from her son. Surely she should have heard by now? Her appetite deserted her and her nights were disturbed by dreams of Jamie calling for her and she couldn't get to him. What could she do? She couldn't even write to his landlady, Mrs Macallister, in Glasgow, for he was not expected there for another month.

The only way she could cope was by keeping busy. Dr Ross had agreed to the redecoration of his patients' waiting-room and Mary, Ellen and Minnie were kept busy moving the furniture and rolling up the carpets. The dining-room table had had its extra leaf removed, and was now at the top end of the dining-room and the waiting-room chairs were arranged around the wall at the far end.

That morning, Mary and Ellen went into the dining-room where Dr Ross and the two apprentices were still sitting over breakfast and Mary said, 'Your first patients will probably be here by half-past eight, Doctor.' She gestured to Ellen to remove the dirty plates.

Dr Ross grunted. 'There was trouble in the town last night,' he said, throwing his napkin on the table and rising, 'that fellow Hamnavoe was in a fight again. This time it's serious. He could swing for it.'

314

'Hamnavoe?' repeated Mary, her face paling.

'Aye. Ye'll know the man by sight, doubtless. Red-headed fellow.'

'I . . . I think so. What's he done?'

'Half-killed some sailor. They were both drinking. Hamnavoe's broken his arm. I'll have to go down to the gaol this afternoon, it won't hurt him to wait. He's too handy with his fists by half. If the man dies and Hamnavoe hangs, I, for one, won't be sorry.' He gave a short laugh and left the room.

Ellen returned with an empty tray. 'Get a move on, the pair of you,' she said to the apprentices. 'I havena got all day.' Ellen didn't think much of the male sex.

Mary went through the rest of the morning like an automaton. What could she do about Mr Hamnavoe? She barely knew him, but he had been good to Jamie—and he had made her the wedge. She couldn't let him languish in the gaol. She knew what such places were like: full of fetid straw, over-run with damp and rats, and gaol fever was rife. Prisoners were not fed unless they had the money to bribe a guard to send out for food, or unless a friend brought something.

She couldn't take him something from the larder. Mrs Johnstone would notice at once and would almost certainly accuse Minnie or Ellen, and Mary did not want it known that she was feeding a felon. She thought of bribing

Mrs Johnstone, but rejected it. That would put her in Mrs Johnstone's power and instinct told her that that would be a dangerous place to be.

She thought about it all morning, and, if it did nothing else, it took her mind off worrying about Jamie. After luncheon, Dr Ross left the house on his rounds—one of which included the gaol, for he was employed by the authorities as the prison doctor and he felt that it was good for his reputation to do something charitable. It gave his apprentices practice, too. Who cared if they messed up the treatment of some poverty-stricken prisoner?

As soon as Dr Ross left, Mary put on her bonnet and cloak and went to Mr Francis Ogilvy's. He had just finished his luncheon when she sent up her name. In a few moments, she was shown in to his office.

'Thank you for seeing me at such short notice,' she said, after the usual courtesies had been exchanged. 'I have come about Mr Hamnavoe. I understand that he's in trouble and I would like to help him if I can. He has been very kind to Jamie.'

'Hamnavoe!' exclaimed Mr Ogilvy. What on earth did Mrs Ritchie have to do with that scoundrel? He steepled his fingers together and looked disapprovingly at her across the desk. 'He's a rough character, Mrs Ritchie, certainly not the sort of man a respectable woman should know. I'm surprised James took up with him. I had thought better of him.'

Mary raised her head and looked him straight in the eye. 'Before Jamie left, I invited Mr Hamnavoe to take supper with us. He behaved perfectly properly.' She saw Mr Ogilvy raise a sceptical eyebrow and, nettled, added that a few days ago she had met him in the street, and that later he had sent her a wedge for her bedroom door. 'I have only met Mr Hamnavoe twice,' she ended, 'and he may be rough, but there are other men in the town, Mr Ogilvy, who are well-thought-of on the surface and whited sepulchres underneath!' She had had far more trouble with Dr Ross that she had ever had from Mr Hamnavoe.

Mr Ogilvy looked at her with a new respect. He had always admired her struggles to do the best she could for her son, but now he saw that she was prepared to risk her hard-won reputation for what she believed to be right.

'Could I bail him out?' continued Mary.

'It would probably cost about five pounds,' said Mr Ogilvy, reluctantly. 'But it would do your reputation no good to have your name as guarantor.'

'Mr Burns, the sexton at the English church, is a friend of Mr Hamnavoe's. I am willing to put up five pounds out of my savings, if Mr Burns would allow me to use his name.'

'Very well,' said Mr Ogilvy. 'I shall ask him. But don't expect to see your five pounds again.'

'We shall see,' said Mary. 'Thank you, Mr

Ogilvy.' She appreciated the fact that he was going to help her, in spite of his disapproval.

She was also doing it for herself, she thought, as she made her way home. Mr Hamnavoe had made her the wedge. It was only right that she helped him when he was in trouble. All the same, her savings were now down to seven pounds. She didn't regret her action, but she felt increasingly vulnerable.

CHAPTER NINE

Every morning, Lady Invershiel enquired after James, and every morning Edward answered that he was doing as well as could be expected. His memory was returning slowly, but he had no recollection of the events which had led to his accident. 'His mind is shying away from some painful recollection,' he finished. 'Too abrupt a recall could be catastrophic.'

'But he'll live?' said Lady Invershiel impatiently.

'Oh yes, he'll live. And in due course he will recover fully, I'm sure.

'Good.' Lady Invershiel smiled and left the room. It was the news she wanted. It looked as though Mr Penicuik were recovering, too. It was time to put her plan into action. If it worked, and she saw no reason why it shouldn't, then she would get Miss Penicuik for John, *and* a handsome dowry into the bargain. The Penicuiks could count themselves lucky to get off so lightly, and, in any case, what she proposed would hardly be news to Mrs Penicuik; she would simply be hurrying things along a little.

No such unpleasant word as 'bribery' crossed her mind. This would be a mutually beneficial arrangement. Madeline would become the Honourable Mrs John Invershiel and, in due course, Lady Invershiel. (Lady Invershiel gave a quick shudder. She, herself, would sink to being the Dowager Lady Invershiel, a prospect she did not relish.) John would be properly settled with a decent income—would a dowry of £30,000 be too greedy? That would be £1500 a year—and he would forget all this nonsense about joining a newspaper.

Of course, once John and Madeline were married it would be as much to the Invershiels' advantage as the Penicuiks' to keep this business quiet, but by then she would have achieved her object. In any case, Lady Invershiel had an aristocratic disdain for scandal. Her husband's ancestors had been involved in massacres and murders too numerous to mention. The mere attack by a man on his natural son was as nothing to the fourteenth-century Invershiel who had lopped the heads off six Frasers before succumbing to his wounds during a clan skirmish.

She rang the bell. A maid appeared.

'Your Ladyship called?'

'Tell Master John that Lord Invershiel and I wish to see him in the library.'

The maid curtseyed and left. Lady Invershiel went downstairs to the library. Her husband looked up, frowning slightly. He hated being disturbed when he was reading, but he knew that look of old. It betokened some maggot she'd taken into her head and he'd get no peace until she'd said whatever she'd come to say. He closed *The Sporting Magazine* with a sigh, and waited patiently.

There was the sound of heavy footsteps coming down the stairs and, a moment later, John came in. 'Yes, Mama?' He hoped it was about him taking up journalism; anything to get out of this dreary place where he had nothing to do.

Lady Invershiel selected a high backed chair and sat down, her spine erect; she never allowed her back to rest against the chair back—so slovenly. She motioned John to sit.

'Edward tells me that Mr Ritchie is out of danger,' she announced, 'and I understand that Mr Penicuik is similarly recovering. I think it is time that we made a move.'

John looked puzzled. 'I don't understand.' he said. As far as he knew, Ritchie had slipped on some scree and concussed himself. What did he have to say to anything?

Lady Invershiel smiled tolerantly. Good, she

thought, no rumours had got out. 'Mr Ritchie is Mr Penicuik's natural son,' she informed him. 'He went to visit his father, who attacked him.'

'Penicuik's bastard!' exclaimed John. 'He attacked his *son*?' He could scarcely believe it. Why had he not heard anything of this? He began to feel uneasy.

Lord Invershiel, too, was frowning. His heart began to race unpleasantly.

'The time has come to stop shilly-shallying,' continued Lady Invershiel. 'John, you have been very dilatory in attaching Miss Penicuik and I must now take matters into my own hands.'

'Miss Penicuik!' exclaimed John. 'But I never—'

'Exactly so. You never see what is in your own best interest. You will be guided by me in this. Miss Penicuik will make you an admirable wife and now, thanks to young Ritchie's accident, we can expect that she will receive a generous dowry.'

John was still looking puzzled. Lord Invershiel sank back in his chair. 'What exactly have you in mind, Lady Invershiel?'

'Why, that a marriage be arranged between Miss Penicuik and John. Mr Penicuik will naturally dower his daughter generously, and everybody will benefit.'

'And if he doesn't?'

'He would be wise to do so,' stated Lady

Invershiel calmly.

'You're going to threaten him with exposure!' exclaimed John, shocked.

'I doubt whether I shall have to proceed to such extreme lengths.' Lady Invershiel gave a thin smile. 'Once I explain the situation—that we have young Ritchie here—I am sure that no harsh measures will be necessary.'

'I think I'll have some of my medicine,' said Lord Invershiel unsteadily.

Lady Invershiel rose and poured him out a measure. 'Come now, Invershiel,' she said, rallyingly. 'It will be all for the best.'

'But what about me!' cried John. 'I like Miss Penicuik well enough, but I don't want to marry her!'

'You will do as you are told,' said Lady Invershiel impatiently.

'Now, I do not want a word of this to get out. Henry will have to know, of course, but that's all. The Ushers are leaving tomorrow, and I think it would be better not to tell Edward unless we have to.' She did not want Edward's conscience making things difficult. Let him be presented with a *fait accompli*. His job was to get Ritchie well. In any case, she was not pleased that he had taken no interest in Georgina Usher, *and* she had had to scotch his *tendre* for Robina. No, she would leave Edward in ignorance.

*　　　*　　　*

John and Henry had never particularly got on. John had resented Henry's arrival when he was two—he hadn't wanted a baby brother who broke his toys and generally made himself a nuisance. Later, he'd resented Henry's being able to go out into the world and do what he wanted, whereas he, John, had had to hang around at home, doing nothing.

Henry, for his part, found John's moody temperament difficult. He'd always mooned about, even at school, and seemed forever in the sulks. His own character was pragmatic and out-going, and John's moods irritated him. Henry didn't particularly want the title, but, even so, it seemed unfair that John would get everything, whilst he himself had to make his own way in the world.

All the same, each saw no real harm in the other. They were just different, that was all.

John was not so self-absorbed that he had not noticed his brother's growing affection for Madeline. His first action, therefore, on leaving the library, was to seek out his brother. He found him up in his room, his law books open on the table beside him, making notes. John knocked perfunctorily, opened the door and entered, closing the door carefully behind him. Henry looked up.

'The devil's in it now,' said John heavily, and sank down on Henry's bed.

Henry turned his chair round to face him.

'What's the matter?'

John told him. 'It seems to me that you're the one who is taken with pretty Miss Penicuik,' he finished. 'Or am I wrong?'

'We're engaged to be married—secretly, of course,' said Henry shortly.

'Engaged!' John had had no idea that it had gone so far.

'I know!' said Henry. 'It's an underhand thing to do and neither of us likes it. But Madeline told me about Ritchie and her father, and I knew that the Penicuiks would never consider me a suitable match. We didn't know what else to do. Madeline will get three times her husband's annual income, and I can't support her on that and what I earn.'

'Look,' said John, with more energy than he'd shown for some time, 'I don't want to marry Miss Penicuik—you do. You'd better tell Mama. No point in both of us being made unhappy. I'll back you up.'

Henry stared at him. 'That's very good of you, John,' he said slowly. He knew how much John hated argument.

John shrugged. 'We're as different as chalk and cheese, but you're still my brother.'

'Thank you. And if ever I can do anything for you, consider it done. Shall we go now?'

'Better not. Papa needed his medicine; Mama's intrigues came as a shock. God, they did to me, too. Wait until tomorrow, after the Ushers have gone.'

Henry nodded.

'I'll leave you to polish your arguments, then,' said John with a grin, and left the room.

*   *   *

Meanwhile, at Achnagarry, Beatrix felt that at last things were getting back to normal. The disagreeable Mary Ritchie business was now in the capable hands of Mr Ogilvy. He would deal with it. Duncan's health was improving. He was still disinclined to move very much, but his mind was beginning to recover—except with regard to Ritchie's appearance and its aftermath, which he seemed to have forgotten. Beatrix vowed to keep it that way, if possible.

With regard to Madeline and Mr Mountsorrel, things were less satisfactory, but there was no cause for despair. Mr Mountsorrel had undoubtedly been shocked by Charlotte's unfortunate accident at the Falls of Foyers, but, the more she thought about it, the less she believed the hints that it had been anything to do with Ewan. Why on earth would he do anything so ungentlemanly, pray? All the same, Mr Mountsorrel was proving elusive.

Even so, Madeline now had the entrée to Dunlairg, and she had improved her acquaintance with the Invershiels, which could be an asset when they returned to Edinburgh. If Madeline had to have yet another Season before she was married off, then at least she would be able to talk of summer excursions with the Invershiels. So, Beatrix came down to breakfast feeling, on the whole, not unhopeful of the future.

There was only one item of post on her plate, and it had been hand-delivered. Beatrix's heart began to beat faster. Could it be from Mr Mountsorrel, requesting Madeline's hand in marriage? It should, of course, have gone to her husband, but Mr Mountsorrel must know that Mr Penicuik was not up to receiving mail. She broke the seal and spread it open.

> *Dunlairg Castle*
> *Monday, 28 August*

My dear Mrs Penicuik
You will be interested to hear, I am sure, that we have a young relative of your husband's staying with us, a Mr James Ritchie. We found him collapsed by the side of the road, with serious injuries to his head and throat. He is now out of danger and on the mend.

I think that the time has come to arrange matters between my elder son, John, and Miss Penicuik. A match between them would be of mutual benefit, don't you agree? Your daughter's beauty and charm, accompanied by a handsome dowry, will complement my son's superiority in rank.

As the Honourable Mrs John Invershiel,
she would be above any scandal that might
emerge if your husband's attack on Mr
Ritchie found its way into the public
domain.

I am sure, dear Mrs Penicuik, that a
woman of your intelligence must see these
things as I do.

I look forward to hearing from you.
Yours etc.

Mary Invershiel

Beatrix folded up the letter with trembling fingers; the breakfast-table seemed to blur before her eyes.

Robina and Madeline, who had both noticed the letter, exchanged glances. 'Is anything the matter, Beatrix?' asked Robina. It was unlike her cousin to be so quiet. She was sitting, staring in front of her, her eyes glazed, as though she had had a severe shock.

'N . . . nothing,' said Beatrix quickly. She gave Madeline a quick, searching glance, then, without another word, she rose, picked up the letter and left the room.

'I'm not sure, but I think it may have been Lady Invershiel's writing,' said Robina. She tried to think back to the letter she'd had from that lady. Surely, that sloping hand was similar? 'I hope that nothing has happened to James.' She didn't think that Beatrix knew that he had been taken to Dunlairg.

'Henry said that he was doing well,' replied Madeline, putting down her toast, which suddenly tasted like sawdust. She was feeling uneasy. Why had Mama looked at her in that odd way? Did she *know* something? If Lady Invershiel knew who James was, and chose to make it public, then it would be impossible for her to marry Henry—or anybody else. Would Lady Invershiel really do that? She was a strong-minded woman, but not vindictive, surely?

'Are you seeing Henry this morning?' asked Robina.

Madeline shook her head. 'The Ushers are leaving today. He has to be there to say good-bye, and didn't know when he would get away.'

'Why don't we go down to the bay?' said Robina. 'We'll see the carriage, and I'd like to say good-bye to Georgina, and perhaps Henry will come down later.'

'Anything to get out of the house,' said Madeline, thankfully. The last thing she wanted was to be called up to her mother's room.

*　　　*　　　*

James woke up from the most appalling nightmare, drenched in sweat and with his heart pounding. His wound was throbbing and the bruises on his neck ached. The atmosphere was so thick with terror that he dared not open

328

his eyes in case he saw the bull-necked man with the purple swollen face lurching towards him. Dawn was just beginning to break when he eventually forced his eyes open—and the room was empty. With shaking hands, he managed to light the bedside candle.

Gradually, the fear receded, and he lay there, exhausted. He now remembered almost everything: the boat trip, the walk up Glen Nevan, giving the maid his letter, his father coming round the desk with a heavy object in his hand—and then, nothing. He didn't know how he came to be in this turret room, save what Mr Mountsorrel had told him: that he'd been picked up on the roadside by Lord and Lady Invershiel.

The grey dawn slowly lightened to pink. Jamie tried to sort out what had happened. His father had tried to kill him and he—oh God!—he had had hold of Olaf's paper-knife and . . . it had gone into his body, slid in so easily. What had happened? Please God he hadn't killed his father! For one awful moment, the bruising round his throat felt like the hangman's noose. His hands grew clammy with fear, and his heart beat so rapidly that it seemed to jump about in his throat.

Olaf had been right. He'd warned him and he hadn't listened. He'd written a number of scenes in his head, covering, so he imagined, any eventuality. Except what had happened. At the back of his mind, Jamie had always had the vague conviction that his mother had misjudged his father. That, surely, once he knew the truth, he would come back into Jamie's life, be proud of him.

He'd invented it, he now realized, because of his own longing for a father. He must accept that Penicuik did not want to acknowledge him; more, that he wished that he had never been born. A few tears trickled down his cheek on to the pillow. He brushed them away angrily with the sleeve of his nightshirt, but still they came. Eventually, he gave in, and wept until exhaustion overtook him and he dozed off.

When he awoke, there were voices on the stairs and, a moment later, Edward came in, carrying his breakfast tray.

'The maid came up earlier, but you were dead to the world,' he said. He took in the gutted candle and twisted bed sheets and drew his own conclusions. He said nothing, but busied himself with the teapot.

'I had a nightmare,' said Jamie, pulling himself up. He took the tea Edward poured him and drank it gratefully.

Edward watched him. He was paler than yesterday, his hair was damp, and the whites of his eyes were bloodshot. He picked up Jamie's wrist and took his pulse. It was higher than it should be.

'Do you want to talk about it?'

'I . . . is anybody after me?'

'No. Not as far as I know,' said Edward, surprised.

Jamie gave a sigh of relief and sank back against the pillows.

Edward released his wrist. 'You should rest this morning,' he said. 'You've had a shock and that will set you back a bit. I'll come up and see you later.' He had just reached the door, when there was a horrified gasp behind him. He turned quickly.

'My mother!' gasped Jamie. 'She'll be frantically worried. I must write. Now!'

'You're doing nothing now,' said Edward firmly.

'I must!' insisted Jamie, trying to swing his leg out of bed. 'Oh my God, she'll wonder what has happened to me. I *promised*!'

He looked so distraught that Edward said, 'If you give me her address, I will write on your behalf and tell her that you had an accident but you are now well on the way to recovery.'

'Yes! Yes!' Where was she? What was that man's—Ross's—address? He *must* remember.

'I'll go and write the letter and you can give me the address when I come back,' said Edward, soothingly. 'You could add a few words at the end, if you like.'

Jamie sank back. 'It will go today, won't it?'

'Of course. Kenny the Post comes at about ten o'clock, I'll make sure he gets it. She should get it tomorrow.'

His calmness had its effect. Jamie's colour

331

returned. He took a piece of toast and began to butter it, and by the time Edward came back, Jamie was more collected. Edward handed him the letter. He'd said nothing beyond the fact that Jamie had had a fall on the hill, that he was being looked after and that the writer expected a full recovery.

Jamie read it, and glanced up at Edward. Did he actually *know* what had really happened? But a fall on the hill was undoubtedly the best thing to tell his mother. He could not tell her the truth. He might tell Olaf, eventually, but not his mother. He would spare her that, at least.

Edward handed him a pencil, and Jamie wrote: *I really am on the mend. Please try not to worry. I will write soon. Jamie.* He gave Edward the address.

'There,' said Edward. 'It will go with Kenny, I promise.'

Jamie lay back and closed his eyes. 'I think I'll sleep now,' he said.

Edward picked up the tray and the letter and left the room.

*　　　*　　　*

Robina's Journal   *Tuesday 29 August*
Something's going on—I know it. But what? Beatrix is saying nothing.
    Madeline, Aeneas and I went down to the bay, but there was nobody from Dunlairg there. We

saw the Ushers' carriage and went to meet it. Mrs Usher was a bit tight-lipped—I suppose all that business with Aunt Honoria still rankles—but Georgina hung out of the window and called, 'She won't forget your puppy, Robin!' as the carriage rumbled off.

I don't want a dratted puppy! But I smiled and waved, and moments later the carriage crossed the bridge over the River Nevan and Georgina was still waving her handkerchief. Madeline decided to go home, and Aeneas and I went to call on Mhairi. Aeneas's Gaelic is coming along very nicely, though he hasn't quite grasped the genders.

Every now and then his mistakes made us laugh. It's lovely to see Mhairi smiling again. She's obviously very taken with Aeneas and, when he had rushed off to see if there were any eggs, she confided that she thought he was a 'Fine, wee laddie'. So he is, bless him.

Later, I went over to the crannog. I hadn't brought a towel, but it didn't matter, I dried my feet in the sun. I was worried lest Edward was there, but, of course, he wasn't. It seems so long ago now.

If only I knew what I ought to do! Part of me feels that I ought to write to Mrs Lambourn and leave Achnagarry. But I can't—not just yet. Things aren't finished. I know that James is still at Dunlairg and I want to know that he's all right. I want to know what's going to happen to Madeline and Henry.

And Edward? Is it too much to hope that Edward learns the truth about what happened? Does he care? I feel as if I'm in one of those Shakespeare plays which hover between comedy and tragedy. Winter's Tale, *perhaps. There, things turn out right in the end; justice and love win through—but not for young Mamillius, who dies of a broken heart, nor for poor Antigonus, who is eaten by a bear. Neither of them deserves their fates, but it happens, just the same. They are minor characters and can be dispensed with.*

Like me?

Oh God, I'm becoming morbid.

I sat on the crannog for a long time and thought about Edward, and Hamish. He *didn't deserve to die, but* these things happen. *One just has to do one's best to cope with what you get.*

*   *   *

The moment the Ushers' carriage had trundled off down the drive, Henry and John followed their parents into the house.

'I'd like a word with you both, please,' said Henry. He turned towards the library and held the door open for his parents, and then nodded to John, who went over to pour his father some of his medicine.

Lord Invershiel sat down, and took the glass offered to him. Trouble, he thought. He had been pretty certain that Henry wouldn't like the plan to entrap Miss Penicuik into marriage with John—what lawyer would? He'd tried to say as much to his wife, but she'd brushed it aside. He drained the glass and looked at Henry. 'If this is about the Penicuiks, don't expect me to interfere,' he said, querulously. 'Once your mother gets the bit between her teeth, there's no stopping her.'

'Well, what do you want, Henry?' demanded Lady Invershiel. She was not going to have her plans overturned. If Henry were indulging in a fit of conscience, she would remind him that he was dependent on his parents to the tune of £200 a year, about half his income. That should bring him to his senses.

'John has told me who Ritchie is and what happened with Penicuik. I can't say I'm surprised; I always thought Penicuik was no gentleman. But what I want to say is this: John can't marry Madeline, because I am already engaged to her.'

Lady Invershiel gasped as if a bucket of cold water had been thrown over her. 'You! It's impossible! A younger son! Your father and I could never agree to that!'

'It's *not* impossible,' replied Henry, calmly. 'I love her and she loves me. If necessary, we shall wait the three years until she comes of age. I shall be very sorry not to have your blessing, but, ultimately, your approval isn't necessary.'

Lady Invershiel, for once lost for words, looked first at John and then at her husband.

'Very good match, my boy,' said Lord Invershiel, cheering up. Henry was his favourite son, why shouldn't he have pretty Miss Penicuik if he wanted her? It boded well for his career at the bar that he could face up to his mother, at any rate.

Lady Invershiel turned to John. He normally resented his brother; she could remember a number of schoolboy quarrels over ponies and whose turn it was with the ice skates. Surely, he would have something to say about Henry's appropriation of the heiress?

John shrugged. 'Henry loves Miss Penicuik. I don't. Does it matter which one of us she marries?'

'The Penicuiks will want a title for their daughter,' stated Lady Invershiel.

'They will get one: the Honourable Mrs Henry Invershiel,' retorted Henry, drily. 'You hold all the cards, Mama. They will have to accept whichever one of us offers. They won't want anything about Ritchie to get out, will they?'

Lady Invershiel decided to reassert her authority. 'What you propose is impossible. Mrs Penicuik would never agree to it. You, Henry, earn little more than a hundred pounds a year. At the moment, you are entirely reliant on allowances from us and your godfather. We could withdraw . . .' She let the threat hang in the air.

'You could, of course,' agreed Henry.

'However, I think you are forgetting Madeline. It's *me* she wants to marry. I have every intention of working hard and succeeding at the bar. I'm good at my job. We may have to struggle for a few years, but I don't think that, in the long run, the Penicuiks will have any cause for complaint.' He turned and smiled at his father, 'Papa, I hope that you will consider it at any rate.'

Lord Invershiel gave a grunt, which might have been approval. Henry smiled, looked across at John, gave him a brief nod, and the brothers left the room.

'Whew!' exclaimed John, when the library door had closed behind them. 'You've more bottom than I have, old boy.'

'Mama's mostly bluster,' said Henry. 'What can she do, after all? It's true that I need my allowance for the next few years, but in five years or so, I'll be independent, and she knows it. In any case, she's been harbouring Ritchie, and that makes her an accessory after the fact; she can't possibly want the truth to get out. Besides, it's always useful to have a barrister in the family, especially as the Invershiels backed the wrong side in the Forty-Five! The law can be expensive. Papa will talk Mama round.'

'I'm not so sure,' said John gloomily. He'd never known his mother change her mind about anything.

*   *   *

Edward was discovering that uncomfortable thing, a posthumous relationship. After Betsy's death, he had done his best to forget her as quickly as possible. It was not difficult. He plunged himself into work, accepted one plant-hunting expedition after another and made sure that he had no time to think about the past, whilst, at the same time, significantly enhancing his scientific reputation. He congratulated himself that he was over all 'that business' as he termed it.

Now, it seemed, 'that business' had not done with him, after all. He'd refused to allow Robina to embroil him once again in the sort of stupid emotional messes Betsy had so loved, but, even without Robina, the old pain of anger, hurt and resentment had shot to the surface, like a suppurating wound that would not heal.

For the first time, he began to look at his side of the marriage, and admitted that part of it at least had been his fault. He'd taken Betsy away from Scotland, where she'd had a happy girlhood, with lots of outings and parties with her cousins, brothers and sisters, and expected her to live miles from anywhere, not knowing the language, and fifty miles, say, from the nearest white female. Betsy had had to do all the adapting. He himself had made no concessions to what *she* wanted. It was not an easy admission.

He began to feel more and more disturbed. He took to going for long walks alone on the pretext of looking for rare plants. But he never came back with any Highland cudweed. He was trapped once again in his life with Betsy; all the humiliations she had heaped upon him; the anguish he'd felt, having to pretend to be the complaisant, tolerant husband, when all the time he was being cuckolded.

He remembered Betsy once saying, 'I have no weapons against neglect,' and thought of it now. Was it really neglect, when he'd gone away for a month or so into the interior? Plant-hunting was his job, she'd known that when she'd married him. He'd warned her what it would be like. Surely, it was for a woman to follow her husband and make a home for him *wherever* he was? She should have knuckled down and made the best of it. Other women did, after all.

But she wasn't 'other women', she was Betsy, his wife. He should have taken her wishes into account. It wasn't as if he were financially dependent on the money from his expeditions, in fact, he was more likely to be out of pocket. What mattered to him was the acclaim, the respect of his peers. What did Betsy get out of it all? Nothing!

But she had not been weaponless, after all. She had fought back with the one weapon which could hurt him: humiliation. God! What a mess! He thought about it endlessly as he strode furiously over the moors, resisting all the attempts of Charlotte, or anybody else, to accompany him.

There had been that awful time in India when Ahmed had had to carry Betsy back to the house after he'd found her collapsed, drunk, in the garden. Ahmed had said nothing, but Edward could see the pity— and contempt—in his face. Edward's eyes closed involuntarily against the remembered humiliation and, the next thing he knew, he had tripped over a tussock of heather and was sitting with grazed hands and wet knees on the peaty ground. It was a long time before he got up. He stayed there, head bowed, and the bitterness of all those years ago overwhelmed him.

He'd always hated intrigue, and here, at Dunlairg, which had once been a place of refuge, he couldn't help but feel, increasingly, that secrecy lurked. Conversations now stopped whenever he and Charlotte came into the room. Even John and Henry seemed to be infected by it, as they stood in corners, talking in low voices.

Every morning, since Ritchie's arrival, Lady Invershiel had enquired how their patient was getting on. She had been anxious that he should have the rest he needed, and Edward had seen nothing in her enquiries but kindly concern. Now, suddenly, she wanted him to be well enough to come downstairs, when only a day or so ago, she'd urged that he stay quietly in his room.

Edward hated not knowing what was going on. And, worse, he could no longer hide from himself that there *was* some mystery surrounding Ritchie. Had Penicuik really tried to kill him? Robina's fantastic story had borne more resemblance to one of Daniel Miller's Gothic tales, which Betsy so loved to read, than sober reality. This was the nineteenth century, for God's sake! How could he possibly ask Ritchie if Penicuik had tried to kill him? Quite apart from his scruples about such intrusive questioning, he knew how near the young man had been to mental breakdown. He just couldn't cross-question him. But there was something he wasn't being told, and Ritchie was the key.

*　　　*　　　*

At about the same time as Edward was reliving his past, Madeline and Henry were sitting by Loch Nevan in their usual place. Henry had just told her of his mother's letter to Mrs Penicuik.

'So *that* was it!' exclaimed Madeline. 'Robina thought she recognized your mother's handwriting, but we didn't think . . . Oh, Henry, I *can't* marry your brother.'

'Of course you can't,' said Henry, squeezing her hand. 'Look, I think I should come back with you and talk to your mother.'

'You . . . you mean, tell her about . . . us?'

'Yes. Ask for your hand in marriage. Of course, I know it ought to be your father, but, fortunately, he's unavailable at the moment.' Just as well, he thought. If Penicuik could attack his son, God knows what he would do to an unwanted suitor.

'Mama won't like it,' said Madeline.

Henry made a face. 'She may not, but she'll have to put up with it.'

'It . . . it may mean that I'm forbidden to see you,' faltered Madeline. It was one thing to agree to a secret engagement, with all the thrill of the forbidden, but quite another to have to cope with heavy parental disapproval.

'Didn't you tell me that there was some lawyer staying with you?' went on Henry.

'Mr Ogilvy? Yes, but he's in Inverness at the moment.'

'Ogilvy, eh? I know him. He must know about this business, surely?'

'I think so. Robina said that he knew about James, so I suppose he must know the rest. But what can *he* do?' So far as she could see, Mr Ogilvy had the power to cut her off without a shilling, if her mother asked him to.

Henry put his arm around her. 'Poor darling. You're worried. I can tell.'

'I'm afraid of what Mama may do,' confessed Madeline. 'I'm sorry, Henry, I thought I would be braver, but I'm not.'

'Would you rather I didn't talk to her?'

'No.' Madeline straightened up. 'I may be afraid, but I'm not a complete coward.'

'That's my girl.' Henry kissed her cheek. 'We may be in for a rough ride, but we'll win through, I promise you. I'm not letting you go.' He rose and held out his hand to help her up, and they began to walk towards Achnagarry.

Even if she were locked in her room on bread and water, it must be possible to get a message through to Henry by Robina or Aeneas, thought Madeline. She wasn't entirely friendless. As they neared the lodge, she gave Henry's arm a squeeze and said, 'You go on. I'll go in the back door. Good luck.'

Henry gave her a reassuring smile. He watched the slender figure walk swiftly to the side of the house, turn, blow him a quick kiss, and then disappear. He went up to the front door, straightened his cravat, set his shoulders, took out his card case, and knocked. Frank opened the door.

'Could you ask Mrs Penicuik if she would be so kind as to grant me a few moments of her time?' said Henry, and handed him his card.

*   *   *

Once again, Charlotte was up in the turret room with Jamie. This time, he was dressed and sitting in a chair by the window. His mind was clearing by the hour and, although in

343

many ways this was a relief, it had brought other problems in its wake. He hadn't realized, for example, that Dunlairg Castle was only a couple of miles from Achnagarry. How much did his hosts know? Even after what had happened, he didn't want to bring any trouble down on the Penicuiks' heads. Jamie, quite as well as Beatrix, understood the scandal that would result from any disclosure. It could affect him, too. Neither Inverness nor Glasgow University would want it known that they were financially supporting a young man who was involved in so unsavoury a scandal. He could lose both bursary and scholarship.

How could he have been such a fool? How naïve he had been And yet, surely he couldn't be blamed for not anticipating that his father would attack him. Nobody could have foreseen that.

Charlotte was watching him quietly. Like her father, she had noticed that there was some secret that the Invershiels were not telling, and she, too, realized that it must be something to do with Jamie. Unlike her father, she had no scruples about asking.

'Are you related to the Penicuiks?' she asked, suddenly.

Jamie turned sharply and then winced, for his neck bruises still hurt. 'What makes you say that?'

'You look like Aeneas,' said Charlotte. Then her mind made another jump. 'Is Mr

Penicuik your father?' She watched Jamie's colour rise, and nodded. 'I thought so.'

'For God's sake, hold your tongue!' cried Jamie.

'I'm not a tittle-tattle,' retorted Charlotte. 'But there's something going on downstairs, and I want to know what it is.'

Jamie's colour faded as rapidly as it had come. 'They're not coming for me, are they? The law?' His voice was scarcely more than a whisper.

'Why should the law be after you?'

'Nothing. Never mind. Look, just go away would you?'

Charlotte got up, went over to his bedside table and poured out a measure of brandy. 'Here, drink this.' Jamie drank.

'What's this about the law?' asked Charlotte, when his colour had returned.

Jamie didn't answer for a few moments, but the urge to tell *somebody* was overwhelming. 'All right,' he said, and began to tell her the whole story. It was an enormous relief, like lancing a boil. She was a good listener, he thought. She didn't interrupt, nor did she exclaim with shock or horror.

'I think you are worrying too much about the law,' she said, when she'd heard him out. 'As far as I know, Mr Penicuik had an apoplectic fit and is recovering slowly. If they'd wanted to get the law on to you, we'd have heard by now. Besides, you could just as well get the law on to *him.* He attacked you first. You were only defending yourself.'

'That's true,' said Jamie, brightening up.

All the same, thought Charlotte, the Invershiels were plainly up to something. It had not escaped her notice that Lady Invershiel had been very keen to get the Invershiels and the Penicuiks together. Did she want Madeline for John? Or Henry? But what had that to do with Jamie?

'It's awful to be hated by your own father,' confessed Jamie. 'I . . . I can't help feeling ashamed, as if there is something wrong with me.'

'Nonsense,' said Charlotte, roundly. 'He's the one who should be ashamed. Why, you're younger than Madeline! He was carrying on after he was married. It's disgusting.'

'Young ladies are not supposed to know about such things,' said Jamie severely, but he smiled. Thank God she *had* spoken. She'd relieved him of his worst nightmare.

Charlotte made a face. 'I know.' She'd decided long ago that lady-like ignorance could only be a grave disadvantage to any female. She glanced out of the window and saw her father, thumb-stick in hand, coming up the drive. His head was bowed and he was walking as if he were exhausted.

For the first time, Charlotte wondered whether he had any interest in what had been going on. How much did he know? Should she tell him? She said nothing of this to Jamie, only rose and said that she'd better go. 'You will be all right now, won't you?' she asked.

Jamie nodded. He was feeling tired again, but this time it was a good tiredness.

'Good,' said Charlotte. 'I'll come and see you again.'

'I can't wait,' retorted Jamie.

Charlotte laughed and left.

*   *   *

Robina's Journal   Tuesday 29 August cont.
I envy Madeline her relationship with Henry. At least he believes her, and takes her anxieties seriously.

I've decided that I'm going to stop hankering after Edward. Do I really want a husband who thinks I'm lying? No, I don't. Actually, I've never found it easy to lie. I refrain from mentioning things sometimes, one has to (I'd have liked to have told Mrs Usher that she should stop trying to manipulate her Aunt Honoria into leaving her her fortune, for example) but that is different.

I'm going to turn over a new leaf. Perhaps I should take Ewan in hand? Teach him archery, or something? No, that's just martyrdom! The problem is that up here there's not enough to do. I suppose I could spend more time listening to Beatrix, but all that would happen would be that either I'd become so irritated that I'd say something rude, or that my mind would wander off and I'd start thinking about Edward again.

I'll think I'll go and see Mhairi. There's bound to be some little job I can do for her, and I can practise my Gaelic.

*   *   *

That same morning, Mary came downstairs feeling, as she had increasingly, the heavy weight of anxiety. What had happened to Jamie? She had no means of knowing. There were no friends who could act for her, who might be prepared to trace his steps for example. And yet, she also realized that, so long as she did not know for sure, then she could at least hope. She both longed for a letter and dreaded the postman's knock.

Jamie was her whole world. Without him, what was her life worth? It was right that he left and went out into the world, but to lose him entirely? No! She wrenched her thoughts away; that way lay madness. There was the patients' waiting-room to be done. The wood had been stripped and primed, the walls and ceilings washed. Today, they would beat the carpet and then clean it.

The jangling of the front door bell shattered her thoughts. She could hear Minnie opening the door. Voices. Then Minnie: 'There's a letter for ye, Mistress Ritchie.' Mary's heart jumped into her throat. She flew to the door, grabbed the letter with trembling fingers and almost ran to the housekeeper's room and shut the door. Only then did she look at it. It was not in Jamie's handwriting, and it was post-marked Fort Augustus.

She sank down on a chair and tried to quell a rush of terror. Eventually, she summoned up the courage to break the seal, read it, and burst into tears. Jamie was all right! He'd had an accident, but he was all right! She kissed the letter in a passion of gratitude. When she'd recovered the tone of her mind, she heard whisperings from the kitchen, and went through. Three faces turned anxiously towards her.

Mary smiled uncertainly. 'It's from Jamie. He had an accident, but he's all right. Oh, Mrs Johnstone, the *relief*!' The tears began to flow down her cheeks again.

'I'll bring ye a cup of tea, and maybe a wee whisky, shall I?' said Mrs Johnstone, and behind her, Minnie and Ellen smiled.

'Tea would be lovely, thank you,' said Mary, searching for her handkerchief.

As she sipped her tea, Mary thought, Mr Hamnavoe must be told. But where was he? She'd had a brief note from Mr Ogilvy, saying that bail had been accepted, but that was all. She would try and get down to Alec Burns's cottage. She could leave a message there. Fortunately, that afternoon, Dr Ross had to go out to see a patient in Balloch and would not be back for a couple of hours, and Mary had the unexceptionable excuse of having to replace the paraffin lamp glass chimneys, for Ellen had dropped one and cracked another, and they were easily broken. It would be safer if she brought them home herself.

However, when she reached the Burns's cottage, there was a surprise. A beaming Mrs Burns, a toddler clutching her skirts, informed her that Olaf was in her parlour. 'He'll be right pleased to see ye, I'm thinking,' she said, indicating that Mary should go through. Olaf was sitting, his arm in a sling, a bandage round his head and a baby in the crook of his good arm. The moment he saw her, he got up, put the baby gently back in its cradle, and went to shake her hand.

'I'm glad to see ye, Mistress,' he said. 'I have much to thank ye for.'

Mary waved it aside and sat down. 'That's not why I came.' She reached into her pocket, took out the letter and handed it to him, smiling.

Olaf read it carefully, and turned it over to look at the post mark. Fort Augustus. The fool must have gone to see Penicuik then. He looked at Mary. Did she know?

'I'm so relieved,' said Mary, wiping her eyes surreptitiously. 'I just wish he had given me an address. I'd have liked to thank the kind people who took him in.'

Olaf watched her. 'At least he is on the mend,' he said. There was a short silence. No, she doesn't know, he thought, and he wasn't going to voice his suspicions. 'Why did ye bail me out?' he asked, curiously.

'Because of Jamie,' said Mary at once. 'I don't know if you can understand, but it's not easy to bring a son up on your own. I . . . I did the best I could, but all the time I was aware that he didn't have a father. It makes a difference to a boy. You . . . you taught him how to fish and catch a rabbit, things that I couldn't, and I was grateful. That's all.'

'I was fair beside myself with worry about the lad,' admitted Olaf. 'Drinking and fighting meant that I didn't have to think.'

There was another pause, then Mary said, 'Do you have any family, Mr Hamnavoe?'

The baby in the cradle began to grizzle and Olaf reached out with one foot and began to rock the cradle. 'I didn't get on with my big sister, she was a mean-minded body, and it seemed to me that she was always telling tales. I was a wild lad. My poor mother put up with me as long as she could and then threw me out. I can't blame her.'

'Is . . . is she still alive?'

'I used to write, but haven't heard from her for many years, not since she went to live with my sister. In the end, I stopped writing. There seemed no point.'

'Mr Hamnavoe, it's none of my business, but I think you should go back and see your mother, let her know that you're all right. I

351

cannot believe that any mother would forget her son and not want to know if he were still alive, whatever he'd done.'

The baby's grizzling quietened and Mary could hear small snuffling noises. She peered down at the baby. He was sleeping, and she could see his mouth making little sucking movements.

'Aye, maybe you're right,' said Olaf. 'Tie up loose ends. Poor Mother. She tried so hard with me.'

'Go and tell her, then,' said Mary with a smile. 'Mothers like to be appreciated.'

'I can't skip bail, though.'

'No, but Dr Ross told me that the sailor is recovering, so maybe the charges will be dropped.'

'They'll be pleased to be rid of me,' said Olaf, ruefully. Yes, maybe he should go back to the Shetlands, see if any of his folk were still there. Mrs Ritchie was right. He couldn't go on kicking up fights and getting into trouble just because he hated his sister. Anyway, he owed Mrs Ritchie five pounds. It was a lot of money, and he knew that she couldn't afford it. If he could see his mother again, say he was sorry, then he would come back to Inverness and try and settle down a bit. He'd never be a pillar of the community, but he didn't have to live the way he did. He knew it was squalid. There must be other ways of living.

Mary returned to Dr Ross's feeling much

happier in her mind. Jamie had written and Mr Hamnavoe was on the mend, too. Things were looking up, at last.

*   *   *

'No, Mr Invershiel! You may *not* marry my daughter! It is quite out of the question!'

Beatrix and Henry were in the drawing-room at Achnagarry, and such was Beatrix's rage that she could scarcely keep still, and Henry was left standing while she paced up and down the room. From the moment that that wretched James Ritchie had come to the lodge, she had endured nothing but humiliation piled upon humiliation, and this was the last straw. If she *must* accept Lady Invershiel's demands, then let Madeline marry the elder son, the one who would inherit the title. At least that need not be explained away; people would understand that she might want a title for her daughter.

'Your mother means to mortify me by every means in her power,' she rushed on, too angry to weigh her words. 'Not only do I have to put up with Ritchie daring to come here and attack my husband, but he also inveigles his way into your mother's good graces, meaning to ruin us all!'

Henry looked astonished. 'No! No!'

'Yes! Yes!' snapped Beatrix. 'Why on earth should I want my daughter to ally herself with a family who has lost much of what prestige and wealth it had, if I weren't forced into it?'

Henry frowned. 'But, surely . . .? Why did you want Madeline to come to Dunlairg, then?'

Beatrix bit her lip. If Madeline had done as she ought and attached Mr Mountsorrel, this would never have happened. She would be engaged by now and the Invershiels would be able to do nothing.

'Ah! I see. You wanted Mountsorrel. But look, Mrs Penicuik, you have got this all wrong, I assure you. My mother has always hoped that Madeline would marry John, but she and I love each other. She is promised to me.'

'She most certainly is not!' A second son, and, from everything she had heard, one who had no fortune of his own. No, a thousand times, no!

Keep calm, thought Henry. He could see that she was in no mood to listen to reason and there was no point in antagonizing her further. 'I understand that you are not happy about it,' he said, quietly. 'But I assure you that I mean to make a success of my career. Ask Mr Ogilvy.'

'Mr Ogilvy!'

'Yes, I think that he will give me a character. I am not a wastrel, and I will do everything in my power to make Madeline happy. Please, give it some thought.' He went to the door. 'I must go and make my peace with my parents; they, too, are not pleased.' He bowed and left the room.

Beatrix heard his footsteps in the hall, he said a few words to Frank and then the front door closed. She sank down on the nearest chair and shut her eyes and a few angry tears trickled out from underneath her eyelids. Henry Invershiel as a husband for Madeline! She might as well marry Kenny the postman and have done with it. And the stupid girl had entered into some agreement about it! She had been indulgent towards Madeline for long enough, and look what had come of it! It was high time that she was brought to heel.

She was just about to summon her daughter, when there was a tap at the door and Frank came in with a card on a tray.

'Mr Gillespie to see you, Madam,' he said.

'Mr Gillespie! Ask him to come in.' He was a man of the cloth. She couldn't say that she was 'Not at Home'.

'I am come to enquire after our invalid,' said Murdo, when they had shaken hands and Beatrix had offered him a seat.

'How kind of you. Mr Penicuik is improving slowly, thank you.'

'I'm glad, but, Mrs Penicuik, you look sadly pulled down by all this. I hope that you are looking after yourself?'

Beatrix took a deep breath. 'It is not Mr Penicuik who is concerning me,' she stated, 'it is the undutiful behaviour of my daughter!'

Murdo drew his chair up a little. 'You may confide in me! I have not held a living for some years now, but I assure you that I have not forgotten that I am in Holy Orders. Anything you say will be confidential.'

Without stopping to think, Beatrix plunged into her woes. If her story bore little resemblance to what had actually happened, nevertheless, Murdo was able to piece together the essential bits: Mr Penicuik had been attacked by a young man purporting to be his natural son, who had then taken refuge in Dunlairg Castle and, by some underhand means, had persuaded the Invershiels to humiliate her by blackmailing her to accept Henry Invershiel as a husband for Madeline. And Madeline was so lost to all sense of propriety that she had actually agreed to an engagement without her parents' consent!

Murdo's exclamations of horror were genuine, but, all the same, he saw at once that there could be something in it for him as well. Doubtless the Invershiels were demanding a handsome dowry for their silence. He allowed Beatrix to talk herself out, which took some time, and assured her of his absolute discretion.

Then he said, 'I am sorry to have to report that I have seen Miss Drummond and Mr Mountsorrel alone together on yet another occasion. I do trust that he is not serious about her. A man in his position cannot be too careful who he marries. I am afraid that this scandal would—quite undeservedly, of course—taint Miss Drummond's reputation as well.'

'If Madeline had attached Mr Mountsorrel, as she should have done, this would never have happened!' declared Beatrix. She was furious at Robina's treachery. She should never have invited her up here—doubtless she had connived at Madeline meeting Henry Invershiel, too. She didn't think she could bear it if Robina, dowdy, thirty-two-year old Robina, married Mr Mountsorrel, when it should be Madeline who became Mrs Edward Mountsorrel.

Murdo watched her face and made a pretty good guess at the emotions she was struggling to conceal. 'What you have told me is confidential, of course,' he assured her, 'but, if you would allow me to tell Mr Mountsorrel, I believe it would be enough to make him think again—if he were considering offering for Miss Drummond.' He paused and added, 'It cannot have escaped your notice that I, myself, hope to marry to Miss Drummond—Robina. And I believe that I have the prior claim!'

Beatrix nodded. 'Tell him. And, Mr Gillespie, if, or I should say, when, Robina weds you, I think I can promise that my husband will see fit to add a further thousand pounds to Robina's portion.' She saw him hesitating and added, 'Possibly two.'

Murdo bowed. 'You are most generous. I am sure that Mr Mountsorrel will see reason.'

And Robina will be at Nevan House, whenever I need her, thought Beatrix with satisfaction, and she would not have the humiliation of seeing her make a far better match than Madeline.

CHAPTER TEN

Mr Ogilvy and his cousin, Francis, did not meet as often as they would have liked, and on this late summer evening, after the steamer had docked at Inverness and Mr Ogilvy had taken a cab to his cousin's, there was much to talk about. They both led blameless lives, and acknowledged a guilty pleasure in observing the havoc which Mr Penicuik's irregular goings-on had wrought in the lives of those around him.

They sat in Francis's snuggery, with a peat fire softly burning, each with a glass of whisky, and discussed what had been happening. Once Mr Ogilvy had told his cousin of James's arrival at Achnagarry and its aftermath, and Francis had responded with the story of Olaf, and Mrs Ritchie's problems with Dr Ross, they realized that they were probably the only two people who knew the whole story.

Mrs Ritchie, they thought, would not tell

James of Dr Ross's importunities, nor would James tell of his disastrous meeting with his father. The cousins decided, with a pleasurable feeling of power, to keep their knowledge to themselves. Lawyers knew many secrets, but rarely one which had such destructive potential.

'Will Penicuik recover?' asked Francis.

'To a certain extent, I'm sure. He's a determined man. But I doubt whether he'll be able to go ahead with his Inverness venture. I have advised Mrs Penicuik to defer its implementation.'

'Very sensible. About Mrs Ritchie. I'll send a boy round with a note asking her to call on a matter which is to her advantage, shall I? Say two o'clock tomorrow afternoon.'

*   *   *

'Two thousand pounds!' exclaimed Mary incredulously, the next day. How could Duncan have offered her that? It wasn't like him. 'Are you sure?'

'It would not look well for a man in Mr Penicuik's position to be taken to court for fraud,' said Mr Ogilvy.

'But . . . but I could never have afforded to take him to court!'

'I hinted that you might.' Mr Ogilvy exchanged a mischievous glance with his cousin. 'He saw the justice of my argument.

My dear Mrs Ritchie, he can well afford two thousand pounds, I can assure you.'

'Then you advise me to accept?' faltered Mary.

'Certainly,' put in Mr Francis. 'This is a full and final settlement; there will be no further contact with Mr Penicuik.'

'Indeed, no,' said Mary, shuddering with relief.

'Very well then.' Mr Ogilvy picked up a quill, dipped it in the inkstand and handed it to her. 'Would you please sign here, signifying your acceptance.'

Mary did so. 'But what am I to do with two thousand pounds?' she cried.

Mr Francis smiled. 'I would be happy to advise you on this. I think a suitable investment in the five per cents, which would bring you in just under two pounds a week would be best.'

Stunned, Mary agreed to his suggestions, and, dazed, returned to Dr Ross's. That night, in the quiet of her room, she thought over the sudden change in her circumstances. She could go to Glasgow with Jamie! Then she thought, no. He was seventeen now, she must let him learn to live away from home. But now she no longer had to work, what did she want to do with the rest of her life? She couldn't just sit twiddling her thumbs, waiting for Jamie's vacations.

Now she had the wedge, she didn't mind

being at Dr Ross's so much, and she liked having people to talk to. Perhaps she could run a respectable boarding house? But she couldn't help thinking that, without a man, she'd be subjected to all the unpleasantnesses she used to have when she first lived in Ardconnel Terrace.

In any event, she hadn't got the money yet, and there was no need to tell anybody. She would think it over.

*　　　*　　　*

Robina's Journal　　　　Thursday, 31 August
What is going on? Beatrix is going about with a brow like thunder and poor Madeline is locked in her bedroom. I crept along, hoping that the key would be in the lock, but no. According to Ishbel, Beatrix is keeping the key personally. She only unlocks the door to allow Morag in with Madeline's meals and to remove the slops in the morning.

I tried to persuade Morag to slip a letter in to Madeline, but she was so terrified that I gave up. If Achnagarry were like the old house, then there might be a gap underneath the door, or a cupboard which linked with the next room, but there isn't. Not sure what to do.

Aeneas and I went down to Loch Nevan and Henry was there, looking distraught. Beatrix had sent him away with a flea in his ear. Told him about Madeline. He gave me a letter, but I said

361

that I wasn't sure I could deliver it.

We then went to see Mhairi. Donald there. He told me that one of the other bedroom keys might fit. Of course, they're all supposed to be different, but when the place was built he thought that the builders hadn't bothered. I shall try mine or Aeneas's.

Interesting about Henry. I confess I didn't think he had it in him to beard Beatrix in her den—not to mention Lady I.! He's grown up a lot over all this. I'd assumed that he was something of a dilettante about his work. Truth to tell, I was never sure that the thing between him and Madeline would last, but I was wrong. Henry has unexpected depths.

Aeneas and I discussed the keys and decided that Aeneas would try his and mine; he'll have to avoid Ewan, but he does that anyway, and, as he doesn't come downstairs for meals, he has the most opportunity. Told him to be careful, though Ishbel says that all the servants are on Madeline's side! Gave him Henry's letter.

Later:

It worked! Madeline now has Henry's letter, and Aeneas is terribly pleased with himself!

How Gothic it all is! Madeline wants to marry a perfectly respectable young man, and suddenly she's locked in her room like Angelina Mountfalcon in The Mountfalcon Heiress*! All we need is a sinister monk to appear!*

Henry said that Edward is wandering round like a bear with a sore head. Good! Serve him right. He wouldn't even listen to me. I am trying to convince myself that I'm well rid of him. Do I really want a man who sees me as some feather-brained female, prone to exaggeration and falsehood?

No, I don't! But it still hurts.

*   *   *

After the recovery of his memory, James's improvement was rapid. His bruises began to fade and left a yellowish stain around his neck, and his head wound was healing as it ought.

'Lady Invershiel hopes that you will feel well enough to come down to luncheon,' said Edward. 'I'll take you down to the solar half an hour before, which is just down one flight of stairs, so it shouldn't be too tiring. Then the dining-room is down another flight of stairs. Do you think you could manage that? I shan't let you stay too long.' Lady Invershiel could be overpowering, he thought.

'I . . . I think so.' Jamie was quite excited at the thought of seeing the castle. Charlotte had told him all about it and he was longing to see it for himself. 'Could somebody shave me?' he asked, feeling his chin. 'I don't want to appear looking like this.'

Edward laughed. 'I had a beard when I arrived,' he said. 'I was far more woolly than you are! But I'll get one of the menservants to come and shave you, if you wish.'

At mid-day, freshly shaved by His Lordship's valet, and wearing a spare suit of Henry's, James set off down the spiral staircase, rather shakily, for his legs felt like cotton wool, and into the solar. Edward led him across to Lady Invershiel and introduced him.

'I am very g-grateful to you for t-taking me in, My Lady,' stammered James. He'd imagined somebody wearing a lot of jewels, but this woman, with untidy grey hair escaping from under her lace cap, looked quite ordinary.

'You should address me as "Lady Invershiel",' his hostess informed him kindly. ' "My Lady" is only for servants.'

'Yes, Lady Invershiel,' said James, with an inward smile. She reminded him of the Latin dominie at the Academy, who insisted on being addressed as 'Magister'.

Lady Invershiel took out her lorgnette and surveyed him carefully. A well-looking young man, she thought, approvingly. Good manners, too. To have taken a vulgar hobbledehoy into the house would have, if not overset, then certainly disturbed her plans, but this young man would *do*. It was important that he be presentable.

'Come and sit down,' she said, in her majestic way, indicating a chair next to hers. 'John, Henry, come and meet Mr Ritchie.' She turned to Jamie. 'My sons, John and Henry.'

Jamie shook hands. What should he call them? Were they lords? He should have asked Mr Mountsorrel before he came down. To his relief, John and Henry sat down as well; there was safety in numbers. Lady Invershiel might look ordinary, but James had the feeling that she was a strong-minded woman and he wasn't sure how much he should say. What did she know?

However, Lady Invershiel was smiling and asking him about his schooling, which was innocuous enough, and he found himself telling them of the Inverness Academy, his bursary and the scholarship to Glasgow.

Looking at him with interest, Henry thought, Madeline was right: he did look like Aeneas. A nice lad, intelligent too. It wasn't his fault that the unspeakable Penicuik was his father.

'Do you fish, Ritchie?' asked Henry, feeling that he had been cross-questioned long enough. 'We can lend you a rod, if you like.'

'Yes, I fish. Sea fishing, though.'

'Shoot?' asked John.

Jamie shook his head. 'I've never had the opportunity.'

'He's not strong enough to go up the hill yet,' said Lady Invershiel reprovingly, shaking her head at John. 'But he might do a little fishing. It is not a strenuous activity, and he would be out in the fresh air.'

There was a sudden dull boom from

somewhere down below, which rose to a crescendo and then died away. James looked up startled. Whatever was it? 'Gong,' whispered Henry. The company rose, and Edward came forward to help James downstairs to the dining-room, where he met Charlotte and Lord Invershiel.

'Come and sit down,' said Edward, pulling out a chair. 'I'll bring you something.'

Luncheon was always an informal meal. Food was put out on the sideboard and everybody helped themselves. James found himself with a plate of cold beef, some salad and a baked potato. 'Don't worry,' said Edward, encouragingly, 'I'll make sure that you don't get over-tired.'

Jamie tried to smile. Everybody was being very kind, but it was all beginning to be a bit overwhelming. It was only now that he was downstairs that he could see just how much of a castle it was. The solar was a large panelled room with a ceiling elaborately plastered in lozenges, with ancient moth-eaten tapestries on the walls, and arched windows. Downstairs, the hall had a massive fireplace at one end, with the family coat of arms carved above it and a number of rusty weapons hung on the walls.

The dining-room was equally ancient, with wall recesses which were several feet thick. God knows how thick the walls were, he thought. The furniture looked almost as old as the castle. He was sitting at a huge oak table, which must have been made in the room, for it was far too big to have come in through the door, and the heavy oak chairs had backs shaped like shields. The floor was stone flagged. He couldn't help feeling that the place must be freezing in winter, but probably they had a house elsewhere, Edinburgh, perhaps.

Conversation over luncheon was more general. John and Henry discussed grouse-shooting, Lord Invershiel complained that he had lost his thumb stick and Charlotte asked if it would be all right if she went mushrooming.

James began to relax.

Then Lady Invershiel said, 'I want to invite the Penicuiks to tea, perhaps tomorrow if they can make it. It is too long since we have seen them all.' Mrs Penicuik had had her letter for two days now, and not a word had she heard from her. That state of affairs must not be allowed to continue. She would write this very afternoon.

James's fork fell to the floor with a clatter. Edward, looking at him, saw that he had gone quite white. What the devil is going on, he thought, angrily.

'I'm not sure that Ritchie is ready to meet strangers,' he said.

Lady Invershiel smiled. 'They know he's here,' she said, calmly.

James sank back in his chair. His wound began to throb painfully. The world started to go round in front of his eyes. Edward jumped up.

'Bed,' he said, pulling out James's chair and picking him up. He turned to Lady Invershiel. 'I don't know what is going on,' he said furiously, 'but if he has a relapse I shall hold you responsible. Charlotte, come with me. I need your help.'

When they had gone, Lord Invershiel said, 'Was that wise? You gave the poor young man a terrible shock. Supposing Mrs Penicuik doesn't want to meet Ritchie?' It would be perfectly understandable, he thought.

Lady Invershiel shrugged. 'If the Penicuiks want to decline the invitation, they may do so, but I don't think that they will.'

'But if Ritchie has a relapse?' said Henry, worriedly.

'He's a strong young man,' stated Lady Invershiel.

As soon as luncheon was over, Henry made his way upstairs to Jamie's turret room. Jamie was alone, lying on the bed where Edward had placed him, and gazing at the ceiling. He didn't turn when Henry came in.

Henry pulled up the chair and sat down. 'Sorry about that,' he said. 'Mama has no tact.' Jamie turned his head. The look on his face was so anxiety-ridden that Henry said at once, 'She knows that you are Penicuik's son.'

'They won't want to meet me,' he whispered. 'My father thinks that I should

368

never have been born.'

'Mr Penicuik won't be coming,' said Henry soothingly. 'He is still recovering from apoplexy. As for the others, I know that Madeline wants to meet you, for she has told me so.'

Jamie pulled himself up. 'I've always wanted to know them,' he confessed. 'W . . . would you tell me about them?'

'Well, there's Madeline, she's eighteen, very beautiful and engaged to me—though neither my mother nor Mrs Penicuik are happy about that—so, if there's any disapproval, we can be in it together. Ewan is about sixteen, and a spoilt brat. He may not like you, but, frankly, he's no loss. The younger son is Aeneas; you'll like him. Then there's Miss Drummond, a cousin of Mrs Penicuik's. She's very pleasant, so, you see, there's nothing for you to worry about!'

'Nothing!' said Jamie with a short laugh, but Henry was relieved to see that his colour had returned.

There was a knock at the door and Charlotte came in. She looked at Henry. 'Your mother is the limit!' she exclaimed.

'I know.'

Charlotte turned to Jamie. 'You're not to worry,' she said firmly. 'They'll all be on their best behaviour tomorrow. As it was Mr Penicuik who attacked James, they wouldn't dare be anything else. Isn't that true, Henry?'

She turned to James and added, 'He's a barrister.'

'Quite,' said Henry. She probably knew more than he did, he thought. 'Have you been up here before, Miss Know-it-all?'

'Oh yes.'

'Does your father know you've been seeing his patient?'

'Probably not. I am allowed to decide things for myself, I believe?'

'I wouldn't dare suggest otherwise,' said Henry truthfully.

Jamie smiled. He could see that he wasn't the only person Charlotte bossed about. Henry and Charlotte stayed a few minutes and then left Jamie to rest.

'Come up to the battlements,' said Henry. 'I want to talk to you.'

Charlotte followed him. Autumn was coming, she thought, as they sat down. The rowan berries were glowing scarlet and the birches were beginning to turn. Soon the geese and swans would be coming down from the Arctic for the winter. For the first time, she thought that she would like to stay in the same place all the year round, just to see how it changed.

'What do you know?' asked Henry bluntly.

Charlotte told him.

'Does your father know all this?'

Charlotte considered. 'No, I don't think so,' she said. 'And that reminds me, I want to talk to you, too. What is the matter with Papa? He's gone all moody. I've never seen him like this before. Do you think he's ill?'

'If love be an illness,' said Henry. It was high time she knew, he thought. And it would teach Miss Know-it-all that she wasn't quite so omnipotent as she thought.

'Love?!' Charlotte looked incredulous.

'He's in love with Robina, and he's given her a very hard time, poor girl. She's very unhappy.'

'In love!' echoed Charlotte, thunderstruck. 'But they're old!'

Henry laughed.

'But he's got me!' Suddenly, she wanted to cry.

'Charlotte,' said Henry, gently. 'He won't always have you, will he? One day you may wish to marry, and then what?'

'But I'm never going to . . .' began Charlotte, and then stopped. For some reason, Jamie came into her head. 'I see,' she said, in a small voice. 'I hadn't thought.'

'It needn't be a disaster, you know,' went on Henry. 'It would mean that you could do whatever you wanted to do with your life, and you wouldn't have to worry about your father as he got older.'

'It's just that I've got used to it being only the two of us.'

'Very understandable. But you're growing up, and things are going to change. They

371

always do. If it isn't Robina, and they seem to have quarrelled so it might well not be, it could well be some other lady in the future.'

'I shall have to think about this,' said Charlotte with dignity.

'I'll leave you then,' said Henry. He dropped a quick kiss on the top of her head, which she brushed away angrily, and left her. Charlotte stared unseeing at the loch below. Her father and Robina? Could it possibly be true?

*   *   *

Mr Ogilvy arrived back at Achnagarry on Friday, 1 September, to be greeted by an agitated Beatrix, who marched him into the study and announced that he must find a way out of Lady Invershiel's pernicious blackmail at once. She showed him the letter.

Mr Ogilvy read it carefully and then said, 'I can see why you are not pleased about it. If it had been Mr Henry now . . .'

'Mr Henry!' gasped Beatrix. 'Why, if he's worth a hundred a year I should be very surprised.'

'He's a very promising young man. A barrister and, if I'm not mistaken, set to rise. If I were Miss Penicuik, I would choose Mr Henry.'

Beatrix was not going to humble herself by confessing that that was exactly what her daughter had done. 'But Lady Invershiel has decided that it is John who is to wed Madeline,' she said.

'You could make a counter-suggestion,' said Mr Ogilvy. 'Believe me, Mrs Penicuik, Mr Henry is by far the better long-term prospect.' Realistically, he thought, she had little choice. He did not think that Lady Invershiel would carry out her implied threat, but Mrs Penicuik would be foolish to take any chances, and sooner or later, something would get out. It always did. 'What dowry will Miss Penicuik have?'

'My husband says three times her husband's annual income.'

Mr Ogilvy shook his head. 'That won't do. Come, Mrs Penicuik, be sensible. Lady Invershiel will expect something in the region of thirty thousand.'

'Thirty thousand pounds!'

'Mr John's income will never be more than a couple of thousand a year, but Mr Henry is a coming man. I should be very surprised if his income does not reach ten thousand a year, eventually—and his rise would be materially helped if his wife had money.'

'This changes matters,' said Beatrix. 'Madeline is a sensible girl. I'm sure she will take my advice on this.'

It was decided that Mrs Penicuik would go and inform Madeline of her good fortune and that Mr Ogilvy would tell Ewan and Aeneas of their acquisition of a new brother. 'It's a man's job,' said Beatrix, firmly. 'I really cannot bring myself to discuss such a thing with them, and you will be able to impress on them the importance of keeping it private. I shall send them down.'

Mr Ogilvy accepted the inevitable. A deeply moral man, he disliked the task intensely—he would make certain that his distaste be reflected in his bill. He barely had time to compose himself before Ewan and Aeneas entered, Ewan looking truculent and Aeneas interested.

'Sit down,' said Mr Ogilvy. They did so. 'I have something to tell you, and I want you both to swear to keep it confidential. Do you promise?'

They promised.

'Do you know about the young man who came to see your father, shortly before he fell ill?'

'Yes,' said Ewan. 'He attacked Father and got away. Have they caught him?' Perhaps he would be hanged, he thought with relish.

'No, he didn't,' said Aeneas crossly. 'Father attacked *him.*'

'Don't be stupid—' began Ewan.

Mr Ogilvy held up his hand. 'Aeneas is right,' he said. 'Mr James Ritchie came to see your father because he is his natural son.'

'Father's bastard?' exclaimed Ewan.

Mr Ogilvy frowned at him. 'Your father attacked Ritchie, who was taken in by the

Invershiels at Dunlairg Castle. You do not need me to tell you, I'm sure, how serious this could be for the whole family if it became known. It is not an exaggeration to say that it could ruin you all.'

'But the Invershiels are nice people!' protested Aeneas, his forehead creased in anxiety.

'No, they aren't,' muttered Ewan.

'Lady Invershiel has proposed a match between one of her sons and your sister. If this takes place, then the secret is safe. Obviously, the Invershiels then will have as much to lose as the Penicuiks.'

'But that's bribery!' exclaimed Ewan. He was shocked, but, all the same, Lady Invershiel rose in his estimation.

'Let us say that is a matter of mutual benefit,' suggested Mr Ogilvy, borrowing Lady Invershiel's phrase.

'That's all right!' said Aeneas, relieved. 'Madeline wants to marry Henry, anyway.'

Both Ewan and Mr Ogilvy turned to look at him, one scowling, the other startled. Aeneas grinned.

*   *   *

Robina's Journal   Friday 1 September Things are happening! Madeline has been released and ordered to marry Henry! No explanation as to Beatrix's sudden volte *face,* but Madeline, of course, is not complaining. Very happy for her. Beatrix is writing to Lady I.

I went up to the den and found Aeneas. Mr Ogilvy has explained to him and Ewan about James. Aeneas obviously not clear what

a natural son is! I explained. Once he'd understood, he was rather excited by it. 'It's just like Tom Jones,' he said. I told him what I knew about James and how I'd bandaged him up. It turned out that Aeneas had seen him briefly when he came to Achnagarry, and thought he looked nice.

Ewan came in. He seemed to think that James was trying to usurp his place. I said that he was going to study Mathematics at Glasgow University and that they'd probably never see him again.

'Good!' said Ewan.

James's existence was obviously a shock to him—which I don't think is a bad thing. It might jolt him a bit, stop him thinking that he's at the centre of everything.

*   *   *

Saturday 2 September
Don't know where to start. Beatrix received a letter from Lady I. inviting us all to tea this afternoon to meet James. Not sure if this is in response to Beatrix's letter or not. Frantic preparations. The maids were rushing round

376

pressing clothes and Frank was sitting in the bootroom with a long row of shoes to polish. Flora was with Beatrix and Madeline, wielding the hot curling tongs and Beatrix was shouting at her. If I were Flora, I'd be terribly tempted to let Beatrix's sausage curls scorch!

Of course, my first thought was, what shall I wear? How could I help hoping that now everything was out in the open, Edward would have learnt the truth? In the end, I chose my dark-green silk with the scalloped hem. When Beatrix saw me, she whispered in my ear, 'Pride goes before a fall, Robina,' with a most unpleasant smile. The cat.

Madeline was looking deliciously pretty in pale blue. Flora excelled herself with her hair, which was caught up into a chignon with floating curls coming down. Beatrix was rather over-dressed, I thought. Too much jewellery, but doubtless she wanted to make an impression. Actually, I felt rather sorry for her; it couldn't have been easy knowing that you were going to meet your husband's by-blow. Ewan and Aeneas were looking tidy, but uncomfortable and, for once, Ewan was behaving himself; perhaps he's worried lest Henry throws him off the battlements if he doesn't!

What has Beatrix told Duncan, if anything? None of us has seen him since the incident, except Mr Ogilvy. I wonder how much he'll recover? What a pity women don't run businesses. I think Beatrix would be rather good at it.

Anyway, we all arrived at Dunlairg and were shown up to the solar.

Edward wasn't there. It can only have been deliberate. I forced myself to appear as usual; I'm not going to allow him to upset me any more. He's not worth it.

Lady Invershiel took Beatrix over and introduced her to James, who, thank God, was looking better. Beatrix had her screwed-up face on, as if she'd just smelled something nasty, and she was obviously preparing for an unpleasant duty. But, to my surprise, it went all right.

James said, 'I'm really sorry to have caused so much trouble, Mrs Penicuik. If I'd realized, I would never have come.'

It took the wind right out of Beatrix's sails. Even she could see that he was a nice lad. She said something about all's well that ends well, and introduced him to Ewan and Aeneas. Ewan bowed stiffly and, rather obviously, didn't shake James's hand. Aeneas, bless him, shook hands and said, 'Madeline and I saw you when you came to Achnagarry, do you remember?' and beamed at him.

'I remember,' said James. 'Which one are you?'

'I'm Aeneas, your new brother.' He was obviously thrilled by it all.

'I've been an only child up until now, so I'm delighted to have a brother,' said James.

I thought it was my turn, so I introduced

378

myself: I said that I was the one who had bandaged him up, though I don't suppose he remembered much about it. We sat down. Madeline and Henry came up, both glowing with happiness. Madeline said that, for her part, she was delighted that James had come as, not only did she now have a new brother, but she was also allowed to marry Henry as well. Very prettily put, and I could see that James was touched.

When they'd gone, I took the paper-knife I'd wrapped up out of my pocket and gave it to James. He went ashen and, for a moment, I thought he was going to faint. I felt awful. I should have thought. I assured him that it had hardly touched Duncan and had in no way contributed to his apoplexy. I said that I didn't want it to fall into the wrong hands.

His colour returned. He told me that a friend had made it for him.

In fact, after a sticky start, the tea went surprisingly well. Henry and Madeline were so obviously happy that it would have been churlish of anybody to have cavilled at the match. Lady I. must have decided to be gracious in defeat—or, possibly she realized that, in fact, the Invershiels had done rather well, whichever it was, she outdid Beatrix in affability. I overheard them arranging that Mr Ogilvy would come over on Monday to discuss the marriage settlement.

The only person who wasn't her usual self was Charlotte. She kept looking at me in rather an odd way. I thought that I might have got a piece *of icing on my face or something, so I checked in the glass, but I hadn't.*

So it was a success and I'm pleased. One cannot have everything one wants in life, and I am far better suited to making my own way in the world than Madeline.

The Invershiels are giving a dinner on Wednesday in celebration of Henry and Madeline's engagement. I shall go to that, and then I think I must leave. There is no reason now for me to stay. I shall book myself a passage on the steamer and go back to London, see if Miss Armin can take me, write to Mrs Lambourn and accept her offer—if it's still open. Perhaps I could take James as far as Glasgow?

It's been a summer of love and heartbreak. One day I'll be able to look back with a smile, but not yet. Not yet.

*   *   *

Edward had received a note from Murdo on Friday morning. It was short and to the point: he had something of material significance to divulge and would Mr Mountsorrel do him the honour of calling at Nevan House at four o'clock tomorrow afternoon? Edward stared down at the note, puzzled. He barely knew Gillespie, and what he did know of the man he didn't particularly care for. All the same, his curiosity was engaged, and the invitation would get him out of attending the tea-party

380

with the Penicuiks; in his present state of inner turmoil, he didn't think he could bear to see Robina.

It was now nearly two and a half weeks since Ritchie had been brought to Dunlairg in a state of collapse, and just over two weeks since he had proposed to Robina. Sixteen days of living in hell. Somehow, the pain of his marriage and his feelings for Robina had become so intertwined that he couldn't separate them. He was smarting under the humiliation he had suffered with Betsy, and struggling with a growing feeling that, in spite of all his reason could argue, he had misjudged Robina.

He realized, wryly, that, over the last couple of weeks, he had had far more posthumous conversations with his wife than he had ever had during the course of their marriage. He had learnt to understand Betsy at last, and, in so doing, to forgive. He hoped that Betsy, wherever she was, had forgiven him, too. What remained was for him to forgive himself.

He sent a note round to Nevan House accepting the invitation, and, the following day set out to see what Gillespie had to say. Murdo greeted him soberly, ushered him into his study, bade him be seated, and went to order tea. Edward walked to the window and looked out. Suddenly, he realized that he could see the shielings where he had met Robina, and remembered her saying that they should move.

He looked down and saw a telescope lying on the window sill. Was that what she feared? That they would be spied on—by Gillespie?

He left the window and sat down. Murdo returned, followed by a maid with the tea tray. Edward accepted a cup of tea and a slice of fruit cake and waited for Murdo to come to the point.

Murdo was in no hurry. He asked Edward about his most recent expedition; perhaps he had come across some mountain avens and purple saxifrage in his walks in the hills? His mother, the late Mrs Gillespie, had been a most accomplished watercolourist, whose paintings of the grass of Parnassus down by the River Nevan were considered very fine. Edward responded suitably.

Eventually, the preliminaries were over and Murdo said, 'Mrs Penicuik is anxious that you be made acquainted with a recent distressing piece of family history.'

'Oh?' said Edward, politely. He had remembered that Gillespie had once aspired to Robina's hand—and subsequently wriggled out of it.

'But first I need to be assured of your absolute discretion.'

'Of course.' A sinking feeling grew in Edward's chest. Had Robina agreed to marry the man after all? Was that why Gillespie had taken on the mantle of guardian of family secrets?

'Mr Penicuik has a natural son, who came to Achnagarry Lodge a couple of weeks ago. He was undoubtedly hoping for money. Finding that Mr Penicuik would not give in to his threats, he attacked him and escaped.' Murdo paused for effect. 'I am sorry to tell you that he is Ritchie, the young man who was taken in at Dunlairg Castle, posing as a climber who had suffered a fall.'

'Ritchie!' echoed Edward. 'Ritchie is Penicuik's son?'

'I do not wonder that you are shocked.' Murdo saw, with satisfaction, that Edward had paled.

'Do the Invershiels know?'

'You may be sure that Ritchie lost no time in telling them. He inveigled his way into their confidence and Lady Invershiel has demanded that Miss Penicuik marry one of her sons as a price for her silence. I need hardly say that, if any of this business were to get out, there would be the most appalling scandal.' Murdo was pleased at the effect his news had had. 'The Penicuiks, together with Miss Drummond, would be ruined socially.'

'Why are you telling me this?'

'A man in your position, with a daughter, cannot be too careful.'

'I see.'

'And you are dependent on public money to finance your expeditions, I dare say?'

'You are right,' said Edward. 'May I ask

383

what your own interest is in this?'

'I am a friend of the family,' replied Murdo with a smile. 'I hope to be even more closely connected one day, but I must say no more on that head.'

There was silence. Edward's predominant emotion was an urge to throttle Murdo—the poisonous little toad. Gillespie had performed his task with a great deal of relish and obviously thought that Robina was his for the asking. All the same, Edward didn't trust his discretion. Whatever had Mrs Penicuik been about to make him privy to such dangerous knowledge?

All was now clear. He remembered Robina saying, 'If it were my secret, of course I should tell you.' He should have guessed. Now he thought about it, Ritchie did look like a Penicuik, Aeneas in particular. He'd allowed himself to be cozened by Lady Invershiel's subterfuges; worse, he had refused even to listen to Robina. He'd imposed his own misguided assumptions about female behaviour on to her, most unfairly, and, if he had lost her for ever, then he had only himself to blame.

But Gillespie's silence must be ensured.

'I must correct you on a number of things,' he said. 'I was there when the Invershiels brought Ritchie to the castle. He was unconscious, and as I have had experience in dealing with accidents, he was put into my charge. He had been hit on the head by a sharp object, which, if it had been an inch or so nearer the temple, would have killed him. There was also severe bruising around his neck. Whoever attacked him, meant to kill him, and he was in no condition to inveigle his way into anybody's confidence, as you put it. Whilst he was still in danger, I allowed nobody to see him.'

'You should have told me that you knew about him,' said Murdo resentfully.

'I did not know that he was Penicuik's son.' But I should have known that he hadn't had a fall, thought Edward, in self-disgust. The signs were there. The bandage round his head, the marks on his neck, even the wound itself. He had been blinded by his prejudices.

'With regard to Miss Drummond,' went on Edward, 'I cannot see how this can possibly affect her. She is related to neither Ritchie nor Penicuik. A marriage between Miss Penicuik and either John or Henry will keep the Invershiels silent about the affair. And, if anybody else thinks of spreading rumours, they would be wise to consider that Mr Henry Invershiel is a barrister, and Penicuik a very wealthy man. That, Mr Gillespie, is a powerful combination.'

'I am a man of the cloth,' said Murdo, colouring with anger, for Edward's inference had been obvious.

'And I am a gentleman,' said Edward. He rose. 'Thank you for carrying out what was, all

385

too obviously, an enjoyable mission.'

He inclined his head and left the house.

* * *

Back at Dunlairg, the Achnagarry party left and Lady Invershiel took one look at Jamie and ordered him back to bed. 'Take him up, Henry,' she said. 'He is done in. We have been going too fast.' As Jamie stumbled to his feet, she said, 'You have done very well, young man. Very well indeed.'

Henry looked at Jamie, and winked.

Later, Jamie lay on his bed and thought over the events of the afternoon. Everybody had been very kind, even Mrs Penicuik. If he had lost a father, he had gained two brothers and a sister, even if one of those brothers was unhappy about it. Madeline had said, as they left, 'I hope we won't lose you now we've met you,' and he had wanted to cry. Perhaps, after all, he had not ruined everything.

Jamie slept.

* * *

Dunlairg Castle
Monday 4 September

My dearest Robina
I know that I have been unjust and deserve
nothing and I am sure that I have hurt you.

I now know all about James and Mr Penicuik and, whilst I understand your scruples and honour you for them, what happened at Achnagarry makes no difference either to my feelings for you or to my wish to have you as my wife. I beg for your forgiveness and, if it's not too late, another chance.

I have been a little mad these last few weeks. I have neither understood myself, nor done you justice, but I have learned. Dearest Robina, this is a clumsy letter, I know, but, if you could see into my heart, you would know that it is, and always will be, yours.

Edward

*   *   *

Robina's Journal   Tuesday 5 September
Edward's letter. I'm scared. Yes, it was wonderful, of course it was. When it came, all the pain of the last couple of weeks vanished in an instant. I realized that any price was worth paying, any, to know that you are truly loved, valued and understood. And that frightened me. I love him, but I'm afraid of it happening again—whatever the 'it' was. I can't marry a man who has moods which he won't explain. I'd be miserable. Not sure what to do.

Later:
Mr Ogilvy spent all of yesterday at Dunlairg

sorting out the marriage settlement. Madeline will get £30,000. She is going around in a daze. She asked me to pinch her just to make sure that she was awake.

I don't know what Beatrix is telling Duncan, if anything. Still, neither she nor Mr Ogilvy seem too concerned. I suppose all this business with James—not to mention Wallace—means that Beatrix feels that she now has the whip hand. There is also talk of Ewan leaving school and working for Penicuik's Emporium in Edinburgh—learning the ropes.

It's not a bad idea. Ewan doesn't work at school, anyway, so what's the point in him staying there? Mr Ogilvy is concerned about Duncan's long-term health. He says that starting up a new venture in Inverness would be costly and time-consuming and that he doesn't think that Duncan's health would stand up to it for the foreseeable future, so the idea has been quietly shelved.

I know it's perverse, but I can't help feeling a bit sorry for Duncan, who has effectively abdicated, though he doesn't yet realize it, On the other hand, Beatrix is enjoying herself immensely and is showing a real flair for business. Mr Ogilvy said that ladies should be protected from the coarsening male world of business, or something similar. Sounds like Ruskin to me. Aeneas piped up, 'What about Florence Nightingale?' Quite.

Mr Ogilvy said that her work in the Crimea

wasn't commerce, and Aeneas argued that she'd had to fight for the medical supplies she needed and that he couldn't see the difference. Has he been talking to Charlotte?!

Henry is leaving on Thursday, after the engagement party, to get a Special Licence, and they will be married shortly. 'I want the knot tied before old Penicuik recovers,' he told me. Good for him.

*　　　*　　　*

Dunlairg Castle had not been such a hive of industry since the raising of Prince Charles Edward's standard in 1745. The hall, solar, and dining-room were cleaned and polished to a shine and sparkle not seen for years; the cook and kitchen maids were busy from morning to night; and Henry was sent out fishing and told not to come back without a dozen trout, for Cook was going to do her speciality, *truite à la Génévèse.*

John, feeling that things were moving on for everybody but himself, announced that Edward had promised him an introduction to a friend of his on the *Glasgow Herald,* and that, when Ritchie was fit to travel, he'd take him down on the steamer, see him settled, and then set about finding himself a position on a newspaper. There were twenty-five newspapers in Glasgow, he finished. He was sure that he could find something.

'Trade!' snorted Lord Invershiel, but his words lacked force. Even he could see the inconsistency in marrying off one son to the daughter of a glorified shop manager, whilst denying the other son a career in journalism. The Invershiels simply could not afford a prejudice against trade.

James, listening quietly, thanked his lucky stars that he had not been brought up to think any honest work beneath him, and he felt sorry for John. He had written again to his mother, this time telling her where he was and reassuring her that he was well on the road to recovery. The Invershiels were very kind and treated him as one of the family. He gave her a graphic description of the castle, but was deliberately vague about its precise location. He did not want to risk his mother guessing what he'd been up to.

After luncheon, Charlotte collared her father. 'Can we go for a walk?'

'Of course,' said Edward, conscious that he had neglected her for the past couple of weeks. 'You can show me the waterfalls on Allt Cam Bàn.'

They set off, Charlotte marching ahead and barely speaking. When they reached the waterfalls, she chose a smooth rock and sat down, patting the stone beside her. Edward sat. Charlotte picked at some lichen. 'Papa, are you thinking of marrying again?' She turned to look at him and saw that he had reddened slightly. 'So it's true!' she said reproachfully. 'Henry said that you were in love with Miss Drummond and I wasn't sure whether to believe him.'

'I do love Robina,' admitted Edward, 'but that does not mean that I don't love you. It's different, that's all.' He saw Charlotte glower and added, 'It's not rationed, you know. You are my much-loved daughter and always will be. I hope that Robina will become my much-loved wife.'

'But you'll want to do things with her and I'll be in the way!' cried Charlotte, only half-appeased.

'It's true that we'll all have to adjust. Look, you were visiting young Ritchie when he was ill against my express wishes—and I'm sure that I would have been in the way there.'

Charlotte coloured. 'I didn't do him any harm. He's my age. Isn't it natural that I want to talk to somebody of my own age?'

'Quite natural. And Robina is my sort of age.'

'I don't want her telling me what to do.'

'I don't think she's that sort of person.'

'No,' Charlotte admitted. 'I like her, truly I do, but she'll have to understand that I'm part of the family, too.'

*　　　*　　　*

Wednesday dawned. Lady Invershiel had done

391

her best to make the occasion a celebration—it had been several centuries since the Invershiels had snaffled an heiress. She had brought out all that remained of the family silver, including a Jacobite rose bowl, supposedly given to a former Lord Invershiel by Bonnie Prince Charlie.

She had gone through John and Henry's wardrobes and found an old black dress coat of John's and some black trousers and a waistcoat of Henry's, and had them freshly pressed for Jamie.

'There may be occasions at university where you will need to look smart,' she informed him. 'First impressions are most important. If you want to get on in the world, you must dress as befits a gentleman.'

'Yes, Lady Invershiel,' said Jamie, amused. 'But I'm not sure that I am a gentleman.'

'Nonsense! You will do very well.' He was an intelligent, well-mannered, good-looking young man; who was to know which side of the blanket he was born on? If he was known to be a cousin, say—no need to be more specific—of Mrs Henry Invershiel, then he would be perfectly acceptable.

Back at Achnagarry, Beatrix was feeling cautiously content. The Invershiels were being pleasingly attentive—nobody mentioned Duncan—and it looked as though Mr Mountsorrel was no longer interested in Robina. Lady Invershiel had confided that she'd mentioned that Robina was virtually penniless—an exaggeration, but one in a good cause. She went up to dress for the dinner in a mood of pleasant optimism.

Robina once again put on her dark-red silk evening dress, and Flora found time from doing Madeline and Beatrix's hair, to slip in and help her with her chignon.

'I'm hoping everything goes well for ye this evening, Miss Robina,' she said, with a significant smile, as Robina picked up her fan and reticule and prepared to go downstairs. Flora had heard from Ishbel, who'd heard from Callum, who'd spotted Miss Robina and Mr Mountsorrel walking together on the hill, and Downstairs was well aware that a match was in the air. She liked Miss Robina, who was always civil, unlike Mrs Penicuik, who shouted at her.

'Why, thank you, Flora,' said Robina, colouring slightly.

Flora smiled at her encouragingly and whisked herself out of the room.

In due course, the Achnagarry party, comprising Beatrix, Robina and Madeline, arrived at Dunlairg, were relieved of their coats, hats and muffs and ushered up to the solar.

Robina looked round and saw Edward. Their eyes met, and the next moment he was by her side.

He bent towards her and said in a low voice,

'Robina, is . . . do you . . . could we . . . ?'

Robina could see the anxiety in his face. 'Perhaps,' she said, but her smile was wary.

Edward gave a sigh of relief. 'I hope we will be able to talk privately later.'

Robina nodded, but there was no time for anything more. She must greet Lady Invershiel and do her social duty.

Charlotte was trying not to watch her father and Robina. Instead, with great perseverance, she talked to Jamie. She had confided her anxieties to him earlier and he'd said, very sensibly, 'Why don't you talk to Madeline? She must know Miss Drummond better than anybody.' Frankly, he couldn't see Miss Drummond bossing Charlotte about, she wasn't that sort of person. Now, he gestured towards Madeline and Henry, who were talking to Robina. They were laughing, and Madeline had one hand on Robina's arm.

Looking at them, Charlotte realized that it would be all right. Miss Drummond wasn't going to demand suddenly that she spend an hour on the back board, or insist that she take up embroidery. Yes, there would have to be adjustments, but there could be benefits as well. She liked her. She didn't have to love her, too, just because her father did. She said as much to Jamie. He nodded. He'd been afraid of his mother meeting Olaf, but it had been

all right. Sometimes, you just had to

394

trust people.

Edward was not able to get Robina to himself until after dinner. The ladies had withdrawn, as was proper, to the solar, and the gentlemen passed round the port (Jamie was privately mystified by this arcane behaviour). The conversation relaxed and Edward said, 'I want to talk to Robina privately. I hope that you will all head off any lady who tries to stop me.'

'About time too, if I may say so,' said Henry.

'You and Robina Drummond!' exclaimed Lord Invershiel. 'Bless my soul!' Well, why not? Robina was far more suitable than poor Georgina Usher. 'Take her to the library, my boy. I'll see that you are not interrupted.'

Lady Invershiel and Beatrix stood no chance. When the gentlemen came up to the solar, both ladies were determinedly flanked by John, Henry, Lord Invershiel and Jamie, and Edward was able to steer Robina swiftly out of the room and downstairs into the library. He shut the door firmly, turned the key, pulled Robina into his arms and started kissing her hungrily. He felt like a man who had been starving. Eventually, he recovered himself enough to let her go. 'It is "yes", isn't it?' he demanded.

Robina, feeling weak at the knees, put her hand on his shoulder to steady herself. Part of her wanted to cry, 'Yes, yes!' and be lost in the delights of love, but she forced herself to draw back. There were things she had to know first. She dropped her hand.

'Edward,' she said, 'why did it all go wrong? I couldn't have told you about James, surely you can see that? Why didn't you trust me?' If it were to happen again, she did not think that she could bear it.

Edward led her to Lord Invershiel's armchair and pulled up another chair to face it. They sat and he took hold of her hands, looking down at them for a moment. She had the right to know, but how could he ever explain those tortured posthumous conversations with Betsy? But he must, he knew that. It wasn't easy, nor was it fluent, but somehow he laid bare the agonies of the last few weeks and the revolution in his thinking.

Robina listened. During that difficult half-hour, they laid the foundation for their life together. 'I hadn't realized . . .' she said, slowly, when Edward had finished. 'Yes, I can see that it must have been difficult.'

'I know that I was wrong not to trust you,' acknowledged Edward, 'but it was all such a muddle inside my head.'

Robina leaned forward and kissed him. 'It's all right. Truly.'

He'd opened his heart to her and she'd understood.

'And you'll marry me?'

'I would be honoured to be your wife.'

Edward felt as if a burden had rolled from his shoulders. This time, he thought, I, no *we*, shall build our marriage properly on truth and trust. Time passed.

Suddenly, there was a noise like a high-pitched drone. Edward raised his head, startled.

'It's the pipes,' said Robina, smiling at his look of consternation. 'It'll be Callum—he's the best piper in Glen Nevan. Lady Invershiel must have organized reels. We'll have to go up, they will need us to make up the set.' She stood up and shook out her skirts.

'Chaperoned by bagpipes,' observed Edward, wryly. But he rose to his feet and held out his hand to Robina. 'Let's go, I want to tell everybody.'

Robina bit her lip. 'I never expected this to happen to me,' she confessed, taking his hand. Neither Lady Invershiel nor Beatrix would be pleased, she knew.

Edward pulled her towards him. 'It's all right,' he said quietly, seeing the doubt in her face. 'If you're thinking about Lady Invershiel and Mrs Penicuik, there's nothing either of them can do. They will just have to put up with it and look pleasant.'

Robina began to smile. 'I know.' It serves Beatrix right, she thought. Who was she to dictate who should marry whom?

'Let's go then.' Edward unlocked the door. 'I haven't danced for years. I hope I don't tread on your toes.'

*   *   *

Robina's Journal
Getting on for midnight. Madeline been here with me, sitting on the bed, snuggled up in the eiderdown. She was very funny about what happened when Edward and I left the solar. Henry, John, James and Lord I. stood shoulder to shoulder in front of the door to prevent either Lady I. or Beatrix from surging out.

Lady I: 'I do not understand what is going on! Henry, what is happening?'

Henry: 'Edward is proposing to Robina, Mama.'

Lady I: 'Oh dear! I feared this might happen.' Thanks!

Beatrix (hissing in Madeline's ear): 'It should have been you, if you'd done as you were told.'

Then Charlotte started to giggle.

Lady I: 'Charlotte! This is no laughing matter!'

Charlotte: 'If I don't mind, I really don't see that it's anybody else's business!' She is a splendid girl. I can see that I'll be signed up to Women's Rights, or whatever it is, in a wink!

Talk about the whirligig of time! One way or another, we've all been caught up in it, spun round and landed somewhere completely different; and almost everybody has gained, although not, perhaps, in the way they expected.

398

Even Beatrix is really better off, though she's behaving like a noble martyr. Wallace is dismissed; she will have the proper income from Achnagarry now, and she'll come round to Henry, I'm sure.

Duncan and Murdo have both lost—but it serves them right.

I am the most fortunate of them all.

Midnight: a new day. A new life.